CONSOLIDATION: BOOK TWO

A Novel of Post Pandemic Survival

by
Lisa Harnish

ISBN: 978-1-7331411-3-0

This novel is a work of fiction. Physical locations, including modifications to places names and structures, are used in a fictional capacity, as a product of the author's imagination. Names and characters are either the products of the author's imagination or are used in a fictitious manner. Any resemblance to actual persons, living or dead, or actual events is purely coincidental. Except for the dogs. Some of them are accurately characterized, because they can't sue the author for defamation of character.

Chapter 1

"So, why do you think the Superflu happened?"

This question was asked by my senior apprentice, Ali, as we were working in the ceramics studio on a lovely March afternoon. Ali was not usually into much philosophical introspection. So I suspected he was looking for opportunity to share his own theories.

I shrugged. "I dunno. Viruses just mutate and spread. Things happen." I paused and then gave him the opening he wanted. "Why do you think it happened?"

Ali plunged in. "I'm not sure, but I can't help wondering if it was some plot to wipe us out. Like, maybe someone weaponized the virus and set it loose and it spread way out of control."

I sat up and looked at him. "Who would do that? And what makes you so sure the target was *us*? Plenty of other countries hate each other, too, you know. Pakistan and India. China and Japan. North Korea and South Korea. Well, North Korea and everybody else." I paused, then added carefully, "Israel and Iran." Ali was a third generation Iranian American. His grandparents had emigrated to the U.S. after fleeing Iran when the Shah fell in 1979.

Ali shrugged. He chose not to take offense at the subtle suggestion that his ancestral home land might have been responsible. "Maybe. Could have been anyone, I guess. It's just, the virus was so lethal. 97%. That kind of success rate doesn't happen naturally. It had to have come from a lab somewhere."

I was about to point out that if it was weaponized, it was probably more successful than its designers had ever intended. But before I could respond to that, one of our newer apprentices, Aaron, interrupted; "Nah, no way; we got crop dusted by aliens who are preparing to terraform the planet. They're trying to remove us like we're a pest." He was grinning at Ali. They had several common interests, including a love of hard core sci-fi books and games. And they liked to horse around and mess with each other, too.

Ali threw a damp sponge at Aaron, to show him what he thought of that idea.

My team and I were doing "wet work" that afternoon. Ali and I were throwing and trimming clay pots. We were making large vessels with fitted lids that would be used to store the ashes of the more than 240,000 dead people of the city we lived in. Well, we weren't going to be able to make quite that many vessels. But we would make as many as our survivors asked for, and more, to trade to other communities.

The Superflu had spread around the world more than seven months ago. Besides being an extremely virulent version of a flu virus, it also had the astonishing characteristic of remaining dormant but transmissible, for many more weeks than previous versions of similar viruses. This meant it had spread uncontrolled, undetected and unknown for weeks before people actually started getting sick. In the end, it had killed nearly 97% of the world's population, so far as we knew. At least, that's what the last news reports had shared, before they disappeared off the airwaves and Internet. I figured there might be some isolated pockets or groups of people with a 100% survival rate, groups who had little or no contact with infected people. Like those primitive tribes in the Amazon River jungle, or maybe high up in the Himalayas. Or in underground government bunkers back East.

The rest of us, the 3% who had not died, had either gotten sick and recovered, as if from a normal bout of the flu. Or had been naturally immune. Or had self-quarantined, until the virus had burned itself out, and was no longer transmissible.

Now, in my suburban city of Chandler, Arizona, in the East Valley region of the metropolitan Phoenix area, we had an estimated left over population of about 1,500 survivors, maybe more, maybe less. We weren't exactly sure how many had survived and were hanging around, and how many had left town, bugging out to find some other place to live. Most of the survivors who had stayed were banding together, working towards long term survival. Several mid-level city management workers were among the survivors, and were effectively "last man standing" in the city organization chart. They had been able to allocate city resources, recruit volunteers and organize work crews to clean up things, once the virus was mostly finished.

Among the surviving city management personnel, was my new best friend, Ariana Mendoza. She had last been head of the municipal sales tax department, but had also worked in several other departments

4

during her long tenure with the City. She was a whiz at administrative coordination, able to turn an idea into action with just a few quick instructions to her staff. She also knew where all the keys were, which had been very helpful in accessing things like garbage trucks, fuel tanks, and storage warehouses. Technically, Ariana was out ranked by the head of the city water management department, Robert Ruckles, but since Robert was primarily an engineer and had specialized almost exclusively in civil engineering projects for water management, he was content to leave the administrative tasks to Ariana. He was exclusively focused on keeping the water flowing through the city infrastructure.

In addition to Ariana and Robert, another critical city team management person was Police Officer Zach Adams. Zach had been a lieutenant commander in the city police force, although I had not found that out until much later. When I had first met him, I had assumed he was a regular rank-and-file street cop. After getting to know him better, I had come to understand that he had his own specialized skill sets in personnel management, resource management, and policy setting, which were proving extremely useful. As with every other subset of the population, the police department had lost 97% of its staff as well. Zach had only a few of his original police officers still reporting for regular duty. However, he had recruited additional people for his force from outside the area, namely, some former National Guard members, who were experienced with military policing operations and procedures.

The new and old police officers were scouring the city looking for survivors, to let them know where to go, and what was available, if they needed help. Survivors would be sent to a weekly Town Hall meeting, where they could learn the current status of the local area, ongoing projects, and where they could help out. Those who were willing to work on assorted types of crews, were eligible for housing and free food from the resources collected and organized by the same city work crews. If they were not interested in helping on the crews, they were left to their own devices. They could scavenge for their own supplies, but fresh produce and meat were no longer available, and canned food got tiresome after awhile. No one was forced to work if they didn't want to, but at the same time, those who did not participate would find life much more difficult, come summer.

Our favorite un-funny joke was to look at each other, and say, in a severe stern voice, "Summer is coming!" Summer in the Valley of the Sun is brutal. Temperatures can easily go up to 115 or maybe even as high as 120 in late June. In early July, "monsoon" season starts, with increased humidity, and nearly daily chances of sudden afternoon thunderstorms with violent winds and sometimes hail. Summer in the Valley requires air conditioning. And air conditioning requires electricity. And electricity was our biggest challenge.

The Superflu had severely compromised the ability of power grid to deliver electricity. Many components of the power grid were automated, and could run continuously. But the systems needed people to respond to fluctuations in demand, and adjust the routing of the power to where it was needed. Power in Arizona used to come from a variety of sources, including coal fired plants on the Navajo Indian Reservation, natural gas power plants scattered about, hydroelectric dams on the Salt and Gila River systems, and solar and wind power. We'd already heard that the few survivors on the Indian reservation were done with burning coal. We did not have the skilled manpower to keep any of the natural gas plants going (nor a way to keep the pipelines moving the fuel, which came from Texas). So solar and hydro electric power were our best options for keeping the AC on during the coming summer.

Happily, my own personal hero and savior had stepped up to the task. Gordon Barriston, my new guy, was an electrical systems engineer, with extensive design experience in routing power to where it was needed. Before the Superflu, he had worked in the private sector, for a large scale contracting company. As part of his former job, he had had to liaison with utility companies for numerous projects, and knew much about how such systems worked. In his former career, he had been mostly a desk jockey, designing plans and reviewing them with the people who would actually install the equipment and lay the lines. But of course, he certainly knew how to do much of that himself. So now he spent a large chunk of his time outside doing the line work, along with a dedicated crew of other people skilled in electrical systems.

Gordon and Robert Ruckles had come up with a plan to route power from the Salt River hydroelectric dams to our city core, and the surrounding zone. Actually, the power was already routed to the area, as part of the existing grid. Gordon and team needed to disable much of the unneeded nodes on the power grid so that they did not inadvertently stress the power load on the remaining network. Too many buildings had been abandoned with the lights on. Automatic thermostats would kick on when the outside temperatures started to go up. Unexpected, unneeded power demands on a grid that had lost more than 50% of its source power could cause burn outs, and possibly electrical fires, damaging transformers and converters and other sensitive equipment. Without the original quantity of kilowatts feeding into the system, unoccupied homes and businesses with appliances left on, were a significant drag on the system. Gordon's plan was to actively disconnect and dismantle power services from entire neighborhoods and store or use the equipment and lines to bolster the zones that would remain powered on. He also planned to move a lot of solar panels around, to supplement the services in the consolidation zone. He and Robert had managed to connect with the few remaining people at the local utility company, who had agreed to help with the project, in exchange for similar services elsewhere, and whatever else they might need, including food and shelter.

The obvious consequence of Gordon's zone consolidation pla, was that many homes would be actively cut off from power, and would quickly become unlivable in the summer heat. However, since 97% of the population had died, that meant that 97% of the housing was now empty. Or, it would be, once the deceased occupants could be cleared out.

In the initial waves of the Superflu, many people had gone to the hospitals for treatment to relieve dehydration, pain and other symptoms. There had been no effective vaccine, and no cure, but the hospitals had been overwhelmed with people seeking comfort care. Once the hospitals reached a point of being unable to accept new patients, they had turned people away. That had resulted in some low grade rioting. But sick people do not make for very effective or enduring rioters. In the final stages of the pandemic, many people had simply taken to their beds in their homes, and died there.

Houses, hospital morgues and funeral homes overflowing with dead bodies, not to mention pets dead from neglect and dehydration, all rotting away in place, presented a potential health threat to the remaining survivors. Too much decomposition could seep into the underground water table, and contaminate it, beyond levels that could be disinfected at the water treatment plant. They could also attract rats and insects which could possibly spread more diseases. And of course, the smells were just plain revolting. And inescapable.

And that was what the work crews were for. They had been organized into small groups of 4 to 8 people, with a truck or two. The crew would enter each house (lock picking skills were highly valued). They would locate and remove any dead bodies, make note of the names of the occupants, and clean up the house. They collected and consolidated any packaged food, water and useful supplies like medicine, cleaning products and personal care toiletries. They also gathered valuables like weapons, ammunition and cash, if any was laying around. Clean empty houses in the "power off" zones had their circuit breakers and city water shut off.

Cleaned houses and apartments inside the "power on" zones, were being allocated to people on the work crews, in exchange for their labor. Due to problems in the grid causing some outages and burnouts, at a rate faster than the consolidation effort could keep up with, we were running somewhat short of empty houses inside the consolidation zone. So the city had implemented a "one person, one bedroom" policy. For example, if a house had four bedrooms, it would be expected to have four people. If anyone voluntarily chose to share a bedroom with a partner (and there were plenty of partnerships forming up), that was fine, too. If anyone wanted to stay in their own homes, in the power off zones, that was also fine; no one was being forced to move, if they didn't want to. However, most people elected to do so, for the safety and security, and comfort, that the plan offered. Most people were willing to work in the crews, as it gave them a purpose and routine, which many found comforting. There were, of course, some people who were too lazy, uncooperative, belligerent or grief stricken, to contribute when asked. And they were left to take care of themselves as best they could.

One of the major tasks the work crews handled was body removal. The bodies were transported to a mass cremation site at the local landfill, where other crews would supervise the burning, with as much dignity and solemnity as could be mustered, under the horrific circumstances. The ashes were collected and temporarily stored in paper or ziplock plastic bags, labeled with family and individual names, when known. These could be claimed by survivors, if they wished. Unclaimed cremains were being stored in an empty warehouse, for the time being.

And that was how Ali, Aaron, the rest of my apprentices, and I were contributing. We were making ceramic funerary urns to contain the cremains, for those who wished to keep their loved ones close by.

My name is Maggie Shearin, and before the Superflu, I had been a studio potter, a ceramic artist, making porcelain pottery to sell at galleries and art fairs. Well, pottery had been my second job. My first job was a desk job, which had paid the mortgage. My first job skills did not have any direct application that my reclaimed community could make use of at the moment. But the rest of the city seemed eager and glad to have someone who acknowledged the fact that we had all lost nearly everyone who ever mattered in our lives. My pots were my way of offering just a tiny bit of enduring comfort. The jars we made were fired clay. In the process of firing, the raw clay was transformed into ceramic, a durable stone substance that would last forever. Assuming, of course, the vessel was not dropped on a concrete floor! The urns could hold the ashes of a loved one for an eternity.

When Ariana and Robert discovered this skill set, they had quickly removed me from the body bagging crews and setup me up in the nearby high school ceramics studio classroom. They had located several kids with varying amounts of experience in ceramics and assigned them to be my helpers. I promptly declared them my apprentices, which meant they got to do all the grunt work, while I, as the master, got to focus on the fun parts. They accepted this reasonably well, for the most part. Especially when I relented and helped them get their own clay working skills up to speed. Of course, it wasn't all sunshine and roses right from the start. There was some training, evaluation and adjustments.

Ali and Jenna were my first apprentices, assigned to me almost immediately after the high school studio was reclaimed and opened. Aaron and Kyrene had joined the operation just a few weeks ago. We'd had another helper, Kyle, who was Jenna's boyfriend, but he was not well suited to the job, and was now working with the city police as a trainee instead.

Ali had been a college student, when the Superflu started, studying architecture. Prior to that, he had also been a student at this very high school, and had taken ceramics classes in this very studio. That had been useful for figuring out how the place had worked. Jenna was only 16, and had taken just one pottery class at different high school, when the Superflu had hit.

I didn't know much about Aaron's background, other than that he was in his early 20's and had been taking classes at the local community college. Kyrene had also been a sophomore at the university, with plans to major in ceramics. She'd had a few classes during high school as well. When she had arrived, we'd all had a good time gently teasing her about her name. "Kyrene" happened to be the name of a neighborhood and street in the nearby suburban city of Tempe. However, my new apprentice been born and raised in California, and her parents had not known that, when they selected her name. She took the teasing good naturedly.

Ali, Aaron and I were "throwers"; which meant we preferred to shape our vessels by using the centrifugal force of the spinning wheel to pull up a cylinder, and then shape it as desired. Jenna was hand building boxes from slabs of soft clay.

And my newest apprentice, Kyrene, worked in a variety of styles, both throwing, hand building, and even some slip casting. Together, the team and I made the funerary urns in a variety of styles and colors to suit anyone's taste.

In addition to the pottery, we were also working on making tiles and bricks. We were working on a community group project to build a public sculpture to memorialize the dead. The sculpture would be an abstract human form leaning over, facing downwards, arms outstretched to comfort and hug something. The space under the head and shoulders would be open, with a floor mosaic of the Earth. Thus, the sculpted figure would appear to be embracing the world and whoever stood underneath it. The surface of the entire sculpture would be covered in a mosaic of tiles with the names of the people who had died of the Superflu. Paths leading to and from the sculpture would be paved with bricks embossed with more names, as well.

We were inviting the community to participate in the development of the sculpture. Anyone who wanted to, could come to the studio and cut out a tile, emboss names, or apply underglazes to decorate them. The studio was part of the downtown high school and was adjacent to the downtown core area. It was inside the zone that would remain powered on. We had established that evenings, from 6 to 9pm, Tuesday, Wednesday and Thursday, were "open studio" times for the public. We were talking about adding a Saturday session, too, to conveniently precede the weekly Town Hall meetings.

The sculpture would take months to build and completely cover with tile, so there was a lot work to parse into small digestible chunks. Ali, Aaron and I were planning another supply run to the west side of the Valley to get more clay. It was a finite resource, and I was very concerned about what would happen when we ran out. The clay supply store was a warehouse and wholesale distributor. The owner had given me the key to the place, when he found out I had survived the virus. He had been sick himself, at the time. And, well, 97% didn't survive. That gave me access to what supplies were there. But it wouldn't last forever. After that, we'd be forced to find some "natural wild" clay deposits, and dig our own. A royal pain the patooty and something I was not looking forward to. Ali wanted to also go around to the other school studios around the valley, and scavenge for whatever was left there, as well. After that, we'd really be scraping the bottom of the barrel. However, that was one of the many problems I was going to put on the back burner, for the moment.

For now, I was focused on today's work, and tomorrow's supply run.

Chapter 2

I sometimes have the tendency to be a bit of an "ostrich with my head stuck in the sand," or a turtle pulling up into my shell. I'm pretty good at ignoring problems that I think I can't do anything about. I put on my rose colored glasses, and go skipping and singing "Fa la la lalala…" down the path. Or, I try to, at least.

Making supply runs to distant locations outside our little city core was becoming quite an expedition. In addition to a big moving truck to haul the stuff, we would be accompanied by a pair of the city cops I was acquainted with: Jake and Randy. I had met Jake several months before, when he stopped me at a road blockade in front of one of the largest hospitals in the Phoenix metro area. He and a couple of his surviving National Guard troops had migrated to Chandler shortly afterwards to continue their mission of supporting and protecting the local communities. By becoming local cops. Now, they were coming along on this trip to provide security. However, they were also turning it into a scouting expedition around the metro area. After our stop at the clay store, they wanted to continue westward, and check out Luke Air Force Base, and then continue driving north through Phoenix, and circle around to Scottsdale before coming home south on the 101. The goal was to see if we could identify any other enclaves or groups of people who were working cooperatively, to share information with, and possibly to trade with, in the future.

Just a month before, I had accompanied a small group on a similar information gathering expedition south of Chandler, to several farming communities. That had been a reasonably successful trip. We had met a fairly well organized group in Coolidge, but other locations were struggling in the aftermath of the Superflu. This time, Jake was assigned as my head of security. He had advocated for a stop at Luke AFB to see if the armory there was still secure, and to see if any kind of official operation was still up and running. If there was any functioning military operation anywhere, Jake, and by extension, his boss, Zach Adams, wanted to know about it and make contact with them. The management team was staying home for this one, though, leaving the first contact communications up to Jake and me.

The box truck was a bit of a gas hog, so we were carrying several extra cans of fuel with us, just in case. Chandler had done a decent job of consolidating and conserving fuel resources, but we were aware that it wouldn't last forever, so we figured we should use it before it oxidized past the point of usability. So in addition to the box truck, Jake was driving the black Hummer we had taken on the previous trip. He also insisted that we take enough camping gear and supplies to be out for a night or two, even though we planned to return that same day. He insisted it was just a precaution.

We left early in the morning, around 7 am. In addition to Jake and Randy for security (dressed in plain clothes, so as not to broadcast their skills to observers), we had Ali, Aaron and Kyle with us to handle the heavy lifting. Kyle was in training to join the police force, so this was seen as an on-the-job training exercise for him. Everyone was also armed, including me, with an assortment of firepower suited to everyone's individual skill level and comfort zone. When out in public, I carried the pistol that Zach had given me, even though I didn't much care for it.

The drive to the clay store was uneventful. We took the freeways most of the way there. Jake explained that while we were rather exposed on the open and sometimes elevated roadway, we would be moving fast enough to evade any potential threats. I asked him what kinds of threats he thought were likely.

He responded, "We've been getting stories about gangs forming, and looting. They're still pretty small, just groups of 4 or 5 people, so far. But if they find someone who has a decent setup or stash of supplies, they're taking it by force."

I had to wonder: "And how are you *hearing* these stories?"

Jake answered, "We're paying attention to the police scanners. There's a few people around the valley who have CB radios tuned to the police frequencies. They're letting everyone know if they observe any incidents. It's pretty informal, and no one wants to give away their personal locations. So they're only talking in generalities, like "a big grocery store was cleared out and set on fire last night", without telling us exactly which one. It's kinda frustrating. Zach is trying to get people to open up more, but then they just turn it around on us, asking how big our group is, and where we are. Zach doesn't want to tell everyone what's going on; he's worried we'd get a flood of people looking for a hand out; more than we can absorb all at once. Or worse, those gangs will come looking for more than just a handout."

I thought for a moment. "When you say, "gangs", do you mean like the criminal gangs, like the Crips and the Bloods, and MS-13?"

Jake shook his head. "Nah. Those were gutted by the Superflu just like everything else. In this sense, we just mean small groups of people who think alike. They don't want to work, or they don't know what to do, except to take stuff from other people or stores. They haven't had time to form the bonds and codes of behavior that the organized criminal gangs had, before. Mostly, they're just looking for supplies and to survive, same as the rest of us. The difference is they'd rather take it from someone else, at gun point, rather than work for it."

I kept asking questions. "And why do you think that is? Why would they resort to criminal behavior and violence, instead of just working cooperatively with people?"

Jake shook his head again. "I dunno. People been trying to figure that one out forever. Laziness. Ignorance. Thrill of the fight, the adrenaline rush, the power, the control."

I contemplated that for a while, and was still baffled. It was a mindset I just could not comprehend. Maybe I was the ignorant one. Or naïve. An ostrich or a turtle.

We arrived at the clay store, and I used my key to open up the back door to the warehouse. I directed a couple of the guys to use the pallet jacks to load up batches of stoneware clay onto the truck. While they started on that, I went to the front retail room, to find some other critical pieces of equipment. There were several assorted sizes of electric kilns on display, but they were a little on the small size. A second check of the warehouse revealed several larger models stored on pallets on upper shelving units. I had the guys pull them down as well.

Initially, at the studio, we had been firing in the large natural gas reduction kiln. However, gas pressure in the line that ran to the kiln had dropped to essentially nothing. Clearly, pumps along the pipelines had stopped working and were no longer sending fuel to us. That was frustrating, as it was a large kiln and could fire large batches of pots and tiles at once. And reduction firing techniques allowed us to do some interesting things with glazes, and achieve a different look, than what we could get from electric kilns. I was hoping to obtain a large quantity of propane, perhaps a full tanker truck, which could be hooked up to the kiln's burners, instead. But I needed someone with more expertise in fuel lines than I had personally.

In the meantime, we could fire small batches of pots in the electric kilns. The school had a couple of them already, but they were getting old and had a hard time getting up to proper temperatures. A new kiln, especially one with an electronic controller, would be much more reliable. I'd already had Gordon move my own kiln from my home, to the school studio, and install the proper electrical outlet for it on a dedicated line. (It was pretty handy having an electrical engineer at my beck and call.) Any additional equipment we could collect would be welcome, too.

I cleared out the retail display space of the rest of the underglazes, pre-mixed glaze pints, books, and small tools. I also took extra kiln shelves and stilts, spray guns for applying glaze, sieves, wax resist, and assorted other odds and ends that made operating a pottery studio easier.

I asked Jake if it would be okay if I left a note at the counter, explaining where all the stuff had gone. I was worried that some other fellow potter in the Valley might also be trying to keep on making things and I was robbing them of supplies they could use. I had mostly reconciled myself to the wholesale sanctioned theft of consumable necessities we were practicing back at home, but taking from a fellow potter felt like bad karma to me. Ceramic artists were a clubby bunch; everyone knew everyone, and word could get around. At least, it did before. Yeah, 97% of us were gone, but the population of ceramic artists in the Valley was at least a several hundred people. So there had to be at least a couple others with me in the 3%. But surviving the Superflu was one thing; surviving the aftermath was another thing all together. If it weren't for the the community I had and the resources, I wasn't sure if I'd still have time to make pots. On my own, I'd probably be struggling day by day just to keep on going. So what any other potters were up to, was a complete unknown to me.

Jake considered my note idea. On the one hand, he didn't like the idea of announcing our presence to any random strangers who happened along. But on the flip side, this was a fairly nondescript building, set well back from the main roads. Signage on the front made it clear there was no food, water, alcohol, firearms or cash inside, so there was little reason for those marauding gangs to target this building. The only people likely to come looking on the inside were fellow ceramicists like me. Being a potter did not automatically equate to being a good person. But I still felt the odds of inviting danger back to our town on the other side of the Valley were minimal.

Jake and I compromised. I worded the letter cryptically, explaining what I took, and why. Instead of saying exactly where we were taking it, I indirectly referred to the school studio by the former instructor's name, euphemistically calling it the "So-n-So Memorial Studio." The former instructor there was reasonably well known in the community. If someone found my note, but did not know who or what I was referring to, they could look it up in the invoice copies in the office. Again, someone would have to be highly motivated to do that, and Jake and I both agreed that the average looter would not be interested in tracking down missing clay.

We left the note on the main counter in the retail space, and locked up again. The boys had loaded all the clay, supplies, and equipment onto the truck. Happily, it did not sag on its suspension, the way my minivan had months ago, when I had hauled a load out.

And, happily, it was still fairly early, with plenty of time for the rest of our excursion. We discussed the idea of sending the truck home with two people, and the rest of us continuing on in the Hummer. I argued in favor of doing that. My main debate points included that it would be better for fuel conservation, and we had not seen anyone around on the highways when we had driven here. Jake countered with the "strength in numbers" argument; meaning, two vehicles traveling together were better than one.

I countered by pointing out that a moving van was not exactly a defensive vehicle, and would not be very useful in a confrontation. I'm not sure if that convinced Jake, or if he just gave in because he didn't want to argue with me, but he finally agreed to send the truck home. We assigned Aaron and Randy to drive it together. Jake, Ali, Kyle and I would continue on in the Hummer. We also escorted the truck back to the freeway entrance, to make sure it got going safely, before turning around and heading west.

Jake took a slow route towards Luke AFB, weaving through side streets, subdivisions and housing developments. He had us mark up maps with highlighters to indicate where we saw solar panels (which Gordon's teams might come back for in the future) and if we saw any signs of habitation. Just as in our own area, most neighborhoods had grown weedy. Grass was dry and burnt out. Occasionally, we found a house or even several houses that had burnt to the ground, for reasons unknown. On the surface, it seemed desolate, and unoccupied. But Jake pointed out some tips on what to watch for.

Smoke from chimneys or maybe yard pits was an obvious sign of habitation. But it was mid-morning in March, so fires for cooking or heat were unlikely at that particular time. It was possible someone could have a trash barrel burning, so we kept an eye open for it, anyways. Other signs were more subtle. We looked at car tires; if they were sagging or flat, that meant the car had not been moved in a while. If they looked even, and more importantly, if there were no leaves and dust settled on the cars, that indicated they had been driven recently. We also watched for other signs that homes were being maintained. A well-manicured landscape, free of trash and weeds would have been a dead giveaway, but no one was that obvious. HOAs were no longer a concern, so yard maintenance was a very low priority. Besides, blending in was the best way to avoid actively calling out those new gangs and saying, 'Hey, come rob me here!'

If we had been searching at night, we could have looked for lights, too. Anyone running power, from solar panels or generators, could theoretically have lamps on, which could be spotted. But in broad daylight, that was not an option. We did take time to smell the air, and rate the level of decay we could detect. We chose to use a scale of 1 to 10, with 10 being "vomit inducing." And we mostly gave ratings between 5 and 8, which told us there had been no effort to remove bodies from homes in this area.

Plenty of businesses along the main streets had been broken into. Glass was smashed, and rarely replaced with plywood. Grocery stores, convenience stores, medical offices, and other places had been looted. We did not try to go in to see how thoroughly they had been cleared out, though. So it was hard to gauge whether it was a systematic approach to consolidating resources, as we had done in our own area, or if it was individuals and small groups just struggling to get what they needed.

Our drive through the central Glendale area did not result in any face to face meetings. We did see a few semi-clean cars that we concluded had been driven recently, but no one was willing to come out and talk to the strangers in the big black Hummer. I couldn't blame them, really. I was not that intimidating, but the guys were, with their long guns, and big muscles (well, Ali was not exactly big and buff, but he was well armed).

After driving through several miles of indistinguishable subdivisions, Jake drove straight on Camelback Road for a couple of miles. I was surprised when he abruptly turned off onto a side street. There was no fancy entrance sign, as most subdivisions had. But it quickly became clear that this was an older area, former farm land that had been parceled and sold as "horse properties" or "mini farms." The lots were probably a half acre up to two acres, and fenced with an assortment of materials, from barbed wire, to wood, to steel poles. Or nothing at all. In addition to the clean, neat ranch houses, many lots had other buildings on them, such as barns or workshops or over-sized garages. Even more encouraging, was finding signs of active habitation. In the center of the little neighborhood was a large cleared field, partially planted with assorted vegetables. A section of the field was fenced off and had a few goats and sheep grazing in it.

Jake had driven to the far end of the enclave, and then weaved his way back to the front, slowly cruising past a variety of ranch houses. Some were very large, fancy and expensive, others were rather modest. We glided to a stop near the corner of the garden field that occupied the middle of the neighborhood, at an intersection of two streets. We waited patiently. We rolled down our windows too, so that we could be seen by others. I examined our surroundings carefully. The vegetable garden was well maintained, lush and free of weeds. Shade netting had been mounted above a portion of the garden, as well. A row of houses was on the opposite side of the street that ran along the length of the garden field. The yards were surprisingly neat, compared to the other neighborhoods we had just driven through. The lawns were dry and tan, but there was no trash lying about blown in by the wind. There were no smashed or boarded up windows. There was also no smell of rotting bodies, either.

After a short wait, a man came out from one of the houses across the street from the garden. He carried a rifle, with the strap over his shoulder. He did not point it directly at us, but it was clear he knew the de facto protocol for greeting strangers.

He approached us slowly and cautiously, but not unfriendly. He was on the driver's side of our Hummer, so Jake spoke with him initially, and I was only able to listen in.

The stranger greeted us first. "Morning. What can we do ya for?"

Jake replied. "Good morning, sir. My name is Jake. My crew and I are just out and about, checking things out, gathering information. We're from the East Valley, but we had an errand over here on the West side, and thought we'd cruise around a bit, see how people are doing."

The stranger eyed us cautiously. "Well, we're fine."

Jake paused a moment, so I prompted him softly. "Compliment him! Tell him the garden looks great."

Jake took my hint. "Your garden looks wonderful. It looks like you're going to be set for awhile. You doing some canning, too?"

The man nodded. "Yeah, some."

Okay, it was clear to me that this was going to require us to give some more, if we wanted to get more. I leaned over Jake and waved. "Would it be okay if we got out to talk a bit? We're not here to take anything from you, we just want to find out some information. We're happy to share what we know, if you're interested in hearing it."

The man still had his hand on his rifle, but had not changed its direction. He glanced around him, at the houses behind us, and behind him. Yep, we were definitely being watched. "I suppose that would be alright." He nodded at us again.

I opened my door on the opposite side, hopped out, and walked around the front. Ali and Kyle also opened their doors and stepped out, but stayed close to the vehicle, so they would not appear threatening.

I greeted him first. "Hi. I'm Maggie Shearin. That's Jake, and Ali, and Kyle." I pointed to each in turn. I turned back to him. I held out my hand to shake, and asked, "…and your name is?"

The stranger was late middle aged, a little taller than me, with colorless receding hair, cut short, a moderately paunchy belly hanging over a big belt buckle, dressed in jeans, dusty cowboy boots and gray t-shirt. He wasn't wearing a cowboy hat, but I had a strong suspicion there was one on a hook just inside the door of his house.

He took my hand anyways, and gripped firmly, but not painfully. "I'm Robert MacDonald. You can call me Rob." My stupid shoulder devil promptly perked up and sang out the line, "Old McDonald had a farm, ei ei ei oh…" Luckily, I did not let that one slip out through my mouth.

We released hands, and I added, "Pleasure to meet you, Rob." I paused, trying to figure out which direction to go in first. I decided to repeat the compliments.

"That really is a nice garden there. That must have taken a lot of work, to get it planted, and keep the weeds out. Do you have irrigation running to it?"

Rob nodded. "Yeah. There's a canal just over there," He waved eastwards. "We can pump the water to it as needed."

I tried a little more flattery. "It's so big – you must have a lot of people here, to help with the work and harvesting."

Rob wasn't that easily assured, though. "Yeah, actually we do have a lot of people here, and several of them are listening in on this little convo here," he touched a radio device at his hip, and an ear piece I had not noticed before. "And they would like to know what you really want."

Okaaayyyyy… silly gushing girl flattery was not going to work on this one. I looked at him, and deliberately slowed down my talk. I had a tendency to talk fast, when I was nervous or excited. It could set people on edge. "We don't need anything. Like we said, we're just looking for information, people, checking things out." I paused to consider my next direction. "We're with a fairly large group, ourselves, in the East Valley. Chandler, actually." Jake gave me the hairy eyeball at that piece of information. "We've organized, and banded together to collect resources, and take care of each other. We have our own garden, growing a lot of the same things you have here. Our gardening team is set to start canning a bunch of stuff in a couple of weeks.

We've also got work crews cleaning up our town, to remove the dead bodies. I don't notice much of that smell; you must have cleaned up your area, too?"

I paused to let him volunteer any information. He accepted the opening. "A little. There's actually not much housing to the immediate west of us, so we don't get a lot of that stink. There's a couple of developments close by to the east and south. We cleared those. Keeps the rats away."

I nodded in understanding. "Smart. So… did you fill up these houses, with survivors you found?" I waved around to indicate just his immediate area. This was a little nosy, so I asked as gently as I could.

Rob kept his tone neutral. "Yeah, we've taken in survivors. Anyone who's willing to do the work, and help out. No freeloaders allowed." I nodded my head in agreement, so he continued. "Anyone who wants to join us has to be willing to carry a firearm, and know how to use it. We have guard shifts patrolling the grounds at night."

That pleased Jake, who had stayed silent since I took over the conversation. He jumped back in. "That's good to hear. That's a nice rifle you're carrying there. I got to train with one of those when I was in the Marines."

Rob suddenly grinned and relaxed a little. Well, duh! When complimenting men, always focus on what's important to the men! Like guns! Why didn't I think of that? Because I'm a girl, of course…

Rob asked, "Marines? I was in the Corp. Was stationed at Fort Bragg and…" Rob rattled off a series of units and locations that I did not comprehend.

Jake grinned back. "No shit? I was in (different unit number)! Semper Fi!"

Rob repeated, "Semper Fi!" And boom, just like that, they were best buds. It was true. Men really were from Mars. And clearly I was from Venus. Or maybe even farther away. Like Alpha Centauri.

Jake and Rob carried on the "Do you know so-n-so?" name dropping game, establishing each other's bona fides. While I leaned back and let them bond, a woman came out from the house behind Rob. She was also in jeans and cowboy boots, with a hand gun in a holster at her hip. She came right up to me and introduced herself directly.

"Hi, I'm Madeline; Maddy for short. That's my husband." She gestured at Rob.

I was puzzled. "Husband? From before?" The Superflu had wiped out so many people, I had not yet encountered anyone who had a close living relative, either by blood or marriage. It was statistically improbable, for a husband and wife pair to have both survived, but not impossible.

"Yep. Yeah, I know, we're incredibly lucky. He got sick and recovered, and I never got sick at all. I guess I'm one of the immunes."

"Wow. That's really rare! Uh, congratulations?" I paused to recover my wits. "Oh, I'm Maggie. Hi Maddy." I giggled at the rhyme, and my shoulder devil high fived my ear lobe.

Maddy smiled too, and gestured me to move off from the guys, who were telling raunchy jokes about soldiers they had both known back in the day. Maddy filled me in on more details.

"Actually, the garden is my personal pet project. I coordinate the work on it."

"It's really nice; it looks so healthy; you're not having any issues with bugs or stuff?" I asked.

Maddy answered, "Not much. It helps to know what you're doing, and I've been gardening all my life."

"Our own garden in Chandler is doing pretty well. We've got a master gardener who knows his stuff too, but he's had some issues with root vegetables like potatoes and carrots. They're not producing well, he says."

Maddy nodded, "Oh, yeah, that can happen." Then she rattled off a bunch of tips and technical terms that went right over my head. When she saw the blank look on my face, she offered, "I'll write some of this stuff down, and you can take it back with you." I was honestly grateful and said so.

She looked around at the men. Ali had moved around the Hummer to be near me. He didn't have much affinity for all things military, so I think I he was trying to keep close to protect me, just in case. Kyle was soaking up the military man talk like a sponge.

Maddy suggested we go inside and have some coffee. She pointed to her matching ear piece, and said, "Okay, Dale, why don't you bring them over, and we'll sit & talk." Clearly, she was giving the 'all clear' to someone else. I wondered how many 'them' was.

I gestured to Jake, who nodded, which made Rob turn, and notice his wife walking back inside. He gestured, and they all followed us inside.

Maddy offered us coffee, and invited us to sit down at the huge oak dining table adjacent to her kitchen. I asked for water, but Jake accepted the coffee. Ali and Kyle politely declined. While we waited for the 'them' to arrive, Rob explained that they'd had this house for years, and hadn't found any reason to leave. When Rob had recovered from the Superflu, he had located and liberated some solar panels from elsewhere, and installed them. He figured between his panels and maybe some supplemental energy from his generator out back, they could get through the summer. They wanted to see how they survived the first summer, before deciding if they needed to relocate somewhere else with a more temperate climate, like California.

While he was talking, several more people arrived. I had glimpsed a couple of them ride up on bicycles, and the rest had walked, so clearly they were from homes close by. Rob introduced the rest of the people, but I promptly forgot their names. Three men and two women. They explained that they acted as a council for their little community, deciding on management issues together as a group.

I gave them a bigger explanation of our own situation in Chandler, explaining that we had actual city employees running the show and sanctioning the work. I explained how we were removing dead bodies, cleaning out homes of anything that could rot and stink, and make the places uninhabitable. I also confirmed that we were collecting resources; food, water, household supplies, toiletries, anything that was consumable and likely to run out. I did not immediately tell them about our power zones plan, but I was willing to share it, if the conversation came back around to it.

Jake got them to open up about security issues, first, though. He started by explaining what he had told me about the police frequencies on the CB radios, and how there was steady chatter about violent incidents. As far as Jake could tell, most of the violence was happening closer to central Phoenix. One of the new arrivals admitted that he too had been monitoring the CB, and had been contributing information about incidents that he had seen, or rather, the aftermath of the incidents. He explained that he was making regular patrols well outside of his little neighborhood, several miles outward in all directions, specifically to look for potential trouble that might be approaching his own group. Jake and the man agreed they should start plotting the locations, timing, and severity of new incidents on maps and a time line, so that they could figure out where the gangs might be based, approximately. This information would tell them if the gangs were relocating, or migrating in any particular direction, and help them assess the threat level. They also agreed to start recruiting more of the other voices on the radio chatter, to contribute the same information as well. It all sounded like police work to my ears.

The conversation then turned a discussion of the general condition of the metro area as a whole. They told us what they had seen. We told them what we had seen. We concluded we'd both seen more or less the same: people were gone, damage had been done, a few survivors were scattered about, a few were forming gangs who were getting violent.

Jake asked them if they knew anything about the status at Luke AFB. Rob did in fact, know. He told us there were a few surviving active military there, but it was unclear what their official mission was, in the wake of the Superflu. As far as he could tell, there were no pilots flying the fighter jets (the base had been a fighter pilot training center, among other things). Or at least, no one was taking off and landing any fighter jets, since last fall. He had seen people in military uniforms driving about in military vehicles, but he had not spoken to any of them. Jake seemed encouraged by this news.

We then brought up the sensitive topic of power resources. Rob and Maddy had already explained their personal arrangements, relying primarily on off-grid solar panels. We explained our plans for rerouting and directing power grid electricity to a zone around our city core, and shutting it off in the remainder of the city. This meant we would ultimately be able to keep city water pumps and filtration going too.

Rob's group quickly grasped the implications of this plan. "What are those people in your power off zones going to do? How are they supposed to survive without AC this summer?"

I smiled. "We're consolidating people, too. Anyone who works with us, gets to move into one of the empty houses in the Power On zone." They goggled at me, so I acknowledged the challenges. "Yeah it's been a bit of struggle. At first, the zone wasn't big enough, for the number of people who wanted to move in. We've asked people to take on roommates, where possible. We're expanding our zone, too, to make more units available. The houses have been cleared, but the power hasn't been restored to those yet. We don't have enough skilled electricians and man hours to make it all happen quite fast enough. It's going to be a stretch."

Maddy looked at her husband and then asked us, "Have you had many 'people' problems? People not getting along? It must be stressful, pulling so many strangers so close together all at once."

I shook my head, but Jake contradicted me. "A few. Some personality clashes. A few fights breaking out here and there. Usually, alcohol is involved, too." He rolled his eyes at that.

I amended, "I don't think it's been that bad. We've got a guy – he's good at matching up groups of roomies. He'll put a motherly type with young kids who are floundering. Or, he'll put a gentle free bird soul with someone who's so traumatized by the Superflu they're afraid of their own shadow now. It's actually pretty amazing, how good he is at match making."

Maddy veered off, "Kids? Do you have many kids around?"

"Oh! Just a very few young ones. But the 'kids' I was referring to are actually, like, 20 or something. We do have some teenagers around." I glanced at Kyle and Ali. Kyle was 18, and Ali was 21. They just shrugged back at me. "Mostly, they had already banded together on their own, before we really got our recovery operation underway. Now they're living together near other adults who are providing a little light supervision." I arched an eyebrow at Jake. He was in one of the apartments near the group of teenage boys that Kyle hung out with.

Jake nodded. "Yeah, they're okay. We keep them too busy to get into much trouble."

Rob smiled and winked, and added, "Marine S.O.P."

I thought then of Gordon's foster son, Micah. "We've found a few younger adolescents, too. The ones I know about have been fostered with any responsible adult willing to take them on. Actually, ditto for some younger kids, too. We've got some 4 and 5 year olds that we've placed with a couple of young women who had experience and training in professional child care before."

Maddy got a sad expression on her face. "No babies? No infants or toddlers?"

I shook my head grimly. So far as I knew, there were no babies that had been found alive. Even if any had survived the flu, or been immune to it (which was even more unlikely), they had probably lost all the adult care givers around them before they could be rescued. They would have died of dehydration and starvation, most likely. There had certainly been plenty of tiny bodies burned in the cremation pits. And that thought made me remember something else.

"So, when you cleared your dead out of the nearby homes, did you cremate any of them?" It was clear this was a smart, sensible group who knew basic public health policy and procedure. They nodded to my question.

"Well," I said a little more brightly. "I have something for you then. A present. If you'll come with me to the car, I can show you." The men looked puzzled, and not entirely sure if they were done with the men talk. But Maddy immediately followed me out of the house and to the back of the Hummer.

I opened up the back hatch, and pulled several green plastic milk crates forward, and pulled out the pots. "These are funerary urns, designed specifically to hold cremains."

Maddy's face formed a big O in surprise. "Oh, this is beautiful!" She lovingly ran her hands over the buttery satin tan glaze on a large ginger jar styled urn. "Where did you get these?" she wondered.

"I made them. Well, Ali and my other apprentices helped, too."

"You made these? How?" She was caressing and lifting several other jars, in turn. We had brought a small variety with us, in our many styles. I gave her my standard spiel about how I made my pots. As I explained, the men joined us, and Ali added his technical details as well, when she examined one of his pots.

I went on. "And that's the other thing: this is what we have to trade, to offer communities like yours. My apprentices and I have a specialized skill set, and we're making urns to hold the cremains of the loved ones that we all lost. We've all experienced the same thing, the same grief and loss, and mourning. This is our community's way of acknowledging the ones who went before us, and that they were important to us. And to all the communities we connect with. I'm giving you these," I waved my arm at the few pots we had pulled out of the crates. "And if you want more and are willing to come visit Chandler, we'd be willing to trade them for labor, special skills, or fresh food." I smiled towards her garden.

Then I remembered something else, too. "Oh, did we mention that we've got our hospital cleaned up and running again, too? It's a small scale operation in a large building, but we do have a few doctors and nurses. They can handle injuries or broken bones and physical conditions, like kidney stones or hernias and stuff. It's probably too far for emergency services, but if you can safely transport a broken bone or other injury, we can help."

Maddy grimaced at one her neighbors. "Like when a guy gets drunk and falls on a cactus?"

I nodded. I suspected there was a story behind that.

Rob asked thoughtfully, "What kind of special skills do you need?"

"Electricians are our most pressing need. Water system people. Truck drivers. Other medical personnel would be nice, too. Police or security guards, gardeners, farmers, or anyone who can handle livestock."

Maddy wondered, "Livestock? You have that too?"

"No, not really. A few chickens and goats. But we want to, in the future. We're thinking about turning the rest of our golf course into pasture for horses and cows. There are a lot of them around our area; they were set loose when the Superflu started, and have gone feral. Some of our people think they can be recaptured and put back to work for us, if we can keep them safe."

"Uh huh. Good luck with that," Rob said skeptically.

I wondered if that meant our project would be more difficult than anticipated. But I turned back to the pots. "Anyways, pick out a few you'd like to keep for yourselves. This is a present. We appreciate the hospitality you've shown us, and we're just happy to know there are other groups out there, working for the common good. You're welcome to come visit us in Chandler at any time. Oh, and peach season starts next month. There's a peach orchard out in Queen Creek! You should come and pick!"

I was girlie gushing again. Jake was eyeing me a little. I wondered if I had gone too far.

Maddy selected a few pots, and had her people carry them back into the house. She also had someone quickly box up some produce that had been picked just a few hours earlier, and gifted that to us. She quickly dashed out some instructions for special care to grow potatoes for us to pass along to Carlos, our head gardener. The reciprocity was lovely and we thanked her profusely. I even took a bite of one of the warm, only slightly dusty carrots sitting on top. It was sweet and crunchy and delicious.

As we reorganized the remaining boxes back into the Hummer, Rob asked Jake one final question. "How did you know to come here? You said you been wandering around, what made you stop here?"

Jake grinned. "Google Maps." Everyone was puzzled, so he explained.

"I got sick early on during the pandemic, but I recovered. While I was getting my strength back, I spent a lot of time studying maps of the area, and printing them out. I was afraid that the Internet would go down, and we wouldn't be able to get that kind of information anymore. Especially the satellite maps. So I printed out close ups of almost every part of the Valley, laminated them and put them in a three ring binder. Before I was released from the National Guard, I studied them, trying to figure out where the good places to survive would be. I figured any place that had mini farms, access to water, and maybe some fencing around it, would be a good place. This was one of those places."

Rob's people nodded in agreement. They had the canal to the east. They also had a dry river bed to the west. During storms, that would flow, and with the right power, they could pump extra water into tanks and pools, to be purified and used later.

We said our final thank yous and good byes, closed up the Hummer, and headed out. It felt so good to have been able to establish contact with another community of survivors. It felt good to know we were not the only ones around doing what we were doing, that other communities were fighting to survive too.

Chapter 3

After leaving Rob and Maddy's enclave, we headed west a couple of miles towards Luke Air Force Base. Jake decided on a direct and open approach. He explained that he was now certain the base was being actively guarded, and since we wanted to establish an ongoing relationship, we needed to be open and straightforward. He drove us to the main front entrance (several secondary side entrances were closed and locked, anyways), and pulled up to the main gate, which was in fact, actively guarded.

Jake identified himself, the rest of us, and showed his National Guard identification. The guards asked the rest of us to show ID as well. Happily, we were all carrying ours with us. It had not yet occurred to me to stop carrying a wallet around in a purse. Even though I rarely had use for it anymore. Jake explained that he was requesting a meeting with the head of the base, whoever that might be. It took a little while for the guards to pass the request up through a couple of layers of gatekeepers, but eventually, we were escorted to a modest office building on the base. We were ushered to an upstairs office suite, with a small conference room, and asked to wait. They even offered us coffee or water.

We only had to wait a few minutes before the head honcho in charge of the base appeared. He was a middle aged man, fit and trim, with a fresh hair cut, and freshly shaved. He introduced himself as Major Pete Bartosik, Air Force, and politely asked the nature of our visit. I was a little surprised as his willingness to set aside whatever he had been working on, and meet with us spontaneously like this. It was a bit of an interruption.

I let Jake do the initial talking, having learned that letting the military men connect on their own common ground was the best way to get the preliminaries out of the way. Jake summarized his own service experience, and concluded by explaining that he had chosen to reassign the three surviving members of his National Guard squad to the City of Chandler, in order to continue serving the community, which was his unit's mission. That wasn't quite how it had originally been explained to me, but I didn't think pointing that out was a good idea at the moment. I also wondered what the major thought of the civilian clothes the National Guardsman was now wearing.

Next, Jake summarized our current status back home, and concluded by explaining our day trip and how we were trying to find out where other organized groups were located. Then it was Major Bartosik's turn to explain the same. He started by congratulating Jake on the progress he had made. It seemed he was assuming Jake was directly responsible for all the progress we had made collectively. That annoyed me slightly. He was especially happy to know that some communities were working to take care of themselves. He went on to brief us on his own situation.

"Luke AFB used to have about 8,000 active duty personnel. After the Superflu died out, some of our survivors went AWOL. We think they headed out to check on their families or just go elsewhere. Some others, including all our remaining pilots, got reassigned to other bases near D.C. or in California. They were ordered to fly their fighters out, to be re-stationed where they could better protect the country from potential threats."

My little shoulder devil was finally fed up with the authority figure. He prodded me to interrupt the major. "What threats? Is any other country even able to mount an attack? The Superflu was worldwide. Don't the 3% in other countries have just as many survival problems as we do? Do they really have the resources, or the will, to do anything to us?"

Major Bartosik looked at me like I was a little kid who should be seen and not heard, but he answered anyways. "I don't know, ma'am. We were ordered to transfer planes and pilots to D.C., Edwards and Vandenberg, so we did. The orders came from the Pentagon, and were properly authenticated. So we did what we were ordered to do."

He turned back to Jake, and continued his main narrative thread. "The orders for the rest of us remaining here were to secure this base, and keep it intact for reserves and future use."

I raised an eyebrow. "So, you're basically just house sitting? What about serving and protecting the greater community?" Major Bartosik did not take kindly having his mission and authority questioned by a civilian.

"Our orders are to secure and protect this base for future use by the U.S. Military." He repeated firmly.

Jake asked, "How much U.S. Military is even left? Who's in charge? Is there even a Commander in Chief anymore?"

Bartosik replied, "The President, the Vice President, the President's Cabinet, and most of Congress, all died of the Superflu. This disease took out everything on the designated succession path. The few remaining congressmen decided to hold an emergency presidential election this fall, and a couple of guys are going around the country, campaigning. Until then, the highest ranking brigadier general left in the Pentagon is in charge of the military. They're actually considering abolishing the 5 branches, and combining what's left into one unified force."

That was rather astonishing news. A presidential election? A unified military?

Jake asked, "And how are you getting this information?"

Bartosik answered, "The Internet. Several Military websites are up and running blogs and a news service. It's not exactly prime time polish, but it's getting the word out."

Jake: "Seriously? I thought the Internet was completely down."

I couldn't help interrupting again. "Not completely. It's a distributed network. Taking out some of it doesn't really affect the rest of it. Some parts of it are still out there. The biggest issue is actually being able to establish connection to a service provider. If you can get to that – which most of us can't, back home – then you can navigate to websites. If know where you want to go. If you have the IP address or URL, just point your browser to it." I paused. I had had no idea that any military websites would still be active, and would never have thought to look for them. The cable modems at our home were pretty iffy, because the servers and provider service, connecting them to the rest of the Internet, were not working well, due to lack of either power, or maintenance, or both. But the city hall building had some direct Internet connections that didn't go through the local provider. I would have to try those when I got home.

Bartosik nodded, and scribbled some URLs on a piece of paper for us to try later on. I collected my thoughts, while he wrote. I finally asked, "So, a presidential election? Will that even matter? How's that going to help us? We still got problems to solve here. Local problems."

Bartosik answered, "I thought you said you were doing fairly well; you're growing food, you've got supplies, housing, power – and that's pretty amazing, by the way."

I blurted out. "Yeah, we got the basics, for now. But we're going to run out of gas, and the power may not be enough. And medicine. We're out of antibiotics. And there's gangs forming, who want to take stuff and hurt people. What are we supposed to do about them? And there's other survivors around, too. Some are doing okay, but there's others who aren't doing nearly as well. Good people who are struggling. How's a new president going to fix that?"

Bartosik managed to keep most of his glare in check. "Well, you'll have to ask him that yourself when he comes through on a campaign trip."

That stumped me. Jake took over. "Well, until that happens, what are you doing in the meantime? What are you guys living on, here? How are you fixed for food and fuel?"

Bartosik resumed his briefing mode. "We actually have a stockpile of food. MREs. We also have a small scale water purification plant on base; it can pump ground water for drinking and sanitation. We have generators to provide power; we're converting some of them to run on aviation fuel, so we can keep on using the regular gas for vehicles." He grinned at that clever adaptation.

Jake: "Isn't that going to piss of the honchos in DC, if you use up all your aviation fuel to air condition this joint?"

Bartosik: "I've only got about 50 people on base. We converted the next building over to a dormitory and mess hall. We've locked everything else down and turned off the lights. It's going to be a while before we use up our reserves. And, as you said, everyone is going to run out of fuel eventually."

I had to butt in again. "What about survivors in the surrounding area? Aren't you doing anything to help them? Families of the service men?"

Bartosik was starting to look a little weary. Clearly, I was starting to poke at known problems. "Ma'am, our mission, first and foremost, is to secure this base. That is what we are focused on."

"But don't you need support? Sooner or later, your food will run out, too. Other survivors around here, non-military people, can help you, if you help them. They can gather more supplies, or start a garden." I paused, not sure if I should tell him about Rob and Maddy. I decided I should at least bring it up, without being specific.

"You know, there's a group of survivors not far from here, a couple of miles away. They've already got a garden going, and some livestock. They've got quite a few people. I'm sure they'd be happy to trade produce to you for gas or security services. If you find other survivors elsewhere, you might be able to house them there, in exchange for extended patrols, to help keep them safe."

Bartosik raised his eyebrows curiously at me. Jake nodded in agreement and gestured for me to go on. I told the Major where the enclave was, and who to ask for. "You should really establish some kind of relationship with them, to trade. Their goods, for your services. You'd both benefit. Helping the communities around you helps you keep this base secure, in the long run. Quid pro quo."

The Major considered the idea. While he was still receptive, I pushed a few more ideas at him. "And, if Rob's enclave gets filled up, you could easily house more people here on base. If you've got the means to pull up ground water, purify it, and keep it circulating through the plumbing, and the power to run the pumps, you could really expand this operation, and be a resource to your region. It sounds like you have a big reserve of fuel. My guys keep telling me it won't last. Use it or lose it. Might as well use it to prepare for the time when you don't have any." I paused to remember what the big picture was. Oh yeah...

"I heard you, when you say you have your orders to protect this base. But don't you also have a bigger mission, to serve and protect this country? This region, this city, is a part of this country. And it needs your help. Gather people. Gather resources. Prepare for the long term."

The major's hard ass military demeanor had slowly eroded. He was now just a man, a fellow human being, in charge of a group of people. He wasn't stupid, it wouldn't take him long to figure out how to break down the problems into manageable chunks, and identify solutions.

He sighed. He spoke, finally. "Protect and serve. That's part of our core principles. Yeah, we could do more, without compromising our orders. I'll have my guys start patrolling a wider area, and dig a little deeper, see what they can find."

I grinned then. "Hey, you like peaches?" He was puzzled by my abrupt change in topic. "There's a peach orchard in Queen Creek; they should start getting ripe next month. You could send some people out to pick them. Or we could send some to you." I didn't offer him any of the urns; it wasn't clear if they had done any body removal. I suspected there had not been a lot of deaths actually on the base; most sick personnel had either gone to nearby hospitals, or to their homes in the nearby suburbs. Therefore, he probably did not need the symbolic comfort of a physical remembrance. Well, maybe he had lost family, too? Maybe next time we met, I'd offer him one.

The Major admitted that yes, some fresh fruit would be a nice treat for him and his people. In anticipation of a potential future trade, he acknowledged that they had a generous quantity of antibiotics and some other hard-to-get medicines in their storage warehouse. He had one of his people gather some for us. He also offered to top off our Hummer's gas tank, too.

We exchanged contact information. He was still able to access email. Phone lines, both land line and cellular, were less reliable. He even had business cards with his current contact info! That was kinda weird, but convenient. We agreed to communicate information regularly, and let him know that his people were welcome to visit Chandler any time. And once again, we packed up, and headed out.

***

It was late afternoon, and the expedition had been more successful than we had anticipated, so we elected not to make any more stops for the day. However, Jake did insist on taking the long way home, by going north on the Loop 101, and circling the northern part of Phoenix and Scottsdale, before going back south again. He wanted to see what there was to see, and watch for any other signs of survivor groups. However, he agreed to just make a note of them, and then go back at another time.

I asked him, "You've got other places in mind as potential enclaves, don't you?" I was thinking about what he had told Rob and Maddy, about studying Google Maps.

He admitted it. "Yeah. I think Cave Creek and Carefree might have potential. They're isolated; not many easy ways in or out. That's good for defense. Big houses on large lots. Not a lot of farming already in place, but that doesn't have to be an obstacle. Bartlett Lake and the Verde River are a few miles to the east. With pumps, they could probably move water where they wanted it. "

I had to point out. "Not many stores close by them, though. They'd have to travel a little farther for their scavenging, more so than most other groups. That means they could encounter more competition.

Jake nodded, "Yeah, that's possible, too. Like I said, it's just an idea. I'll come out some other time, and see if there's anybody around."

I thought about his reasoning, and tried to apply it to other locations. I asked, "Anthem? New River?"

Jake said, "Maybe, but probably less likely. Those are a little more spread out, not as many resources nearby."

"I wonder if there's some formula or way to predict if a neighborhood or a city has a good likelihood of surviving. You know, X number of grocery stores plus Y power sources plus Z water system infrastructure, divided by number of houses, equals an index of survivability."

Jake glanced at me like I was touched in the head. "I doubt it," he responded. "You're forgetting the most important factor."

"What's that?"

"People. Enough people with the will and the skills to survive. You know, that's the real reason that Randy, and Darren and I chose to relocate to Chandler. We had other contacts, other places to go, but they were smaller, not as well organized. I even considered going back to Payson." His face got stony for a moment. I knew he was thinking about his wife, who had died in the pandemic. He rebalanced, though. "But after meeting you that day in front of the hospital, I decided we had to check out Chandler, and give it a try. Mind you, it's not any more special than any other suburb around here. But it does have the right group of people who are willing and able to work together. And that meant something to my guys."

"And you?"

"And me."

I smiled. It was actually pretty touching, to know our encounter had impacted him so much. At the time, I had mostly just been annoyed at the obstacle his road block made, and his refusal to let me through. I'd had no idea he had made a conscious effort to find and choose people who thought like he did.

We were quiet for the rest of the ride home. The freeway was mostly clear. A few cars were pulled over to the side of the road, and we could see dead bodies in them, but they were not blocking traffic. The surface streets we had driven through Phoenix and Glendale had been a little more crowded with disabled cars, but not impassible.

We arrived back in Chandler a little before sunset. Jake stopped off at the hospital, first, to drop of the supplies of drugs that Major Bartosik had given us. Then he took us downtown, where we had all originally met up. We all lived within walking distance, and the Hummer was reserved for city use, so it was usually kept downtown. We quickly found people we knew, hanging out on the promenade of little shops that lined the downtown area. Randy met us first, and confirmed that they had gotten the truck full of clay back to the studio with no issues. I reminded the guys to bring in the veggies that Maddy had given us, and they took them into the restaurant that usually prepared food for the work crews. I saw Carlos talking to a group of people. I waived to him, and pointed to the box that Kyle was carrying past me, and waggled my eyebrows at him. He got the message and nodded at me.

Then Ariana came up, and I knew we had to share a lot of details with her, including contact info. That would require a sit down, so I ordered some food. I had only just realized that we'd never gotten around to eating any lunch, and I was starving. I let Jake do most of the talking, while I scarfed down some fresh salad. Our own gardens were producing nicely. The produce Maddy had given us were things we did not have growing well in our garden. But we did have plenty salad veggies. As I was eating, Gordon turned up and joined us. I promised him I would fill in the details he had missed before arriving.

Jake was filling in the details of the story for the rest of my gang, when Kevin suddenly appeared from nowhere, and sat down on my other side.

"Hey, Maggie!" he greeted me. "I heard you been making your own little trips out and about. I'm beginning to wonder if I've got some competition for the long distance information gathering business." He winked, to show he was teasing me.

"Don't be silly. Today's trip was mostly to get clay. I didn't know Jake would be reaching out to not one, but two other community groups." I told him.

"Yeah, I know. Just kidding. Anyways, I just wanted to stop by, say hi, let you know I'm heading out on another run of my own."

"Really? Where to this time? You going back East already?"

"Not quite yet, it's still a bit early; don't want to get caught in any late winter snowstorms out there."

I nodded appreciatively. Glorious weather here usually meant it was pretty awful most everywhere else in the country.

He continued, "I'm just making another quick run around the state, check on some of the groups I found up north, see how they survived the winter."

"Okay. It's been a pretty mild and dry winter down here. So they probably didn't get much snow in the mountains, either."

"Yeah, not so much worried about people getting snowed in, as I am about just getting six months on down the road from the Superflu."

I nodded in understanding. People still grieved, and grief could make them do crazy things.

Another thought also occurred to me. "Hey, if you get to Show Low or the White Mountains, let them know we connected with a group of people in Coolidge, and that those people are still planning on going up there for the summer. They probably already know that, so sharing the info will just let them know that you're connected. Your own personal node on the face-to-face social network. Oh, and stop by the studio and grab some of the urns, to give away!"

Kevin nodded his own understanding back. "You got it, boss. Will do. Anyways, I'll check back in with you after this trip, in about a week, before I really do go back East," Kevin finished.

"Okay, see you soon." I called after him as he stood up and moved out of the crowd. I turned back to my companions.

Jake was still talking and had gotten to the part where we found out there was going to be a presidential election in the fall.

I asked Ariana, "Did you have any idea such a thing was coming? Is anyone following any news from outside of this area?" I looked around at my companions. Robert Ruckles had joined us, too.

Ariana answered, "Yeah, I've heard that. Our ham radio guy, Paul, told me the same thing. And we didn't know how credible the information is. It's unclear who's running against the guy. I mean, it's not much of an election, if there's only one guy running." We nodded at that.

I idly wondered, "And how are they going to collect the votes? Who's going to put together a ballot, and tabulate it, and pass the counts back up the chain?"

Ariana said, "That's a really good question. Balloting was always handled at the county level. The cities had to pass along the applications for the elected positions to them, and County would generate the ballots, and distribute voting machines and stuff."

We pondered the logistical problems this new information presented.

Ariana spoke again, "Actually, this brings up something that Robert and I have been talking about. Remember when you said we need to hold city elections for a new Mayor and a city council? Robert and I have been going along, doing stuff that needs doing, but there needs to be an officially elected person in charge."

"Someone to take the blame when things go wrong?" I snarked. My shoulder devil was acting up again.

Ariana grinned. "Among other things, yes."

My brain raced along. "Well, if you're going to do that, you'll need to collect nominations. And setup a ballot of your own. Since there's no county government left, then you'll just have to design your own. Keep it simple, just boxes to check off on a piece of paper, and stuff it in a locked box."

Ariana was staring at me, but my mouth was running along without my brain. "When do you think you'll want to hold elections? You should give people enough time to campaign for votes. Is three months enough? That puts us into July; the spring harvest will be finished by then, and most of the house clearing, too. So everyone should have time to focus on other stuff…"

Ariana, Robert, and Gordon were glancing back and forth at each other, with serious expressions. "What? What's going on?" I asked. A little frisson ran down my spine.

Gordon grinned at me, but didn't say anything. Ariana got a little sheepish. "Actually, we're nominating you."

It took my brain a moment to apply the brakes to my mouth, and switch tracks. "WHAT??? Oh No. Hell No! No, no, no, no…. negatory, cancel that. Not happening. No way, no how. I am not Mayor material."

Ariana ignored my whining. "And we're holding the election in two months, not three. We're accepting nominations at the Town Hall this weekend. We already put up announcements for it on the bulletin boards. We'll accept anyone else's nomination, but we think you'll be the winner."

I looked at Gordon. He was still grinning that shit-eating grin that drove me nuts. "Did you know about this?" I asked him. He laughed, winked at me, but didn't say anything.

"You know I don't like to be told what to do," I said, pointing at him.

Gordon, still grinning, said, "We're *asking*, not telling. And it's *nominating*, not drafting."

Ariana was still pitching. "And get this, Pastor Daniel has already informed me that he would like to run for Mayor, himself. He doesn't know yet that we're nominating you."

I rolled my eyes. Pastor Daniel was the local Baptist minister. He was rather ardent about his faith, and tended to assume that everyone already shared his belief, or was just waiting to be told the good news, and when they heard, they would fall to their knees in front of him, begging for his divine forgiveness. Pastor Daniel meant well, but he did not have a lot of room in his heart for people who thought differently than he did.

"Are you even allowed to do that, to make nominations yourself? Isn't that a conflict of interest? Don't they have to come from a disinterested third party?"

"Oh, we'll have someone take care of that. We've got lots of people who can make the actual nomination. Anyone I've even mentioned it to, says they'll vote for you."

"But I'm not Mayor material!" I practically shouted this, and several nearby heads turned to stare at me. A few of them snickered and grinned at me. In a quieter voice, I hissed, "Not cool! I didn't ask for this. I'm a potter, not a politician!"

Ariana giggled at my tantrum. "Too bad. You are being called to serve. Would you really turn down all these people in need?" She gestured around us.

"Why are you doing this to me?" I tried whining. That also did not work.

Ariana answered, "Because for once in my professional life, I'm in the unique position of being able to pick my own boss. And I think you'd make a good boss. You're easy to get along with, you have good ideas, you're generally cheerful, most of the time." Gordon snickered some more at that.

I looked at Robert. He said, "Hey, don't look at me. I'm not supposed to be in charge, either. I just want to work on my water systems. I'm way out of my depth on all this other stuff; food and consolidation, and resource management, and security, and law and order. Somebody has to step up."

I shook my head at them, but couldn't find any more words to object. Neither could my shoulder angel, or my shoulder demon. I needed time to think up some better avoidance strategies.

***

Gordon walked me home after that, and laughed at my continuing blustering and bitching. But he did not let me off the hook, nor did he tell me that I could opt out.

At home, we entered through our front door, which immediately triggered a flood of canine affection upon us. We flopped on the living room couch, and played with the dogs. I had been gone all day, and my boys were eager to be close to me. My littlest one, Tyrion the Chihuahua, jumped on me and crawled up my chest to lick my nose. Amex, my big pit bull, rubbed against our legs, jumped on Gordon and brought us toys. Oreo, the rat terrier, tried to get close too, for a couple of head skritches, but he wasn't much of cuddler. Gordon's two dogs also joined in the reunion. His little silkie terrier, who I called by any name other than her gawd awful given one, Godzilla, snuggled in with Tyrion. And his big stately golden retriever, Duchess, just lay calmly on the floor beside the couch, content to watch the other dogs' shenanigans.

One of our roommates, Carlos, also had a dog, a Jack Russell named Jack, but he was not hanging out with the other dogs. I assumed he was probably with Carlos. And I'd last seen, Carlos was downtown, eating dinner with some other people.

We had other humans in the house as well. Micah immediately joined us as soon as he heard the canine commotion. We had found Micah a couple of months ago, on Christmas Day, and had rescued him from a feral dog pack. He was 12 years old, and had been doing surprisingly well on his own, given the difficulties he faced. But he had leaped at the offer to stay with Gordon. We could tell he was pretty happy to have some adults take over for him. He was pretty clingy and usually hung out in the house with whoever was around.

Our last roommate, Dillon, followed Micah into the main living room. They explained they had been playing video games in Dillon's room.

We settled the dogs down after a time, and Micah and Dillon brought me up to date on their day's activities. Dillon was one of Gordon's linemen, helping to reroute power. Gordon and Dillon were teaching Micah the basics, and called him their apprentice. They had all been at work most of the day. Micah chattered away about lines and inverters and transformers and things I had no clue about. It occurred to me that a 12-year-old should not be 30 feet off the ground in a cherry picker box, playing with live electrical circuits. He should be in school. But school had been canceled when the Superflu broke out, and of course, no one had a clue how to get it started back up again.

So I smacked Gordon, lightly, and interrupted Micah's monologue. "And that's another thing! This kid should be in school! I just made a mental mayoral note to get school started up again. And the very fact that I even have to start a mental mayoral "to do" list is all your fault!"

Gordon was confused, but he was also still very amused at my reaction. "How is this all my fault? We're keeping the kid out of trouble. He's learning a trade. What's wrong with that?"

"Because you didn't put a stop to this nonsense! If you didn't have him 30 feet up in the air in a cherry picker, I would not be thinking that he should be in school! This is crazy. Insane!"

Gordon looked at the other guys. "They told her about the elections."

Dillon nodded, and said "Oh yeah… that. Not taking it well, is she?"

"Yeah, that!" I snapped back at Gordon. "Do you have any idea how much work this is going to be? How am I supposed to get anything done in the studio?"

Gordon, "Don't worry about it yet. It's mostly a ceremonial position, you just have to be there to cut ribbons and hold shovels with big bows on them. It's not that big a deal."

I glared at him. I had a feeling he was way off on that assumption. I had a feeling that yes, it would be a big deal. I wondered if there was an official, detailed job description around. I'd have to ask Ariana.

Gordon was still laughing at my indignation, when Carlos came in with his own dog. He had the paper that Maddy had written out her instructions on. I explained the source of the information, and he was glad to have the context. He agreed that her suggestions sounded good. He had sampled the produce she had sent, and thought it was excellent.

The household settled down after a while. I filled in the guys on the details of the trip around the Valley. They were as pleased as I was, with what we had encountered. Then Gordon herded the dogs outside to take care of business before bedtime. I went into the kitchen. I was cleaning up the dishes left over in the kitchen from our morning breakfast, when Gordon came back in and put his arms around me from behind to give me a big bear hug.

"I'm sorry you were so surprised by Ariana and Robert's idea. I honestly thought it would be a good idea. We just didn't get to break the news to you the right way. But I do think you'd be a great Mayor."

I turned around and leaned into him. He was just enough taller than me, that I could nestle my head perfectly in the crook of his neck. "It's going to be a helluva lot of work, you know. I don't know anything about running a city."

"You don't need to. You'll have a council, too. You just need to listen to everyone else's ideas, sift through them, and then turn it over to Ariana. You know she'll just run with it."

I sighed. "And I don't like being told what to do."

Gordon squeezed me even harder. "When you're mayor, you get to tell everyone else what to do."

I rolled my eyes, even though he couldn't see me doing it. "Ha. You really think so? Cause I don't really think so."

Gordon leaned back and looked at me. "Look, it's going to be okay. You have help. You have resources. I'll support you. Everyone will."

I sighed and leaned back on him. We stood like that for a little bit, and then we went to bed.

I had moved into Gordon's master bedroom only a couple of weeks before. Gordon had quickly claimed one of the biggest, nicest houses in the gated community surrounding the resort golf course, early on when the power zone project had gotten started. Then he had convinced me to move out of my own house several miles away, because the power would be going off soon. Initially, I had taken up residence in the little casita adjacent to the main house. Then within weeks, after our new relationship became more serious, I had agreed to move into the main house and share his bed. We were still adjusting to each other's presence. We both snored, so adapting our sleep habits was a bit of challenge. The dogs were still adapting to the change in routine, as well. Tyrion was used to sleeping in bed with me, and insisted on positioning himself between the two of us, most of the time. And little Zililly usually wanted to occupy the same space, as well. It was an ongoing discussion, convincing the little dogs that a king size bed was big enough for all of us.

We had also briefly had one other roommate in the house, a young woman named Yarelie. However, she had committed suicide by gun about a month before. It had devastated me. I had barely even known the woman, and felt guilty because of that. I felt that I had not made enough of an effort to get to know her better, or to see how much pain and grief she was in. Everyone had their demons. Everyone had lost their entire families, friends, and social circles. But most people I encountered seemed to be making an effort to continue to function. Having something useful and meaningful to do seemed to help a lot of people. But I had missed the signs that Yarelie was not coping as well as others. It still saddened me, but I kept on going, anyways.

I added another item to the mental "to do" list, to let Caleb know we had room for additional people. Caleb had taken on the project of assigning people to housing. It might be good to have more people around the house. Maybe another woman or two. Gordon's house already had plenty of testosterone. We needed some more feminine balance. Okay, *I* wanted some balance.

Chapter 4

During the several days that followed, people that I ran into told me they'd heard I was going to be the next mayor, and preemptively congratulated me. I had to remind them that there was a process to go through, including nominations, campaigning and elections, and that nothing was a done deal yet. Nobody seemed phased by any of that.

Saturday's Town Hall meeting arrived. Town Halls were generally somewhat raucous events. There wasn't a lot of organization to them. The meetings usually attracted around 200 to 300 people. I knew we had identified more than a thousand survivors, but not all of them came regularly to the meetings. More showed up for the after-party, but plenty more found other things to do on their Saturday evenings. The Mercados restaurant on the city promenade had been handing out meals prepared from the packaged food collected from the local grocery stores. And lately the food was supplemented with produce from the community gardens. Mostly it was simple things, like spaghetti and meat sauce, or maybe baked enchiladas or some kind of casserole. Sometimes they had to get a little creative.

I wondered if city-sponsored feeding of people was becoming an issue yet. I wondered if the people coming in for food were the same ones who had been on the work crews all day, or not. There were enough people around now, that I wasn't entirely sure who was on a work crew, and who was just hanging out.

There was a craft breweryand pub next door to Mercados restaurant. Some old codger character had claimed it and had managed to get the vats brewing again. For now, he was willing to share the beer freely, so long as everyone was drinking responsibly. Meaning, not getting into fights or harassing people. And of course, no drunk driving. He also promised people that he'd start charging for the beer as soon as he started running low on supplies like wheat and hops. I didn't know what currency he planned to ask for, but I suspected gold coins would be high on his preferred exchange rate.

***

Gordon and I walked to the open park in the downtown area where the meeting was held. Micah came with us, but he quickly found the few other pre-teens around, who he was becoming friends with. They took off on bicycles to go do whatever kids did when allowed to roam unsupervised.

Robert Ruckles called the Town Hall meeting to order a few minutes after 4pm. Ariana and her assistants had handed out the agenda for the meeting as people were arriving and taking seats. This session included brief updates about ongoing projects (houses cleared: 10,000; water quality: safe to bathe with, please keep boiling any drinking water; Power: On in the consolidation zone, coming back on in an additional expansion zone, going down in the power off zones). Then they moved onto the meat of the meeting.

Robert banged his gavel to get a wave of chatter to subside. "Okay, folks, as you know, my team and I have been doing the best we can to run this city. However, it's time we got some proper leadership in place. This city needs a mayor and a City Council to determine policy and set our course for the future. If you've looked at the city website recently, or seen the notices on the bulletin boards around town, you know that we're accepting nominations for the position of mayor, and five City Council seats. We'll be holding elections in June, with the new term to begin in July. In the election, the person with the most votes will be mayor, and the next highest number of votes will be first Council member and so on, until the five open seats on the Council are filled. The mayor and two of the five Council members' terms of office will be four years, plus six months. That will bring those positions back into sync with the former electoral calendar the entire country used to follow. The other three Council member terms will be two years plus six months. When those terms are up, November elections will fill those open seats to start a new four year term the following January. That way, we'll have continuity of leadership in place at every election cycle. Does that make sense? Anyone have any questions about how those terms will work?"

A bunch of hands flew up into the air. Robert had to go through it several more times, before everyone was fully up to speed.

After that, Robert began the nomination process. He explained that anyone who wanted to nominate someone to a position had to stand up and announce their nomination verbally. They also had to turn in a short form indicating the person's name and a brief explanation why that person should be accepted onto the ballot (the forms were being distributed as he spoke). The nominee also had to sign their acceptance of the nomination on that form, as well. Robert and Ariana wanted this process documented in writing, just in case any electoral oversight committee came along some day, from the county, state or federal government.

I had been growing increasingly tense and nervous throughout the meeting. I had Tyrion in tow for this meeting. I was hoping he'd serve as a comfort/therapy dog, but he seemed more interested in randomly barking at odd things, instead of calming my nerves. Gordon was holding Zoe-illa and Amex on their leashes.

The first person to speak up was not one my backers, though. It was a woman whose face I recognized as a member of Pastor Daniel's church parish. I didn't know her name. She raised her hand, and was called on first. "I nominate Pastor Daniel Johannsen for Mayor. He's been a good shepherd to his flock, seeing to our needs and our comfort. He has a lot of great ideas for this community and I think he should be the next Mayor." There was some polite applause while she passed her filled out form to the meeting attendant on the side. I assumed it was already signed by the Pastor.

Robert said, "Very well. Our first nomination. Thank you!" He motioned for the next hand. Someone else I did not know shouted out a name I also did not know, and a justification, and turned in his paperwork. That happened several more times. Each nomination was followed by a short round of applause. Finally, Darren, one of the deputy patrol cops working for Zach, was called upon. He was dressed in plain street clothes, to indicate he was operating as a private citizen, not a city employee. He grinned at me, and spoke loudly.

"I nominate Maggie Shearin for Mayor. She's smart, she has lots of ideas on what needs to be done. She listens to what anyone has to say. She's compassionate, caring, and is building that beautiful monument for us." The same applause followed, and the paper form was brought around to me to sign my acceptance. They had thoughtfully remembered to bring a pen, because I certainly had not brought one.

My stomach was doing dread flip flops over this. But my shoulder angel poked me and told me to suck it up, stand up, smile and wave. So I did.

And just like that, I was running for mayor.

***

As usual, my friends joined Gordon and I for dinner and beer after the meeting. We claimed one of the picnic tables on the promenade, in front of Mercados. This put us out in full view, and it was already a pretty common practice for random people to interrupt us with questions, or to report some tidbit of information to the administrative team. For once, Zach Adams was out of uniform, so technically he was off duty. However, a cop never seems to really be off duty. The lack of a uniform didn't stop people from approaching him.

Zach congratulated me on our meetings with the west side people earlier in the week. He'd been especially glad to find out that the Air Force Base had not been abandoned. Too much military grade hardware and resources in a place like that, to leave unsecured.

Then I asked him for an update on our own local security. "Jake was telling me about some of the gangs that are looting and setting fire to buildings in Phoenix. Are you seeing much of that here in the East Valley? I've been mostly stuck in the studio, and haven't been paying attention in the last few weeks."

Zach answered, "There's been some minor incidents, so far. We've caught a couple of people having mental melt downs, when they find that their favorite store is empty. Survivors that slipped through the net before, or were farther out in areas we haven't thoroughly screened yet. They had been surviving by raiding their closest stores and weren't even close to emptying them, when the truck crews came in and hauled everything out. Those people just couldn't handle it. They didn't know about the operation we've got going here. We took a couple of them over to the hospital for treatment. But no, we've not seen the gangs yet; no organized opposition, no random recreational violence, yet." He grimaced at that turn of phrase.

"What about that Russian woman who came in last winter and

threw a hissy fit about her house? You said that you think she might be cooking and dealing meth?" I asked.

Zach nodded, "Petra Vasilov. Yeah, we still think that, but it's been really difficult to catch her or her team in action. We *are* getting a handle on who she's recruited to help her, though. In a way, she's forming a new old school gang, criminal style. She's gathering people to who can cook, transport and sell the stuff. We think she's got a facility in Phoenix, or maybe Ahwatukee, but definitely outside Chandler city limits. And we're trying to keep our official patrol cars within city limits, or close to them. Unofficially, I don't mind sending guys after her outside city limits. But it's too easy to spot a tail, when there's no one else on the road, so it's almost impossible to follow her. If she sees any of my guys, she just stops her car and waits until they go away. We can't do anything to her for just driving around."

I thought for a moment. "What about drones? Can any of your guys operate a drone, and follow her from up above?"

Zach was startled at this idea. "I'm sure they'd love to learn how! That's actually a good idea!" He waived Randy and Darren over, and relayed instructions for them to find some equipment and start practicing. He suggested that if toy versions available to average consumers were not up to the job, they could try to find a U.S. Border Patrol office and see if there were any there.

Gordon was grinning at me. "See? This is why they want you to be mayor. You've got ideas." The tiny muscles at the back of my eyeballs were starting to ache from all the rolling.

Moments later, we were interrupted by the head doctor from the hospital, Dr. Reddy. I didn't know the man well, but that didn't stop him from claiming a few minutes of my time.

"Miss Shearin, congratulations on your nomination." I nodded. He went on. "And thank you for the antibiotics that were dropped off a few days ago. I don't know if anyone has briefed you on the progress we've made at the hospital. But I wanted to let you know about a special project we're working on. We've actually started culturing some home grown antibiotics and vaccines. We've put together a lab and gathered some pharmaceutical grade raw ingredients from some Phoenix warehouses. We're actually going to start making some medicines of our own, in small batches."

"You're kidding! That's wonderful news! No, I didn't know anything about it." I smiled at him, and made room for him on the bench next to me to sit down. I gestured for him to tell me more.

Dr. Reddy plunged on. "However, they will be mostly in liquid or semi-liquid form. Forming the ingredients into dry pills is still a challenge for us, at this time. And that's why I wanted to talk to you. We need apothecary jars. Small bottles that can be sterilized, filled, and sealed. We need to be able to label them and distinguish between many varieties."

I raised my eyebrows. "You couldn't find enough plastic pill bottles that you could use?"

Dr. Reddy shook his head and explained, "Plastic is fine for dry pills, but does not work well for liquids, creams or pastes. The caps leak. However, ceramic can be sealed with wax or cork or rubber stoppers. Glass would be even better, but so far as I know, we do not have any glass blowers around. Do we?" He asked that hopefully. I shook my head. I'd always wanted to learn glass blowing, but had not gotten around to it before.

Dr. Reddy was sketching sizes of bottles in the air with his hands. "I'd need them sized to hold 1 to 3 ounces, or about a hundred milligrams of material. They need a flat smooth surface that we can apply a sticker label to. Different colors, so we can categorize them by drug class." Dr. Reddy was getting excited at the prospect of getting what he needed.

I interrupted him. "What kinds of drugs do you expect to make, besides antibiotics?"

"We'll be able to culture some vaccines. We'll still need to vaccinate kids against chicken pox, mumps, polio, all the usual childhood diseases. And tetanus, pneumonia and shingles vaccines." He paused. Carefully, he added, "I think we can develop vaccines against future flu viruses, too. It's too late to do anything about the Superflu; that strain has burned itself out. But others mutations could still pop up."

I thought over what he had said. "What about insulin? Does anyone even need insulin anymore? I would have thought all the diabetics got wiped out by the Superflu. It seemed to take out anyone with any kind of underlying condition that made it hard to fight off infections."

He explained. "Yes, mostly. I don't have any active cases of diabetes at the moment. But it can always develop later on. Also heart disease. But most everyone who survived is much more active now, and getting enough exercise from their work. They do not need drug therapies for diabetes or heart conditions very much right now. But we still need vaccines against infectious diseases."

"Wouldn't most of the kids that are left already be fully vaccinated?"

Dr. Reddy smiled at me. "There are some new pregnancies. In a few months, there will be the start of a small baby boom."

My eyes widened. I knew some people were hooking up. Heck, I was one of them. But I had been blithely ignoring the obvious consequence of that normal human behavior. Maybe my subconsious thought my birth control lecture to Jenna had percolated to the entire population? Well of course not, silly!

"Oh," I said. "Okay, yeah, they'll need vaccines eventually. Right. Okay, so, little jars. Wouldn't small glass bottles work, too? I said you raided a pharmaceutical storage warehouse, to get the other drugs; didn't they have empty bottles waiting to be filled?"

Dr. Reddy shook his head. "They had some, and we are using them, but it will not be enough."

"What about those little airplane bottles of alcohol? Those should be the perfect size."

Dr. Reddy was still shaking his head. "Also, just 'some'. We can use some of them but it will be difficult to properly reseal a cap on them. The little metal caps won't be sterile, once they are removed to pour out the alcohol. And they are a thin poor quality of metal for re-sterilizing and resealing. And the bottle mouths are very small for other types of stoppers."

"Okay, so you really want ceramic apothecary jars, made to very exact specifications. I'll get started on them ASAP. You should know that while ceramic can be sterilized, it takes some care. Ceramic has to be heated evenly, to avoid thermal shock. That might be an issue for you. If you can find a good source of more glass vials, you should take advantage of that."

"Yes, Miss Maggie, understood. Even so, it would be nice to have small pots that were made locally. I think it would help people with community connections. Even if we use glass for some of the vaccines, we plan to produce some ointments as well, which might be better dispensed from a shallow jar with a wide mouth, like a ladies moisturizer jar, for example."

I nodded my understanding. Certain types of drugs could be administered topically, through a cream or ointment on the skin. Especially useful for treating cuts, scrapes, minor burns and rashes. I could accommodate that.

Dr. Reddy had one more thing to point out. "And jars made by you; wouldn't that be, what did they call it before… "branding"? If we send out medicines to other communities, packaging them in your pottery will help remind them where it came from."

I grinned at that. He had a valid point. I wondered if I could come up with a unique design that would still produce a nicely functional small vessel. Gordon was grinning at me again, when Dr. Reddy left. "And that's the flip side; other people have ideas, and you're good at helping them make them happen, too."

"Well, duh! When the idea involves making a pot, it's right there in my own wheel house. But there's plenty of other stuff I don't know about."

Gordon gripped my hand. "Maggie, it's going to be fine. People trust you. You just need to trust yourself. Come on, you ready to head home?"

I was. We gathered up the dogs, and did just that. Micah cruised up on his bicycle at that moment, and we paused to let him grab a burrito from the restaurant, to take home to eat. Our friends had mostly been dragged away from our table earlier to listen to other people's suggestions, ideas or complaints. So I waived at Ariana and gave her the universal hand signal for "Call me later!" even though we rarely could reach each other on the phones. She knew I meant that metaphorically, not literally.

We walked home while Micah cycled off ahead of us. I contemplated the information that Dr. Reddy had given me. "Gord, did you catch that part about a coming baby boom?"

Gordon answered, "Yeah, I was right there."

I wasn't sure how to maneuver into the thing I really wanted to say. "You know, we never really talked about babies, before. That would typically be third date material, and, well, we haven't exactly been following a typical pattern in this." I waved my free hand between us.

Gordon jumped way ahead of me. "Been there, done that, not doing any more poopy diapers." He was referring to his grown daughter, who had died of the Superflu while she was half way across the country at college. Then he added, "We've got Micah now, that's enough child rearing for me. He's at that fun age, where I can teach him stuff. It's like the enthusiasm and hero worship of an 8 year old, wrapped up in the body of a teenager." He grinned.

"Careful, Gordo. He'll be turning into a real teenager in no time at all, and just like that," I snapped my fingers, "he'll hole up in his room, playing the most obnoxious music he can find, at top volume, and dying his hair into a purple mohawk, and acting like you're the biggest dork on the planet."

Gordon grinned at my teasing. "Nah, Micah's not like that. He's too needy and desperate for approval. Superflu trauma." He paused. "I wonder if we can call that a thing. Like PTSD, only, ST?"

"I think PTSD applies to Superflu survivors, as is."

"Hmm. I think it's a thing now," he said.

"Anyways, the point I wanted to make, about the babies..." I hemmed and hawed a little bit. "Well, there's not going to be any, here, between us, I mean." I was waving my hands between us again. "I had some ovarian cysts when I was in my 20's. Bad ones. Required complete removal. Of the ovaries." I paused, and waited for his nod of understanding. He stopped and gave me a sympathetic look.

"Mags, I'm sorry. Did you *want* to have kids?"

"Actually, no, that's the thing. I never did, and I still don't. I was glad when it happened. it meant I didn't have to worry about birth control and accidents. It was pretty liberating, actually."

Now Gordon was confused. "Really?" He paused. "Well, that explains why you didn't ask me to get condoms."

"We should have, you know. They're good for disease prevention, too, you know."

Gordon pretended some mock indignation, "Hey, I'm clean. I survived the Superflu, you know. If we can fight that off, we can fight off anything."

"Uh, no, it doesn't quite work that way, and you know better. But you're right. It's too late now to worry about what we can give each other, at the moment. And yes, I'm clean too; haven't been with anyone for years, before you. It was a long dry spell." I eye rolled again.

Gordon responded, "Oh, well, that explains a lot..." I smacked him on the arm. I seemed to have to do that a lot lately.

"Anyways, I just wanted to make sure you understood, about not having any kids. I mean little ones. Besides, it is way too late for me to be having babies. Yeah, I know women older than me have done it, but I'm not going to be one of them."

"Older? I thought you were 25?"

"Do I have to smack you again?" I said, sarcastically.

Gordon laughed at me. "Don't worry about it. Like I said, I'm *way* past the poopy diaper phase. I'd be fine if I never had to change another diaper again in my life."

"Gordon, *no one* likes changing diapers. That's not unique to you. So, you're sure you're okay with it?"

"Yeah, trust me, I'm fine. I gotta feeling there will be plenty of opportunity to be around babies in the near future. And the great thing about other people's babies, is you can play with them and have fun, and then turn them back over to their parents, when they're not fun anymore." He grinned.

"Right. Grandparents, and honorary aunts and uncles."

Gordon nodded. "Exactly."

I grinned back at him. This had gone much better than I had anticipated.

We arrived home and caught up with Micah, who was eating his burrito at the kitchen counter.

"Looks like a pretty good burrito, there, kiddo." Gordon commented. Micah was practically inhaling the food. It occurred to me that I wasn't doing a very motherly job at keeping him fed. I should have made him sit down and eat a regular meal with us, earlier. Yet another example of how I was not good mother material, let alone mayoral material.

Gordon rummaged around in the freezer, and pulled out two pints of ice cream. Part of his original scavenging stash. I didn't think he had many of them left. He grabbed three spoons from a kitchen drawer. He looked at me with a gleam in his eye, and asked, "Peanut butter or chocolate?"

"Chocolate!" I said gleefully.

Micah chimed in, "Both!"

Gordon grinned, and handed me a spoon and the chocolate pint. He kept grinning and asked me another question: "Coke or Pepsi?"

Me: "Coke!"

In rapid fire rhythm, Gordon kept going. "Kermit or Miss Piggy?"

Me: "Kermit, duh!"

Gordon: "Optimus Prime or Pikachu?"

Me: "What?"

Micah: "Optimus Prime, of course!"

Gordon: "Mac or PC?"

Me: "PC."

Micah: Mac!"

I improvised one, quickly: "Android or iPhone?"

Gordon: "iPhone."

Micah: "Also iPhone!"

I shook my head at both of them and passed them the chocolate pint to share.

Gordon took over again: "Bruce Willis or Vin Diesel?"

Me: "Ugh. Bruce Willis, I suppose."

Micah: "Who are those guys?"

Gordon waived it off. "Knight Rider, or Dukes of Hazard?"

I scoffed. "Knight Rider, of course!" I looked at Micah. "Sorry, kiddo, Gordo's hopped into the way back machine."

Gordon snickered at me, and continued, "College football or Pro football?"

Me: "College. Easy."

Gordon: "Golf or tennis?"

Me: "Yuck. Neither."

Gordon: "Michael Jordon or Kobe Bryant?"

Me: "Magic Johnson!"

Micah: "Who's Magic Johnson?"

Gordon, "Oh, *now* who's getting into the way back machine, huh?" I flipped my hand at them and took the chocolate ice cream back.

Micah tried one: "World of Warcraft or Call of Duty?"

Gordon responded instantly, "Call of Duty!"

I didn't respond. I stuck a spoonful of ice cream in my mouth.

Gordon looked to me. "Got any more?"

I answered. "Gimme a minute. I'm thinking. Keep going. I'll come up with something soon."

Gordon looked thoughtful. "Okay, for Micah: Nikes or Reeboks?"

Micah: "Nikes!"

Gordon: "French fries or mashed potatoes?

Micah: "Fries!"

Me: "French Fries." Micah and I fist bumped.

Gordon: "Chocolate chip or oatmeal raisin?"

Micah: "Chocolate chip!"

"Ditto!" I said.

Micah: "What does that mean?"

Gordon snickered. I suddenly felt old. The way back machine was starting to squeal on rusty gears. I answered, "It means, 'same thing,' or 'me too.' Okay Gordo, how about this: San Francisco or New Orleans?"

Gordon: "The teams or the cities?"

Me: "Cities, as a travel destination."

Gordon: "San Francisco. New Orleans was a dump, even before it got schmucked by the hurricane."

Micah: "I dunno. Never been."

Me: "Okay, how about this one, Micah: Disneyland or Sea World?"

Micah: "Oh, that's a tough one, too. I pick Disneyland cause it's bigger. There's more to do there."

Gordon was still grinning, and nodded. "Ditto too."

"Okay, boys, I'm running out of ideas. And I'm tired. I'm going to bed." I handed the ice cream back to them. I was pretty sure they would finish off what was left, but that was okay. I gave Gordon a peck on the cheek, and headed off. They must have decided to play a few rounds of Call of Duty, because I was asleep before Gordon came to bed.

Chapter 5

On Sunday morning, I was puttering about aimlessly. I no longer had an established routine to fall back on. And that made me restless. So I wandered around the house, looking for something to do. I took care of some minor chores. I started a load of laundry. I boiled up a fresh batch of clean water. We had a huge restaurant grade soup pot that we keep on the stove. Every other day or so, we filled it, boiled it for two minutes, let it cool, and then siphoned off water into bottles to carry about. Or used it for coffee or cooking.

Those chores did not take me long. Before moving in with Gordon, I would have spent my weekends in my garage studio, making my own work. Or sleeping in. In the last few months, I'd sometimes struggled to find my motivation to get up and get moving in the mornings. Recently though, getting vertical was getting easier.

Now, since I spent my entire work week at the school studio, I had given myself permission to take weekends off from the clay. Over the last several weekends, I had been slowly working on moving from my own house, to Gordon's casita, and then into his main house.

Gordon's house had been mostly furnished, so I'd only brought my clothes and personal things and some family pictures. The process of moving my stuff hadn't been terribly difficult. But we'd also moved a lot of my studio equipment, including my kiln, to the school or to Gordon's garage. And then we had trekked over to some furniture stores in Ahwatukee, to get some matching bedroom pieces, like dressers. All that running around had seemed to take up all our time over the last several weekends. And then I had switched from the casita to Gordon's master bedroom, so some of the stuff got moved again. Finally now, that phase was complete.

Gordon had left the house early to check on a couple of projects that his guys had been working on. He'd taken Micah with him. They had promised to be back by midday, and that we'd go do something fun in the afternoon, a family outing. We hadn't decided on what, just yet, though.

The other roomies had also made themselves scarce, so I was left to rattle around the big house alone. Gordon's house was big, probably 3,000 or 4,000 square feet; I didn't know for certain. It was roughly square, organized as a series of rooms wrapped around a small central courtyard. The courtyard had a short breezeway to a larger back yard with a pool. The dogs loved the huge yard and spent many hours wandering, sniffing and marking it as their own territory. The property had several mature trees, including eucalyptus, orange, grapefruit and lemons. I decided to try to collect the last of the oranges, and squeeze the juice to freeze. It was getting pretty late for oranges; they were usually ripe around the end of February. Which was all the more reason to clean up the last of the good ones, before they got too dried out, fell off and rotted.

I tried listening to an audio book while I worked, but was having a hard time focusing on it. The nomination and election stuff was buzzing around in my brain. I picked several buckets full of oranges, and carried them into the kitchen. I was cutting them in half, and squishing the halves on the electric juicer. When enough juice had collected, I transferred it to plastic bags set in Tupperware boxes, and moved those to the freezer. Once frozen solid, the blocks could be stacked and packed neatly in the deep chest freezer in the garage, for longer term storage.

Naturally, my hands were sticky with juice and pulp when the doorbell rang. I managed to open the door by covering my hands with a towel, to find Ariana on the doorstep. The doorbell had also attracted the entire pack of dogs, who greeted her enthusiastically and noisily.

Once we calmed the fur alarms down, she followed me into the kitchen so I could finish my project. She sat down on one of the bar stools opposite me, and explained her visit.

"I saw Gordon and Micah drive off a while ago, so I thought I'd mosey up here and see what you're up to."

I gestured at the mess of squished orange halves, and filled boxes. "Just hanging out, puttering around. It's supposed to be my day off, and I have no idea what to do with myself. I haven't had a day off in…, well, I can't remember how long. What are we supposed to do with these again?"

"Beats the heck outta me. When my husband, Vargo, was around, he'd watch sports all day. Football in the winter, baseball in the spring and summer. But, so much for that, now."

"Yup. So, I was thinking I should redecorate around here. This place is pretty generic. I was thinking I should go get some more of my art from my house, and put it up."

"Oh, that would be cool. You going to do that today?"

"Not sure. I only just thought of it a little bit a go. I should check with Gordon, see if he minds. It *is* his house…"

Ariana said, "It's yours, too, now. You have to make it your own; put your style on it. Turn it into a home, not just a house."

I smiled at her. She had a good point. "Do you know who was living here before? I don't think I've ever seen any family pictures from the people who lived here before? It seems kinda rude to just shove their stuff aside, like they never mattered."

"No, I don't." She thought for a moment. "Actually, I think this house might have been up for sale, when the Superflu hit. I think it was already empty, and had been staged for selling. I mean, really, who puts up crap like this?" She was pointing at the huge stylized fork and spoon mounted on the kitchen wall. They were about 3 feet long, and vaguely stylized to look art deco-ish.

"Yeah, I don't like them, either. They gotta go."

Ariana asked, "Are you going to put pots in here?" She pointed up at the tops of the cabinets, which had plenty of open space above them.

"Probably. I have a bunch of pots on my cabinets in my own house. I could bring them over."

Ariana nodded, and was just opening her mouth to say something, when the radio belted to her hip buzzed. She unclipped it, held it to her ear and responded to the call. I could hear a tinny voice, but could not make out what was being said. I watched her face carefully. She got a very serious expression. After a couple of moments, she said,

"Actually, I'm with her right now. We'll be right down."

She looked at me, and said, "Get cleaned up, we gotta get downtown. There's visitors, and they're asking for you.

That was weird. What kind of visitors would come here unannounced? Maybe the Coolidge group? Why were they asking for me?

59

I washed my hands, changed tops, and ran brush through my hair. I scribbled down a quick note for the guys, and handed out dog treats to the puppies. I considered bringing Amex with me, but decided he was just too hyper for this. I belted on my gun holster; that was enough weapon. I didn't need a pit bull, too.

Most of the time I walked to and from the downtown area. However, since this seemed urgent, and Ariana had driven over to my house, she drove us downtown. We arrived to find several unfamiliar trucks and SUVs parked along the promenade. I also noticed a dusty green Jeep that was familiar to me. A large group of people were standing around on the corner, including Zach, in uniform, and a couple of his deputies. There were about 15 or so people that I did not recognize, dressed in an assortment of desert and jungle camouflage, with serious looking assault rifles on their backs, and heavy gear belts weighed down with more weapons, ammo and tools. I also noticed Kevin, standing beside Zach, looking relieved to see me.

I strode up to them, with as much confidence and purpose as I could muster. Ariana trailed after me. "Hey, guys. What's going on? Hi Kevin, good to see you back." I nodded at Kevin.

"Here she is, she's the one I've been telling you about. Mr. Stettner, this is Maggie Shearin. Maggie, this is Patrick Stettner." His voice was fast and excited, and just a touch higher than normal. He gestured to a large man standing opposite him. The entire group had formed a rough circle, with Stettner and his people on one side, and Zach and our people on the other. Even with Ariana's and my arrival, we were still outnumbered. There were not many other locals around the area this early in the morning.

It took me a moment to be sure I was looking at the correct man. I tried holding my hand out to shake, and stepping into the circle, but the big man did not respond. He was taller than I was, a stocky build, with brown hair in a receding hairline, brown eyes, and mustache. He just eyed me carefully. I dropped my hand, but it took all my grit to not step back. I remained a couple of steps in front of the rest of my people.

"Mr Stettner? What can I do for you?" I asked him neutrally. Stettner didn't respond right away. He was clearly sizing me up, assessing my bearing and backing. I was still pretty confused about what was going on, but I could sense that I'd better be straight with this guy.

He finally asked, "Kevin says you're in charge of this little operation here. Is that correct?"

I glanced back at Kevin, who looked a little embarrassed. "Uh, not quite, no. It's a group effort. Technically, the head guy in charge is Robert Ruckles, the town's water quality manager."

Stettner frowned at that. "Kevin told us that you were the Mayor."

Kevin spoke up, "Uh, I said she's *going* to be our Mayor. When we hold elections."

I amended that. "Well, I've only just been nominated for the position. Elections are in a couple of months. And of course, there's no guarantee what will happen. There's several other candidates running, too."

Stettner was still frowning. "So, if you're not in charge yet, why would you send this man out to spy on us?"

I frowned back at him. Spy? That was not the verb I was using for Kevin's activities. I wanted more info first.

"Uh, where are you folks from? How did you meet Kevin? Why do you think he was spying on you?"

Stettner thought for a few moments, and decided to share a few tidbits of info, in order to get his own questions answered. "We're from Oak Creek Canyon. My group took possession of the canyon last fall, when the Superflu hit. It's ours now, and we don't much appreciate strangers knocking on our front door. We turned him away politely last fall. But then he showed up again this spring, and we can't help but wonder what he's really after."

Okay, now the puzzle pieces were getting sorted out. Oak Creek Canyon was north of Sedona. With only one main paved road that traversed the entire narrow, deep canyon, it was easy to seal off from outsiders. Some parts of the canyon opened up wide enough for some small scale gardening. And there was trout in the river. They probably had horses, and maybe a few cows, too. There was an assortment of cabins, small houses and woodland resorts scattered throughout the canyon, as well. And the creek flowed year round, an excellent source of water, if they took care not to pollute it. The canyon had been a popular tourist destination, known for its scenic beauty and cooler-than-the-valley temperatures.

I answered his question. "Kevin is not a spy. He's a scout. I've asked him to collect information on what other people are doing to survive, all around the country, and maybe to help establish some trading partnerships."

"A scout." Stettner said skeptically.

"Yes, a scout. Someone who collects information, and brings it back," I said.

"I know what 'scout' means. And I also know a scout is usually reporting information about an enemy back to a military unit."

Oh geez, this guy was going to be a hard ass. I could feel my shoulder devil starting to perk up. I turned back to Ariana and asked her, in a clear calm voice, loud enough that everyone could hear me, "Is there anyone in Mercado's yet? Do you think we could get some beverages out here, some coffee, maybe some of that fresh orange juice?" She nodded, and turned to go inside. I felt a twinge of guilt for treating her like my assistant.

I turned back to the group. "Why don't we sit down here, and have a talk." I gestured at the same picnic tables I'd been hanging out at last night.

Stettner and his people looked at each other, and nodded. He and a couple of his people took a seat across from me, while the rest widened the circle a little bit, scattering farther about. Several faced away from us, scanning the surroundings. Zach took a seat on one side of me, and Kevin on the other. Zach's deputies remained standing behind us, backs to the shop windows facing the street.

"Thank you," I nodded to them. "Look, clearly, we're not a military unit. We're not spying on you, or anyone. We're just interested in establishing contacts with other survivor groups. We're just a city, a little one. Heck, by some definitions, you could call us a 'village' now. And I'm not in charge, but yes, I did ask Kevin to go collect information. Honestly, it was just a way to refocus him on something positive. Kevin doesn't do well when he's sitting still in one place. He's not the usual work-a-day kind of guy. He used to be a long haul trucker, before. He's got a case of wander lust, likes to travel. So, I sent him out and asked him to let us know what he finds. He found your group last fall, and he went back to see how you survived the winter.

Spring is here, and he's getting ready for a bigger trip soon, but we agreed that a short trip in-state would be a good idea before he goes back East."

Kevin was staring at me. I don't think he'd realized my personal perspective on his own behavior patterns before now. I ignored him.

Stettner was eyeing me, too. I waited to see if he would accept what I had told him. Finally, he asked, "And what was the deal with all the pottery?" His tone was neutral, carefully controlled.

Kevin interrupted. "He smashed them, Maggie. Pulled them all out of my Jeep, and smashed them on the road." He looked sad at this.

I put my hand on Kevin's arm, to silence him, but waited a moment before I said anything. Stettner did not deny it; the expression on his face remained stern.

"Well, that's a real shame. I made those, you know. As trade gifts. They're funerary urns to hold the cremains of your loved ones." I met his brown eyed stare evenly.

Kevin spluttered again. "He thought they were bombs, IEDs." I squeezed Kevin's arm gently, and he stopped talking.

Stettner finally looked away. When he looked back, his voice was a little softer. "I just found it extremely weird, some stranger arriving with a load of pottery, of all things. If you wanted to trade, why didn't you send liquor or ammo? Those are the preferred trade goods, these days."

Now I was confused. I still kept my voice even and slow. "Are they? Who's trading that with you?"

"Some people. We've been meeting with a couple of groups in Verde Valley and Cottonwood."

"And they're trading ammunition to you, for... what? Food?"

Stettner: "No, the other way around. We've traded our ammo to them for fresh food. Verde Valley has a lot of vegetable farms. Some hay and grain, too."

"I see. Aren't you growing any of your own food?" Still keeping it neutral and even. At that moment, Ariana walked out with one of the Mercados staffers who was carrying a pot of coffee, and several mugs. She passed these around. Another one of the restaurant people followed her a moment later, with a large pitcher of orange juice and a tray of glasses. I poured myself a glass of the juice and offered the pitcher around, as well. Ariana sat down beside Zach.

After Stettner had sipped some of his coffee, he answered my question. "We're growing some food, but it's difficult. A lot of the soil in the canyon is very sandy. Sometimes, things don't grow every well there. We've caught and smoked a lot of trout, though."

I nodded encouragingly at that. That was a potential trade good there, something we couldn't produce locally.

"Are you running short on food then? Are you interested in trading with us?" I was starting to get a little hopeful.

"No, we're not short, we have enough MREs to last for awhile yet."

Hmm. My shoulder devil was cranking the calculation wheels in my head. "MREs? Those get pretty boring after awhile. I'll bet your people were happy to finally start getting some fresh food."

Stettner smiled thinly. "Yes, they do appreciate that."

"So, how many people do you have, just out of curiosity?" This was a nosy question, and I wasn't sure if he'd take it well. He didn't. He just stared at me some more.

"Alright, I'll tell you mine first. Chandler used to have a population of almost 250,000 people. The Superflu killed off 97%, so that should have left around 7,000 people. We think, of those, about half, maybe as much as three quarters, bugged out, went elsewhere, or died from other causes. We have a little over a thousand people that we've identified, and we think there's maybe up to another thousand or so still hiding out in their homes. We've got patrols and work crews going door to door, to identify survivors, and remove the dead. If there are no living occupants in a house, we clean it out and turn off the water and power. If there are survivors, we encourage them to move into our consolidation zone here. We've got electrical crews turning off some neighborhoods, and rerouting major trunk lines to keep this area powered on. We're also moving solar panels and installing them here, to supplement grid power, too." I paused, and then asked, "There, is that enough information for you?"

Stettner's face had gone from carefully blank, to astonished.

"Seriously? He said you guys had power, but I didn't believe it. Nobody has had power for months." He had pointed at Kevin.

I looked around. It was early morning, another bright sunny day, so there were no street lights on, or other obvious indications that we had power.

Ariana spoke up. "Your coffee is hot. The juice is cold. You can go inside the restaurant there. The ceiling fans are working. The kitchen is open. The cook might even fix up some eggs for you, if you ask nicely."

Stettner was still surprised. "*How* do you still have power?"

I waggled my head. "Well, the answer is a complicated technical one. The short version is, we got lucky to find some very talented and skilled people. It's been a lot of work. Gordon can give you the details, if he happens to come around. I'm not sure where he is at the moment. Anyways, no, the power did not just snap off like a light switch, here in Valley. Much of the grid is automated, and flexible enough to adapt to changing conditions. Some of it is not. Some places have had problems, but our team has managed to avoid those, and keep power flowing here." Out of the corner of my eye, I sensed Zach and Ariana communicating, probably wondering if they should summon Gordon, but neither stepped away. So I guessed they decided that Gord's presence was not immediately required.

Stettner asked another question. "And you're seriously cleaning out *all* of the houses? What are you doing with the bodies?"

"We have to. It's a public health issue. They stink, they attract pests, they leak into the water table. We don't want to poison ourselves, by leaving rotting bodies laying around. We've been cremating them. That's what the urns are for." I said this last part gently.

Stettner asked, "And how is that all working out, exactly?"

"It's slow going. A four person work team can clear about 15 to 20 houses in a regular work day. We've got several dozen work crews just for basic body clearing and house clean out work. There are also some specialized crews, to handle businesses, retail, apartments, or unusual situations, like mini-farms and horse properties. We figure they've cleared maybe half or three quarters of the city so far. We have them working from the inner core outwards. We also have some other special crews just going door to door looking for survivors. We check on those regularly, too.

Stettner asked, "And how are you keeping up with all that cremation? Bodies don't burn very easily; too wet."

"We have some pits at the city land fill. Yes, it takes awhile to get them properly reduced to ash. We have a very special group of people handling that chore. One of our religious leaders is in charge of that operation. He does a lot of group praying. We also have them keeping track of names, so that we can properly memorialize them."

Ariana interrupted, to add. "The cremation process is pretty backed up, but we're doing our best to keep track of everyone. And the weather is helping, actually. It's getting warmer and drier, so the bodies are starting to mummify now."

Stettner stared at Ariana for a moment, and then turned back to me. "And you're making pots to hold their ashes? Seriously?"

"Yes, seriously. I'm a potter. I make pots. When the Superflu was first getting started, I got an order from one of the local funeral homes. It just kinda went on from there. It was pretty clear we'd need a lot of funerary urns, so that's how I've been contributing to this community." I paused. He was still looking dumbfounded. "Would you like to see the studio?"

"Is that really the best use of your time? I mean, if you're going to be the mayor, shouldn't you be, oh, I dunno, *leading* people, or something?"

I stared at him for a few moments before I responded

"I make the urns because our people need them. Everyone lost everyone. We've all lost our families, our friends, our parents, our spouses, our children. We all grieve. We all mourn. My urns are a way of letting everyone know that we understand that their people were important. That they existed, they were a part of this world, they had an impact. My urns are the physical reminder and remainder for the thousands who are gone now.

"You can't be planning to make urns for the entire Valley, can you?"

"Of course not. There's not that much clay, or time, or power to accomplish that. So, we are also building a monument to memorialize them. See that park over there?" I pointed to the north, where the open grassy area was now staked out with small flags. Some dirt was churned up, and some construction equipment lined the parking lot.

"That's where we decided to build our memorial. Would you like a closer look?

Stettner agreed to the impromptu tour. He brought his coffee mug with him, and listened as I outlined the basic design of our memorial.

His face got stony, as he listened, and watched me wave my hands to sketch in the air. When I finished the explanation, I paused to give him a chance to respond. He stared at the torn up ground, and looked around.

Stettner's face was a little sour. He didn't seem to approve of our art project. "You're going to need some serious foundation work here, to support all that weight, you know." He said, waving around. I thought that was what the little flags in the ground were for, to indicate where to pour the concrete. But I had turned over that phase of the project to a construction team that had been carved out of the work groups. So I just nodded to agree with him.

Stettner's next question was a change of topic. "I understand you've also got a community garden going?"

I wondered how candid I should be about this. I glanced back, and saw that Zach was following closely, and his deputies were not far away. I also saw a variety of people with familiar faces who had gathered, materializing from nowhere. They were hanging out on the patios and park areas around the downtown area. They were not approaching too closely, but they were allowing their presence to be known. And they were armed. I felt protected. I decided to go all in. "Yes, we do. It's just around the corner, and a couple of blocks down the street. I can show you that, too."

I turned, and walked him the few blocks to the small pedestrian gate entrance to the golf course.

It took Stettner a moment to recognize what he was looking at. "Was this a golf course? In the middle of the city?"

"Yes, it was. We just walked past the backside of the resort hotel. This course was part of the resort. We've decided to repurpose the first three holes. Those were fairways, before we replanted them. We haven't plowed up the rest of the course yet; we haven't completely decided what the best use would be. Either more garden acreage, or maybe pasture for horses and cows."

Carlos, of course, was hanging out at his garden work station. Even when he wasn't working, he could usually be found somewhere in the vicinity. He joined the group. Not all of Stettner's men had followed us, but they were still a large enough group to attract attention. I introduced Carlos, and asked him to explain his layout strategy, and what kinds of things we had been growing.

While he did, I hung back, and sidled up to Kevin and Zach.

"Kevin, they didn't hurt you, did they? How long have they been holding you?"

Kevin shook his head and answered, "Only a couple of days. I went to Sedona last, instead of first. They didn't hurt me, just kept me locked up in a room."

"Okay, that's good. We'll talk more after wards." I turned to Zach. "Your assessment?" I asked him.

"Preppers," he said instantly. "Possibly with a militia mindset."

"Yeah, that what I was thinking, too."

Carlos walked Stettner and his men back to us. I wondered if I should walk him to the studio, and show him that operation as well, but I didn't think it would sit well with him. I decided to just walk back to the city promenade, where the rest of his team was waiting.

As we walked, I asked him questions.

"So, are you willing now to tell me how many people you have in your group?"

He shrugged, and thought a moment before answering. "About 250, including women and children."

I wondered if that completely filled up all the housing in the canyon. I wasn't sure what kind of capacity was available, given the resorts and rental cabins there.

"And, you're okay for food, you said?"

"Yeah, we're fine, for now. But we don't have much power. We've got a few solar panels, and some generators and fuel, but we use those only for the highest priority items like freezers and fridges. I've already told everyone to be prepared for no air conditioning this summer."

"And you have medical services? Doctor, nurses, supplies?"

"Not much, actually. We've got some former military people trained in combat medicine, and a couple of nurses. Don't have nearly enough pain medicine or antibiotics. We've had a rash of injuries, too. The rocks in the creek are slippery; people falling, breaking limbs."

"We have an orthopedic surgeon over at the hospital. Actually, he's the head guy in charge over there. I'm sure he'd be delighted to take a look at something that's actually within his personal specialty."

Stettner was dumbfounded again. "You have a working hospital? I thought they were all destroyed in the rioting last fall."

"Well, ours took its fair share of damage, but not as bad as the Phoenix hospitals got. After the flu burned out, the surviving medical personnel cleaned the place up. Any other survivors we found with medical experience of any kind were sent over there, too. Even a couple of vet techs. They ended up shutting down most of the building, because it's too big, but they consolidated everything they need into just one wing off of the emergency entrance. They can do surgeries, medical checkups, prescriptions, birth control. And, they're going to start culturing some vaccines for regular stuff, like measles, mumps and chicken pox. For kids. And tetanus shots. They've cultured that, too."

Stettner got a wondering look on his face. "Do you have kids?" He immediately realized the awkwardness of that question, and tried to recover, "I mean, not you personally, I meant in the community."

I smiled gently. "A few. We found some survivor kids, ages 4 or 5 and up, but no toddlers or infants. At least, not alive. However, there are a few pregnancies in their first or second trimester. And we have plenty of adolescents and teenagers around."

We had arrived back at the promenade, and resumed our seats at the picnic table.

I looked at him. "So, are you interested in trading with us, or not? You don't seem to need much of what we have to offer, so I'm still not entirely clear what you want from us."

Stettner was back on his guard, thanks to my directness. He looked at me thought for a moment. "Look, I just don't get it. This guy here," he pointed at Kevin, "shows up in our town, poking around, acting like he's casing the joint. We figure he's gathering intel for a possible invasion. So, we grab him, and he says he's doing exactly that, gathering information, only not for an invasion, but just because his people 'want to be friends.' That you're just looking to trade. So we come down here, to see what the heck is going on, and find that your people are just puttering around, planting gardens and making art. In the middle of the frickin' Sonoran desert. It gets hot here! Really hot! Who lives in the desert where it gets really hot? And no water? And another thing, where is your defense perimeter? Where are the guards? Where's your armory? This place is wide open, you don't have any kind of natural or man-made barriers. How do you keep the looters out? I don't get it."

I stared at him for a moment. "Well, where would you like me to start?"

"Security. How do you protect this place?" He asked me promptly.

I glanced at Zach, but he was still doing his silent cop thing. He had donned some mirrored sunglasses at some point.

"Zach, would you please fill in Mr. Stettner here, with the basics of our police security policy?" Zach glanced at me, but gave him the basics. We had regular uniformed cops on patrol. We had an armed citizenry who were mostly living in tightly packed, close proximity, and thus, able to notice and sound an alert if intruders were detected. We had little that was of extremely high value to looters, such as fancy cars, super huge mansions and other luxury goods, so there was little incentive to loot, compared to other locations, such as Scottsdale, Paradise Valley, Carefree, or Sedona. Our biggest threats, so far, had been from feral dog packs. Nevertheless, our patrol units were constantly on the look out for looters and gangs. They were also building up a police radio network with other communities, which shared information on looting and violent incidents happening elsewhere in the Valley.

While Zach spoke, I took the opportunity to down some more orange juice. My throat was getting a little dry. When Zach finished, Stettner was still perplexed.

I took my shot. I worked hard to keep my tone level and even. "How about I tell you what've I've figured out about you, so far? You're preppers, aren't you? You've been stockpiling supplies like MREs and ammo and water purification tablets in a bunker. You or one of yours had a cabin in the canyon, and when the shit hit the fan last fall, you sent up the bat signal, and everyone went running. You probably self-quarantined for a few weeks, or maybe some of you got sick, got better and then bugged out. Once enough of the regular people who were already living in the canyon got sick and died, you took over, blocked the road, and called it private property. How am I doing so far?" I paused.

Stettner was glaring at me now. He responded, "Yeah, I've been preparing for the apocalypse for years. We all saw it coming, we just didn't know what form it would take. But we protected our own, made sure everyone was safe and cared for. So, what I don't get, is how a whole suburban town of people who did nothing to prepare, can possibly be surviving? You're in the worst possible place. A sprawling suburb in the middle of a barren desert. You have no barriers, no guards, no water, no nothing."

I couldn't hold my tone any longer. "Did you not hear anything we just said? We *do* have water. We have power. The power pumps the water from the underground aquifer or the canals to the treatment plant, and then pumps it to the consolidation zone. We have food; we're growing it, lots of it. I just showed it to you! We have police, we have medical, we have electricity, we have air conditioning. Hell, we even have fresh craft beer!" I was waving my arms around. We were both glaring at each other now.

I took a deep breath and deliberately calmed myself down before I went on.

"Out of all the possible apocalypse scenarios this world could have faced, this was the best one that could possibly have happened. I've read the stories, watched the movies. I know about the all the different ways it can go tits up. EMP. Coronal mass ejection. Terrorism on a massive scale. Nuclear holocaust. Economic collapse. Asteroids. But we didn't get those. We got a massive species die off from a wildly successful virus. That left all the infrastructure in place. We didn't get bombed back to the stone age, we just got a generational reset, to about late 1800s. We still have roads, and dams, and buildings, and best of all, we still have the knowledge, in our heads, in our books, in our libraries, about how to make this world comfortable. We can save the equipment, and the infrastructure. With that knowledge, our children can rebuild water systems and power distribution. And maybe, a generation after that, they'll be able to start manufacturing complex machines, like engines, again. And in a generation after that, they'll have new computers, and a new Internet. Four generations, to get back to where we were a year ago. Given that its been about 250 years since the start of the Industrial Revolution, that doesn't seem too bad to me. But hopefully, those future generations will have learned the lessons that went right over our heads. To preserve the natural resources, to not overpopulate the planet, to not stress the ecosystem so much that it has no natural defense against a simple little virus."

I paused to gather my thoughts again. "Look, I don't know why the Superflu spared us, but it did. We didn't ask to survive it, but we did. I got sick, and then got better. So did a lot of people. And some people never got sick at all. The Superflu didn't give a shit about who prepared for disaster, and who was totally clueless. We survived the disease, and now we're just trying to survive the surviving. We're here because this is our home. We don't want to take your home away from you; we have our own. We're just developing our own specialized niches, so that we can trade with others, who have things we don't have, but might enjoy. We just want to preserve as much of our lifestyle as we can, and live happily ever after, same as anyone does."

I stopped. I waited. Stettner stared at the table for few moments. Then he looked up at me. There was a little gleam in his eye and a small smile appeared. He asked, "So… would you be willing to trade for some of that craft beer?"

I smiled back gently. "I think something can probably be arranged."

Chapter 6

The tension with the visitors eased. We broke up into smaller groups to chat. I noticed Zach talking to Stettner one on one, smiling. I also observed that they shook hands, too. Maybe the start of a great friendship? I hoped so.

Ariana and I relaxed at one of the picnic tables on the promenade for a little while, waiting to see if anyone else had questions for us. Ariana was watching Stettner and his men carefully, as they packed up to head out. Stettner and his men worked out an arrangement for kegs of beer with the pub's guardian, which I suspected had involved gold coins, they said their goodbyes and headed back to Oak Creek Canyon.

I spotted Kevin approaching us, carrying a tray of food out of Mercado's. We waved, and invited him to join us. Kevin sat down with us, and started scarfing down his food. His plate was filled with fresh eggs, scrambled with peppers and onions from the garden. We watched him for a moment. I said, "Geez, Kev, didn't those Oak Creek Canyon people feed you at all?"

He knew I was teasing him. He spoke around his food. "Yeah, but it was just those MREs. They're kinda nasty. At least, the ones I had were. I get it, that they're convenient, and easy to carry, and they'll keep you alive, but this food is much better." He shoveled another bite of scrambled eggs into his mouth.

"You realize those veggies in there came from the new gardens?" I asked him. He'd not been wild about the concept of having to grow his own food, last time the topic came up.

He looked up at me, squinted, and stuck another forkful of food in his mouth.

I decided I didn't need to tease him any more about about that, and got down to business. "So, you wanna tell me anything else about what happened up there? Anything else I should know?"

Kevin swallowed his food, and answered. "It was pretty much like he said. I was wandering around Sedona, and they just came outta nowhere and grabbed me. They were searching my Jeep, and took all the pots out. They took the lids off and looked inside, and could see they were empty, but one guy said he thought they could still be IEDs, with a hidden compartment or something." Kevin snorted at this. He was right. It was pretty difficult to build a hidden compartment into a fired vessel, and then fill it with explosives, or shrapnel, without being able to feel all the extra weight in it. My jars were large enough to fit a hand and arm inside, so it was easy enough for anyone to feel all the way to the bottom, and judge the foot and wall thickness and the overall weight, for themselves.

Kevin finished his explanation. "So they smashed them on the ground, just to make sure. Actually, once they realized there was nothing wired into them, they did look a little embarrassed. But by then it was too late." Kevin looked sorry, too, about the broken pots.

"Don't worry about it, Kevin. I can make more pots. I'm not out of clay yet. But let's not offer up any more to them, either, until they're ready for it. They don't seem to appreciate the art or the sentiment behind them, quite the same way other people do."

Kevin nodded, and returned to finishing his breakfast.

"So," I continued, "are you still going on that long trip back East?"

"Yeah, planning leaving in a day or two. If you still want me to, that is."

"Yeah, I'd still like to find out more about what's going on in the rest of the country. Have you thought much about what specifically you'll be looking for?"

Kevin nodded, and held up a hand in the "wait one" gesture, while he finished chewing and swallowing a large bite of food. When he could speak without spitting all over me, he explained his plan.

"I still want to try for D.C. Based on what I've seen in other large cities, it might be kinda hard to get there. Most cities are pretty wrecked from the riots and looting, before most everyone was gone. But in the little towns, where they got ham radio operators, they're saying there's still some government operating there. Military and stuff. It'd be nice to know just how much they're doing, and if they can help or not."

I looked around again. Our downtown area was actually looking pretty normal. Cars were parked neatly, people were walking or riding bikes around, chatting with each other. The landscape was also cleaned up. I also knew this was an isolated oasis, and most other city streets and public areas were overgrown with weeds and untrimmed plants. Elsewhere, cars were abandoned and pushed to the sides of streets. Plenty of stores had had windows smashed out, too. However, we'd made an effort to cleanup our downtown area because a lot of us were spending a lot of time here.

"Kevin, how much help do you think we actually need?" I gestured around us. He looked around as well. Then he looked down at his plate of food;

"I dunno. I just thought we should find out. I mean, we all paid all those taxes for years to the IRS. I'd like to see a return on my investment, as my dad used to say."

Ariana spoke up. "We kinda got the benefits of those taxes already, you realize? We have roads, and a power grid, and communications, and a military. A lot of federal money got redistributed to states and cities, too, before."

Kevin was frowned at Ariana. He was probably not well versed on federal distributions policies. So I redirected.

"Okay, never mind. You know what I'd really like to know? I want to know if there's going to be any way to get resources from other communities, things we can't get here. Like flour; wheat doesn't grow here in desert. The plains and Midwest have the best climates for growing corn and wheat. I also want to know if any oil refinery along the Gulf is back in production yet, or if there are any plans to get one going. And pharmaceuticals – is anyone going to be able to manufacture more antibiotics soon? I want to know if they're going to reestablish the dollar or any other form of currency. Those are the things that we can't grow or make for ourselves, and will need help and guidance from a national authority."

Kevin was nodding. "Yeah, but don't you want to know what caused this whole thing? I don't know about you, but I never did get a good answer on what caused the Superflu."

Inwardly, I was shaking my head. I could see Ariana rolling her eyes. No answer was ever going to satisfy that question for anyone, on any level. In a steady, level, calm voice, I said, "Kevin, the Superflu was a virus. It mutated from other viruses. It got really powerful, and could kill almost everyone it infected. It took a long time to make people sick, so it had plenty of time to circulate widely. It infected the whole world, before the doctors could do anything to prevent it or stop it. I really don't think there's much more to it than that."

Kevin looked skeptical. "I dunno… I heard some theories."

I nodded. "Yeah, I've heard the conspiracy theories too: it was a weaponized form, it was an alien invasion, it was retribution from God, blah blah blah. None of that matters. It got the whole world. Tracking down the cause isn't going to change the outcome. We're here, we go on."

Kevin and I just looked glumly at each other for a moment. I went on. "Okay, so go to D.C., learn what you can and come on back."

Kevin nodded. I got up to leave. I gave him a pat of reassurance on the shoulder, as I moved past him.

Ariana dropped me back at home, where I met up with the rest of my makeshift new family. Gordon and Micah had just arrived home as well and were grabbing a quick lunch. They were munching on granola bars and some of the orange juice I had just packed to freeze. Oh well. The dogs bounced around us, sharing their own personal perspectives on the conversation.

I told them about the impromptu meeting with the Oak Creek Canyon people, and how they seemed to be real hard asses about survival and preparedness. Gordon shrugged, and said, "Well, they're not wrong, you know. There is something to be said for being prepared for disasters, having enough food and water and stuff."

"Yeah, I know. But they just had such a militant attitude about it. You should have seen the rifles they were carrying. Serious weaponry."

"And that's where they lose me," Gordon replied. "My idea of preparedness is making sure the power stays on. Its what I'm all about. You understand that's why I do what I do? I did it before, and I'm still doing it now. Making sure that electricity gets to the places and people who need it."

I nodded. "Yep, I get that, and that's what makes you my personal hero." I gave him a saccharine smile and a peck on the lips. Micah groaned at us. Gordon then pointed out, yet again, that the way I handled the situation was exactly why everyone else wanted me to be mayor.

Then they asked me what I wanted to do for the afternoon. I brought up the idea of wanting to decorate the house more. Micah rolled his eyes; he was quickly developing a dislike for any "girlie" activities, especially the ones that might involve shopping. I started to explain that I wanted to get some of my own art. And then another idea occurred to me. I hadn't been to my mom's house in months. In fact, I couldn't even completely remember if I'd been there since my own recovery from the Superflu. During the few weeks between her death, and when I had gotten sick, I had gone there several times to start cleaning things out. My parents had managed to gather a nice art collection of their own; including several large pieces that I had always loved. I occurred to me that they would work well in this big house. I suggested the trip to Gordon. He considered the idea, and offered a counter proposal.

"Okay, but if we're going down there, I want stop at the range and pick up some more ammo. We should all do some target practice. You haven't done that in while, have you?"

No, I hadn't. Zach had given me a pistol for personal protection, last fall, and had taught me how to shoot it. I'd followed up with a few practice sessions, but of course, I'd gotten lazy about that, and hadn't done any in a couple of months.

"And, if you're acquiring militia groups for trading partners, it would probably be best for you to brush up on your own skills," Gordon added. "You know, so you can walk their walk, talk their talk, if you have to?"

I nodded. He had a point.

Micah got excited, "Can I shoot too? You promised you'd show me how!"

Gordon nodded. "Yes, that's exactly what I was thinking, too. I've got a small shotgun that I think would be perfect for you to learn with. And I could use some practice, too."

Micah was overjoyed. "Awesome! I'm in! Let's go!"

We gathered up our gear, gave the dogs their "goodbye" treats, and headed out. We decided to go to Mom's house first, and then stop at the range on the way back. Mom's neighborhood had not yet been cleared by the work crews. I was mildly surprised that there was very little smell in the area. After some consideration, I concluded that the elderly population in her retirement community had probably gotten sick during the early phase of the Superflu, and had mostly died in the hospitals, rather than at home. There might not be very many bodies around this particular area. And as long as fridges stayed closed, any rotted food odor was contained.

Of course, all the pretty landscaping was going to seed. Mom's neighbors had always been especially proud of their natural desert landscaping. Retirees with plenty of time on their hands, and a fascination with plants that were unlike anything they were familiar with, tended to develop some especially interesting collections of cacti and yard art.

I had the key to mom's house, so entering was easy. I was pleased to see that everything was exactly as I had left it. The air was a little stale and stuffy, though. And dust had settled onto everything. I gave Gordon and Micah a quick tour of the house, and explained how my parents had collected their art works. They had been firmly in the "I don't know much about art, but I know what I like" style of collecting. And they liked paintings of landscapes, animals, and some abstract art. To my eye, everything was tasteful and attractive. My parents' experiences with art had directly influenced my own idea of what it meant to be a successful artist. Because they bought their art at art fairs and galleries, that formed the basis of my desire to sell my pottery through those same venues.

I picked out a few of my favorite pieces, boxed them up and put them in Gordon's truck. I told Gordon and Micah they could pick out something that they liked, as well. Gordon actually liked several of the outdoor sculptures my Dad had acquired years before, and wanted them for his courtyard and back yard. Micah was uncertain and pretty uncomfortable with the whole thing, and declined to pick anything for himself. He was at that age where posters of manga characters were his idea of high quality art.

We also cleared out what little packaged food remained in mom's cabinets. There wasn't much, really. Condiments, soup, some stale crackers. We left a note on the counter, explaining that we had already cleared the house, so that when the work crews finally came through, they would know who had done it, and that they could just move on to the next one. We shut off the water and electricity at the fuse box, too.

And next, as agreed, we went to the gun range. Our city police patrol had setup an informal gun range a few miles south of the downtown area. They had re-purposed an empty industrial building with a large fallow field behind it. They had moved a variety of targets and obstacles into the field, backed by old hay bales. Inside were more shooting galleries. The office space at the front of the building had been organized and secured to stock an assortment of ammunition and weapons recovered from the cleared houses. Just as Zach had encouraged me to carry a gun when out and about, most people were openly carrying now. Feral dog packs were usually the most common, immediate threat. And, of course, there was potential for one or more of those Phoenix gangs to come around some day.

Gordon carried in a duffel bag containing his weapons, and I had my own pistol on me in its shoulder holster. A young man I did not happen to recognize was working as a front desk clerk. He helped me pick out several kinds of ammo to experiment with in my pistol. He even gave me a quick refresher on how to load the gun and the magazine, which I appreciated.

Gordon began the standard safety lecture for Micah. He explained that a gun was not a toy, and he should never, *ever*, 'fool around' with any gun, no matter what. He then explained the particulars of his old small hunting rifle to Micah, showing him how to work it, how to load and unload it, the different types of bullets it could fire, and how to choose the right ammunition for hunting game or in self-defense situations. They squared off in one of the booths, and Gordon fired a few shots first, and then let Micah try. Micah was pretty shocked at the powerful kickback he got in the shoulder, but he adapted quickly and set to practicing conscientiously.

While Gordon supervised Micah, I spent some time in a separate booth practicing with my own weapon. I tried the several different types of ammunition, and learned that each had a different feel in the gun. They each had their strengths and weaknesses, and were intended for different scenarios. So learning how each type felt and handled was useful information.

My arms and shoulders quickly got tired from the unfamiliar activity so I took a short break to observe my guys. When Gordon saw me watching, he stepped back to stand next to me. We watched Micah, who was practicing firing while lying on the ground, as if he were hiding in the grass and targeting a deer.

"You never told me about your prior experience with guns." I prompted Gordon.

"I didn't? Well, my Dad taught me how to shoot, on that very gun, probably when I was around the same age." He nodded at Micah. "That hunting rifle was the first gun I ever owned. After I learned how, we'd go deer hunting every fall. We usually brought back a kill most years. Venison chili was one of our favorite things back then. One time, we went goose hunting too, but we decided we didn't like goose meat, so we never hunted those again."

"So hunting was about hunting, then? Eat what you kill, don't waste it?"

"Yep. We took one and only one deer each season, we didn't need more than that. And my mom didn't much like the venison, even though Dad and I did. My dad learned to hunt from his Dad, so it was a family thing, too."

"And when did you learn hand guns?" He had been practicing with his own Glock pistol, as well.

"When I was in college. Or just before, rather. Again, Dad taught me. He wanted me to know how to protect myself. Once I had proven to him I could be responsible with a gun, he got me one to take to college. This was back in the days before they prohibited them from college campuses, of course."

"Of course." I repeated.

"It was an old Colt 45 revolver. That thing packs quite a wallop, you know. I still have it, back at the house. I didn't bring it with me today, but I can show it to you if you want to see it. But for daily carry, I like this one better." He patted the holster at his hip, where he had placed his semi-automatic. "Holds more bullets, easier to use. Well, I think so, anyways."

I wondered if it bothered him that carrying guns around was now a routine thing. I wasn't quite sure how to ask him, though, so I fished around and tried another angle.

"There's still so much I don't know about you – I don't even know if you were in the military."

"Nope. Went from high school to college to graduate school and straight to work. Never saw much need to go into the military, personally. I respect them and all they did for us, of course." Gordon got a thoughtful look on his face. "Can't help wondering what happened to all our assets and bases overseas."

I shrugged. "Same thing as happened here. 97% gone, 3% left. I told you about the Major we met at Luke Air Force Base, didn't I?" Gordon waggled his head at me. I know I had mentioned him, but I wasn't sure if I had mentioned this part: "He said he heard that the Pentagon is consolidating all five branches of the military into one."

Gordon looked mildly shocked. "Seriously? I wonder how that's going to work."

"I dunno. But all his fighter pilots and most of his planes got moved to California, or Washington, D.C. It sounded to me like they're trying to put resources on the borders, in a defensive posture."

Gordon scoffed, "Defensive? Against who? Who has the means to attack us now? Superflu was worldwide."

"I know! That's exactly what I said."

Gordon pondered the idea. "What about submarines? Or maybe Navy ships? If any of those were out on patrol missions, they might have avoided exposure. And if that's so, they might still be fully staffed. And if any of our subs and ships are fully operational, then maybe other navies have some, too. Those could be a threat."

"Maybe." I shrugged. The conversation was not going where I wanted, so I decided to just ask him, point blank.

"So, did you ever learn to fire assault rifles?" I asked him. He was not carrying one in his duffel, but that didn't mean he didn't have one, back in the gun safe at the house.

He nodded. "Yeah. This gun club I used to go to once in a while, before, would rent out ARs and other types. They were fun to shoot, but I never saw the need for one of my own. Until now." He eyed me curiously.

"And, *do* you have one now?" I prompted.

"Nope, but Zach said he could get me one, if I felt I needed it. But I've not taken him up on his offer yet. Too awkward to carry around on the job. But I'm sure Zach will be handing them out like candy to anyone who wants one, if something comes up. Like, those guys from Oak Creek. What did Zach think of them, anyways? You said he was there?"

"Zach thought they were militia style preppers, too. He doesn't seem immediately concerned, though. I got the sense they were just trying to figure us out, not that they're a direct threat. I saw Zach shaking hands with them, before they left."

Gordon studied me. He finally clued in on what was bugging me. "You don't much like this, having to have guns around all the time, do you?"

"Nope, not really." I looked at him. "Look, I'm not an anti-gun nut pacifist or anything. I never wanted to take them away from anyone else. But I never saw a need to have one, myself, before, either. I'm pretty uncomfortable with them, actually. And I'm sad that it's become a necessary thing. And I'm really hoping we don't ever need to use them for real."

Gordon sighed. "I hope we don't, either," he said. He wrapped me in a bear hug for a few moments, until Micah noticed and audibly gagged to express his disgust at adult displays of affection.

We let go. I suddenly felt motivated to practice my own gun skills just a little more. So did Gordon. We worked through a few more boxes of ammunition before calling it a day, and heading home.

Chapter 7

A day later, I headed into the studio with "a pot in my head." That was my favorite expression to describe the creative urge. I would get an idea for a new vessel, and the desire to sketch it out in clay was nearly irresistible. In this case, I was noodling on how throw small bottles. I planned to try "throwing off the hump" which was a technique where a large mound of clay was centered on the wheel, and then small amounts were pulled up to form the desired vessel. Once the piece was formed, it was cut off of the hump and set aside to dry and cleanup later, leaving the bulk of the mound centered, ready for the next piece. It was an efficient method: center once, throw many.

I headed into the studio and got to work. My apprentices arrived shortly afterwards. And the moment they walked in, I could tell something was up. Jenna's eyes were slightly red and puffy, and the guys immediately made themselves busy elsewhere. Ali, in particular, looked tense and annoyed. Kyrene hovered near Jenna, with a worried look on her face.

I absorbed the new vibe, and considered. Oh goody. Millennial drama was on tap for the morning's entertainment.

"Good morning, ladies. How's everyone, today?" I asked them neutrally. They mumbled "fine", and set to work uncovering their pots, and checking on progress. I continued throwing little jars off the hump. Once I had made about a dozen small jars from the lump of clay on my wheel, I stood up to stretch. The girls were seated at a nearby table.

"So, you wanna tell me about it?" I asked them carefully.

Jenna looked up, startled. I raised my eyebrows at her. "I can tell something is going on. Better to just get it out. Maybe I can help. I can at least listen."

Kyrene nodded at Jenna, to go ahead.

"It's Kyle. He's such a shithead. We had a huge fight last night." I nodded, but didn't say anything yet. Jenna launched into it, kinda starting in the middle, and wandering around.

"I went over there last night, to hang out with him, maybe watch a

83

movie together. But I caught him looking at some porn DVD on his computer. And then he gets all mad at *me*, when I tell him that's gross. He says its not gross, and besides, it doesn't count as cheating, and anyways, he says I'm the cheater because he caught me talking to a guy on Saturday, and that's way worse because its in person. But it's not, because all I did was talk to Rayson for a little bit, and it's not like we were alone or anything, Kyrene and the others were there, and we *just* talked."

Jenna paused, and looked at me for validation. I stayed neutral. She went on.

"So, then, Kyle tells me I shouldn't have worn that top, the cute red one with the scoop neck, that it's too tight and 'revealing'. Like, he gets to tell *me* what to do. I keep telling him to cut back on the video games, but does he do what I tell him? Noooo! So why should I have to do what he tells me? He was working on Saturday, patrolling. I didn't want to just sit around at home, I wanted to go to the meeting, and hang out with my friends afterwards. I shouldn't have to be alone just because he can't be there with me. So I went out. What's the big deal?"

She threw up her hands.

"Oh, and then – get this – I'm sitting on the couch, waiting for him to say sorry about the porn, and he asks me to start a load of his laundry! I don't even live there! So, I told him to do his own laundry, and he just blows up on me, tells me I'm lazy, and flaky, and that I don't want to help him. He said he wouldn't even need the porn, if I would just move in with him. But you told me not to, not right away, and I like living with my girl friends, our house is much cleaner, than his ratty old apartment. His roommate is a total slob, and he won't do anything about it. I think he's just wants me to move in so I can keep the place clean for both of them."

She stopped gushing, finally. I waited, to see if any more drama was coming. When I was certain she did not have anything else to add, I held up my fist. "Okay, let's parse this out."

I flipped out a finger for each major point I was about to make. "So, Kyle was working on Saturday, so you went out with your friends. You had a conversation with a boy. Were you flirting with the boy?" Jenna shook her head.

"Was he flirting with you?" She shrugged. Kyrene nodded her head, and eyed me significantly.

I flipped out another finger. "Okay, next day. You went to Kyle's place to watch a movie. Did he know you were coming over?" She nodded.

"And did you arrive at the time he knew you were coming?" Another nod.

"And when you arrived, you found him watching porn?" Nod. "I take it the roomie was not around?" (Because that would have been a little creepy). Jenna shook her head.

"And you told him that porn was bad?" Nod. I put my third finger out. She added, "It's gross, and sick, and... what's that word?" she looked at Kyrene.

Kyrene said, "Demeaning. To women." Jenna nodded at that.

I continued. "And then you waited for him to apologize for what he did?" Nod.

"And he did not apologize. Instead, he asked you to do laundry and clean up after him. And when you refused, he got mad. Did you leave after that?" Nod.

She smirked, and added, "I slammed the door so hard, the little doohickey hanging on the wall beside it fell off." Kyrene shoulder bumped her in solidarity, grinning at her.

"Okay, does that basically sum up everything that happened?" I had all my finders out now.

Jenna: "Yeah, I guess so."

I thought for a moment. I put my hand down. I had lots of opinions, but it occurred to me that she really needed to be led to the conclusions, not told what to do.

Okay, let's start with the laundry thing. Is that the first time he's done that?"

"Yeah."

"And did he *ask* you, or *tell* you?" Jenna was confused, and had to think for a moment.

"I guess he was asking..."

"Does he actually know *how* to do laundry? Have you ever seen him complete an entire load before?"

"Not very well. He ruined some socks and underwear, when he mixed them up with the darks. They got all gray."

"So, Kyle, is what, 18? 19? I'm guessing he was still living at home with his parents, before the Superflu? I'll bet his mom was still doing laundry for the whole family, before. I wonder if anyone has ever taught him the finer points of sorting by color and water temperature selection…" I raised my eyebrows thoughtfully at her. She looked startled.

"Do you really think that's it? He just needs to learn how?" she asked.

"You know, most guys usually aren't very good at asking for help. They don't like to admit when they don't know things. They're supposed to be the problem solvers, not the problem havers. It's actually a good sign when they admit they need assistance. They don't like to admit to a weakness, including a lack of knowledge. It puts them in a vulnerable position. You might consider rewarding that behavior, instead of jumping all over him. Maybe use it as a learning opportunity."

"Huh." Jenna was thinking hard.

"Okay, So, let's a little farther back. When you were flirting with that boy, what was his name?"

"Rayson. And I wasn't flirting with him."

"Right, Rayson. When you were talking with him, were you having a good time? Laughing, smiling, telling jokes?" Jenna nodded.

"And Kyle saw that behavior?" Nod.

"So, how would you react if you saw Kyle doing the same thing with a girl? Sitting at a bar, laughing, talking, smiling? Maybe he's with other people, maybe he's alone? But you see him and were not expecting it. What would you do?"

Jenna squirmed. I waited.

"I dunno. I might get mad, I guess."

I kept on waiting. Kyrene jumped in.

"Wouldn't it depend on how they're behaving? I mean, is he touching the other girl? Is she touching him?"

I clarified. "Nope. They're *just* talking. Other people are with them, but they get up to get a pitcher at the bar, or go to the bathroom, or whatever. Maybe the other people are having their own conversations. Kyle and the girl are *just* talking, but he's smiling and relaxed." I looked at Jenna expectantly.

"I guess I'd still be pretty mad," she admitted, looking down at her hands.

I sighed. "Okay, context is everything. What if Kyle was behaving pleasantly, but keeping a little distance between himself, and the person he's talking to? Holding himself a little stiffly, being polite, but not overly friendly? What then?"

Jenna pictured the scenario in her head. "Maybe that wouldn't be so bad. I wouldn't want him to be rude to other people."

"But if you saw Kyle behaving the way he saw you behaving on Saturday, then you would be pretty mad?" I asked.

I paused to let her consider this. Then I went on.

"So, next, the porn. Guys like porn. Guys are visual. But you think porn is gross. Is it, really?" I looked at both Jenna and Kyrene.

Kyrene answered first. "It's disgusting. It's demeaning to women. The women who do that, are only in it for the drugs and the money. Or because some scumbag sleaze ball boyfriend forced them to do it."

I considered Kyrene. "All porn? And how do you know that? Have you worked in the porn industry? Do you have friends or relatives in it?"

Kyrene froze, a shocked look on her face.

"What about amateur porn, married couples filming themselves. Is that demeaning? They're doing it of their own free will…" I kept my tone neutral. No response from either girl. Now Kyrene was confused.

"What about how-to tutorials, for newlywed virgins or the inexperienced? Is that demeaning?" Still no response.

I looked at Jenna. I continued speaking calmly and slowly.

"So, the fact that Kyle enjoys watching porn means that Kyle is exactly like nearly every other guy on the planet, past and present. Guys like porn. The question to answer here is, what do *you* really think of porn? Have you seen enough of it to actually form your own opinion, or are you just repeating what others have said?"

Jenna shook her head. "I only saw just that little bit, on his computer."

"So, if you watched the DVD for yourself, how do you think you'd feel about it? Do you think watching other people have sex is wrong? Is having sex wrong, or just watching other people have sex, the wrong part?" Jenna's mind was slowly blowing up. I went on.

"So. *Lots* of guys have this stuff. Does that make them bad people? What do they get out of it? Is it affecting them in a bad way? Does it change how they behave with real women?"

Jenna answered in a small voice. "I don't know…"

"Those are the questions you should be asking yourself, and asking Kyle. *Why* does he watch it, what does he like about it? What kind is he watching? Is it good or bad porn, in *your* opinion? How are the people in the videos treating each other, and what does he think about that?"

Jenna and Kyrene were both stumped, now. I could practically see the wheels spinning in Jenna's head, turning over the new perspectives I had given them.

After that drama calmed down, I went out to the kiln courtyard, to check on the guys, who were loading and unloading kilns. I gave them the 'all clear' signal, so that they could come back in whenever they wanted. Ali looked especially relieved. I went back to throwing little pots.

***

A little while later, Ariana walked into the studio, and dragged me back out, to get lunch together. We walked over to Mercados. The weather was yet another beautiful day, so we sat out on the back patio, which was slightly more private than the front promenade.

Once we had our salads in front of us, Ariana asked me, "So, are you still freaked out about the elections? Still mad at me?"

"I wasn't mad at you, personally. I'm annoyed at the situation, not mad at you." I paused. "But I'm still not convinced I'm the right person for the job."

Ariana: "Well, let's break that down, and figure it out. What did you say you did before, for your real job?"

I eyeballed her, wondering if she had the studio bugged, and had heard my earlier discussion with Jenna and Kyrene. "I was a content developer for a small software company. I helped build the help manuals. Or rather, the online help guides. We hadn't published on paper in at least 15 years. It was all built into the software."

Ariana asked, "Okay, and how many people worked for your company?"

"Uh, lessee… anywhere from 20 to 50, at various times. We had some real ups and downs, financially."

Ariana nodded, "Okay, and did you get any supervisory experience there?"

"A little. I was team lead, for a group of 4 people, at the end, when everyone got sick."

"And what did you learn about supervising other people?"

"That I didn't like doing it. Well, that's not completely right. I didn't mind working with my little team, as they were pretty self motivated and generally did whatever needed to be done. I didn't have to spend a lot of time telling them what to do. They already knew. But there was a brief period, quite a while ago, when I was in charge of another group, a customer training and service group. They were supposed to help teach our customers how to use the software. It was kind of a second tier support thing. If a customer was having a problem, and called in for technical support, the first tier would work with them, to solve the problem. Except, sometimes there was no problem, it was just customer ignorance. They didn't know how to use the software, and needed to be educated on it. So, they'd get bumped up to second tier, my group. If the customer was already on a service plan that included a certain amount of training, fine, no problem, my people could just jump in and take off. But if the customer was not on a plan, we expected them to pay for the training. We were selling it in one-hour blocks. So my guys had to also sell the service, as well as provide it. That was a big challenge for them. I had one guy who was good at selling, and several other people who were good at training, but no one who was good at doing both. The theory behind the way our group was organized was that the seller would influence the trainers, and the trainers would influence the seller, and everything would be great. Unfortunately, it didn't exactly work out that way. I also had a couple of idiots who weren't good at anything. That whole project lasted about 9 months, before management realized the error of their ways, and sent me back to content development."

I gave her the "what can you do?" shrug. It was all ancient history, now.

Ariana considered that. "So, what did you learn from that?"

"Well, that sellers should sell, and trainers should train, and idiots should be fired?"

"Uh huh. Now, extrapolate that and apply it to what we got going on here." She spread her arms wide to indicate our current community. I thought about it.

"Well… Electricians should hook up power systems, truckers should drive trucks around, cops should keep us safe, gardeners should grow food, potters should make pots, and if you used to sit at desk doing something that's completely useless now, you can excel at cleaning houses?"

Ariana smiled. "Bingo! Well, sort of. The point I want you to get, is that everyone is good or experienced at something, it's just a matter of finding out what it is, and applying it. Find the skill, and apply it to the job that needs doing. Find the knowledge, and get it shared to those who need it. "

"What if there's jobs that need doing, but not enough skilled people to do it? Gordon keeps saying he doesn't have enough people."

"Yeah, I know that's hard. That's where the creative problem solving comes in. Finding ways to cope, alternatives solutions, temporary stop gap solutions. Like, when you had the idea of collecting the food from the houses, to supplement what was left in the grocery stores, until we could start growing fresh stuff."

I was still worried. "There still so many problems to be solved. Things are not exactly perfect, yet. Don't you ever get overwhelmed with it all?"

"Yeah, sure. Deep breathing exercises help. And beer." She winked at me. I grinned. "Okay, here's some paper and pencil. Let's figure it out your campaign platform." She pulled out a notepad from her shoulder bag. I idly wondered why she even bothered to carry one around anymore; it was not like we needed our wallets for anything, at the moment. Of course, women carried all kinds of different things in their purses, including paper and pens.

"We can't exactly solve everything all at once, you know," I commented.

"I know, but we can sketch out the main issues, then break them down into smaller components."

"Like what?" I asked.

Ariana said, "Like, electricity. Write that down." She pointed at my paper. I did, and thought, and started writing more items.

- Electricity/Power
- Food
- Clean water
- Fuel
- Security
- Housing
- Health services
- Transportation
- Communications

Ariana leaned in to read what I had written. "That's good. Next, most of those can be broken down into smaller chunks, so add some subtopics. Like, for Health services, there's physical health, and mental health. We've got physical health mostly solved."

I nodded. "Sort of – but they're still struggling with medicine supplies. Did you know they're going to start making their own? They've got a lab, and Dr. Reddy asked me to make some apothecary jars!"

Ariana grinned. "Yeah, I knew that – I told him to ask you. See? The problem was: 'how to store medicine,' and the solution was: 'find someone who can make small containers.' Voila!"

Well, of course she knew that. "I don't think it's always going to be that simple. And the better solution would be to find a glass blower to make glass vials."

Ariana said, "See? There's often more than one solution, too. But for now, the easy solution is ceramic. Okay, keep going. Mental health?"

"What about it? Everyone's got their grief, but it seems like most people are getting it together, aren't they?"

Ariana shook her head. "Not so much. There's still a lot of people who just aren't responding to the call to join up with us. They're still sitting in their houses, staring at blank TV screens, or drinking or whatever."

"Really? How many is 'a lot'? I don't know if we can do anything about that..." I paused. "Gordon thinks that Micah has 'Superflu

Trauma'. I don't think that's a thing yet, but maybe it *is* a thing.

Ariana wobbled her hand. "Yeah, could be. Sounds like a good way to describe what some people are going through. So, what can we do about it? Let's brainstorm some ideas. Those houses are going to get hot soon, and there's no power there. How can we help them? Apply that creativity…" She looked at me expectantly and gestured for me to start filling in the blanks.

"Well… Do we have any counselors or psychologists over at the hospital? Maybe get some support groups going? Or maybe get Pastor Daniel or Caleb to pay a house call? They could offer some spiritual support and consolation. I guess we need to find a way to assess their condition, find out just how bad off they are. Do they need medication, or just a slap in the face to snap out of it? If they're religious, then call in the spiritual guidance counselors. If it's physical, offer them medication. If it's just general malaise, same as all of us, show them how everyone else is coping. Drag them out on a field trip, no commitment required, just show them what's going on around here."

Ariana straightened up, and smiled. "A field trip! That's exactly what I was looking for! A basic idea, a strategy that I, the Administrator, can now run with and implement. I can reassign some people from the work crews to make regular check ins on our shut ins. We can ask the good doctor to build a psych questionnaire, to help identify who needs professional help, and who just needs a kick in the butt. And from there, we can apply the resources we do have, to help them." Ariana was grinning at me. "See what I mean? Problems have solutions."

"Seems to me like you already knew that particular solution. You didn't need me to tell you that." I looked at her sourly.

Ariana shook her head. "Oh, but I do. I need executive leadership above my job role, to direct my actions. It avoids… whaddya call it…? It avoids conflict of interest and personal bias. See, if I'd been working my own solution, my first thought would have been to ask the pastors and bible study groups to go pray with them, maybe schedule a memorial service. I wouldn't have considered drug therapy, as a part of the solution."

"Yeah, another way of saying that, is C.Y.A. You're just covering your ass." I answered her.

She snorted back at me. "No, I'm not. Seriously, I can't do all of this alone. I need a team, and that includes a public face, who can take input from the community, digest it, get creative, and identify the beginnings of solutions. *Then* I can run with it."

She paused, and pointed at my list. "That is the start of your campaign platform. Expand out on those topics, break them down into sub topics. Decide on what you think should be done. That becomes your policy platform."

"Some of this is already being taken care of. We have the garden, Gordon is taking care of the power, Robert is handling water."

Ariana said, "Exactly! See? Half the work is already done! Once you're Mayor, you'll get to just sit back, put your feet up, and rest on your laurels."

"Yeah, not buying it. I may be naïve, but I'm not stupid."

Ariana waved off my comment. "Anyways, your homework assignment is to build out that list. Get it on computer, too. It's going to become your main talking points when we have the candidate debate next month."

"Debate? What debate? Who said anything about a debate?" I nearly screeched.

Ariana just snickered at me. I was getting the distinct feeling that I was being shoehorned into something, and I wasn't sure I liked it.

After lunch, back in the studio, I thought over all the things she had shared with me. I had not realized there had been so many problem people still stuck in their own houses. What were they doing for water? If the power was out, they probably didn't have any water pressure left. If they had pools, they could take a dunk in the pool to get clean. But without power, the pumps to clean the pools wouldn't be working either, and without pumps and chlorine, pools would get gross eventually, too. And what about water to flush the toilets? Yeah, we had to step up our game to get more people consolidated. I made a mental note to address that personally.

Chapter 8

A couple of days later, Zach popped into the studio for an unexpected visit. He was in cop uniform, so that meant he was in Officer Adams mode. He asked me if I could take a ride with him on a home visit to someone. He told me that Ariana had told him what we had discussed previously, and that it was time for me to practice what I would be preaching. It was time for a personal intervention.

"We've got a woman who hasn't left her house in months, as far as we know. She's in one of zones that's been cleared of bodies. The power was shut off a few weeks ago, but she's still not budging."

I looked at him. "What else? Why do you think I'd be the right person to talk to her?"

"Well, I think you'd have a lot in common with her. I think she's about your age. She seems to like art, and I think maybe she used to work in technology. And… She's been losing weight. I think she was pretty big, before, but now her clothes are practically hanging off of her."

I'd been losing weight, too, thanks to the more active lifestyle and fewer processed carbohydrates in my diet. I was walking to work, and moving about the studio, instead of sitting at a desk. And there wasn't much flour left to make bread with, let alone any chips or other salty snacks, which I had been so addicted to. I didn't really think I was over my carb addiction; rather, it was on hiatus, due to circumstances and not by choice. Nevertheless, I was glad I had lost the weight that I had, so far. I was certainly not skinny, by any means, but I did feel better in my clothes.

I agreed to the field trip with Zach, and covered up my wet pots with plastic, so they wouldn't get too dry. I was schmeared with clay so I washed my hands and arms and knocked off the largest chunks from my clothes. I decided the rest of it didn't matter.

I also gave Amex one of the "I'm going away and you're not" treats from a jar on the instructor desk. The dogs got to take turns visiting the studio with me, and it was Amex's turn that day. I asked my apprentices to keep an eye him for me, and that I would be back soon.

We got into Zach's cop car, and headed south. As he drove, Zach glanced at me, and asked, "So, you wouldn't happen to know anything about why my deputy trainee is in such a snotty mood this week?"

"You mean Kyle?" I asked.

"Yeah."

"Yeah, he and Jenna had a big fight last weekend. She caught him watching porn, and then he asked her to do his laundry."

Zach snorted, and smacked his hand to his face.

"Yeah, it was a real 'kids are idiots!' moment. But I talked her through it, helped her see some alternative points of view. I suggested some other ways of looking at the situation, and maybe a different way of communicating."

"So, are they going to kiss and make up?" Zach asked me.

"Probably, at least for now."

"You think they're going to last, long term?"

"I doubt it. They're too young to know what they want. Might be the community's very first breakup. I'm just hoping they can do it with a little grace and dignity. We're a pretty small group, now. Can't have hurt feelings and teen angst polluting the environment around here. But for now, crisis is averted."

We pulled up to a random house in a nice subdivision. It was a fairly large house, two stories, fancy entrance. Red tile roof, expensive sedan in the driveway.

Zach and I walked up to the front entrance. I rang the bell, since the button was closest to me. I could hear a dog barking inside. We waited a few moments, but the door did not open. Zach tried knocking loudly on the door, and called out, "Sharon, its Officer Adams. I wanted to check on you. Can you open the door?"

After a few moments, I heard some shuffling inside, and then the door opened wide. A woman stood there, looking a little disheveled. Her medium blond hair was lank, but pulled back off her face in a clip. She was barefoot, and dressed in a ratty t-shirt and sweats, which were hanging off her frame, as Zach had indicated. She was still large sized, like me, but yes, I agreed with his assessment that she too had apparently lost a little weight recently.

Zach greeted her. "Thank you for coming to the door. Sharon, this is Maggie Shearin." He gestured to me. "Maggie, Sharon Walker."

Sharon, could we please come in for a moment?"

Sharon was staring rather blankly at us. She loosed the door to let it open even wider, and turned away from us. She walked to small den off to the side of the entrance way, with a large couch, and a big blank screen TV. A medium sized mutt ran out from behind the couch, barked at us, and ran away again. He did that a few more times, while we followed Sharon into the den. Sharon flopped down on her leather sofa.

The coffee table in front of the sofa was littered with water bottles and paperback books. I pushed a few aside, and sat down on the table so that I could face her.

I wondered where to start. She was ignoring me, staring blankly into the middle distance. I picked up a few of the books, and looked them over. There were several books from the *Sookie Stackhouse* series, by Charlaine Harris.

"Hey, I've read these. Well, I listened to the audio book versions. How are you enjoying them?" I tried.

In a surprisingly clear and level voice, she said, "They're stupid. Vampires aren't real. People don't come back from the dead. You think we'd be in this mess, if that were the case?" She waved vaguely around.

Oh goody, she had reached the anger stage. But, an opening was an opening. I tried. "And which mess is that? Because I've got a lot of them right now. We've all got a lot of them."

She glared at me. "Hello? The Superflu killed the whole world!"

"Not all of it. Just 97% of it. There's still plenty of world left to go around. But Officer Adams tells me you haven't left the house. So it doesn't seem like you've had much chance to encounter any of it."

"What for? What's the point? The Superflu killed everyone I know. It killed my parents, it killed my friends, it killed all of my co-workers." She paused. She had started out angry, but was rapidly shifting over to despair. "It killed my fiancé."

"I'm very sorry for your loss." I said this as slowly and meaningfully as I could. "We've all lost people. You're not the only one."

"You don't understand!" she wailed softly. "He was the One. We were going to get married! He actually picked me. ME! Look at me, I'm fat, and ugly, but he didn't care about that. He liked me for who I am. We liked all the same things, we thought the same way. We bought this house together. We were even talking about having kids. It was absolutely perfect. I had finally found the One, and now he's gone. He was the only guy I've ever been with, and now he's gone. Everyone is gone."

Sharon's dog had come out from wherever he was hiding, and had crawled into her lap. She was gently massaging his neck. He looked up at her adoringly.

I tried some more sympathy. "Sharon, I'm so very sorry about your fiancé." I sat quietly for a few moments, trying to think of what to say next. She just stared down at her dog.

After a bit, I tried a more normal conversational tone. "You haven't been eating much. Zach here thinks you're losing weight."

She was momentarily confused by the name; she only knew him as "Officer Adams." But she caught on. "Yeah. I just can't handle the idea of food. It all tastes like glue and sawdust to me, right now."

"Well, it looks like you're drinking plenty of water. That's good. Are you getting any exercise?"

"Some. I take him for walks." She nodded down to the dog in her lap.

"Cool. And how about a shower? It looks like maybe you could use one." I said this as gently as I could, as well. But she scowled at me anyways.

"Can't. Water stopped working. Power, too."

Oh yeah. Zach had told me that.

"Well, tell you what, if come with us, we can set you up someplace where the water and power are still on. You could get a hot shower, put on some clean clothes, eat some hot food. It might make you feel better."

"I'm not leaving my house!" She snapped at me. She glanced over her shoulder at Zach behind her. "I've told you! I'm not leaving!"

I hung my head, and thought for a moment. I glanced out the sliding glass door to her large back yard. The grass was yellow and patchy. I noticed a bucket setup in the corner, with a toilet seat on top of it. Right, without power, or running water, no easy way to flush the toilets, so she had created a mini-outhouse for herself. The doors were shut, so I had not noticed any smell. I turned back to her.

"Listen, no one likes being forced out of their home. I didn't want to leave mine, either. But you know what? This will still be your home, even if you're not staying here. It will always be your home. Maybe someday you can come back. Maybe someday we can get the power and water back on in this area, too. But for now, it's safer if you're closer to the rest of the people near downtown. They've got clean running water. Toilets that flush. And power for lights, cooking, air conditioning, and everything."

She stared angrily at me for a few moments, not saying anything. Clearly, I needed a stronger connection to the woman. I looked around the room. It was a pretty nice house. The sofa was leather, and there was some nice art on the walls.

"So, what did you do for a living, before?"

"I was in I.T."

I arched my eyebrows, trying to draw her out. She didn't take the bait. "So, what kind of I.T. work? Programming? Help desk? Networking? Web design?"

"I was the CIO for my company. I was in charge of everything. Telecommunications, directing network installation and upgrade projects, systems migrations, sourcing our hardware and software, managing the internal help desk staff. You name it, if it had to do with computers, it was my responsibility." She actually rattled this off with an air of pride and professional buzz speak.

"Wow. That sounds pretty important," I said.

I wondered if maybe her company had ever used my company's software, back before. "Did you ever hear of or use the cloud apps from…?" I dropped my own company's name. She nodded.

"Yeah? Well, I worked for that company. I wrote the help manuals for some of those applications," I said.

Sharon's eyes widened. Bingo. I'd finally made a connection with her. Time to reel it in.

"So, who were you working for?" I asked her.

She named a company I had never heard of, and explained what they did. As she did, my shoulder angel was pointing out that she could help out with city I.T. stuff. I was pretty sure that Ariana was understaffed in that area, and could certainly make use of her.

When she finished her elevator pitch, I responded. "Huh. You know, we could really use your skills. The city is kind of hurting for technical help. They've got a guy, but he's stretched real thin right now."

Sharon was puzzled at that. "Doing what?"

"Well, anything and everything. They've been collecting a lot of data on everyone who died, so we can keep track of it, memorialize them, or at least be able to answer questions, if anyone ever comes looking for their lost relatives. But I don't think they've done much to organize that data properly. A good DBA would probably be a help. Or someone who can pick the right software, and get it installed for them. They've got admins, to do the data entry. But no programmers. Also, they could use anyone who can help restrore the telecommunications network. It needs to be extended to the rest of the city - houses, businesses, etc. A network admin would be really useful, I think."

I raised my eyebrows inquiringly at her. She got a considering expression of her own, as well.

"If you would come with us, we could introduce you to a few people…"

She scowled again. She was not stupid. But she was coming around. Behind her, Zach pointed to the radio speaker at his collar, and nodded at me. He stepped out of the room. I understood that to mean he was going to make a couple of calls, to get balls rolling.

"Look, it's a pretty simple arrangement. Come help us rebuild this community, and in exchange, you get a roof over your head, fresh food, hot running water, and cold air conditioning. You have skills the city can use. We need you. And you can't stay here for much longer. It's going to get hot soon and you don't have power."

I stopped there, and let her process the offer. Finally she sighed. "And my dog?"

"Of course. We'll find you a pet-friendly home." Zach nodded to me, to indicate he was already making the appropriate inquiries.

She sighed. She tipped her head back on the sofa. I could practically see the wheels spinning in her head. Finally, she nodded. "Okay. Fine." She didn't seem very happy about her choice, just resigned.

I went with her upstairs, to help her pack a few clothes into a suitcase. She also changed into some clean clothes that she dragged from the back of her closet. Probably smaller sizes she hadn't worn in a couple of years. I let her know that she could come back for more stuff, later on. It also occurred to me that it was good that we would be driving her downtown. Until she had fully made the transition into the community, I didn't want her driving her own car. I was afraid if we let her drive herself, she'd run away, come back here, and go back to hiding from the world.

Sharon also packed up some food and supplies for her dog. She told me his name was Buster. We then headed downtown. We took her to Ariana's office first, and explained her skill set. Ariana was indeed glad to have her join her office team, as the I.T. department primarily consisted of Tim, who had been previously help desk support for the city employees. He was overwhelmed with too much work, most of which was beyond his skill set.

While Ariana and Sharon talked, I slipped out to find Caleb. I found him in the conference room he had claimed for his workspace. He had a huge map of the city on the wall, with the Power On zone outlined in red ink. Additional maps, enlargements of various neighborhoods, were tacked up around the main map's perimeter. Various houses were marked with post it notes.

"Hey, Caleb. We've got an emergency placement for you. We managed to talk one of the shut-ins out of her house. She hasn't showered in a few days, and is still shell shocked by the Superflu. I think we need to start calling it 'Superflu Trauma', or ST, for short. It's a thing now."

Caleb smiled at me, and stood up. "Hi Maggie, nice to see you too."

"Oh, sorry. Yes, nice to see you," I said sweetly. Then in my more serious business tone, I went on. "Now, can you help us out?"

"Okay, yeah, I talked to Zach on the radio. He told me the basics. Female; with a dog. How old do you think she is?"

I told him what little I knew about Sharon. I added, "Look, she's still deep in her grief trauma. She needs to be around someone who can supervise her pretty closely, without being obvious."

Caleb folded his arms, and tapped at his face for a moment, while he thought.

"How about Gideon? You know the old guy who's running the bar?"

"The old codger guy, with the droopy mustache? Looks like he belongs in some Old West re-enactment tourist trap?"

"Yep, that's Gideon. He just lost a roomie, who moved in with someone else, so he's got a room free."

"Maybe… Is he around during the times when she would be? She might need rides to and from places. We've kinda separated her from her car, for the moment. I'm afraid of her sneaking off, and going back to hiding out again. And Gideon is kinda keeping bar hours; starts his day late, ends late."

"Good point. Well, how about… lessee…" He studied his wall map. "You know who JoAnn Ashby is? She's got a spare room still."

I shook my head. "Never heard of her. What's she working on?"

"She's mostly doing body detail crew work. Was a teacher her in her former life."

"Uh, not sure she'd have much in common with Sharon. Any other options?"

Caleb looked sideways at me. "Well, how about your place? Don't you and Gordon have a spare room now?"

Whoops. I had not seen that coming. And it was an entirely valid option. It had been over a month since Yarelie had committed suicide. Gordon and Dillon had removed the blood soaked mattress and found a replacement bed for the room. It was just waiting for a new occupant. For that matter, the casita was available, too. And I had been meaning to let Caleb know about that, too.

"Uh… I'm not sure if that's a good idea. I'm trying to avoid what happened to Yarelie."

Caleb looked at me compassionately. "What happened to Yarelie was Yarelie's choice. You had nothing to do with it. It was not your fault."

Nice words, but it still didn't stop me from feeling guilty, like I should have done more. And Sharon seemed to be in just as bad a place, emotionally, as Yarelie had been. I wasn't sure I could take it, if it happened again.

Caleb offered another point, as well. "It also doesn't sound to me like Sharon is suicidal. It's been almost six months since the Superflu hit. She's had a lot of time already. If she were going to do it, I think she would have already, by now."

That was an interesting perspective to consider. And, it also occurred to me that if Sharon was going to work in the city offices, she'd be keeping regular business hours, like I was. Our schedules would be in sync, which meant I could keep a close eye on her. I wondered how Gordon or the rest of the guys would feel about it. Of course, it would be nice to have just a little more estrogen in the house, too. And then there was her dog, Buster. That would be Dog #7 in the household. That was getting to be a lot of dogs. But she did have nice taste in art, based on what little I'd seen in her own house.

I nodded. "Okay, we'll take her. At least until she's on her feet, and ready to be on her own. Thanks for the help, Caleb!" I headed out of the office to go find Sharon and Ariana. It occurred to me that Caleb had not actually done anything, other than offer a couple of unsatisfactory suggestions, which made his final alternative, and the obvious solution, seem more attractive to me. That was pretty clever of him. I'd have to remember that strategy for the future. I wondered if maybe he should be my vice-mayor. Was that even a thing in this town? And could I appoint one, or did the position have to be elected?

I found Ariana and Sharon where I had left them, in Ariana's office. They were chatting casually now. I burst in. "Okay, it's all settled, you're staying with us. I mean, me and my guys. We need another woman around the house. And, we have dogs. Oh my God! I left Amex at the studio! We have to go get him! Come on, we can walk there, and then walk home."

Ariana was laughing at me. I was getting just a touch manic, for absolutely no reason. It was still early afternoon. And Amex would be fine at the studio. My crew knew him, and would keep him safe until I returned.

Ariana spoke up. "Actually, that's perfect; yes, she should move in with you. Sharon, you'll start here first in thing in the morning. Go with Maggie, and let her help you get cleaned up and settled in."

We passed Zach in his own office, and explained the plan. I asked him if he would, pretty please, take her suitcase, which was still in his cop car, over to my house, so we didn't have to drag it around. I explained that he didn't need to drive us because we needed to go by the studio to pick up my forgotten beast. Her own beast was with her, following politely on his leash. Zach agreed to play valet for us, and take her bag to her new home.

We juggled ourselves out of the building, pausing while Sharon let

Buster sniff the bushes and pick the perfect one to water. She was momentarily out of ear shot, so I grabbed Zach as he headed to his car. "Hey, don't be too quick to give her a gun, please. I don't want another Yarelie in my house, okay?"

He understood what I meant, and nodded. He took off in the car, while I walked her to the studio across the street and up a block. I explained a little about some of the customs and routines that were starting to develop, like the Saturday Town Halls, and dinners at Mercados after wards. Then I introduced her to my apprentices, who greeted her politely. Amex and Buster had a good sniff at each other, and promptly tangled their respective leashes. Amex did not seem too offended to have been left in the studio for a couple of hours. He hadn't exactly been alone, and he was familiar with the place. I had all of the dogs on a regular visitation rotation.

Next, I walked her through the little downtown area, pointing out various points of interest. We cut through the back side of the resort complex, and crossed over a portion of the golf course, which had now been partially converted into the vegetable gardens. Sharon was rather surprised to see that. I could practically see her appetite for fresh food coming alive.

And finally, we arrived at Gordon's house, which was now my house as well. We walked in, and of course, were promptly mobbed by the rest of the dogs. I introduced Sharon to each of them in turn: Tyrion, Oreo, Zilla, Duchess and Jack. Since Tyrion was the loudest barker of the bunch, I picked him up to quiet him down. The rest of them took turns giving Buster a sniff. Poor Buster was overwhelmed by all the attention. He crouched on the floor, and peed a little on the tile entryway. Sharon was very apologetic, but I explained that I kept lots of floor cleaners and towels around, since Oreo was prone to doing the same thing, for much less reason.

Next, I led Sharon and the dog pack to the kitchen, where we found Carlos in the kitchen, preparing dinner for a crowd. It wasn't officially a group dinner night, but Carlos did not seem surprised to see us. He explained that Zach had already been there, and Sharon's bag was waiting in the bedroom assigned to her. I had not told her about Yarelie, and was not going to. She might get creeped out at the idea of being in the room where another girl had killed herself. In fact, I was a little creeped out, and felt guilty about that, too. I knew I could let her have the casita, but it was just isolated enough that we would not be able to keep as close an eye on her. Maybe I could offer her that option later? I could stall for the moment by saying I hadn't cleaned out all my stuff yet…

I gave Sharon a quick tour of the house and showed her to her bedroom. I hadn't been in it since the guys had replaced the mattress, when I had made it up with replacement sheets and comforter pulled from the house's linen closet. The room was still kind of bare and plain. I pointed out the bathroom and closet. I suggested she go ahead and take a hot shower, then come join us in the kitchen. I shooed all the dogs except Buster out of her room, to give her a moment to collect herself. I went back to the kitchen to see what Carlos knew. He was surprisingly good at finding things out before anyone else and keeping them to himself. In this case, what he knew was courtesy of Zach.

Carlos and I were chatting when Gordon, Dillon and Micah arrived home. I was sitting on one of the bar stools at the kitchen counter, watching Carlos prepare a huge salad. He had chicken breasts pulled from the freezer stash, thawing and waiting to be grilled outside. The guys walked in, shedding their work gear. They routinely carried around a lot of heavy duty equipment, including safety helmets, tool belts, heavy work boots, thermoses for water, and hand guns for personal protection. Most of the gear was stored in the mud room off of the garage. Gordon had also installed a large gun safe there as well.

Gordon stopped in the kitchen to talk to Carlos and me, before going to take a shower. I got up to give him a peck on the cheek, and pitched him first.

"So, remember when you brought me Oreo, and said he needed to be rescued?" I asked with a light innocent tone.

"Yeah…." He cocked an eyebrow at me as he pinched a piece of red pepper away from Carlos and the carving board.

"Well, we have a new rescue now. The good news is she doesn't pee in the house like Oreo does."

"And, what's the bad news?" he asked me, looking around at our milling pack, trying to count them and identify the newcomer. I had Tyrion in my arms again, as he was being particularly barky this evening. It was the only way to get him to shut up.

"No bad news. The even better news is that this rescue is the two legged variety. The even bestest news is that she comes with a dog of her own."

Gordon looked at me. Dillon and Micah had caught the drift of the conversation as they moved from mud room to kitchen, on the way to their own rooms and showers.

Gordon was still looking around. "Where?"

Dillon butted in and asked, "So, that brings it up to, what, seven dogs now?"

Micah just groaned. We had assigned him the regular chore of picking up the dog poop from the back yard. "Please tell me it's not a big dog. No more big poops."

I pointed at Micah. "Hey, you should be glad for big poops. They're easier to find. Little ones get lost in the grass."

Micah rolled his eyes, and said, "Yeah, I know! That's my point!"

I laughed at him.

"So, where is our new roomie?" Gordon asked.

"She's taking a shower, she'll be out in a little bit. Listen, she's had a rough time of it. Let's go easy on her, okay?"

Gordon frowned at me. "Whaddya mean, rough time? What's going on?"

I shook my head at him. "Not now, later. It's a long story. We'll see if she can tell some of it when we sit down to eat. Why don't you guys go get cleaned up, as well, and then you can grill that chicken for us."

I sent them off to their showers. The work they were doing was nearly 100% outdoors, in the full sun. They usually came home sweaty and dusty. So, I had implemented my grandmother's old policy of making them bathe after work, instead of in the mornings, like they used to when we were all office workers. Another benefit of this strategy was that it left more hot water in the heater for me in the mornings. I hoped Sharon would eventually see the brilliance in that schedule, as well.

After a few minutes, Sharon herself reappeared, with damp clean hair, clean clothes, and Buster still on his leash.

"Hey, you certainly look better. Do you feel better?"

"Yeah, that was heavenly. I ran into a guy in the hallway, though.

Said his name is Dillon?"

"Yep, that's one of our roomies. Did I explain about the 'one bedroom, one person' policy?" Sharon shook her head, so I did. I concluded with, "So, this house is huge, it has five bedrooms, so five occupants. Gordon and me, Micah, Dillon, Carlos here, and now you." I gestured towards Carlos.

"That's six people." Sharon pointed out.

"Well, yeah, but Gordon and I are in one room. We're, uh, together." Sharon looked at me oddly. I realized it was pretty insensitive of me to flaunt my newish relationship in front of her, given how raw her own wounds were.

Gordon walked in at that moment, also freshly showered and in clean clothes, put his left arm around me, and kissed my cheek. He turned to Sharon, held out his right hand to shake, and grinned. "Hi. I'm Gordon Barriston. You must be our new roomie. Welcome aboard! We're glad to have you here."

I tried to fill in the gaps. "Yes, this is Sharon Walker." They shook hands.

Gordon bent down to try to greet Buster, but Amex took that as an invitation, and jumped on him. So Gordon sat down on the floor in the middle of the kitchen, to wrestle with Amex. Duchess brought him a tennis ball, which he threw towards the living room for her to chase. Zilla also darted in and out of his reach, yapping excitedly. I put Tyrion down to join in the fun. He barked even more than Zilla did. Oreo kept himself behind me, where I could not see him. And Jack stayed at Carlos' side, who kept on working on the food. Eventually, Gordon was able to say a proper hello to Buster, who hesitantly approached him.

Gordon was still on the floor playing with all the dogs, when Micah and Dillon finally rejoined us. Dillon pointed at Micah, and said, "You used up all the hot water, dude."

Micah retorted, "Nuh uh. You did."

Sharon's face fell. "Oh gosh, I'm sorry, that was probably my fault. I haven't had a proper shower in days, and I was in there for a really long time, and I had just finished when you guys got here…"

Gordon stood up to rejoin the humans. "Don't worry about it, Sharon. It was just bad timing. We'll do better next time." He turned to

Carlos. "So, what's for dinner?" He snatched a piece of carrot from the salad bowl.

Carlos was also preparing several packets of a seasoned rice mix, to go along with the chicken and salad. I had noticed several boxes of pasta on the back counter, but Micah asked about them first. Carlos explained that he was also going to fix a pasta salad for everyone to have for lunch or dinner the next day. One session of cooking, multiple meals. He was rather proud of himself. That also explained why he was chopping so many extra vegetables, too.

The guys were chattering away, drinking beer, preparing the grill, marinating the chicken. The meat had been pulled from Gordon's deep freezer chest and there was more than plenty to go around. Sharon was looking a little bit like a deer caught in the headlights. I realized it had been quite some time since she had been around so many people, all talking at once, and goofing off. I'd be having a minor panic attack, too, if I were in her place. I tried to stay close by her side, keeping calm, letting the commotion just wash over us. I wasn't so sure my calming efforts were having any effect, though.

We sat down to a lovely dinner. The dogs had finally settled down, as I had a strict "no feeding them from the dinner table" rule. They could hang with us, but no begging was allowed. And of course, the guys constantly competed to come up with subtler ways to break that rule. As we ate, we backfilled our origin stories for Sharon. She also asked us about the house rules. Aside from the dog management rules, we had never formalized anything, so far. So we ad libbed it.

I started with the obvious. "Tidy up after yourself. Don't leave messes behind in the communal areas. Your room and bathroom are yours, and we'll respect your privacy, but please, don't do anything that will attract bugs, like leaving plates of unfinished food in your room."

Gordon added, "If you go out, let someone know where, with who, and when you expect to be back. You're not a teenager; you don't have a curfew. This is just basic safety stuff."

Dillon offered his advice. "This dinner is an extra, but our regular group dinner night is Fridays. Other than that, you can eat what you want, whenever you want."

Sharon responded to that, "Oh, I don't really eat very much anymore." Dillon frowned, but did not get a chance to followup on that. Micah piped up next.

"No peeing in the pool." That made everyone laugh aloud

Carlos spoke up next. "Actually, I have a new rule for everyone. We're starting a composting project. So, everyone has to collect the kitchen scraps and set them aside. I'll setup some buckets outside. Once they fill up, I'll take them to the main composting bins we're building over on the north side of the golf course."

Finally! I'd been meaning to ask him about that. The house had already had a plant composting bin in the side yard, but so far as I knew, nothing was being done with it. "So, what took ya so long? Shouldn't we have started doing that months ago?"

Carlos answered me, "Eh, it doesn't much matter. It was not warm enough, in January, to get a good compost pile going. It requires some heat, and a lot of time, you know, to "cook" out the bad microbes, and break down the material. And, a few months ago, we were still eating so much packaged food, and doing a good job of eating what we prepared, and not letting it get wasted, that there was very little to compost. Now, with the gardens producing, there's a lot more vegetable scraps that can be composted."

Gordon looked thoughtful. "I've always wondered, but never got around to googling it. Why aren't meat scraps put into composting?"

Carlos answered him. "They can be composted, but it requires a slightly different process, a different set of microbes, to break down the proteins. It also requires a slightly higher temperature, to kill off any harmful bacteria. So, if you're going to do it, you have to keep it separate from plant-based compost."

Micah jumped in. "What about dog poop? Can we compost that?" He looked hopeful.

Carlos nodded. "Yes, but it also requires a different process as well. I was planning on keeping animal manure and meat scraps separate from vegetable matter. I have separate bins, and will keep them on separate cycles. Also, the compost from the protein sources will not be used for food crops, only for other plantings around the course. Just in case some bacteria does happen to survive. We don't want to pass that along into the food we're growing for ourselves."

Huh. Well, I was learning something new. Micah's face fell, however, when realized that he'd still have to collect the dog poop from around the yard, in order to get it into the buckets for transfer to the big bins.

Sharon spoke up, after having been quiet for a bit. "How did you people manage to get such a huge garden growing? It seems awfully big, for just a few people."

Carlos looked at her with surprise. Gordon answered first. "We're not exactly just 'a few people.' There's several hundred, maybe around 1200 or more, actively working on city-sponsored projects. And its estimated there could be another thousand or so people within the city limits, who are still surviving on their own in their own homes, much like you were." He said the last part gently.

Sharon was shocked. "That many? I had no idea. When Officer Adams kept telling me to come downtown, I thought there'd be maybe 40 or 50 people around. Wow."

Gordon went on, to give her some perspective. "This street we're on? Almost all the houses on it are already occupied. I think most of the houses within the gated section are already occupied, in fact." He glanced at me for confirmation, and I nodded. Sounded about right to me.

Gordon explained, "This entire city square mile, is our primary "power on" zone. In fact, we had to expand that to include the next sections south and west, as well. They're moving people in there just as fast as they can."

Sharon asked the next obvious question. "And who decides who gets what house? What if someone doesn't want roommates, and would rather live alone?"

Gordon gestured for me to take over. He stuck a forkful of food into his mouth. So I sat up and started filling her in. "Well, simple question, complicated answer. Basically, if you're working with us, helping, contributing, in some way to our mutual survival, you get housing in the Power On zone. If you're not directly helping, you can still get housing, but it might take a little longer, and it might not be your first choice or preference. There's a lot of other factors too, like what your own situation is; do you have still have power and water at your own home or not, etc. If you want to live alone, there's some older, smaller homes to the east side of the zone. Some of them are not in as good a repair as the newer homes are, not very energy efficient. We're routing power to the entire quadrant, but aside from that, there's no guarantee the AC is working all that well in those older homes. And, the "head" person of any house is responsible for upkeep of the landscaping and home in general. If someone doesn't have the skills or equipment to do something themselves, like, say, fix a broken window, they can request help, or offer a trade. There's also some apartments and condos in the zone too, for those who don't like roommates."

Sharon's mind was starting to spin up over all the interrelated issues this conversation was bringing up. "And that's another thing: what are you doing for money? I thought the economy completely collapsed, and money was basically worthless. How are you paying people?"

Gordon grinned at me. "Should I get everyone more beer?" He knew this was a philosophical topic, and in his mind, any heady intellectual topic required a libation.

I answered Sharon. "Yeah, the economy collapsed. We're basically not using any money at all, at the moment. We ask people to work, and if they do, they get a meal. If they do a lot of work, they get a house. At the moment, it's essentially a very primitive form of communism. 'From each, according to his ability; to each, according to his need'." I sighed. "It's not going to last, though. It works while there is plenty of everything to go around – food, water, electricity, fuel. Once that becomes scarce, or difficult, we need a mechanism to ration it. Pretty soon we're going to have to adopt some form of currency. Something that converts labor to value to goods and services."

Sharon scrutinized me carefully. "Economics major?" She asked me. I wobbled my hand. "Econ minor."

Sharon went on. "And what *is* the deal with the power? Why can't it stay on everywhere? Why did it go off? If it was on for five months since the Superflu, why couldn't it just stay on?"

I grinned back at Gordon. "Your turn." I said back him and dug into my own food again.

He grimace grinned back at me, and said "Why, yes, I would like another beer. Thank you, honey." I decided that was a reasonable request, and got up to get him a bottle. Dillon nodded for one more, but Carlos waved it off. Gordon ran through his lengthy, technical explanation about rerouting the grid power, and solar power, and preserving equipment for future use. By the end, Sharon was looking a little stunned.

I asked her, "Too much information?"

She responded, "Yeah, kind of overwhelming. I wish I had known all this was going on." She paused. "Well, I guess that's not really fair to Officer Adams. He's been trying to get me out of my house for a couple of months. I don't know why I didn't believe him, or come see for myself. After I recovered from the Superflu, I made a couple of massive supply runs, but I haven't left my house for months since then. I've just been sitting around, watching TV and reading books. Did you guys know that the cable OnDemand service was still working? Well, it was until I lost the power in my house a week ago. I watched almost every single HBO show in the archive."

I said, "Huh. Which was your favorite?" So not the point of the conversation, but I was a tiny little bit tipsy from the beer, too.

She answered, "*The Sopranos*. Best show ever made, I think."

"Really? I thought *Breaking Bad* was the best show ever made. Kind of like a classic the way *Moby Dick* or *Tom Sawyer* are American classics."

Sharon said, "Never saw it, but I've heard that before. Maybe someone has it on DVD? I should give it a try."

Before we could get into a detailed debate over the finer points of modern television story telling, Gordon reeled us back in.

"So, anyways, ladies, it's actually getting kind of late. There's always time for more talk tomorrow, but I want to get an early start. It's starting to get hotter, which means us linemen have to start working earlier." He nodded at Dillon, to suggest he do the same. Dillon and Micah headed off for their nightly round of video games.

Sharon helped me clear the dishes. "So, what's the deal with the kid, Micah? He's not actually your son is he?"

I smiled at her. "No, he's Gordon's foster son. Gordon and I found him on Christmas Day. He was the only survivor in his family, had been in his house, alone, for 2 months. Gordon invited him to come stay with him. Actually, Micah moved in here before I did. Micah practically worships Gordon, and thinks Dillon is like a big brother."

"Wow, that's awfully generous of Gordon, taking in a strange kid like that. I'm not sure I'd be able to do that."

"Yeah, Gordon really is pretty generous." I smiled.

"But what's with the child labor thing? Is he really dragging that boy out to the job sites?"

I smirked. "Well, it's not like Micah can go to school. There isn't any of that, anymore. And going out with Gord and Dillon is better than leaving him at home, unsupervised. Micah would rather be with the guys, than alone. And he likes helping them. So Gordon is treating it like an apprenticeship, teaching him the business."

She thought that over. "And you and Gordon? You two are a thing, then?"

I grinned again. "Yeah, a very new thing. It's only been a couple of months."

I let her absorb that information. She was still pretty raw over her own losses. I didn't think she understood that she was also back on the market, and so was most everyone else. I also didn't see much need to point that out just yet. She'd gotten stuck in the mourning process, in the grief and anger phases. Hopefully, getting her out of her house, and finally experiencing life again, would get her back on the path to the acceptance phase.

Chapter 9

Within weeks, Sharon seemed to be reclaiming her own life. She may have been a little behind schedule, compared to everyone else's recovery, but she worked hard at catching up. We felt confident in her commitment to rejoining the world, so I drove her back to her house, to get more clothes and personal items, and then let her drive her own car back for her own daily use. Mostly, we walked to and from our respective jobs, since they were so close. Letting her bring her own car home was a mostly symbolic gesture. Not that I told her that, though.

Sharon also brought back some of her art work, for the house. The big house on the golf course had originally been decorated with some very generic desert landscapes. Some had been removed and replaced with my own art (or my parents' art), but those were smaller pieces. Sharon had several large scale dramatic paintings that we happily hung in the living room. It made me feel all warm and fuzzy to see her engaging in living life.

Life for everyone seemed to be getting both better and worse, simultaneously. Maybe "complicated" was the most appropriate term. Carlos was having some wonderful success in the gardens, but power was getting wonky. Even in the Power On zone, sometimes unexpected system surges caused brown outs. Sharon was helping reconnect City Hall and residents in the zone, to the Internet. But finding useful operational sites and services was still a challenge. Robert was still not having much success in assuring that fresh water supplies were properly treated to be safe for drinking. And, on top of that, pumps in the power off zone weren't working, unless a generator could be connected to them. This was affecting water pressure throughout the system, which motivated any remaining survivors to push for their relocation into the consolidation zone.

Meanwhile, the city had marked off a portion of the downtown park for the new memorial monument, but assorted construction specialists were bickering over methodology, foundation, and support for the structure. I kept reminding myself that problems had solutions, but then my little shoulder devil would point out that every solution just led to new problems.

***

On a beautiful sunny April weekend, we received our first official visit from an outside delegation. The Glendale group we had encountered the month before, had taken us up on our offer to visit. They had been in somewhat regular communication with us via VoIP phone lines, so we were aware they were coming. Ariana arranged to have some rooms in the resort hotel aired out, in case they wanted to stay overnight. The plan was to meet in front of City Hall, for a short visit around town and show them what we had accomplished so far. Then we planned a group trek out to the peach orchard in Queen Creek. Our contact there told us that some of the trees were just starting to ripen. We were pretty excited about this tangible evidence of spring. As if the cactus flowers had not been enough proof.

Rob and Maddy MacDonald and their entourage arrived at the expected time. Rob and Maddy were in the lead, driving a large pickup truck, stocked with an assortment of shallow plastic crates that would be ideal for taking peaches home. They also brought with them some varieties of produce that they thought we might not have. And even better, they brought an assortment of exotic seeds that they had harvested, dried, and prepared for storage, along with instructions about when and how to plant, water and harvest the crops. Carlos and Maddy immediately fell to talking shop, and he offered her the tour of his own gardens, to show off his own progress. He was especially excited to show her his composting bins. I figured it must be a gardener thing.

The MacDonalds were accompanied by several other vehicles, as well. The most impressive one was a long fuel tanker. Rob explained that several of his people had figured how to access the fuel depot in southwest Phoenix, and transfer fuel to tankers. They were leaving this one with us, and we could bring it back any time to fill up again. And, oh, where would we like it to be parked?

That was an especially welcome gift, but I think our police force was even happier with Major Bartosik's contribution. Bartosik had established his own neighborly relationship with Rob & Maddy's group. And, he had personally driven a heavy duty vehicle mounted with a rocket launcher, and a supply of grenades to use in it. Jake quickly stepped up to greet the Major and introduce him to Zach. They shook hands and grinned at each other. Zach seemed very impressed with the artillery. He gestured for the Major to follow him a little ways away, for a private conversation. I frowned at their departing backs, wondering if I should tag along, but I was distracted by Ariana. She was herding us cats into trucks and SUVs for the trip out to Queen Creek.

We gathered up our gear and headed out. I was seated in the back of one of the SUVs with one of the Glendale people, a woman I had not met before. She had also dropped off a gift case of homemade soaps, so I asked her about her craft process, out of professional curiosity. She explained the basic overview, and indicated she was prepared to ramp up her production quantities, if I felt there was a market for it yet. I wasn't sure there was much market for soap, just yet; that was one of those things that the stores still had plenty of, and we'd also collected it from empty homes. However, it occurred to me that sunblock might be useful. Commercial sunblock lost its effectiveness over time, usually within a year, so new product would be needed. If not this year, then definitely next year. I offered her some powdered zinc oxide from my ceramic glaze supplies. I hoped she could find a way to mix it into creams or lotions for application. She was excited by the prospect, and promised to work on it.

We arrived at the orchard farm to find a small contingent of locals waiting to greet us. Between the Glendale people, and our own Chandler people participating in the outing, there were about 30 of us. It was starting to feel like a party. Everyone was making friends and was excited by the project. The Queen Creek farmers showed us to the ripe trees. They had moved picnic tables under the peach trees, which made it easier to get to the upper parts of the tree. Less up and down, than using ladders. They had also collected an assortment of packing crates for our use. They shared some tips on how to determine if something was ripe or not, and the best way to separate it from its stem.

Carlos and Maddy were a little late to join everyone, as they had been side tracked by the garden tour in Chandler. Then they got equally distracted looking at the orchard's vegetable garden. I discovered that the orchard caretaker's name was Eugene. I had not known this before. When we had previously met a few months ago, he had not told us his name, out of distrust or shock or fear. Today he was welcoming and happy to have someone appreciate the work he had done to keep the place producing.

Micah and a couple of his friends had elected to skip their apprenticeship work for the day, with their supervisors' blessings, and had joined us for the excursion. I set them to work on picking the fruit and loading it into trays. They took to it reasonably well, although there was some tossing, pitching and hurling of imperfect, bruised fruit. I tried the well worn line, "Its all fun and games, until someone gets an eye poked out!" but they didn't seem to comprehend it, so it wasn't very effective. I finally resorted to sending them to the trees farthest away from the other adults, to minimize harm to the innocent.

After about an hour of picking, my arms, shoulders and back were tired of the reaching up motion. I shouldn't have been surprised. While the concept of fresh fruit was enticing, the actual work involved was exhausting. I took to shuttling filled trays back to a shady staging area, for convenient loading into the vehicles later in the day.

At midday, we brought out hamburgers and fixings and side dishes, and treated our guests and hosts to a barbecue. Last winter, some of our city residents had managed to butcher and freeze the meat from some of the mini-farm cows that were not going to survive. Although most of the local dairy herds had died, we'd still managed to successfully process a few dozen of the cattle that were wandering, or trapped, unable to be cared for properly. And our storage warehouse had a freezer section, with an industrial scale generator hooked up, just in case the grid power failed. Between the amateur butchering, and the commercial meat that had been safely recovered and frozen for longer term storage, we had plenty to share. So we were comfortable with sharing out the meat freely. Eugene's people seemed especially grateful. I suspected they had not had much protein in their diets lately.

I spent the afternoon hanging with Carlos, Maddy, and Eugene. Ariana wandered back and forth between tree picking, and hanging with us too. Mostly, I just listened to the gardeners discussing their craft, sharing tips and tricks. Maddy was a big advocate of canning. But

Carlos pointed out that dehydrating didn't require as much storage space, work, and processing supplies. He had 'borrowed' my original three food dehydrators, as well as any others he could scrounge from the Walmarts and other kitchen supply stores around town. However, they all ran on electricity. He wanted to use the natural power of the sun, to maximize the quantity of stuff that could be preserved. After all, the sun was our greatest resource, and it seemed foolish not to take advantage of it. However, he was struggling with ways to keep insects and birds off of the produce.

They brainstormed various options, and came up with an idea to use mesh screens (that they were sure they could get from Home Depot), mounted on wooden frames. The framed screens would form trays that could be stacked and racked. The fruit could be sandwiched between trays, protected from intruders and pests. The racks could hold the trays at a slight angle, to ensure direct sun and good air circulation through the layers of mesh. And the racks could be mounted on caster wheels, so that they could be easily moved about, into and out of the sun as needed.

I wondered aloud if they would be able to effectively clean the surfaces in between sessions, to prevent the spread of bacteria or parasites. They believed the mesh screening they had in mind would be plastic, and a grade that could tolerate being bleached and sanitized. I pointed out that the wood frames might not take sterilizing too well, and suggested they consider PVC piping for the frames. They could wrap the mesh around it, or secure it with steel crews. PVC would not tolerate sunlight for more than a few years; most plastic degraded and oxidized in UV light; it was just a question of how long it took. Some types did better than others. So, I also suggested they be prepared to rebuild their trays every few years, or develop other alternatives, too.

They were excited by the ideas. Eugene rustled up some paper from somewhere, and they sketched out designs. They included variations that would work better for drying meat. They considered using different grades or sizes of piping for frames, so they could segregate types of racks for different types of food. 'Wetter' foods like peaches would be on one type of tray, while dryer types of foods, like carrots, would be on other trays. Meat would be completely separate, on trays reserved exclusive for meat, to avoid potential cross contamination.

All in all, they were preparing for a lot of large scale food preserving. This was encouraging; Carlos and his team had planted a huge garden. I was not entirely sure he hadn't over planted, and that we might not have some excess that would go to waste. But everyone was sharing ideas on how to preserve excess food for the long term. It might even make for trade goods, in the future. Carlos also pointed out that he wanted to make sure all the pets in the community had plenty of food for the future, too.

Late in the afternoon, we packed up and headed back to Chandler. Ariana slyly pointed out that we would probably miss the Town Hall meeting, oh darn. And, she was almost right. We arrived just in time for the tail end of it. Before Ruckles was allowed to wrap up the meeting, Ariana spontaneously amended the agenda, to tell people to come and grab a flat of fresh peaches, if they wanted any. Most did so happily.

As we usually did on Saturday evenings, many of my friends gathered at the long picnic tables stretched in front of the promenade between Mercados and the brew pub. We took turns getting plates of food and pitchers of beer. We introduced the Glendale people around, including to Gordon, who they were especially eager to talk to, about power and electricity for their area.

While they discussed specifics, I deconstructed the day with Ariana.

"You know, I'm not sure that Eugene and his people are doing all that well. They still seem to be struggling, to me. I mean, I'm grateful for how they treated us today, and the orchard looks great. But I don't think they have much else besides that."

Ariana looked at me questioningly. "How so?"

"I think they're struggling with power and fuel, still. They need pumps to move irrigation water to the fields. And they need electricity to keep their houses cool this summer. I don't think they have enough of either." I paused, wondering how to phrase the next part.

"Do you think we could split off one of Gordon's sub teams, to install solar panels on their houses? There doesn't seem to be as many people around in that town as we have here. So there's probably only a few houses that need it. And it's too far a commute to move them here, and send them back out there to work every day."

Ariana nodded slowly. "Seems reasonable to me. Will solar panels be

118

enough for air conditioning?"

"Gordon says if they're the right kind of panels, and enough of them, and enough battery storage capacity, they can independently power a whole house year round. As long as there's enough sunlight, too, of course. Which usually isn't a problem here." I winked.

Ariana said, "Well, I don't have a problem with splitting off a crew; if it's just a few houses, it shouldn't take too long. As long as Gordon is okay with it, I am too."

"Fabulous. Thank you. I also think we should ask Rob or Maddy about a fuel truck for Queen Creek, too. They have generators, but they're going around car to car for gas. They haven't figured out how to siphon it out of the underground tanks at the gas stations, nor do they have a good way to transport lots of it at one time. They're just using small portable gas cans."

Rob must have heard me say his name, because he turned to me inquiringly. I explained how Eugene and his little team had generators for irrigation pumps, but they had difficulty getting enough fuel to them. Rob was willing to help. He had a couple of people who had specialized in fuel management, before, and those people were teaching others how to access the big above-ground storage tanks, transfer it to trucks, and move it to other areas. He promised to send out a team in a day or two. And to bring some more generators, for strategic distribution, as well.

Ariana was smirking at me, I noticed. "What?" I said.

"See? Problems have solutions."

"Oh, stop. Not right now, please. This is supposed to be a fun evening," I said.

And that was when Aaron and Ali ran up to us and burst into the conversation. They had spent their day out gathering more ceramics supplies from other studios around the Valley.

"Hey, Maggie! We saw giraffes!" Ali hollered at me.

I was baffled by this non-sequitur. "Huh? What? I don't get it. What are you talking about?"

Aaron and Ali rushed to fill me in on their adventure.

Aaron said, "We were driving up Hayden Road through Scottsdale; you know that long strip of park that runs along it? The golf course and ponds and bike path and stuff?" I nodded. "We saw five giraffes there, eating leaves off the trees!"

I stared at them, turning this over in my mind. Ali announced the obvious conclusion as it was forming in my brain. "They must have gotten loose from the zoo. It's not that far away."

I nodded. "They were probably eating acacia leaves. That's an African tree, that's pretty common around here." There were actually lots of African and Australian plants in the metro area. They were well adapted for the arid, sunny climate. And people liked exotic things, so they thought nothing of installing non-native plants, when designing a landscape. Bet they never thought their exotic plants would attract exotic animals, too.

Aaron continued the story. "We wondered how they had gotten loose, so we drove over to the Zoo, to see what was going on. Maggie, the place is wide open. Somebody let most of the animals out of their cages!"

My eyes grew wide at that implication. "Everything?"

Ali tapped into the conversation. "Almost everything. The Reptile house was still locked up. But most of the big animal cages were open. Elephants, baboons, antelope, zebras, all gone." Ali looked at me meaningfully. "But the African lions cage was still locked up. We saw a dead one in the enclosure."

I asked him, "What about other big cats? Leopards, tigers?"

Ali said, "Not sure. They looked like they were still locked up, but we didn't see any others, alive or dead, inside."

Aaron asked, "Why would some turn all those animals loose? Can they even survive?"

My brain had been working through the implications. "Well, yeah, actually, a lot of them probably can. The zoo had a pretty strong African animals exhibition, because the climate those animals live in, is similar to what we have here. They also had a really strong native animals program, but it wasn't as big or splashy as the African ones. Any of the herbivore herd animals can probably do okay around here. I think the giraffes will be fine – there's plenty of acacia trees around. The elephants will probably also be okay, too, but they need a lot of water. I know they're plant-eaters, but I'm not sure what kinds. They're probably sticking close to the river… The antelope and the zebras – same thing, as long as they can find water to go with the stuff they're grazing on, they might survive. They have a strong drive to migrate, but I'm not sure they'd know where to migrate to and from, or when, so that might cause them some problems."

Then another animal occurred to me. "Hippos! Were there any hippos in the zoo? Were they set free too?"

Ali knew what I was thinking. "Yeah, there was a space for them, and it was open, too. Not sure how many were there."

"Oh geez. They probably made their way down to the river, too. That marshy wetlands area east of Tempe Town Lake is probably perfect for them." Even though hippos were herbivores, they could be really nasty tempered. And then it occurred to me that rhinos were even worse, and didn't need to spend as much time in the water, and thus, could range farther.

"Rhinos?" I asked them.

"Yeah, same thing. Probably one or two of them, gone." Ali answered.

"Alligators?" I asked.

Ali answered, "Well, there were crocodiles as part of the African animals display, but they were gone too. They might be in that little pond by the zoo entrance. Unless you think they could have made it to the river, too?

I popped my eyebrows in the "I dunno" shrug. The zoo was part of a large city park adjacent to the Salt River. Most of the Salt River area was actually more of a dry riverbed, since the dams upstream had blocked and regulated most of the water flow years before. The same dams that generated the electrical power that Gordon was working so hard to stabilize and reroute. Although the dams released a controlled supply of water, the drought conditions of the last two decades had dried up most of that. Once the river reached the metropolitan area, most of the water had sunk into the ground, or evaporated, leaving only a thin stream of water to travel down a plowed furrow, through central and west Phoenix.

Where the city park met the riverbed, was Tempe Town Lake, a man-made lake two miles long, that had been formed when giant rubber bladders had been installed at each end, further blocking the water flow. Initially it had been filled with an allotment of ground water, pumped up and into the space. It was a fairly shallow lake, no more than 20 feet deep. Like all major governmental projects, this one had its share of supporters and protesters. The people in favor of the project had wanted to build a water feature attraction, which would generate more development in the downtown area. The objections included costs and impact on the river ecosystem. In spite of the objections, the project was approved, and had been fairly successfully in encouraging more development. A number of projects for condos, offices and light retail sprang up along side the new lake. Park space was also developed, and hosted numerous festivals which drew lots of visitors.

Overall, the project was mostly successful. But a few years ago, at the peak of the summer heat, the rubber baffle at the west end had ruptured. The rubber had dried out in the nearly constant sunshine and heat, and pressure from the water behind it had stressed it to the breaking point. All the water in the lake had rushed out, leaving a muddy smelly mess. It had taken months to get a replacement baffle installed, and several more years for the entire west end dam to be replaced with a steel one that would not degrade in the intense UV light.

I wasn't certain if the rubber baffles at the east end had ever been replaced, though. A few years after the lake was first filled, an unusually wet winter occurred (comparatively speaking, of course). Excess rain in the mountains northeast of the Valley sent extra water down the Salt River, where it was blocked by the baffles at the east end of the lake. The water collected, rising up high enough to cover the baffles, spreading and forming a marshy wetlands area. Assorted grasses and reeds took root, and numerous types of birds, both migratory and permanent, took advantage of the bounty. Much of wetlands formed under the intersection of two major freeways, which were raised hundreds of feet in the air. This created plenty of shade which helped the micro ecosystem thrive, as well.

In other words, that marshy wetlands area just a few miles upstream from the zoo might be very attractive to African wildlife, like hippos, crocodiles and elephants.

I eyed Ali and Aaron speculatively. "Well, it's good to know about this, but I don't think there's much we can do about it, other than warn other people to be on the look out."

Aaron asked, "Don't you think we should try to find the crocodiles, and remove them?"

"No, every ecosystem needs some predators at the top of the food chain. The crocs will eat small game, fish, and anything stupid enough or old and weak enough to get in their way. That's called "thinning the herd." No, my worry is if people aren't aware of it, they might stumble into something they didn't expect. Hippos and rhinos can be pretty aggressive, and can do a lot of damage if you mess with them."

Ali grinned. "I dunno, I thought it was pretty cool seeing the giraffes. Kinda nice having them around."

I grinned back. "Yeah, and elephants too. I wish I knew if they were around too." Then I frowned. "Of course, they're not native, so that makes them an invasive species. Not sure how well they'll adapt to living in the urban wild. They might do really well. Or they might not be able to find the right kinds of food they need. Also not sure if the small number of starter animals is enough to grow into a big herd. Might not be enough genetic diversity to be healthy. And, most of those animals species have a serious migratory drive, but I'm not sure where they would go, or when, here in Arizona." I paused. "Well, there's much we can do about it, regardless. Except to spread the word to people, to be on the lookout."

And that was when Zach, Jake, and Major Bartosik arrived, looking dirty, sweaty, and smug. I squinted at them. "You've been playing with big toys, haven't you, boys?"

Zach grinned back at me. "Nope. We were working. It was just very successful work, is all."

Ariana and I glanced at each other. She didn't know what he was talking about any more than I did. Gordon and Rob were a few spaces away from us, talking to each other, but they caught the new vibe, and turned to focus on us as well.

I looked around at each of them. Bartosik practically had a metaphorical victory cigar clamped in his teeth.

"Care to explain what's going on?" I asked them.

Jake snickered, but Zach took control of conversation. "Well, let's just say that we took care of the Petra Problem." He grinned.

I frowned. "Maybe you should backup, and explain the whole situation, for the benefit of our guests here." I gestured to Rob and

Maddy.

Zach focused on our guests and said, "Sure. See, we had this incredibly rude rich bitch Russian lady, named Petra Vasilov. She owned one of the houses in the gated community before the Superflu, and was pretty pissed off, when she came south like a snowbird in January, and found her house occupied by a bunch of strangers. She promptly kicked them out. Since then, she's been running around all over the East Valley, gathering up supplies, and recruiting people to cook and sell meth. She setup a lab in an empty store in a strip mall in Ahwatukee. We tried to follow her, to get solid evidence, but it's pretty hard to follow someone by car, when you're the only two cars on the road. So, thanks to Maggie's suggestion," he gestured at me, "we started following her with a drone camera. We finally got the conclusive proof we needed just a couple of days ago. We've got video surveillance of her people unloading chemicals used to make meth, and more of them moving cases and boxes of finished product back out again. We found some of the people she's been selling to, and they were high as kites. We seized some of the product from the customers, also. So, I let Major Bartosik know what was going on and asked for his assistance. I've been in touch with him, also thanks to Maggie." He was grinning at me.

Zach went on, "So that's why he came along on this little expedition with his special toy car." He paused for dramatic effect. "We setup a stake out, near her facility and just waited for her to come in for work. When we saw her go into the lab with a bunch of her people, we sent three rocket propelled grenades into the building. The lab has been completely flattened."

I was stunned. Ariana was stunned. She yelped out loud before I could. "You just killed them? Just like that? Why didn't you arrest them?"

Zach's face fell. This was not the reaction he had been hoping for.

He answered, "Say we did arrest them? Then what? We've had this conversation before, Ari. We don't have the means to legally prosecute anyone at this time. No lawyers, no judges, no way to hold them for trial, or properly imprison them, if found guilty."

Ariana was still appalled. "You just murdered those people!"

Zach put on his Officer Adams face. His voice got serious, almost stoic. "Murder? Ariana, those people were criminals. They were distributing a highly lethal product. We know of several recent deaths caused by meth overdoses. The same meth that she's been cooking. Our drone has captured video of them meeting a small group of people driving cars with California license plates. They've been selling product to both local users, and out-of-state groups. They had the capacity to ramp up production to deal to the entire southwest region. They were poised to become the head of a brand new drug cartel. That would have attracted a significant amount of attention, and traffic – the kind that we don't want. The kind of people who come in and raid homes and businesses, to find the cash to buy, or the supplies to make more of it. The kind of people who hurt innocent people who get in the way of them getting what they want."

Zach didn't stop there. "By taking them out, we have eliminated an old style criminal gang, destroyed their inventory of product, their equipment, and their supplies for making more. This will prevent numerous future deaths from meth overdoses, and collateral damage. Today, we *solved* a problem."

Now he stopped and stared at us. I was thinking about that old line, about forgiveness being easier than permission, and wondered if I should say it out loud. I could tell Ariana had a lot more she wanted to say, but she was stuck and couldn't get any more words out at the moment.

A complete non sequitur ran through my mind. "Cash? She was selling for cash? Why would she do that? Cash is worthless now." I blurted this out, before I could consider the potential impact.

Ariana huffed at my irrelevant tangent, threw up her hands, and got up to stalk away. I was pretty sure she was heading home. I'd catch up to her later.

Zach answered me. "Actually, she was taking mostly gold and some silver. Coins, if people could get it, jewelry if that was all a potential customer had. We recovered a lot more of her revenue at her house, before we came here. We've impounded it. The City is going to need to start minting coin soon, and that seizure will be our seed stock, as well as keeping the supply tight."

Well, that was actually a sound economic strategy.

Zach softened a little, and said more quietly to me. "Look, you've heard of 'plausible deniability'? That's another reason we went ahead with this. You're not Mayor yet, and if I asked for your or Robert's authorization for the mission, then you or he would be culpable, as well. On the extremely unlikely possibility that the FBI or any other reconstituted government agency comes around investigating, you can blame me, fire me, and still have a functioning operation. It would be far more damaging to have the head of our city government have to take the blame for it. In this case, the buck stops here." He tapped his chest.

I sighed. That was a reasonable explanation, actually. And his previous point was also valid; he *had* solved a problem. I just wondered what other new problems would pop up because of it.

Bartosik interjected, "Actually, just so you're aware, I ran this operation up the chain of command. And it was approved. My superiors examined the information, and considered the meth production lab to be a threat to the communities in this area. They authorized my contributions as an official military strike against an enemy."

Well, good to know someone was crossing the t's and dotting the i's. I nodded my thanks. I'd share that with Ariana later.

I turned back to Zach, and asked him, "Who was actually buying the meth? I don't see too many people around who look like meth addicts. Or am I just too naïve to tell?" I gestured at the crowd around us.

Zack explained that, too. "Addicts don't do work, they just get high. The only work they do do, is to scavenge for the gold to get their drug, so they can get their high. They're not hanging out around here." He repeated my gesture. "A lot of them took up in some of the really big houses around the area. I think some were coming from Phoenix or Scottsdale, too. Whatever, they don't care about things like clean water, air conditioning and quality food. The only thing they care about is their high."

"And now that their supply has been cut off, do we have to worry about an invasion, when they go looking for a replacement?" I asked.

Zach shrugged. "Maybe. We should probably post some more guards around. I don't have enough fully qualified police officers yet. But our first cohort of new trainees is coming along nicely. And speaking of, we're planning a joint training exercise in a few weeks.

We've worked out a deal with those preppers in Sedona. They've got a problem with some squatters and need more bodies to roust them out. It's a good exercise in urban patrolling for the trainees. He's bringing his men along, too." Zach nodded to the Major. Bartosik nodded back to confirm.

"And to make it a fair trade, we're bringing Gordon along. They're giving my boys some training in urban patrolling, we're training their people in solar power installation." Zach added nonchalantly.

"Oh? And does Gordon know about this?" I wondered. I looked at him, seated a few spaces away from me. He nodded at me.

Zach said, "Yeah, he knows. He agreed. Don't worry, he won't be anywhere near the training exercise."

"Okay, that's good to know. More patrols and guarding is probably a good idea, for lots of reasons."

Zach nodded back, obviously relieved that I wasn't freaking out over his actions today.

Gordon and I walked home after that. I back filled him on the conversation about the released zoo animals, which he had not been paying attention to. He agreed that it was kinda cool to have such exotics around. Hopefully they would survive and adapt to the environment, as well.

Gordon also pretty much agreed with Zach's reasoning and choice regarding the Petra problem. He was actually not all that surprised at the action. He confided to me that Zach had previously told him they had been planning this for more than a week, and that he'd been sworn to confidentiality, as part of the "plausible deniability" aspect.

We stopped at Ariana's house, which was just down the block from ours. However, she was not ready to talk yet, saying she need more time to process. We let her alone, and headed home.

Chapter 10

On Sunday morning, Ariana joined Sharon and me downtown for breakfast at Mercado's. I had the little dogs with me, and Sharon had Buster. Ariana had calmed down somewhat. While she could understand Zach's reasoning, she still didn't approve. I told her what Bartosik had told me. She thought about that for a moment, and said, "That still doesn't make it okay. Zach made a decision, and that decision has consequences. People are dead. People we might have been able to save."

I sympathized with her position, but I'd had time to get over the shock. I had decided I actually kind of agreed with Zach's reasoning. I had enough tact to not say so, quite so blatantly, though.

Instead, I tried a couple other angles on her.

"You realize, of course, that with the meth supply gone, we might be able to avoid any more overdose deaths. Remember that argument we had, where I said we should just let people do that, if that's what they really wanted? Take themselves out of the gene pool, stop being a drain on resources, and all? Well, that may not happen now. So, it looks like you've won that argument after all."

She glared at me. Nope, that was not going to work on her.

Ariana had little Zulilly, the three pound teacup Silkie Terrier, in her lap. She was feeding the dog bits of left over eggs from her own plate. The tiny dog was politely licking the food from Ariana's fingers. Tyrion was sitting in my own lap, but was staring at them, and whining. He wanted leftover breakfast, too.

I tried another angle on Ariana.

"So, another thing to consider; there's another big empty house available, inside the gated zone. Maybe you could move Tucker and his friends back into it?"

Tucker and several other people had briefly occupied the house before Petra had shown up several months before. She had thrown a royal hissy fit over finding strangers squatting in her house, and demanded their eviction. She had then taken up solo residence in her own house, but she had not made any effort to participate in civic life.

Nor had she welcomed any roommates, either. Of course, she also had wisely not tried to claim any of the civic resources, such as food from the community warehouse, either. Had she tried, she would have been met with stony refusal.

Ariana answered neutrally. "Tucker's fine where he is. I think I'll tell Caleb to reserve the house for special needs. Maybe long term guests, or something."

I thought for a moment.

I tried my last diversion on Ariana. "I know Zach said this last night. But if we had a functioning court system, he could have handled things differently. So, maybe it's time to find a judge, and some lawyers? They'd have to be the kind who can run criminal cases, like DUIs, fights, stuff like that. I don't think we need any corporate lawyers, at the moment."

She sighed theatrically. I already knew it was one of the thornier problems. I went on. "And is there even a courtroom, and jail, in the City Hall building?"

She answered, "There's a joint municipal/county court, just across the street. Used to handle traffic violations, civil disturbances, stuff like that. The holding cells are pretty simplistic; they were never designed for long term imprisonment, just holding people while they waited on courtrooms and judges. I suppose I could send one of the handymen crews over there, to install some beds. We'd need guards, too. I'll have to see if Zach can reassign any of his people." She brightened. "Now that they're not spying on Petra anymore, maybe they'll have more free time, and can handle some guard duty."

I had a feeling Zach might feel a little differently, but I just said, "I'm sure Zach will have some ideas on how to fix up the jail and assign some guards. They'll need bathrooms and showers. And food. And a kitchen to prepare and store the food, too."

Sharon had not said much during the conversation, as there was a lot of back story she was still piecing together. But now she spoke up. "If you actually convict someone for something big, can't you just send them to Florence?" She was referring to large prison complex in the small desert town to the southeast.

Ariana and I shook our heads simultaneously. Ariana back filled the information for her. "Nope. No one left there. 97% of the inmates died, too, just like everyone else. The rest were either released or…"

Sharon interrupted her. "There's convicted criminals running around loose? Shit! Why aren't you rounding them up and putting them back in jail?"

I took over. "The ones that were released had been convicted of non-violent offenses; DUIs, possession, embezzlement, stuff like that. And apparently, they took off for parts unknown, and are probably not anywhere near here. The really violent ones… well, the last remaining head warden over there, shot them."

Ariana pressed her lips tightly together. She had not been happy to hear about that, either, but was in no position to argue about it. Florence was not her town, nor her prison, nor had the choice been made by anyone she knew personally.

Sharon was a little shocked as well. She looked at me. "Is that why so many people go around carrying guns? It's kinda weird, you know."

I set Tyrion down the ground. He was getting heavy in my lap. "It's not all that weird. I'm no gun nut, mind you, but the point is protection. We're not really all that worried about criminals. The bigger issue is problems with feral dogs running around. Guns work to scare them away, as well."

"Feral dogs? What the eff?"

More and more, it seemed like Sharon really had been stuck in time warp. She still had a lot of catching up to do.

"Yeah. When people got sick with the Superflu, a lot them just opened up their back yard gates and let their dogs run loose, to try to fend for themselves. They probably thought it was better than letting them die for lack of food and water in their houses. I'm a little surprised you didn't see any. Didn't you say that you had been walking Buster pretty regularly, at your own house?"

"Yeah, we did a lot of walking, but it was inside a gated community."

Huh. I did not remembered driving through any gates to and from her house. Well, whatever.

"Well, they are around, and they can be a menace." I said.

Ariana added in, "Yeah, we even had them inside our own gated community for a bit. But they've been driven out, now."

Sharon asked, "Do you think I should get a gun? I've never had one before…"

Ariana widened her eyes at me. I managed to keep my voice level and normal. "If you think you'd feel safer with one, I'm sure Zach can arrange something. But you probably don't need it quite yet. If you're out and about, make sure you're with someone who's armed. And here inside the consolidation zone, there's not really a problem with the dogs anymore. Too many people to chase them away. If you're going to work, or hanging out downtown, you don't need a gun. Only if you go outside the zone. And if you're doing that, it's usually best to go with someone. And they'll probably be armed."

Sharon said, "Oh. Okay." She thought for a moment, and looked a little sheepish. "I was actually thinking about going out. I could really use some new clothes. Nothing fits me right, anymore. All my old stuff at home is either too big, or really old and worn out."

Ariana brightened visibly. "Time to go shopping!" she practically squealed. She really did love shopping. I barely tolerated it, and only for the sake of hanging with friends, or if there was something specific I actually needed.

I grinned back at them both. "So, there you go! We'll carry our firearms, so you won't need one." I looked at Ariana. "The mall again?"

She nodded gleefully. "The mall!"

Sharon, Ariana and I got up to leave. We stopped off at home, so that I could pick up my gun, which I had not taken to breakfast. I let Gordon know what my plans were. We had not specifically made any plans to spend time together for the afternoon. But I kinda thought he might object to me going off to do girlie things. But he didn't. He just grinned, and told me to find something pretty to wear to dinner that evening. Guys were so weird.

We showed Sharon the basic tricks for getting into the mall, like which doors were unlocked, and why it was a good idea to carry flashlights. We poured over racks and racks of autumn and holiday themed clothing, to much frustration. We did manage to find some neutral basics to boost up our current wardrobes, and that was enough for the time being. That project took most of our afternoon. But I did have just enough spare time at home to squeeze in a nice little nap, too.

At sunset, Gordon and I walked back to Mercados. We joined our usual friends for the evening. While Sundays were a slightly smaller crowd than on Saturdays, there were still plenty of people hanging out and eating dinner. Apparently, a lot of people did not like to cook for themselves. Huh. Thankfully, we did not have as many interruptions as we usually did on Town Hall days.

Dinner was delicious and pleasant. I even had a couple of beers. I was feeling pretty relaxed, and getting comfortable. So, when Gordon got up, and joined several people on the small music stage in the corner of the room, the "hey, WTF?" bells started going off in my head. A guy from Gordon's electrical work group picked up an electric guitar, while another guy I did not recognize, turned on an electric piano keyboard. Gordon himself took a seat behind a drum set. Gordon played the drums?

One last guy who I did not know, took up the microphone at the front of the stage, and greeted everyone. "Hey everybody, if you don't mind, we'd like to play a couple of songs for you." The lead signer didn't wait for anyone's permission, the band just launched into the opening chords of The Beatles' song, "Get Back."

Gordon was grinning at everyone, but mostly at me. I just stared back, stupefied. He was rockin' out with the band, tossing his nonexistent hair around his head, mugging for the audience. He kinda reminded me of Animal, from the Muppets. I could hear my mom's voice in my head, reminding me that my dad always warned me to stay away from musicians. Sorry, Dad. Too late now.

The band with no name played several more songs, also without asking for permission, but no one seemed to mind. Everyone in the restaurant was thoroughly enjoying the impromptu performance, clapping hands, bobbing heads and singing along. I was just astonished. I couldn't remember the last time I'd heard any music performed live. The band went on to play "Free Ride", and "American Pie." They had chosen the kind of classic rock songs that everyone knew, and could sing along with.

Once the band finished their short set, the crowd applauded them enthusiastically. The lead singer explained that was all they had rehearsed, but they'd have more in the future, if that would be okay? More cheering and applause. The band broke up, and returned to their respective tables, to rounds of many questions from their companions.

I asked them of Gordon, as well.

"W.T.F., Gordo! Since when do you play drums? How come you never told me?"

Gordon laughed, and said, "Since about age 10, when I joined middle school band class. And because you never asked." He was grinning his usual broad grin. "You surprised?"

"Well, duh, I'm surprised!"

"We've been practicing in secret for a few weeks. And this afternoon. We thought it would be something fun to do."

Well, yeah! I looked around the room; everyone did seem to be pretty happy.

"Are you going to play more in the future?" I asked him.

"Yeah, as long as you don't mind the practice time. I already work pretty long hours as it is. That doesn't leave a lot of time for date nights with you, you know."

"Well, we've got those open studio sessions in the evenings, for people to make their tiles. I need to be there for those. You could practice on those evenings."

Gordon nodded in agreement at the proposed schedule. We walked home, hand in hand. I reflected on how I was still learning things about this guy that I had thrown in with. I wondered what other surprises he had in store.

Chapter 11

Around us, the town was a mix of problems and solutions. Power was getting shut off in the outer neighborhoods, section by section. But the water flow was much more erratic. Some areas had dwindled to nothing. Other areas still had full pressure. Survivors were still being discovered, too. Pressure was mounting to get everyone moved into the consolidated safe zones.

The studio had become one of my de facto sources for news about the community. Some people had stories to tell of their lives before the virus, or how they survived. Some had information on current happenings about town; who was moving into which house, the odd ball discoveries in a neighborhood that was being cleared, etc. Some just had gossip to share. Others had more significant stories to share.

One evening, Jake made an appearance. He explained that he had just gotten back from the Sedona training exercise, and he was fed up with being with the rest of the cops, after a long day, and long drive back. So he had made a beeline for the studio, instead of heading to the brew pub where the rest of the guys hung out when not on duty.

I tried to get him to work on a tile, but he insisted he had no creative talent at all. And he confirmed it by quickly cutting out a simple rectangle of clay, and just stamping his deceased wife's name onto it. I encouraged him to try some other embellishments, but he was happy with it as it was, and politely declined. It quickly became clear that the tile was just a pretext, and he really wanted to share something else with me. He sat with me at the work table where I was carefully stamping names from a long roster, onto freshly cast bricks of cement. It was an experiment we were playing with.

"So, you heard about our little adventure today? " he asked me.

"Yeah, a training exercise in Sedona?" I asked him back. "But I didn't hear the details on how it got setup."

Jake answered. "Well, after you smoothed that guy's, Stettner's, ruffled feathers a few weeks back, he was talking to Zach, and asked if there was any one who could train them how to install solar panels."

I nodded. "Yeah, Zach mentioned it, after the raid on Petra's lab."

"Right. So Zach asks him if they could provide some training to our newbies, in exchange. Zach says he needs our boys to improve their urban patrol skills. Asks him if his people could provide any reciprocal training."

"Aren't you guys doing that already around here?" I asked.

Jake answered, "Well, around here, this is police patrolling, for civil situations. How to deal with drunks, or domestic disputes, looking for survivors, stuff like that. But the boss is getting concerned about more organized gang activity, large scale looting, stuff like that. When it's more than just a few people, and they're heavily armed, it takes on a military quality. Detecting, assessing and responding to those kinds of threats requires a different skill set."

I nodded again. "So they finalized a deal then? Solar panel installation skills for urban searching and clearing skills?"

Jake nodded back at me.

A thought occurred to me. "Didn't Bartosik and his people also go along?"

Jake answered, "Yeah, he did."

I narrowed my eyes at Jake, and asked, "They really just wanted to get a look at the operation up there in Sedona, didn't they?"

Jake grinned at me. "You catch on quick, Maggie!"

"And, they wanted to take advantage of a situation that highlighted the difference between a legitimate military operation, and a half baked unprofessional militia op?"

Jake said, "Two for two, so far."

"Okay, so, what happened? What did you guys find out?"

He answered, "Okay, so Zach gets it all put together, sets it up that we're taking our newbies, and a couple of Bartosik's squads. We all meet up at the butt crack of dawn this morning, and drive up there. We meet Stettner's people at the designated place, they escort us into the canyon, to their main camp area. They've got a lot of their people housed in a old neighborhood of little houses and mobile homes, right next to a great fishing spot on the creek. That's where they're getting all that smoked trout from."

I nodded. Jake continued.

"We drop off Gordon, and he goes off with their electrical people, to teach them about solar panels and stuff - that all went fine, by the way."

I was still nodding. Gordon had told me yesterday that he was going. And he had left the house so early that morning, that I had not even woken up enough to notice.

Jake continued, "So, we meet their guys, and they outline the plan for the day. Turns out, they've got a squatter problem in one of the ritzy areas in West Sedona. There's a bunch of huge mansions up in the hills, and they've been taken over, turned into mini fortresses. The people in there are raiding all the other homes, the businesses, the stores in the area. There's not very many grocery stores in Sedona, and they cleaned those out months ago. They've been raiding as far away as Camp Verde and Cottonwood, they said."

"And how is that any different than what Stettner's own people are doing? Or us, for that matter?" My shoulder devil stood up and saluted.

"Ah, the difference is that these squatter groups are killing anyone who gets in their way. They either grab people, and make them work for them, or they kill them."

I frowned. "So, its every prepper's worst nightmare? Looter gangs?" Jake nodded sagely to me.

"Okay, so what did they want to do about it?" I asked.

Jake said, "They wanted us to help take them out, of course."

Well of course, that much was an obvious conclusion. "Was Zach aware of this before he took a bunch of young, untrained newbies up there into a live fire situation?"

Jake wobbled his head. "Sort of. He knew they had a live target to work on, but he didn't know the scale of the problem. But that's why he reached out to Bartosik, to help out. Bartosik brought along his RPG truck again." Jake had a broad grin on his face.

"Again?" My shoulder angel shook her head. Boys and their toys.

Jake said, "But we didn't tell them about it, right away; we left it parked on the side of the road, hidden in some brush, a little ways outside of town, before we met up with Stettner's people. Just in case." Jake waggled his eyebrows at me, and went on.

"So, we sit down and go over a bunch of maps, and Stettner shows us where the squatters are based. We work out a plan. We pair up the newbies with the Luke guys, and Stettner's guys, in four man teams.

They're going to circle around on the back roads, and hike down the hills from above the mansions, and observe. They'll be picking spots for sniper positions. Meanwhile, the rest of us are going in via the regular paved streets into the neighborhood. The area is pretty brushy, but not a lot of tall trees. So, coverage is only moderate. The incoming teams might be pretty visible to anyone above them. So those teams are going in Bartosik's armored vehicles. The exercise part of the exercise, is that they'll go from house to house, on foot, clearing each one, for the last mile or so, until they're in firing range of the squats."

Jake paused to take a long swallow of his half empty water bottle. Story telling was thirsty work.

"So, what did they find?" I prompted him.

Jake continued, "Pretty much exactly what they said. The usual scenario; heavily armed men holding a bunch of other people like slaves. Forced to work to keep a roof over their heads, or maybe someone's kid is held hostage to motivate a guy to do what they want, like looting the stores and stuff."

"And what did you guys do about it? Were the gang people out and about in broad daylight?"

Jake answered, "Sometimes. We setup a few sniper positions, and picked a few of them off. Of course, once we started doing that, they all scrambled for cover, so that wasn't very productive. And once they did that, we had to crawl up to the buildings, and tear gas them. That flushed everyone out. Then it was just a matter of sorting out the good from the bad. The women and kids rolled over on the leaders real easy, told us who was running the operation."

"And what did you do with them?"

"We had way more people than they did, so it was easy to overpower them. We hand cuffed them, put them in chains, and loaded them into a box truck. There was a lot of discussion about the right way to handle them. One of Stettner's people, his number two guy, just wanted to shoot them right then and there, but Bartosik and Zach didn't like that idea. Felt they might take too much heat for it. On top of what we just did to solve the Petra Problem. He suggested they just drive the gangers out to the desert a few hundred miles, and leave them. In the end, that's what they ended up doing. A couple of Bartosik's' guys were taking them out to the Mohave desert, somewhere past Kingman. Way too far to be easy to get back. If they survive that, maybe they'll just go to Vegas, instead of coming back to Sedona."

I pursed my lips. "Creative solution."

Jake nodded, and in a slower tone, he added. "The thing is, Maggie, those a-holes were living like pigs up there. The power is completely off up there, so there's no pumps to move the city water. They were dumping their shit down the nearest arroyo. I mean that literally. They were using buckets for toilets, and just pouring them down whatever little gully they had nearby. The whole area stunk to high heaven. They were completely trashing the houses, too. Those gorgeous huge houses were filled with bags of trash, and food waste laying all over the kitchens, empty bottles of liquor, ashtrays overflowing with cigarette butts, weird stains on the floors. They had generators, powering their TVs and video games. But the pools were turning green, because they didn't think to connect the pool pumps to the generators."

Jake was shaking his head sadly. "How can people live like that?"

I shook my head with him in sympathy for his confusion.

"One guy we pulled out of there was a real jerk. He didn't understand why the place was turning into a dump. He actually blamed Stettner's people for it. He was yelling, 'this is all your fault; this was a nice place before, but you didn't think we're good enough for you, so you cut off the water, and stopped picking up the trash.' Maggs, how can anyone be so idiotic? How can they think they're entitled to just have heaven handed to them on a silver platter?

"I don't know, Jake. Some people just never make the connection between cause and effect. Hard work and rewards," I said.

We sat for a few minutes. I stamped out more names. Finally, I asked him, "So, you never did use the RPG truck then?"

Jake answered, "Nah. We talked about it, but we couldn't figure out how to get the innocents out of the houses, but leave the gangers inside. Too much risk of collateral damage."

"Good. What about the people that were rescued? What did you do with them?" I asked.

Jake said, "They went back to Oak Creek Canyon. Stettner agreed to take them in, get them food, water, medical care, housing. There was about 25 or 30 of them, and maybe 15 or 20 gangers that got dragged off."

"What were the rest of Stettner's people like? Did you get to meet many of them?"

"Most of them are okay; just people, just like us. Just trying to survive. Oh, but get this: Stettner has a daughter. A blood relative, I mean, not just a stray foster that he took in, like all the kids around here. Her name is Cassandra. They're both recoverers." He had been grinning over this odd coincidence. But then his face grew serious.

"You might want to give Gordon an extra hug or something, soon. When he was introduced to the girl, he got that look on his face, you know, the one when we're reminded of someone from our old life?"

"Yeah, Gordon had a daughter, before. How old was Stettner's daughter?" I said.

Jake squinted into the air. "Uh, I'm guessing around early 20's, give or take?"

I nodded. "Gordon's daughter was in college. So that must have been an unpleasant reminder."

Jake said, "I think he's okay now; he got over it quick. But I just thought I should mention it." Jake paused, then got back to his main line of thought.

"Like I said, most of Stettner's people seem decent. But there's factions in there. Stettner's number two guy? I think his name was Javier... the one who wanted those gangers executed on the spot? He and Stettner seemed to be having some kind of private argument over things. Not in words. It was just a sense I got. Body language and stuff. That that guy was even more hard core militia than Stettner was. And he had some people backing him up."

Hmm. That was interesting information. I thanked Jake for the story. He helped me clean up the studio for the evening, and walked me home, which was on the way to his own apartment.

At home, I found Gordon still awake, but in bed already, reading. I gave him that hug, and asked him about his day. He told me how his own training session had gone, and what he had heard from the guys out on the patrolling exercise. He agreed with Jake's idea that there might be factions within Stettner's group, saying that he'd noticed that vibe as well.

***

Other studio visitors had less exciting, but more chaotic stories, than Jake did. Sometimes I had to pry information out of people, sometimes it came freely. A day or two after Jake's visit, another story was reported to me by a studio visitor, about a friend who had gotten very sick with diarrhea. So sick, that she had to be hospitalized for dehydration. The visitor reported that she was not the only one, either. There seemed to be a mini epidemic of this going around, she told me.

That news was pretty alarming. The following day, I skipped the studio, and headed straight into City Hall, to see what else the team there knew. Ariana had just received the same information, courtesy of reports sent over from the hospital. We gathered in one of the large conference rooms, which had city maps already mounted on the walls. It took a while to locate Robert, who was out working on the various projects, but he eventually got the message and joined us in person.

Once we brought him up to speed, he was as alarmed as we were. We started working on maps, identifying the homes where the affected people were still living. This required some calling over to the hospital for address information, and other radio calls to work crews and other people who had mentioned their water problems. It was getting harder and harder to find and call people. Most people had turned off their cell phones, since the cell service providers had gotten erratic. And if they were working on crews, they were out and about, and not at home to answer their land line phones. That was also another ongoing dilemma: which communication technology to try to salvage: cellular service or land lines. But for the moment, the expanded network of police radios was our best way to reach work crews and other segments of city operations.

After hours of radio chatter and phone calls, we were able to identify that the people who were getting sick, were still living in neighborhoods south of the water treatment plant. Robert and his people had been focused on making sure the treated, potable water flowed northwards, to the power on zone. Water in the piping systems to the south and east had mostly been left to operate on autopilot. Someone else also pointed out that there were numerous mini farms, and not-so-mini farms, including several of the dairy farms, in the same areas where the illnesses had been reported. Early on during the Superflu pandemic, dairy herds and other livestock had died by the thousands due to neglect and dehydration. Thousands of carcasses had been incinerated right where they had died. But the cleanup crews had not finished a thorough sweep of the mini farms yet.

Several people in the room looked around at each other. I went ahead and asked the question aloud: "Is it possible the dead livestock seeped enough gunk into the ground, to contaminate the drinking water?" Robert shrugged his shoulders.

"Robert, help me understand how it works: the treatment plant produces water that is safe drink, bathe, clean with, etc." Robert nodded.

"And that water gets pumped through concrete pipes outbound, to regions, cities, neighborhoods, and then houses." Another nod.

"And it's kept separate from waste water, from sewer water, which is flowing the opposite way, or somewhere." Another nod.

"So, is it reasonable to assume that the pipes that are moving the clean water, are pretty well sealed?" Robert did not nod at this one. He waggled a hand instead. We waited. Finally, he elaborated.

"Its complicated. A water pipe is not a perfectly closed system. Pipes are not one solid line; they are a series of segments joined together. And those joints may not always have completely perfect seals. It's theoretically possible that a contaminant could leak into the piping, from a bad joint or a failing seal. Chemicals in the soil, usually. Usually, the clean water is flowing at a fast enough rate and volume, that any contaminants that might be picked up, are so widely distributed, in terms of parts per million, that they are not statistically significant, or harmful. However..." He paused to gather his thoughts.

"However, the water to the south has slowed considerably, and volume is decreasing as well, as fewer and fewer people were using it. We tuned the pumps down, because there was less need for water to be drawn out, but that meant the water that was there, was taking longer to get from processing plant, to final destination. In other words, it had more time to pick up more contaminants. And if piping goes through locations where livestock carcasses were decomposing for any length of time, yes, it might have picked up the microbes that cause dysentery."

Well, crap. Literally.

Ariana asked the next question: "Why is this just showing up now? The dairy herds were incinerated months ago. How do we fix it? Can we ramp up the pumps, to flush stuff out?"

Robert shook his head slowly. "We're already fixing it, by moving people out of those areas, and into the consolidation zone. We're just not doing it fast enough."

I turned back to Ariana. "How can we ramp up the relocation effort?"

Ariana turned to one of the assistants, and asked her to bring Caleb in. Caleb was using a similar conference room, down the hall, as his office. She turned back to the impromptu meeting.

"A lot of the people didn't want to leave their homes any sooner than they absolutely had to. They had stocked up on supplies, and even without power, as long as they had water, they were okay with staying in their homes, without electricity. It hasn't gotten quite hot enough to need air conditioning (well, at least, not until this week). They were eating food that didn't need cooking, or taking meals downtown."

I turned to the nurse we had summoned from the hospital. We needed help with the medical background information. The nurse's name was Loren. I asked her, "Do all the people who got sick know *how* and *why* they got sick?"

Loren nodded. "Now they do," she said.

"Did they know they were supposed to boil their drinking water?"

She shook her head. "A lot of them missed that one. But even if they are boiling drinking water, if they're showering in contaminated water, they still have a small chance of picking up the vector that way."

At that point, Caleb joined the meeting. We brought him up to speed on the situation, and asked again, what we could do to ramp up the relocation process. He thought for a moment, and then responded.

"Well, there's several reasons why some people resist moving: they don't want to leave their own homes, they don't want to live with roommates they barely know, they haven't been able to locate trucks and enough strong backs, and time in their schedules, to move their stuff, and, until now, they haven't had enough justification for it."

We pondered that. Caleb elaborated. "Many people are doing physically difficult work. They're already spending 8 or 10 hours a day hauling bodies, trash, food, supplies, in and out of houses and stores. They're exhausted at the end of their shifts. The last thing they want to do is box up their own stuff, and load it onto a truck and haul it around, too. A lot of the people who are doing the dirtiest, hardest work, are doing it because they don't have the skills to do the other stuff, like electrical work, engineering, gardening, cooking, administrating, or making pottery." He smiled at Ariana and me.

"Or assigning housing," I quipped back.

Caleb answered, "Right. Anyone who had skills or backgrounds that are completely useless now, are doing the stuff that doesn't require any special skills. The difficult, sweaty, hard grunt work. So, they're tired, exhausted. So, they've stalled on relocating as long as they could. We have not been forcing anyone to move. There's no stick behind the carrot, and some people just don't find that carrot to be rewarding enough on its own."

My little shoulder devil came up with the obvious metaphor extension: "So, how can we turn that carrot into carrot cake? Make the reward more enticing? I don't think anyone wants to get a bigger stick."

Caleb said, "I've had a few ideas on that, actually." We nodded at him to go on.

"Well, to counter the 'I don't like roommates' objection, we can hold mixers, get togethers where people can meet others who are in the same situation. Maybe an old fashioned ice cream social, or something. We could organize some simple 'get acquainted' games, to help people find others they could at least tolerate living in the same house with."

I frowned at that. "I thought you were some genius whiz kid, at matching up groups of people who would work well together."

Caleb: "Well, I'm doing my best, but in order to do that, I have to interview people, find out a little bit about them, what they like and don't like, stuff like that. And that takes time. It bottlenecks the process. I've got some assistants to help, but there's only so much through put we can handle."

I nodded. That made sense. "So, what are your other ideas?"

Caleb said, "Well, it really boils down to continuing to refine the plan we're already working. Expand the zone to add more housing. Keep power in those zones. Make sure the water in those areas is clean and flowing at the right pressure. Spread the message to the outlying enclaves and groups, make sure they know to boil their drinking water."

Loren spoke up. "I don't think any of the dysentery cases came from the group enclaves. Most of cases were from individuals living alone in their old homes. So, the mini-farm groups are practicing the proper hygiene. I think you can leave them alone."

I nodded. I looked around the room. "So, anything else we can do? Are we concluding then that we just need to work the plan a little harder? Get the message out, keep encouraging the solo survivors to come downtown?"

Everyone nodded. Ariana covered a small smile behind her hand, though.

The dysentery investigation and brainstorming session had taken most of the day. Ariana and Caleb had quickly zoomed in on some ways to setup gatherings for unmatched, unmoved people, and had wandered off to take care of their own tasks. I headed out and stopped by the studio, to make a quick check on my apprentices, who were doing fine. Then I headed home.

The week had been a trying one, but I tried to keep some perspective. We had helped the Oak Creek people solve a thorny problem in their area. I was teaching city residents how to make tiles and encouraging them to let their artistic creativity flow. I had helped analyze and diagnose systemic issues in the water supply. I knew that an ice cream social was a pretty weird way to solve a dysentery epidemic. But ultimately, I was feeling pretty good about the way things were going, overall.

Which, of course, is why Murphy and his inevitable law of karmic balance decided I needed a smack down to keep me humble.

***

On the sunny Saturday morning just a day after the dysentery brainstorming session, Ariana insisted that I join her for brunch. She said she had several pieces of important news that I needed to be aware of, and she needed my help with something. First, she updated me on the progress she and Caleb were making. And then she told me that the Oak Creek Canyon group had contacted her earlier that morning. They were requesting permission to return to town, bringing a couple of their people who needed special medical attention. They promised a nice supply of smoked trout, for the help. Then she told me a news story that she had just found out about only hours before.

A group of a dozen or so people had taken over a small cluster of houses in a horse property area off Warner Road, near the city border. The homes they were occupying were well away from the main roads, so they were fairly well hidden from casual view. The cluster was mostly fenced, but had several entrances with pole gates. The houses were shielded with mature shade trees and other bushes, which obscured some lines of sight. There were several barns and storage sheds around the perimeter of the compound, as well. They also had a full array of solar panels for independent electricity, so the inhabitants have never felt the need to reloate to the city core zone.

During the middle of the night, the enclave had been raided by a gang. Motorcycles and cars had come bursting onto their properties from multiple directions, crashing through the gates. They had quickly assaulted their targets, with an enormous amount of loud engine noise (thanks to the numerous Harley motorcycles). That caused confusion, and made it hard for the residents to respond quickly and effectively. Many had been asleep. Others did not have weapons handy, or were unable to see where their targets were and thus, could not shoot at them.

The raiders set several houses on fire, as a distraction, while others kept up the cacophony of noise. While the residents were focused on escaping the fire, and trying to figure out what was going on, several trucks pulled up to the storage barns and proceeded to load up pallets full of supplies. The raiders had even thoughtfully brought along their own pallet jack, to speed the process along.

When the residents came out of their houses, either escaping the fires, or trying to stop the raid, the raiders shot them dead. A few people hid inside, and tried to shoot at the raiders from cover. A few shots even succeeded, but the gang overwhelmed the residents by sheer numbers, and ultimately, burned down two houses, and removed an entire pole barn's worth of supplies. Ten residents were dead, along with four of the raiders. Two people survived, but were suffering from smoke inhalation and minor cuts and bruises.

The two survivors got themselves to the hospital, where the staff was able to notify the police, who came and examined the scene. Zach Adams had summoned Ariana and the city management team to a debrief about the raid that morning. And now Ariana was telling me about it. After we finished eating, she wanted me to go with her to look at the raid site and then visit the survivors at the hospital, to offer our condolences.

We were sitting in the hospital's waiting area, while the two survivors were getting getting some tests done. We speculated on how the raiders even knew about the compound, and what they had. We didn't have any good answers for that yet. I was thinking about how Murphy's Law was making sure I didn't get too uppity about being able to handle stuff. That was when we saw Patrick Stettner and several of his people arrived in a large van. They carefully carried in two other people on stretchers. They were taken into the emergency area, where Dr. Reddy pounced on them almost immediately.

Stettner noticed us, and came over. His face was tight with concern over his injured people.

He greeted us. "Ladies, I didn't expect to find you here." We nodded our greeting to him.

He explained, "As I mentioned on the radio, we have a couple of people who need more medical help than we've been able to provide. My daughter, Cassandra, took a bad fall from a horse, and broke her leg. We tried to reset the bones, but something isn't right. We don't have an X-ray machine, so we can't tell if there's a small fragment out of place, or what."

Ariana nodded at that and smiled reassuringly. She gestured at the personnel buzzing around the new patients. "They have an X-ray machine. And the doctor over there," she pointed at Dr. Reddy, "he's an orthopedic guy. Specializes in bones. He can fix her up."

I spoke up. "Jake mentioned you had a daughter. He was one of the guys on the training exercise a couple of days ago."

Stettner nodded. "Yes, she and I both survived the Superflu. We know it's really crazy coincidence."

He paused, and explained further. "The other guy we brought in; he's got a broken collar bone. Our combat medic hasn't even tried to reset it; it just happened yesterday. We just focused on stabilizing him for transport, and getting him down here."

We both nodded at him. This was exactly the kind of work the hospital team was happy to have. Dr. Reddy was practically salivating, at the prospect of getting to use his personal expertise.

Ariana and I both peered into the emergency treatment area through the counter window. We couldn't see the patients, but we could see the medical people moving about quickly, assessing the new patients, while still keeping the raid victims comfortable. Stettner spoke up.

"Is it always this busy around here? Are you sure you have enough personnel to handle the load?"

Ariana jumped in. "No, it's not usually this busy. You just caught us at a bad time. We had a little incident last night, and they're taking care of couple of other patients, too."

Stettner cocked his head at her. "What kind of little incident?"

Ariana and I looked at each other. I wasn't sure how much information we should share. Ariana plunged in, though.

"There was a raid last night. On a housing compound. 10 people died, and 4 raiders. They burned down a couple of houses, too."

Stettner scowled. "How did that happen? Where was your defense? Why weren't your people out patrolling?"

Ariana's shoulders straightened up. She was bristling like a cat. She didn't like the implied criticism any more than I did.

"The group was outside our city core. They'd been living on their own and hadn't relocated yet. The raiders came in the middle of the night, crashed in, and set the houses on fire. Everyone was asleep, and couldn't see anything in the dark. The gang had dozens of people."

Stettner was not about to excuse the incident, though. "And that kind of scenario is exactly why you're supposed to have guards patrolling, *all* the time!"

Ariana said, "Look, we had no way of knowing this was coming. The raiders were a huge group, well planned, well coordinated. We don't even know where they went, afterwards. And the victims – they chose to live in their compound. We've made it clear to everyone, the benefits of living downtown in the zone. But they didn't want to leave their own homes. Don't go blaming the victims, here."

Ariana sat down with a huff.

Stettner paused, thinking. "You know what, yeah, I *am* blaming the victims, here. They failed to post a guard. If they had, they would have been warned something was coming, and could have evacuated, or fought back."

Then Ariana completely shocked me. She jumped up out of her chair, and starting spewing a loud harangue of Spanish at him, pointing and poking her finger at him. The tirade went on for a minute. Every time she took a step closer to him, he took a step back. His eyes got very wide. Then they narrowed and he leaned forward. When Ariana paused for a moment to suck in a breath, he started shouting back at her, in Spanish as well. I had no idea what they were saying. My own Spanish language skills consisted solely of: "Bean burro, enchilada style, por favor." The other people in the waiting area turned to stare at Ariana and Patrick, as well.

After a few more shorter, but equally loud exchanges filled with exaggerated syllables and wide gestures, Ariana harrumphed, and flopped back down in her seat beside me. Then she jumped up again, grabbed her bag, and said, "Come on, Maggie, we're going." She hurried out the door, while I trailed after her.

Once we were in the car, naturally I asked her. "Uh, you going to explain what that was all about?"

She shrugged. "Stupid shit. Same stuff I said before. I told him he was being an ass, and that it was not our people's fault."

I was turned sideways towards her. She was driving the car. "Uh, you went on for, like, a minute. There had to be more to it than that."

She glanced at me and grimaced, "Well, I may have cast some doubt upon his mother's quality of character."

"Seriously? What else?"

Ariana added, "Well, I also told him it was really impolite of him to judge us, if he wasn't prepared to step in and help us. I said we didn't have the skilled manpower to be running patrols around the external groups outside the zone, and if he wasn't prepared to loan us some men, weapons and training, then he better not criticize the way we do things around here."

"The 'put up or shut up' argument. Always a favorite. But you know, he *did* help our guys out, this week. They did do that training thing."

Ariana tossed her hands. Her face was angry.

"So, what did he say to that?" I prompted.

Ariana answered, "Well, he said that if we'd been following the rule book, like we're supposed to, we would already know how to do things."

I kept on starting at her. I made the 'and...?' gesture.

Ariana grimaced, and said "I told him to send us a copy of that rule book, because ours got lost in the mail."

"That's it? You couldn't come up with anything better?"

Ariana threw up her hands again, and then re-gripped the steering wheel: "I froze. I realized everyone was staring at us. I couldn't think of what to say next."

I frowned at her. "Ariana! What on earth got into you?"

Ariana looked at me. Her face crumpled. She went from scowling anger, to completely stricken anguish. In a softer voice she said, "Maggie, I'm going to marry that man."

I screeched. "*What?* What are you talking about? Are you crazy? You barely know the guy!"

Ariana shook her head. "Nope. I knew the minute I first looked in his eyes, that first time he came here. He's mine, and I'm his."

I shook my head. "No. Just... No. That is about seven different kinds of fucked up."

She shrugged again. "Doesn't matter. When he started spouting off about how we're doing it all wrong, I just had to stand up to him. I had make sure he could stand up to me." She smirked a little bit. "And he did."

"Ariana, I seriously think you may have gone off the deep end. I think the stress is getting to you. Has gotten you. Has taken you, and chewed you up, swallowed, barfed it back up and chewed you up again. You're delusional. Turn the car around. We need to get you to a psych doctor."

"You can call me crazy all you want, but that man has my name tattooed over his heart. He just doesn't know it yet."

I shook my head at her some more. When Murphy smacks down the uppity, he really does it with style.

Chapter 12

Summer in the Sonoran Desert is brutal. Zonies have lots of favorite cliched sayings to summarize how we cope:

"It's a dry heat"

"100 days over a 100, but only 60 days below 60."

"We're just paying our dues."

Memory is a funny thing. In the winter time, I can look back on the last summer's miserable heat, and think, *oh, well, it wasn't that bad, we can get used to it*. And then summer rolls around, and I wonder why on earth anyone thought this was a good place to live.

It starts getting hot as early as mid-April, but the humidity is so low, no one minds, much. Around Mother's day in early May, we usually see our first 100 degree day. Most people will say, 'Eh, 100, 105, it's not that bad'. That early in the summer, we're only feeling the heat that flows down from the sun. But by the third week and fourth week of June, we get that super hot blast, where temperatures are in the upper hundred and teens: 115, 118.

The heat bakes into the ground, pavement, and buildings, and every object around, and radiates back outward and upward, as well as still pouring down from above. There's no escaping it. On a record setting day years before, we even hit 122. Everyone is pissing and moaning by this time of the year, or retreating to their air conditioned hibernation hives. Or, if they have the option, they just leave the Valley for the summer. San Diego, or Colorado are favorite destinations, but really, anywhere that's not here is fine with most people.

Now, of course, those places seem like they are on the opposite side of the planet.

It was still only May, but our house was starting to warm up too. We had the swamp cooler and fans going, but Gordon was stalling on switching over to AC. His reason was valid: since he worked outdoors all day, he needed to train himself to get used to the heat. But that didn't keep him from radiating lots of body heat into the sheets and mattress, and by extension, to me. And our two littlest dogs, Tyrion and Zilla, were also very proficient bed warmers. And they could not be convinced to find other sleeping locations. The combined heat input was greater than the cooling output, and thus, I was not sleeping well.

***

The Saturday Town Hall meeting in late afternoon, after the scene at the hospital, was pretty typical. Robert briefed the crowd on the raid, and as usual, people shouted out questions and concerns. Mostly, they boiled down to, "Could it happen here?" and "What can we do to make sure it doesn't happen here?" and "Where did the raiders go? Can we go after them?" Of course, he had no concrete answers for that.

After the meeting, the group dinner was somewhat subdued, compared to previous ones. But it did feature some smoked trout I'd not had before. I was pretty sure it was from the Oak Creek group, in exchange for the hospital services. I spent a big chunk of the evening chatting with Sharon, and learning more about her back story. Stettner did not attend the meeting, or the after-dinner. I assumed he was still at the hospital with his daughter. Several of Stettner's people attended our Town Hall, though, and Ariana greeted them, and made sure they got food afterwards.

So, between the raid fallout, Ariana's personal form of crazy, and the newly arrived heat, I was already a bit cranky, when I got up on Sunday. And then all the dogs yanked me around the golf course for a long walk before breakfast. So I was all sweaty, too.

Gordon, Micah and Carlos were sitting at the kitchen table, eating breakfast when I came in. Gordon was explaining the principles of large scale power distribution to Micah. Gordon was talking.

"... so that's the primary level. On the secondary level, you've got the transmission power lines that go from region to region, neighborhood to neighborhood. At the thirdary level, the transformers change the power down..."

"Tertiary" I interrupted.

Gordon looked up at me. "What?"

"Tertiary" I said again. "Thirdary is not a word. The word you want is 'tertiary'."

Gordon looked blank. "Thirdary makes more sense. No one knows what 'tertiary' means."

I rolled my eyes. "Gord, you can't just make up words! And you do too know what 'tertiary' means."

Gordon said, "Sure I can. Google wasn't a word, until it was. Those guys just made it up, and everyone liked it, so now it's a word. Its even a verb." He was starting to smirk at me.

"No, you can't. It's not a word until everyone agrees it's a word. And thirdary is just dumb."

Micah jumped into the crazy pool with us. "I like 'thirdary'." He nodded at Gordon. Carlos was starting to smirk, too, but was hiding behind his coffee cup, trying to keep me from seeing it.

Gordon nodded back at Micah. "Thirdary it is, then." He smiled at me.

I shook my finger at him. "You can't just go corrupting the Queen's English, the language of the great Bard himself, by making up words."

Now Gordon was grinning that smart ass grin. "You know, the Bard himself made up words all the time. If it worked, it worked. You yourself have told me that English is always evolving, always changing and adapting. People make up new words all the time."

"Not when there's a perfectly good word in use already. 'Tertiary' works just fine. And it has a nice ring to it." I sounded the word out grandiosely: "Terr-shee-arry,"

Gordon raised his eyebrows at Micah. "Thirdary?"

Micah nodded. Gordon added, "Fourthary?" Micah grinned and nodded even harder.

Carlos, still smirking, said, "Fifthary has a nice ring to it, too."

Gordon and Micah both repeated "Fifthary" and grinned back at Carlos.

I rolled my eyes. "Well, are you gonna say 'oneary' instead of 'primary', then?" I snapped at them.

Gordon sounded that one out thoughtfully. "Oneary. Nah, too close to 'ornery'. 'Primary' is fine."

I considered telling them to get themselves to a nunnery, but that quote was the wrong gender.

Gordon looked to Micah. "You know that 'primary' means 'first", right?"

Micah nodded, but countered, "Why not firstary? Firstary, secondary, thirdary, fourthary, fifthary."

All three of the guys were laughing out loud now. I threw up my arms and started walking out of the kitchen. "Get thee to a mannery!" I tossed back at them. For once, I had managed to get the last word, but only because I walked away from them while they were still lolling. I went to take my shower.

***

After a shower, and getting my own breakfast, I retreated to the casita, where my laptop was still stationed. It was time to do my homework to prepare for the upcoming mayoral debate. And the heat crankies were good fuel.

A small election commission has been assembled from volunteers who were not previously involved in any city management work, in order to avoid any potential conflicts or improprieties. They planned two public sessions for the candidates. The first one would be a simple positioning presentation. The commission had come up with a short list of questions, and each candidate would have five minutes to answer. In addition to preparing my own answers, I wanted to flesh out my ideas for my platform.

While I was still annoyed at being put up to this by my friends, I had decided I didn't want Pastor Daniel to take over as mayor. He'd been avoiding me ever since I'd forcefully declined to attend his church. But Ariana, and others, reported he was still full of ideas, and was actively suggesting them to anyone who would listen, and then acting affronted when they were not immediately implemented.

I opened up a word document, and started jotting down notes. My goal was to organize my thoughts on what my campaign platform included. Essentially, I tried to identify every major area of concern that the city was facing, and how we could respond. I wanted to figure out what my goals would be, if I got the job.

Maggie's Platform:
Safety/Security
- Increase safety patrols, to detect intruders. Similar to how

private security guards supplement a police force.

- Establish drone teams to run reconnaissance/surveillance, to detect people coming into city limits. Intercept as needed.
- Recruit more people to go through training to join the Police force.
- Hire services from partnership organizations (Luke AFB, Oak Creek group)

Relocation project

- Increase amount of available of houses by improving efficiency of the assignment process.
- Expand the city core power on zone to have at least 15% to 20% excess capacity of livable housing. Need excess capacity to handle possible population growth.
- Incentives to relocate?

Food

- Continue to develop our community gardens, including additional locations.
- Identify locations and resources that can be scaled up for large quantity production. Need staple crops: Corn, beans.
- Identify regional trading partners for foods that we cannot grow or raise locally (beef, pork, seafood, wheat, rice)

Water

- Maintain ongoing service;
- Seek to improve water quality, to previous level of potability (safe to drink from tap)

Medical services

- Promote hospital services as a trade good to wider regional groups.
- Develop a task group who can investigate and respond to public health problems.
- Develop veterinary services?
- What about preventative medicine? Regular checkups, dentistry, birth control, midwives?

Electricity

- Pester Gordon to make it work perfectly.
- Ween off of power generated by fossil fuels, focus on locally generated power (hydro, solar, wind).

- Identify locations for more solar panels to collect. (What about the university? Even farther away?)

Fuel

- Identify efficient ways to collect gas from abandoned vehicles, and where to transfer it to.
- Identify ways to maximize length of fuel storage time, in order to make it last as long as possible.
- Monitor and track vehicle usage to maximize fuel usage, before it becomes unusable. May need to conserve fuel; may need to try to use it up before it goes bad.
- Find out if oil is being refined anywhere, and what it will take to get some (what will they trade for?)

Transportation

- Fuel efficient forms: motorcycles, hybrid cars, other high efficiency specialty vehicles.
- No fuel forms: golf carts, other electric carts.
- Muscle power: Bicycles, horses, oxen. Feet.

Non-food supplies

- Continue consolidation of manufactured goods
- Essential supplies: soap, cleansers, paper products, shoes, clothing, bedding, linens
- Non-essential supplies: housewares, entertainment, sporting goods
- Should we expand collection and consolidation efforts beyond city limits? Depends on presence of organized communities who have jurisdiction.

Communications Technology

- Determine if land line telecommunications can be salvaged, restored
- Determine if cellular telecommunications can be salvaged, restored
- Determine if Internet services and resources can be restored
- Develop and maintain two-way radio communications networks (police, city)
- Develop short wave radio operations, to collect and share information outside of region (backup/alternative to phone, Internet, and broadcast channels)

- Collect and consolidate communications hardware, for replacements. Be prepared to deal with planned obsolescence: batteries, hard disks, computer components eventually fail. Need to secure enough replacement equipment to ensure uninterrupted service, until manufacturing of new equipment can be restarted (could be 1 to 2 generations in the future).

Community Relations

- Conduct outreach efforts, to connect with similar survivor groups in the region, for trading.
- Send scouting parties farther out, to collect information from other parts of the country, and provide contact info
- Improve screening of newcomers for valuable skills and assess their willingness to participate in the community (recruit newcomers?)
- Encourage social development and growth of community bonds
- Festivals, entertainment (plays? movies?), music
- Encourage all forms of worship and faith
- Marriages certificates
- Birth certificates

Economics

- Establish a form of currency, which can be easily converted for exchange with other communities
- Establish the means to produce and circulate the currency.
- Start a weekly market (traders, gardeners, crafts, etc).
- Start monetizing services that are currently provided for free: food distributions, Mercados, hospital services, rooms at the hotel
- Encourage development of private businesses.
- Services: hair salons, dog grooming, message running.
- Products: custom made clothing and shoes, specialized crafts (soap? Honey? Goat's milk products? Craft beer!)

Education

- Get schools restarted!
- Higher education?
- Encourage more apprenticeship programs
- Does the library need to be improved? How complete is the

collection? Should any additional material be added? (Where to find them?) Check with the University?

Justice

- Get courts restarted!
- Find lawyers, judges
- Reopen jail/prison
- Develop schedule of when/how enforcement of laws will resume. For example, put high priority on prosecuting drunk driving, assault and violent crime. Low priority on prosecuting minor property crimes like shoplifting from abandoned stores.
- Should laws from before Superflu be re-evaluated? Re-ratified by entire community? Would provide opportunity to discard unneeded/unwanted laws, and change others. I.e., legalize marijuana)

Memorializing the dead.

- Issue death certificates
- Collect names of the dead for community memorial sculpture
- Commission histories of Superflu; stories, memories. Record for posterity.

Wow. I was kinda shocked at what I had written. It looked like I was practically trying to reinvent modern civilization. Seemed awfully ambitious, especially for someone who kept saying she didn't want to be mayor…

Next, I turned to the questions the panel had come up with. We had been advised that reading from a prepared statement would be acceptable. I took some time to write up my planned responses. I decided that it would need some review and editing. I also needed to consider ways to adapt them on the fly, in response to issues my competition raised. But it was a good start.

***

The campaign work had taken me a couple of hours. But now that the chore was done, I set the crankies aside, and decided it was time for fun. Gordon had promised to leave his afternoon open to spend time with me. Months before, we had resolved to have a weekly date, but unfortunately, we were both pretty bad at carving out the time to actually devote to one-on-one relationship building. But today, he had firmly sent Micah out to play with his new friends. Some of the roomies were still hanging around the house, so we decided to do a mini-bug out.

We packed a simple lunch, and drove out north on the Bush Highway along the Salt River. It occurred to me that this may not have been a very fuel conserving activity. The concepts I'd been doodling over were still rattling around in my brain. But Gordon justified it by saying he wanted to check out one of the smaller dams on the river, to assess its condition. He'd report back his findings to his contacts at the power utility, who were eager to know, but were too busy with their own work, to visit in person.

We drove past several small recreation sites – pullouts with picnic tables under awnings – along the river. We stopped at the Saguaro Lake recreation area. The parking lot and nearby grounds were grown over with weeds – nothing surprising there. But the desert was in full bloom. It was hot, but there was nice breeze off the lake, and in the shade, it was actually pretty tolerable. We setup at a table under the shade ramadas, and ate our food.

We chattered about various little things for a bit, but then I pinned Gordon. "So, if this is supposed to be real date, we have to talk about the typical things that people talk about on dates."

Gordon raised an eyebrow at me: "Really? Like what?"

"Well, the usual 'getting to know you stuff.' Like, where you went to school, what you wanted to be when you grew up, where you wanted to travel someday, other things you like to do for fun. There's still a lot I don't know about you."

Gordon was still looking at me sideways, but he was smiling. "I already told you where I went to school. Northwestern. And haven't we already had this conversation?"

I rolled my eyes. "Come on, work with me, here. Did you ever try any online dating? Match.com or eHarmony?"

Gordon said, "I tried Match. Once." He shuddered.

"Okay, so, think about all those profiles you had to wade through; everyone says what they like to do, what they're looking for, blah blah blah."

Gordon tilted his head back for a moment to think. "Okaaayyyy.... It's been so long, I barely remember what I said in my own profile, let alone what I read in others. Oh, you know what really bugged me about that whole scene? Everyone always said the same thing: 'I love to laugh!' Like, have you ever heard anyone say, 'no, I hate laughing'?"

I giggled. "Exactly! Yes, everyone says that, and it *is* stupid. And they all say they love music, and travel, and good conversation. Geez! Who doesn't? Hardly original. But work with me here. Imagine if one those online sites had paired us together, and this was a first face-to-face, what would we be talking about?"

Gordon thought for a moment. "Uh, how about travel? Wasn't that a thing? Everyone had to go through their top ten bucket list destinations, and they had to be cool, or you weren't getting a second date."

"Right! Okay, let's run with that." I squeaked up my voice an octave, and faux twirled a lock of my hair. "I really want to go to Bali, and London, and France, and Casablanca, and Fiji, and Dubai and the Hamptons. How 'bout you?" I pretended to bat my eyelashes at him.

Gordon grinned back, and lowered his own voice and gruffed it up. "Yeah, right after I finish that motorcycle race up Pike's Peak, I'm going on safari in Kenya. Then I'm gonna hitchhike down the Amazon River, and swing over to Machu Pichu. After that, I'm going fly my personal glider into Burning Man, and set him on fire myself!" He returned his voice to normal. "Like that?"

I was laughing so hard, I could only nod. Finally, I wiped the tears from my eyes, and asked him, "Yes, exactly like that. Exactly. Okay, what else do total strangers talk about on first dates... Oh, here's a good one: the hypothetical 'what would you do if you won the lottery?'"

Gordon was grinning, and motioned for me to try it first. I had to think for a moment. I went back to my squeaky blond voice. "Well, I'd buy a horse ranch up in the mountains, and start a program to help disabled kids get their self-esteem back by riding blind horses."

Gordon grinned at me. "That's not too bad. Lemme try." He lowered his voice again. "Well, if I won the lottery, I'd throw the party to end all parties. I'd take the Most Interesting Man in the World out to dinner, and then fly him and 20 of my closest friends, in my private plane, to Monaco for a night of black jack. And then we'd go out to Mick Jagger's Caribbean island for some leisure time, and finish off the party with a private concert by Kanye." He squinched his face up to show me what he really thought of that plan.

That had me laughing hysterically again. When I finally calmed down enough, I said, "Okay, you're much better at making up crap than I am. You win. Congratulations."

"Why thank ya, thank ya very much." He slurred his words like Elvis. Then in his normal voice, he said "Okay, so let's hop back to reality here. Since the idea of traveling anywhere else for fun is a non starter at the moment, let's talk about where we *have* traveled, why and what was learned. You go first."

I leaned back and looked up in thought. "Oh, geez… where do I start? Well, I was blessed to have wonderful parents who took my brother and I on vacations pretty regularly. As I kid, we traveled all over Michigan. We had special trips to Montreal and Toronto. We went to see my grandparents in Florida for spring break a few times." I paused to gather my thoughts.

Gordon prompted me. "What was the most special thing or time on those childhood vacations that you remember?"

"Hmm. Probably the trips to northern Michigan. We'd visit Charlevoix, Petoskey, Harbor Springs. We'd go to art fairs. One time, Dad insisted we have a dinner picnic on this rocky beach next to Lake Michigan. Actually, it wasn't all that different than this one." I gestured around us.

"Dad wanted to show us the green flash. Do you know what that is?" Gordon shook his head. "It's this atmospheric phenomenon, where just a moment after the sun sets behind a body of water, it appears to almost rise up just a little bit, with a green flash of light. Something to do with how the sun's light is refracting through the water. Dad was real focused on making sure we got to see that, and we did. It was a perfectly clear evening, and perfect viewing conditions. I think I treasure that memory now, because it shows how my dad was a man of science and observation but could still appreciate the strange wonder and beauty of the natural world."

Gordon was sitting with his chin in his hand, listening intently. "That's a good one. What else?"

"I dunno. There were special moments on lots of trips. Mom and Dad both believed that travel "broadened the horizons", that it was important to get out and see the world, see how other people lived. They encouraged me to do a foreign study program, my junior year in college. I went to France."

"Really? You can speak French?"

"Not any more. I wasn't all that good in the first place. I could communicate. I could understand it better than I could speak it, at the time, but I was never fluent."

"And what else did you see while you were in Europe?" he asked me.

"All over France, of course. The Loire Valley. The Cote d'Azur. And Paris, of course. Any time I went anywhere, I had to go through Paris to get there. I was studying in Lyon. I also visited Switzerland and Germany and London. Never made it to Italy, though. Back then – this was the late 80's – our school program director advised against women traveling to Italy or Spain on their own. They said it wasn't safe for solo women travelers."

"That's a shame. So, would you go back to Europe, to go see Italy? Assuming the Superflu hadn't happened, and everything was like it was, of course?"

I shook my head. "Nah. I saw enough of Europe. Lots of cathedrals and old architecture. I'm done with that. My bucket list was focused on Asia. I wanted to see Japan, and Korea, and China. Southeast Asia. I really wanted to go on an Asian cruise."

Gordon responded. "I went on an Alaskan cruise with my Dad a few years ago. It was fantastic. Fjords, glaciers, whales, all kinds of great stuff. Took zillions of pictures. I should dig out my computer and show you one of these days."

"Yeah? What else? Where did you go when you were a kid?"

"We did the Florida thing a lot, too. Disney World was my favorite. Absolutely loved Space Mountain. I did some Spring Break road trips to Daytona with my buddies in high school, too. In college, my frat brothers and I would go to Mexico, to Acapulco or Zihuatanejo. After I got married, we went to the Caribbean a few times. But once my daughter came along, we kept the travels closer to home – it was just easier, when traveling with a kid. Actually, we started coming out here, to Arizona, a lot, when she was young. My parents retired out here, so visiting them was a convenient way to see a lot of the southwest."

I nodded at that. Also a familiar experience for me, as well. "So, out of all the wonderful things here in Arizona, what's your favorite?" I was expecting him to say the Grand Canyon. It was the state's best known attraction, of course. He surprised me though.

"Canyon de Chelly on the Navajo Rez. It is just stunningly beautiful. I've been a couple of times now, but the first time I saw it, was about mid August. They run these jeep tours up both arms of the canyon, and we got lucky. The monsoon rains had forced them to cancel a lot of trips, but the day we were there, it had been dry for a couple of days, enough so that the dirt tracks were firm enough to drive on, but the grass on the canyon floor was green and lush. A few of the tribes' members live in the canyon, and they run cattle and horses in there. At one point, we came out of this shallow wash, and startled a little herd of horses, and they stampeded away from us. They were running across that green grass, with those red rock walls behind them. It was like living inside an old west painting, or something. Beautiful."

He stopped, and looked a little sheepish, at his gushing. I just smiled, but didn't interrupt him.

"Anyways, it was also a good trip, because of the wonderful hospitality we experienced. Those Navajo were so kind and generous and friendly to us. We stayed in a little hotel in the town just outside the canyon. It was nothing fancy, but it was clean and comfortable, and the food was good. It was just a really relaxing, enjoyable trip all around. Or maybe it just seemed that way, because it was the first big trip my daughter and I took together, without her mother. I think it was a little while after the divorce was finalized, but before I moved out here myself."

I reached out, and covered his hand with mine, and squeezed. We sat quietly for a few moments, just enjoying the afternoon.

I finally asked him gently. "So, that's another topic that's commonly covered within the first few dates. Past relationship history; and why it didn't work out. You haven't really told me much about that, before."

Gordon eyed me. "I tell you mine; you tell me yours?"

"Sure."

"Well, the usual reasons, I guess. College sweethearts. Got married just a year after we graduated. She worked in corporate finance, and was working her way up the company ladder. Took us awhile to realize we had very different ideas about what we wanted out of life. She wanted a lifestyle that I didn't. She liked going to society events, and the theater, and classical music concerts, and charity fund raisers. My idea of a classic music concert is seeing U-2 at Wrigley field." I grinned at him. "I liked playing golf, she hated it. She didn't like playing it with me, and didn't like it when I played without her. She liked going "antiquing" and I hated that. She thought we should be sitting on charity boards and foundations, and going to black tie fund raisers. I wanted to watch movies at home. After a while, we were just making each other completely miserable. I could see it, but even then, she still wouldn't admit it."

Gordon paused. His face had gotten serious now. "I tried talking to her over and over, explaining, trying to get her to see my point of view. We even tried counseling. Finally, I just moved out, got an apartment a couple miles away. It kinda killed me a little bit, inside, to leave Jenny, though. It took us both a while to get her to understand it was not her fault. Eventually, she came around, but it was a rough couple of years. That trip I just told you about, when we saw Canyon de Chelly, that was the major turning point, in getting my daughter back, getting her to understand. After that, she was okay with me moving here full time, and eventually convinced her mom to let her move out here, too, full time. She spent her high school years here in Chandler, before going back to my old alma mater for school. Northwestern."

"Right." I nodded that I remembered that.

Gordon nodded at me. "Okay, your turn. Hit me with your best shot." He winked.

I grimaced, and plunged into my own story.

"I dated a little in college; nothing serious. Couple of very short relationships in the first couple of years after college. Then a dry spell. I moved out here to Arizona, and then right away, I met Rick. It got very serious, very fast. It just seemed so right at the time. We just clicked. It all progressed so smoothly. He managed to fit himself into my life perfectly, like it was meant to be. I thought I'd found the love of my life. He seemed so happy to be with me, too. He was thrilled to adopt my lifestyle. Then he started doing really well at work, got a few promotions. We made friends with his coworkers, and we started doing 'couple' things." I paused to figure out where to go next.

"I realize now, that those few years were just a costume he was wearing. A template he was fitting himself into. See, all his life, he'd been modeling the various phases of his life after stereotypes, caricatures. It was, like, his lifestyle defined his identity, when it should have been the other way around. One's core identity should define how they live their lives."

"But at that point in his life, the 'good boyfriend, upwardly mobile techno geek who shall inherit the earth (or at least rule the Internet)' was a good role for him to play. But then some other roles came along, some other lifestyles that were more attractive to him. He started hanging out with other coworkers. And they were nice people, too, but they liked to party. And I mean, *party*! Like, all weekend long, getting wasted and high, and goofing off. Well, I'd already done that, back in college. Been there, done that, and I no longer found it all that fun anymore. At least, not at that stage in my life. So, like you and your ex, we just wanted different lifestyles. Basically, Rick changed out of his "nice boyfriend" costume, and put on his hard partyin' stoner costume, and that was the end of that. Of course, it took a few months for it all to actually go down. I did a really good job at ignoring the signs for a long time. But eventually, it all imploded, and he just up and moved out. And I haven't been with anyone since then. I'm well over it, mind you. I just hadn't found the opportunity or candidate to pursue since then, is all."

I paused, and then added, "And then, well, the Superflu epidemic came along."

Gordon looked at me out of the corner of his eye, and asked, "Was it an epidemic, or a pandemic?"

I shrugged. "An epidemic is when your neighbor gets sick. A pandemic is when you get sick."

Gordon snickered at my quip. Then he asked, "So, did you ever hear from him, after you broke up?"

"Rarely. And not for many years, now. I don't even know if he's still in Arizona. Or was. I guess the Superflu probably got him."

Gordon nodded. "Thanks for sharing that with me. I see what you mean about how the first few dates are a critical period for information sharing. It would have been weird to have discovered all that years from now."

"Yep, that's the point." I nodded back. We thought for a few moments. Gordon asked me, "You think we'll make the same mistakes again?"

"Nah, we'll make different ones." I smiled at him to take the sting away. He grinned back at me.

We sat side by side, facing out towards the peaceful lake, enjoying the afternoon. We could hear cicadas buzzing, animal sounds, the gentle breeze. Out here, the heat didn't' seem like such a bad thing, for the moment.

Chapter 13

By early May, the community garden was in full production mode. The typical growing season in the Valley of the Sun is weirdly offset. It's much too hot in mid summer to grow most things, so smart gardeners know to plant early and harvest early. Carlos had managed that first cycle well.

I hadn't realized it before, but the watering system for the golf course was easily adapted to the garden's needs. Carlos had learned a lot from Maddy, library books and other resources. He had clustered some plants together in large batches, and other were mingled together to take advantage of each other (like tall tomato plants providing shade for smaller pepper plants). Shade netting was stretched over some sections; other areas were left in full sun. Compositing bins were aligned along a back wall, and clearly marked according to type of waste they each processed.

Carlos had repurposed the resort's large tent structure, adjacent to the golf course. It used to host wedding receptions. Now it was his work space. Tools and machines were stored on one side. On the other side, tables were set up in rows for food processing, where they peeled and cut freshly picked produce. His work crew had cobbled together assorted types of drying racks, and were cycling batches of tomatoes, green beans, peas, carrots, squash, and zucchini through them. He also had plenty of electric dehydrators running constantly. If anything was marked for canning, pickling or freezing, it was trucked over to the food distribution warehouse down the street. Seeds from non-hybrid varietals were also set aside for future plantings in the fall and winter.

Fresh produce was available to anyone who asked. City residents could come and pick up whatever had been recently harvested, or even go out into the plots, and pick their own, so long as they didn't damage any other plants.

All in all, the success of the community garden was lifting up people's spirits. Too bad the plans for the community memorial project were counterbalancing it all, like an anvil sitting on the other end of a see-saw.

Several people with construction experience had stepped up to help with the memorial, but they said that the weight of the planned sculpture would require preparing a specialized foundation; otherwise, it would be prone to cracking and possibly collapsing. Building a suitable foundation would require digging up several feet of the ground layer, and relaying it with specialized materials that could tolerate the weight, and the environment. Locating the proper supplies, equipment, skills and manpower was challenging.

Our plan was to build a huge concrete amorphous form, like a giant figure reaching out his arms to hug the world. The base of the figure would be sheltering walls. The head, neck and chest would lean out over the space being encircled. The part that I had not anticipated during the original design phase, was that the head would need several steel i-beam supports. Unfortunately, if they were just vertical posts from ground to head, it was going to detract from the overall effect. It would look like our protector was getting stabbed in the face.

With the help of our graphic art designer, Kaycee, we came up with an idea to build a web of curving horizontal supports from the arms and hands, to the head and neck, which could be left exposed. Essentially, they would all join in a central point, which would be effectively inside the figure's head. The web would be a dome, with half of it encased inside the sculpture and half of it exposed between and in front of the arms and head. We decided it could symbolize our own interconnectedness as a community.

Once the supporting structures were erected, layers of chicken wire, and other construction mesh materials would be applied, to smooth out lines, and form the figure. Concrete would be built up to the desired thickness and shaping. Once dried and cured, we could start applying the surface tiles.

The modifications to the planned design had to be reviewed and ratified by those who cared to participate, during the town hall meetings. The cycle of revisions and adaptations showed signs of going on for a long time yet. Which was pretty typical, for any kind of design-by-committee project. Or so I was told.

Between coaching clay novices on tile making, supervising the construction details, checking in at City Hall, and listening to other people, I had little time to make urns myself these days. I could bang out a couple dozen little bottles for Dr. Reddy, and three or four large urns, in a morning's worth of throwing, but then people would come along and want to talk to me, or share their idea for something, or want me to look at some odd find in a house that had just been cleared. And I'd wander off, or drive off, and get side tracked. Most of the time, Ali was glazing my pots for me, as well as loading them into the kilns. Many finished pots went straight to the cremation pits, where Pastor Daniel was still praying over the dead. Once filled with ashes and labeled, they were moved to a storage warehouse. Other urns were handed out to who ever wanted them, or boxed up to distribute to other communities.

Townies were regularly visiting the studio in small batches, to make tiles with the names of friends and family members who had died in the pandemic. Some were simple square or rectangle tiles. Others let their creativity flow and made more symbolic representations. My assistants had collected cookie cutters and craft store templates for people to use. They cut soft clay into the shapes of flowers, plants, animals, cars, hearts, stars and many other abstract shapes. Names were hand written, or stenciled, or stamped in. Textures were rolled onto the soft clay, or carved out. Colors were applied with underglaze, slips, or glazes as the spirit moved them. My team fired the tiles as soon as we had full kilns, and collected the finished pieces into big tubs for installation later on.

One visitor to the studio surprised me, though. It had been one of the first days of the season to reach more than 100 degrees, and the studio had grown quite warm. We had a swamp cooler running, but between the open doors, and 15 or so people working inside, it was hard to cool the space down. Amex was with me that evening, for his designated studio visitation, as well. I had fed him his dinner, and was playing with him a bit, as he had grown restless with the inactivity of being in the crate all day. We were playing tug o'war with a favorite toy, when Patrick Stettner walked into the studio. Amex noticed the new stranger immediately and went to greet him (since he had already slobbered over everyone else in the studio).

I went to control my dog but Stettner didn't seem to mind the attention. He had squatted down to Amex's level to make friends with him and scratch his head. I told Stettner the usual basic info about

Amex and let them get acquainted.

When they finally seemed to have arrived at a mutual level of canine-to-human admiration, I butted in. "So, what can do for you this evening?"

"Well, I wanted to thank you for letting us bring our people to the hospital. My daughter is recovering well from the surgery. The doctor said it was a pretty complex break, which was nearly impossible to set by hand. He put a bunch of metal into her to fix it up. Plates, and screws and whatnot. He showed me an x-ray after the surgery; it looks like there's more metal than bone in there now."

"Well, I'm glad she got the surgery she needed. But you don't need to thank me; I didn't do it. The doctor did the work."

Stettner clarified, "Well, I meant the whole town; everything that everyone is doing. To make it possible for the doctors and nurses to do what they're doing."

I nodded. "Very kind of you. It *is* a team effort."

We stumbled to a stop, not sure what to say next. Stettner was looking around the studio curiously. I tried again.

"So, this is the studio, where all the magic happens. Would you like to try your hand at making a tile?"

Stettner shrugged, "Oh, thanks, but that's not necessary… I mean, this is for Chandler people, right? I didn't live in Chandler, before."

"I don't think that really matters. It's for anyone. It's a memorial to all the people who went before us, who helped make us who we are, who brought us to be here, in this city, this state. You can put a name up, if you want. You must have someone you want remembered?"

Stettner paused to think that over. "I do, but I'm not sure what to do." He was looking at a small group at a nearby table who were painting flower tiles in bright underglaze colors.

"Well, you can cut some clay into a shape you want, and then write or stamp a name into it. Is there any particular shape or symbol you think you might want?"

Stettner frowned in thought for a moment. "She liked music…" he said softly.

I smiled, and said, "Tell you what, let's look through this book of shapes, and see what appeals to you." I grabbed a children's coloring book off of an empty table. It was filled with shapes of music symbols and instruments. The images could be used to trace a shape onto a slab of clay, and then one could cut out the design.

While Stettner leafed through the book, I grabbed a slab of clay that had been rolled out earlier, and left on a ware board to stiffen up. We had taken to preparing these ahead of time, as most people found it awkward to work with very soft clay, if they were not experienced with it. Slabs that had stiffened up held up to cutting and carving better. I also grabbed a set of tools for him to use.

I guided him to an empty table, and got us settled. Stettner showed me an image of a graceful music symbol, a clef sign. "Is there way we can do this?" he asked me.

"Sure. Let's pull the image out of the book, and then trace over it gently with this." I handed him a stylus tool, a small steel ball mounted on the end of a wire, wrapped in a wood handle. He extracted the image out of the book by carefully tearing it from the spine. Then he gently laid the image over the clay, and traced it, sticking closely to the edge of the lines. When he was finished, he peeled the paper away, to see his design.

"Okay, good. So, the nature of that particular design is that it's all line, and no substance. If we try to cut it out exactly as is, those thin parts will probably crack and break." I pointed to the thin swirls.

"Oh." His face fell.

"But, we can use it as the relief part of a larger piece." Without actually touching the clay, I sketched in the air, a diamond shape around his symbol. "If we cut out this larger shape around it, and then just cut away part of the surface around the symbol, it will stand up above the base. That's called relief carving."

Stettner looked confused. "May I?" I asked him, and pulled his board over to myself. I drew the outer diamond shape and cut away the outside clay. Then I used a small loop tool to gently carve down through the thick slab of clay, about a third of the way down, along the outer side of part of the symbol. I scooped a small piece of clay out, revealing a divot in the surface. I repeated that for several more strokes along the bottom of the symbol, and then peeled a little more away, farther away from the symbol, to show how the piece would be left.

"Relief, in this context, means something that stands up and out from the surface. The clef will be in relief above the main tile, once you finish." I handed him my tool and pushed the ware board back to him. He considered it, and started to repeat my gestures. He was a quick study; it didn't take long for him to grasp what I was doing, and then do the same. I sat quietly and watched him for a time, to make sure he understood what to do. Most people would have asked a zillion questions, like, what if I go too deep, or cut through it. Stettner didn't. I watched him for a bit, and scratched Amex, who was sitting with me. Until Aaron signaled that he needed help with something. I stepped away for awhile to attend to other visitors, and answer questions.

After about thirty minutes, I went back. He had carefully carved away the outside border around his clef symbol. He had even thought to leave a raised lip around the outside perimeter of the tile, to frame the whole thing. He had thickened up the longest stroke, which crossed the vertical strip at a diagonal, making it thicker than the original image had been.

"Is it okay if I write her name here?" he asked me, pointing to it.

I smiled at him "Of course." He selected a thin needle tool and carefully wrote "Marlene" across the stroke.

"Your wife?" I asked him. He nodded without looking up at me. He continued to carefully peel away the top third of the clay in the space around the design, and smooth it.

"You know, you're incredibly lucky to have a daughter who survived. I haven't heard of very many people who have a surviving relative."

Stettner nodded again. After a moment, he spoke, still without looking directly at me. "She's the one who made me come here. She heard about this project from one of the nurses who's taking care of her. She wanted her mom's name on a tile."

I nodded. "Well, I'm glad we could make that happen."

I got up again, to help with the cleanup chores. I didn't want to rush him, but it was getting late. For me, at least. I was still cleaning up my own wheel, across the room, when I noticed Stettner get up and look around for me. I went over, to review the final piece. In the carved away area, he had scratched in some more words. "I don't dance, but I'll always dance with you." Clearly some kind of inside joke or promise to his wife.

"That's beautiful" I told him. He asked me what to do next, and I showed him where to put the tile to dry for the bisque firing. I didn't think he'd be around for the glazing stage, so I asked him if he had a preferred color for the piece. I figured I'd take care of it for him. He thought for a moment, and said his wife's favorite color was green. I made a mental note of that.

He asked me what he needed to do to clean up his work space. I gave him the instructions, which were simple; just pack up his tools into the little basket, and place them on the shelf with the other kits we were sharing with other visitors. And then scrape up the scrap clay and put it in the recycle bin. He then noticed that we were the last two left in the studio, so he offered to walk Amex and me out. I shut off the lights and closed up, and explained that I was heading over to the brewery, to see if Gordon was there, as it was on my way home. He often was, if I was working late. Stettner agreed to walk with me.

Stettner said, "So, I'm actually heading back home tomorrow morning. My daughter can't travel yet with us. She needs to stay in the hospital for a few more days yet. And even after they release her, they want her to stay close by."

"Really? We can probably arrange something for her…" I started, but he continued.

"Actually, Ariana said Cassandra could stay with her until the doctors say she can come home."

"Ah. Did she now. That sounds like Ariana." I said dryly. I wondered how much ulterior motive she was still working. Apparently, they had made up, after their shouting match at the hospital. Ariana and I hadn't talked about her crazy outburst since the day of. I wondered if Ariana knew about Stettner's late wife. Then I wondered if Stettner knew about Ariana's late husband.

"I was kinda surprised. I don't get it. After that big fight, last week, I didn't think she'd even talk to me. You think it's okay for me to leave my girl with her? Cassandra is already planning on it. Apparently, Ariana has been visiting her and they're becoming friends."

"Uh, how old is Cassandra?" I remembered that Jake had said she was in her 20's. And that impression had been reinforced when she'd been wheeled past me in the hospital.

Stettner confirmed, "She's 22."

"Oh. Well, I think at that age, she's old enough to make her own decisions, isn't she?" I tried to say this as gently as possible, even though my shoulder devil was snarking it up.

"Yeah, I guess. We just haven't been apart much since we recovered from the bug. I just worry."

"Well, every parent does. She'll be fine with Ariana. I'm close by, and can keep an eye on things too."

We had arrived at the brew pub and, as I had suspected, Gordon was sitting on the patio, finishing a beer, and talking with Robert Ruckles.

"Hi guys. You remember Patrick Stettner, right?" I gestured to him.

Gordon grinned at us, and hugged Amex, who jumped on him. "Of course!" Patrick and Gordon renewed their acquaintanceship by shaking hands. Gordon explained to Robert, "We met when I went up there for that training trade."

Then Gordon gestured to the pitcher on the table. "Anyone want a beer? Have a seat! It's a nice evening, it's finally cooling off!"

Gordon was his usual cheerful self. I was tired, and wanted to get home to bed, so I declined. Patrick agreed to share the last of the pitcher with them, and sat down. I left them to their conversation. I figured they were grown men and could make friends, or not, without my assistance or prodding. I pecked Gordon on the cheek, pulled Amex away from his manly love fest and headed home.

***

That following Saturday was the first mayoral debate. The term, 'debate' was a little misleading, as it was really more of a presentation. But most everyone was using the term, regardless. We already knew the questions, and knew that we would each have five minutes to answer. Our speaking order would be randomized during each question, so different people would be going first, last and in the middle. Since there were seven of us running (for six open slots, one for mayor, and the rest for City Council), the meeting was going to take at least a couple of hours. So, the regular Town Hall meeting was canceled, in favor of the debate.

Since it was getting hot, the debate session had been moved to the school auditorium. The original city high school was right next to the downtown area, and was easy for everyone to get to. The air conditioned auditorium could seat 2,000 people, so it was an obvious solution.

I had spent several hours thoughtfully crafting my replies, to each question. Of course, since I didn't know what order we'd be speaking in, I tried to leave some wiggle room to be able to adjust my responses, to counter what others has said before me. Sharon had spent an evening listening to me practice my mini-speeches and providing helpful feedback.

On the day of the debate, I put on a nice blouse, dark capri pants, and a simple blazer jacket. I wanted to look business-like, but still be comfortable. Gordon drove us to the auditorium, since it was over 100 degrees, and I didn't want to get sweaty just walking there. We agreed to leave all the dogs at home this time.

We made our way to the front of the auditorium, where I greeted the election commission on the stage, and took my seat with the other candidates to wait for the event to start. We were seated at tables with large name cards positioned, for everyone to easily read our names. Other than Pastor Daniel, I didn't know the other candidates. Their faces were familiar to me, but I had never been good at keeping names matched to faces in my memory. Apparently neither was anyone else, since we all had to introduce ourselves to each other politely.

At the top of the hour, the head of the election commission called the meeting to order. He introduced each of us to the audience. The auditorium was a little more than one third full. On the one hand, that looked pretty empty and disappointing to me. But then I remembered that it could seat 2,000 people. So I figured there were about 750 people, give or take. And given the post-pandemic population who had been consolidated, and were actively participating in our community, I realized that was a pretty good turn out for a bunch of boring political speeches.

The commissioner next explained the rules of the debate to the audience. Then he announced the order that we would go in, to respond to the first question. The first candidate would be Richard Forchik, followed by Pastor Daniel. Then one of the other candidates, whose name I had already forgotten (I couldn't see the name placards), then me, then the other two candidates.

The commissioner read the first question aloud. "Candidate, what steps will you take to make sure our town is protected?" He then gestured to Richard to start. He stood up and launched into his prepared mini-speech, reading from his notes.

"This town has done a lot to recover from the Superflu. But we are still not secure. Felons have been released from prison and could be threatening us right now. Unauthorized looting is draining away our resources. Drug addicts are breaking into homes, and stealing whatever gold and silver they can find. People from other parts of the Valley are migrating here, to take what we have, because we're just giving it out, for free. This needs to stop. It's attracting too much attention. We need to keep the criminals and looters out of the core zone. We need to manage our resources to develop a better security profile. Supply collection should focus on communications equipment, weapons, hardware, and fuel. My plan is to apply my business management skills to effectively use our resources to safeguard our consolidated perimeter."

Richard nodded to the audience, and sat down. The commissioner thanked him, read the question aloud again, and asked Pastor Daniel for his response.

Likewise, the Pastor stood up. He had note cards in hand, but was not reading them word-for word. He clearly had his response memorized, and was able to look the audience in the eye as he spoke.

"This town's sense of security and safety has been sorely tested. We all grieve for the lives that were lost in that senseless raid on the Warner road compound. Raids by godless heathens must never be allowed to happen again. As mayor, I will work with our police force to increase their ranks. Our very capable officers must train up more of our strong young men to be defenders of the community. Every citizen must be armed, and prepared to defend themselves, and their families, from all external threats. We should establish road blocks at all border intersections. We can use abandoned cars for this. If any intruders with malicious intent do not take heed of our warnings, they must be dealt with swiftly and decisively. In this way, we will protect all that we have struggled to rebuild."

And he too sat back down. The same process repeated for the next candidate, whose name I could not remember. His speech was even less memorable.

Next, it was my turn. Again, the question was read aloud: "Candidate, what steps will you take to make sure our town is protected?"

I stood and also gave my speech.

"Until very recently, we have not experienced any serious threats to our physical safety, from organized outside groups. We also know that is starting to change. I also believe that we should increase our police force. My plan has four components. First, we need to start a police academy, to train more people to become full fledged police officers. Second, we should negotiate for security services and resources from other communities, such as the military personnel at Luke Air Force Base, or the people from Oak Creek Canyon. We will have to determine what they want for compensation and if we have the resources to provide that. The third part of my plan is to deploy a supplemental force of security guards who can patrol and identify anyone who approaches our borders. And finally, we can use drones to monitor areas that the security guards cannot. The drone operators can then communicate with the police and guards to evaluate the potential threat, and respond appropriately. My intent is to rebuild Chandler into a regional trade hub. Blockading visitors who may have valuable resources to offer in trade, will not serve us well, in the long run. I firmly believe that a combination of solutions, resources and wise application of skilled people can secure our community to keep it a safe haven for all of us."

I sat down, and waited. The final candidates proceeded in turn, offering similar statements, saying yes, we needed to do more to protect, without actually saying *how* they would do it.

When the first round was completed, the commissioner thanked us, and launched into the second round. The question for the second round was: "How will you make sure that we have enough power, food and clean water for our long term future?" Then they announced the order that we would speak in. Surprisingly, my name was drawn first, followed by Pastor Daniel, and then the others. When he indicated, I stood up again, and gave my response. This was the one I was most worried about, as I was afraid it would go over the five minute limit. Sharon and I had worked on trimming it down, but it was still tricky to address all three components of future survival effectively. I started:

"Power and water are complicated networks. Electricity is vital to our comfort and survival here in the desert. Electricity can be generated by the hydro electric dams on the Salt River for generations to come. However, moving that electricity from its source, to us, requires careful management of the equipment on the grid. At the time of the pandemic, power was widely distributed to a very large area. However, now that 97% of the population is gone, the devices using that power at the end points are shorting out, starting fires, and causing damage that spreads back into the grid. The electrical engineering teams have been focusing on blacking out some portions of the grid, so that electricity can continue to flow uninterrupted to our community, and other communities around the Valley. This is an ongoing process, and it is a long way from being finished. Solar panels are being relocated to supplement the grid power, to compensate for uneven distribution of power. My goal is to make sure that operation continues.

Water is also a vital resource, necessary for our very life itself. And it is an equally complicated network. Likewise, clean water must flow outbound from the treatment plant, at steadily and smooth pace. When 97% of the homes and business stopped drawing water, the volume was reduced. Pressure was maintained by pumps (which were powered by electricity), but the quantity of water was moving more slowly, allowing it to pick up contaminants that it otherwise would not have. Many of those electrically powered pumps are in sections of the electrical grid that are being shut off. So, the water department has been turning off and blocking sections of the water network as well. This ensures that the remaining portions will have a steady flow of clean water. A robust distribution system ensures that the water that arrives in your home, will be as clean as it was when it left the processing plant. My goal is to restore the water grid to that former state of robustness, so that we can all use it with peace of mind.

Food, much like solar and wind power, is a renewable resource. Human beings are omnivores. That means we can eat food that comes from both plants and animals. Until about 250 years ago, growing crops and raising animals was how every family survived. The Industrial Revolution made it possible for large portions of society to remove themselves from the work that directly related to the growth of food. The Superflu kicked us back to a pre-Industrial Revolution state. So, now we have the community garden. We can raise animals or hunt for game. We can trade with other communities, for diversity in our diet. We can learn to take advantage of what the native desert around us has to offer. Its hard work, but we're not going to starve.

Clean water means clean plants and healthy animals. A strong power grid, means we can apply labor saving tools to make it easier to grow our food. With power, we can cook and preserve our foods for the future. My plan is to use our carefully managed water and power to grow our food in the most efficient manner possible, for the health, safety and comfort of everyone."

I nodded and sat back down.

I must have made it to the end of my message before the five minute warning, maybe with only seconds to spare, because no one was complaining. The commissioner moved onto Pastor Daniel. He read the question again, and gestured to the Pastor to begin.

"I too am proud and pleased with the work our engineering teams have performed, to preserve our electricity and water. I am also very impressed with the community garden, which seems have sprung up from nowhere, overnight. I give thanks every day for the abundance we experience. As Mayor, my goal will be to ensure that these gifts are not taken for granted, but are strengthened and shared with all."

That seemed pretty short and non-specific. Everyone paused, expecting him to go further, since the pattern had been established. But he just sat back down. So the commissioner pointed to the next candidate, who also gave an equally short response. In turn, Richard stood up, and gave his prepared response:

"We need to wean ourselves off of expensive, unsustainable fossil fuels and focus on securing renewable energy sources. We should acquire more solar panels and install them on every house, store and office building in the city core. We need to conserve fuel for use by farming equipment. We need confidence in the quality of water that comes into our homes. We need to identify, grow and harvest crops that are well suited to this desert climate."

He paused for a moment. "Many of you may not be aware of this, but before the pandemic, I was the CFO of a company with over 500 employees. I've supervised as many as half of my company's departments, to ensure they were performing effectively, and meeting established goals. If elected, I will apply those same managerial skills to our power, water and agricultural departments, to ensure the long term viability of each."

And then Richard also sat down. The remaining candidates also gave their answers. It was getting hard to distinguish between the babble. Everyone was more or less starting to sound the same. I wasn't the only one who thought so, either. I noticed a few audience members were dozing off.

The commissioner announced the final question: "How will you make sure that resources are distributed equitably in the future?" and then the order we would respond in. This time a couple other candidates when first. Then Richard had his turn.

"As I mentioned before, I have extensive financial and managerial experience in the corporate world. I've spent years coaching people on the best ways to manage their budget to accomplish their goals. Distribution of resources is the same thing. We have to allocate those resources out to those who will make the best use of them. For example, lots of calories to the people doing the heavy lifting. Fuel to the trucks that are bringing in more supplies. Clean water for the community gardens. Electricity to the hospital, and occupied homes. I've managed resource allocation for years in the corporate world. Now, I'm ready to put my skills to work for this town.

Pastor Daniel responded next:

"This community is rich in many resources. We have actively consolidated thousands and thousands of pounds of food and supplies. There is still much more waiting to be collected in the homes and stores beyond our borders. The good folks at the community distribution center have been generously distributing that wealth to all who request it. To ensure that we can continue to do so in the future, we will adopt guidelines to ensure that the proper amount of nutritious food is provided to every family. We will assign housing to maximize comfort and compatibility, and encourage the growth of new families. We will make sure that all occupied homes have a steady supply of clean water and electricity. We will eliminate waste and unnecessary drains on our resources. For example, instead of consuming food intended for people, pets can be released to forage for vermin, which will help keep our town clean and safe. In this way, through hard work, we can build our long term prosperity.

The final candidate gave her answer next. To my ear, they all seemed to be missing the point of the question. When my turn came last, I pounced on the key takeaway I wanted people to think about.

"You just heard my opponents talk about how many resources we have, and can get in the future. And that's true, for the most part. We do have plenty of some kinds of resources, and limits on other types. But let's reconsider that question: "How can we make sure that resources are distributed *equitably*. "Equitable" is the key word here. Distribution of resources is the function of any economy, and the primary lubricant of any economic engine is money. Since the pandemic, the value of our old monetary supply has completely imploded. Paper dollars are worthless, as are our debit and credit cards. But we're all still working hard. That work needs to be compensated somehow. After a long day of hauling bodies around, I know most of you just want to relax and have a beer. So far, Gideon has been generous with his resource." I paused for a few audience chuckles. "But soon, he's going to want some form of payment. Currency is the mechanism that converts your hard work into goods and services. Ideally, that currency needs to be something that is transportable, transferable, and valuable to all who participate in the economy. It needs to be valuable to people outside our community, as well. The supply of money needs to be limited, in order to keep demand high. It needs to be issued to those who have earned it. Once it starts circulating, money will be the lever that guides the distribution of resources. A lazy man who only does 4 hours of work, will get 4 units of money. He'll only be able to buy 4 units worth of food with that money. The industrious man, who works 8 hours, can get his 4 units of food, and still have 4 more units to spend on other things. Maybe he needs a hair cut, or someone to fix his car. His labor will directly determine how many resources he can consume.

"But wait, it gets more complicated. What about people from outside our community? What if a visitor also wants a hair cut, and has a bushel of apples to trade? Will he accept the unit of money the industrious man has to offer? My goal, to ensure an *equitable* distribution of resources, is to re-establish a currency system. We also need to establish a marketplace for the exchange of goods and services. My goal is to have people with specialized skills, services or products, to open up businesses. My goal is to let a robust, functioning economy manage the distribution of resources. If you work, you earn. If you earn, you can buy. If you buy, you have *equitably* acquired the resources you want. We don't need some committee or manager telling us how much we can have. If you want something, you work for it. You earn money, and then spend that money to buy the resources you want. That is how we should *equitably* distribute the resources."

With that emphatic conclusion, I sat down. The audience started applauding politely. Many stood up. It was flattering to think that it was for me, and what I had said. But I think the real reason was because their butts were tired of sitting on the hard chairs, and they were just happy to have an excuse to get up and move about.

Once the audience had quieted a bit, the commissioner thanked everyone for their participation in the event. They also explained the next event, a question and answer session, to be held in one month's time. Then they closed the meeting, and everyone happily scattered out of the auditorium.

Gordon and our roomies joined me, and congratulated me on the performance. I wasn't sure if it had been good, bad, or just boring. It was all a lot of wonky policy stuff, which most people didn't care much about.

We wandered over to Mercados for dinner. People were patting me on the back, telling me I did a good job, but I wasn't sure if they were right or just being supportive. Dinner was a constant string of interruptions by strangers who wanted to tell me their own ideas about security, currency, or resources. Mostly, I just listened, and absorbed the input without committing to anything, since I couldn't actually do anything yet.

When my eyes started getting glassy from too much input, Gordon guided me home, and sent me to bed.

Chapter 14

On Sunday morning, Sharon and I took the dogs out for a morning walk. Since afternoon temperatures were probably going to be over 100, we had resolved the night before, to get up early, before 6am, to accomplish the chore of exercising our pack. We both agreed that a tired dog is a good dog. And early morning, preferably before the sun rose, was the coolest time of the day now. I would have preferred to get up at 5am, but I also preferred relaxing in bed, too. We compromised and set our alarms for 5:30, with the goal of getting out the door by 6am. I consoled myself with the promise that I could take a siesta nap later on if I wanted.

Naturally, most of the dog pack loved a good walk. Tyrion was known to occasionally turn down the opportunity, but not this time. All the other dogs were making too much noise for him to ignore it or be left out. So, I leashed Amex, Tyrion and Oreo, and Sharon took her own Buster, along with the well behaved ladies, Duchess and Zilla. Gordon and the rest of the guys were either still sleeping, or already working on their own chores.

We navigated out to the golf course, which looked a lot less like a course, and more like an overgrown field, except for the parts that had been planted with vegetables. A paved cart path wandered around through the space, and made an excellent dog walking circuit. The dogs yanked me around, trying to sniff and mark every bush, post, and odd object that had ever been visited by another dog. It took a good 20 minutes for them to empty their bladders and settle enough to start making any serious forward progress.

Once the dogs had gotten their yah-yahs out, Sharon and I congratulated ourselves on having the self-discipline to get up so early, and wasn't it nice out, while it was still so cool and fresh? Weather is the one topic that *everyone* has in common.

I asked Sharon, "Have you looked at any weather websites lately? The ones I liked aren't posting any fresh data. Granted, the only thing to know about the weather right now, is that it's getting hot, and going to get even hotter. But once monsoon season gets here, it would be nice to see some forecasting. Or a radar map."

Sharon answered, "Yeah, I know. Most of those sites are useless now. Radar and satellite maps were doing pretty well on their own, for quite a few months. That was all automated. But something must have gone down on the servers that stitched it all together for the time lapse videos. And with no one there to get the servers back up, well, they're mostly hosed. There's a couple of regional weather satellites still posting images, but they're stills, not video. Do you want me to send you the site?"

"Yeah, it might be handy, in monsoon season. But there's nothing that shows what temperatures are expected, or anything like that, is there?"

Sharon answered, "No, not anymore. That kind of stuff had to be entered by a meteorologist, after he cranked his other systems to come up with a forecast."

I grimaced. "What I suspected. So how is the rest of the Internet doing, anyways? I stopped looking at it months ago, when my own feeds stopped posting anything new. The news sites I liked went dark too."

Sharon brightened. "Well, the good news is that there's still plenty of data centers and high capacity trunk lines are functioning just fine. The problem is that there's no people to input new data. No writers to post news stories. And of course, a lot of homes can't connect through their modems, if they don't have power."

"Wouldn't the power shut offs be affecting the servers, too?"

Sharon: "Not necessarily. You ever seen a data center?"

I shook my head. I knew some things about how the Internet worked, but Sharon knew way more than I did.

She went into lecture mode. "So, anyone who was anyone, and running any kind of serious data, hosted their data on remote servers. Media companies, banks, retail operations, travel, everything, practically."

I nodded. That much I knew.

"So, no server is an island. They all get backed up to co-locations; multiple servers running the same stuff simultaneously. Helps relieve the pressure. If one server goes down, the others keep going, so that the end users don't notice it. That's the "cloud." Distributed computing."

"Right." I nodded at her again.

"So, those servers are mainly hosted in massive data centers. I got to visit one here in Phoenix a few years ago, when my company was renegotiating its contract. They gave tours to their customers, just prove how secure they are. They showed me just enough to prove they couldn't show me much of anything. Most data centers are giant warehouses that have been specially designed for the job. They're situated near major, industrial grade communications trunk lines and power lines. Obviously, given the amount of data going in and out. They have generators and backup generators, and backups for the backups. There's custom electrical equipment just to regulate the power flow at a steady rate. They have heavy duty air conditioning and fire suppression systems up the wazoo. The floors where the servers are actually located are raised up above the base layer, just so the fire suppression and air conditioning can circulate under, as well as overhead, and all around. The servers are racked in cages, in rooms that have heavy duty security protocols to get into. The center I've visited, I wasn't even allowed to get near my own machines!"

She popped her eyes at me in remembered disbelief. Clearly Sharon was fascinated by her own experience. I let her keep gushing.

"Of course, placement of a data center is important too. When the Internet was growing in the early 90's, Silicon Valley had a lot of demand for this kind of service, so a lot of them were built in California. And on the East Coast, too. But, of course, California gets earthquakes. And the East Coast gets hurricanes. So they started building more co-lo's all over the mid-west. Iowa, Minnesota, Canada. And there's plenty here in Phoenix too. And all over the world. So now, we've got all those heavy duty reinforced server farms ready and waiting to spread their data to the world."

She stopped for a moment to collect her thoughts.

"What was the point I was trying to make?" she asked.

"The state of the Internet?"

"Yeah, it's still there. Its just a question of how to connect, and who's going to generate the content. Who's going to write the stories, upload the video, churn the information and build the replacement websites. How do we consolidate the data, the way you've consolidated people, and houses, and food and stuff. We need anyone and everyone who can still access the Internet, to use the same sites, to post to the same blogs. And we need to communicate what those sites are so everyone knows where to go."

I asked her, "So, do you mean a specific site, like Facebook or Twitter? Or a blog?"

"Yeah. Twitter is up and running, but Facebook seems to be a little glitchy. Something about their advertising algorithms; probably. If an advertiser's contract has lapsed, and they don't reactivate, the algorithms can't insert any content into the placeholders. And if they can't fill all the spots with ads, the pages won't display. That's their business model; gotta show the ads along with the posts."

"Doesn't Twitter get it's revenue from advertising, too?"

"Yeah, I think so. Maybe their system has a looser set of rules for what to fill into the spots, though. Or maybe an employee or three survived and is still plugging away on it, pushing enough ads into the stream to keep the flow going. They don't have to be real ads, just an image file, and a data record that says it's paid for."

"Huh." I pondered that. "Fake ads to keep real news flowing!" I smirked. Sharon grinned back at me.

"Okay, so what about telecommunications? Is there any hope of salvaging land lines or cellular networks?"

Sharon answered, "Oh, that's a toughie. I know it's probably not what anyone wants to hear, but of the two, I think we're going to have to focus on land line technology. I know it's not sexy or fun, like cell phones are, but the underlying technology is more robust. Literally. Most phone lines are buried underground, protected. Cell phone towers are just sticking up in the air, and can be damaged in storms. And they're connected to the regular power grid. Power goes off, the tower can't pass along the signal."

"Wouldn't that be true of regular phone lines, too?"

"Sort of, but it's different. Phone lines *are* a type of power line; they transfer power, along with data, when they push the signal through the wire. And they're segregated from the regular power lines. They only need a little bit of electrical power at the starting and ending point. As long as both the caller and receiver have power, the call can transmit, even if the line is crossing an area that doesn't have grid power anymore. That's why land line phones still worked, even when a thunderstorm took out the power in a neighborhood. It was designed that way, so that people could call for help."

"Yeah, but cell phones still worked, when the power got knocked out."

Sharon nodded, "Yeah, mostly. If the nearest tower that your cell was pinging still had power, or had a generator supplying backup power, or if your device was close enough to a tower in an area that had not lost power."

She went on. "However, I still don't think cell phone networks are going to be easily restored. Maybe in some other areas, but not here. I don't know of anyone in our group who has enough experience at building and maintaining the networks. I met one guy who used to work for a company that put up the physical towers, and attached the receivers. But that was just following a set of packaged instructions. He wasn't designing the network, and had no clue what to do to make sure the incoming signal got passed along to where it needed to go next. I sure don't know how to do that. But I can work with land lines, and voice-over-IP lines."

I was kinda bummed at that. Most everyone I knew was still frustrated that their gadgets were seriously compromised. Most people still carried their cell phones and took photos, played games, or wrote notes or whatever. No one I knew was ready to give up on the whole package of benefits those tiny little computers provided.

Sharon spoke up again. "Here's another reason why the cell phone network isn't going to be back any time soon. Planned obsolescence." She looked at me, and I nodded for her to go on. I was familiar with the term, but wanted to hear her explanation. Besides, the golf course hills were getting me winded. We had slowed down, as everyone was getting hot, including the dogs.

"Mobile devices, by definition, are battery powered. Batteries have to be recharged. There's a limit on the total number of charges any battery can absorb. Good ones can take more, cheap ones can take less. And what do we do when our battery won't take a charge or drains too fast? We replace it. Sooner or later, we're going to run out of batteries that can be recharged. And by "sooner", I mean, sooner than some manufacturing plant can tool up to make more of them."

I nodded glumly. "And, that doesn't even factor in broken devices, cracked screens, buggy apps, and whatnot. There's a limited supply of new devices, too. Until we can manufacture more."

"Right. There's enough stuff still in it's original packaging in stores and warehouses, to supply the surviving 3% for a good long time yet. But the technology is basically locked at it's current level of development. For now."

I sighed. We had rounded the back half of the course, and were approaching the gardens. Now that the dogs were calmed down, I had dropped Tyrion and Oreo's leashes. Oreo would stay right with me, but Tyrion was prone to wandering off to shady spots to sniff and putter. We frequently had to stop and wait for him to catch up. I held onto Amex's leash, though. He was not trustworthy off the leash.

A thought suddenly occurred to me. "Hey, isn't that same battery issue a problem for land line phones, too? My phone system always crapped out on me after a few years; I had to keep replacing them. Planned obsolescence. " I repeated.

"Yeah, cordless phones have crappy batteries. We may have to revert to corded phones. Plugged into the lines, physically. Remember those old bakelite rotary phones?"

I groaned. "Oh gawd, please no…"

Sharon grinned at me. "Well, it probably won't get that bad. But they were seriously heavy duty. A lot of modern office phones are built to last a long time, too. We should consider installing a lot of VoIP phones in the zone houses. Plug them into a power source, and an Internet modem. Connect them to the city phone system, program them with an extension, and voila, working communications. Sort of like a big Fortune 500 company system. Only spread out through a neighborhood, instead of a big office complex."

"Well, alrighty then; I delegate that project to you, Madam City CIO person." I pointed at her.

She laughed back at me. "Hey, you're not my boss yet!"

We had rounded the back half of the golf course, and were approaching the front portion, near what used to be the first hole. The pro shop where golfers could change clothes, buy shirts and book their foursomes had become Carlos's office. The pro shop had a small patio café/bar, which was convenient for visiting or taking breaks. The big semi-permanent tent style building that Carlos used for storage and food processing was about fifty yards away.

There were actually a dozen or so people scattered among the rows of crops, bending over to pull weeds, or pick produce. Apparently, they were not keeping the Monday to Friday bankers hours that most everyone else was.

Carlos was on the café patio, talking to a few people, and waived to us to come join him. He had his own dog, a Jack Russell Terrier with him, the seventh member of our household canine pack. The dog was named Jack, which I found rather unimaginative. Jack barked at the rest of his canine roomies, who barked back. Carlos turned from his conversation, waved at us, and went to fill several water bowls for the dogs. After they had their fill, Sharon and I sat down at a table in a shady area to visit for a little bit with Carlos.

I pointed to the composting bins stationed against the course's border wall. There were five large metal trash dumpsters, with holes that had been cut into their sides, and trap doors installed in the walls, close to the bottom. They were labeled, "Fruit & Veggie scraps", "Meat & Bone scraps", "Dog Poop", "Yard Waste" and "Rose Bushes."

"What's the deal with the one that says "Rose Bushes"? I asked Carlos, when he joined us.

"Ooohhhh, I didn't tell you about that one? Rose plants make the best fertilizer, better than any other kind of plant. They're like magic. People use to pay big bucks to those West Valley rose growers, for their plants whenever they got old, and weren't producing, and had to be ripped up and replanted. So, I tell the cleanup crews if they find rose bushes around the neighborhoods, that are dying or dead, to just bring them here."

Carlos seemed very pleased with himself, for setting up a collection system to get this prized element. It occurred to me that this recycling process was probably diverting a big chunk of the community's current waste stream, and that was a good thing, too.

Trash pickup had been prioritized for resumption of duty early on after the Superflu had burned out last fall. The City had had to make some adjustments in how they handled things. The recycling program was canceled completely; there was no one to process the collected material to be re-manufactured into something else. Trash pickups had to be requested; they weren't regularly scheduled, outside the consolidation zone. And they had had to find some drivers who could figure out how to operate the trash pickup trucks – the levers and mechanisms were not exactly commonplace. Residents were encouraged to consolidate their trash by sharing bins or clustering them together when put out for requested pickups. And now that there were no HOAs to give an eff, a lot of people were burning combustibles like paper and cardboard, too. And somehow, Carlos had manage to get people to segregate their compostable scraps, and deliver them to his bins regularly.

I watched someone dump a bucket of leaves and twigs into the bin labeled "Meat & Bone." "Wait, aren't they putting that stuff in the wrong bin?" I asked Carlos.

"Oh, that one needs some plant stuff to get stuff going. Helps keep the chemical reaction under control. Otherwise, it just turns into a disgusting greasy stew. It's okay to put some plant stuff into the meat one. They just can't put any meat into the plant ones." Carlos looked confident in his response. Sharon and I just said, "Oh."

Carlos, Sharon and I continued to chat for a bit. Carlos brought us up to date on what was growing best in the garden in the moment. Sharon asked if the people out working in the crops were his regular crew, and did he have them on a 7 day rotation, or what? He explained that some people were just picking for themselves. But some of his regular workers had decided to modify their work schedule, to get their work done during the coolest part of the day, the early mornings. Instead of a full day of work Monday through Friday, they were doing half days, or three quarter days, from 4am to 9 or 10am, six or seven days a week.

We could see those workers moving about with rakes and gardening tools, and small carts.

Sharon spoke up. "Hey, that guy over there, in the white t-shirt, is his name …?" She rattled off the name of someone I had never heard of.

Carlos responded, "Yeah, that's him. Do you know him?"

Sharon answered, "Vaguely. Met him a few times at some networking events I went to for this association I was a member of. He was a real big shot in that crowd. Really knew his technology stuff. Gave a lot of talks and speeches and things. I should draft him to be on my telecomm crew." She winked at us.

Sharon stared at the guy, who was hundreds of feet away and couldn't hear us. "But it's weird to see him here, pulling weeds and stuff. Really 'out of context', you know?" she asked me.

I just nodded. My shoulder devil squinted at her, and wondered if she was going to point out the irony of a big shot corporate drone was doing field work, while a Hispanic man whose own parents might have been immigrant field workers, supervised them. But she didn't go on. Maybe her own shoulder angel was making sure she kept her foot out of her mouth.

Carlos managed to deftly change the topic. He put an excited look on his face. "Hey, any puppies want a treat?" He looked around at the pack, who were sprawled around us on the cool slate tiled patio, doing their best "play dead" poses. Several of them perked up their ears at him.

Carlos quickly walked to his tent barn, and returned carrying a medium sized watermelon and a big serrated knife. Amex stood up and started butt wagging. He knew what was coming. It didn't take Tyrion long to catch on, either. The others were mostly confused.

Carlos set the watermelon on a nearby table, and started hacking off large chunks. Then he trimmed the red fruit away from the rind in big drippy wet pieces, which he handed out to the dogs. Amex demanded his first. Jack knew what watermelon was, and politely sat to request his portion. Tyrion yapped loudly for his fair share, and a little more. Zilla, Duchess, Oreo, and Buster had to be coaxed into the trying the treat. But once they had a taste, they realized it was good stuff, and wagged happily as they slurped it up. It was pretty funny, watching them trying to pick up pieces, only to have it fall apart on them and drop out of their mouths. Once every dog had a nice pile, they stopped growling at each other. Duchess the Golden Retriever tried to be the lady that she was, and eat hers delicately, but the long fur on her legs and feet still managed to get dragged into the juice and bits that were rapidly spreading over the ground. By the time they had scarfed up all the fruit, they were all sticky and wet. I wondered if Gordon would let them into the pool for a bath.

Carlos promised to bring another watermelon home, for human consumption, later on. Sharon and I gathered up the pack, and headed back to the house. It was really warming up quickly, even though it was still early.

On the return back to the house, I finally asked Sharon about one of the many other topics on my mind. "So, how are you feeling about being back in the world now?"

"Huh? Oh, yeah. Okay, actually." She paused, and came up with a metaphor. "It kinda feels like I've moved half way across the country, and I'm now getting to know my new home. I mean, technically, I've lived in this town for eight years, but since I left my house and moved here, it feels like I'm in a brand new place, and there's new people and customs to get to know. In some ways, it reminds me a little of being a freshman in college – overwhelmed with a new environment, so much information, and so many new people, and so much stress... You know what I mean?"

"Yeah, I do. That's a good way to put it. You got work to do, and clubs to join, and friends to make. You even got a bunch of co-ed roomies!"

We both snorted at this.

Sharon extended the metaphor. "And, we even go out to the bar on the weekends!"

I grinned. "Well, of course. It wouldn't be the Apocalypse College's School of Modern Survival without beer!"

We giggled some more at ourselves. But then Sharon's face sobered a bit. "And it's like my fiancé is the home-town honey I left behind, and I can't find the time to call and talk to him. I'm too busy with my new friends and classes and stuff, so he's getting stuck on the shelf."

I quieted too. After a moment, I said, "I really am sorry that you had to lose him. You know, everyone lost almost every single person in their world. We *all* grieve for our lost ones. There's some grief counseling groups around, if you want. Support groups."

Sharon nodded. "I know. Ariana told me. But I think I'm okay now." She smiled wanly at me. "Or at least, I will be, soon."

I nodded at her. "Good. You kinda had Zach worried there, when he couldn't get you out of your house."

"And I'm sorry about that. I didn't realize how stuck I was. It was

191

like time was standing still. I thought I could just sit around and read books forever."

"You should come to the studio and make a tile for your fiance, too." I reminded her. Like I hadn't been talking about the project endlessly for weeks, to everyone in the house.

Sharon nodded. "I'm working on that, too."

We had reached our house, and were passing the side where the casita fronted the street. Sharon nodded at it, and said,

"And, speaking of getting me out of my house, what's the deal with *that*? How come you didn't let me move into the casita?"

"Uh… well…" She had me pinned, there. I didn't really have a good excuse. "Well, that space would be perfect for a couple, or anyone who's got a child they're taking care of, or other special needs. And, at the time, I hadn't gotten all of my stuff out of there. And, well, I really wanted to keep a close eye on you, and having you in the main house kept you closer to the group, than the casita does. I was afraid you might slip back into that stuck zone, if you were in the casita, and we weren't stumbling over each other."

She raised an eyebrow at me, but accepted the answer for now.

We took the dogs into the house through the front door, and then immediately dragged them out to the back yard, to encourage them to jump in the pool. Which Gordon happened to be cleaning with a skimmer net. Duchess was clearly well acquainted with pools and needed little encouragement to locate the steps. Amex had never been around pools before this one, and even in the few months we'd been here, he had not yet been in the water. Until now, he thought it was just an odd blue object in the middle of his yard. I tried picking up one of his toys to engage him in a round of fetch. He was interested in the toy, until I tossed it into the middle of the pool, where it floated. That confused him.

Gordon interrupted us. "Uh, what are you doing? I just got this thing cleaned!"

I answered him. "They all had a bunch of watermelon over at Carlos's HQ. They're all sticky. They need a bath." I could see Duchess's long fur floating out of her, as she happily swam to retrieve Amex's toy. The other dogs were barking at her, confused by the fact 90% of her was gone, as far as they could tell. They didn't seem to understand the concept of how water refracts and deflects light.

Gordon said, "Uh, I was planning on this being a dog free zone… We've got too many of them, too much dog fur, it'll clog up the pump."

I grinned at him. "Well, Gordo, you should have thought of that before you started bringing me rescues. Besides, Duchess is the one with all the fur."

As I was chiding him, Zilla happily jumped into the water at the shallow end and paddled after Duchess. Clearly, she had been previously taught that pools were fun things, too.

Amex was still whining about his toy. I tried stepping onto the first step and calling him to me. It didn't take long for me to get him to step down onto the first step, which came partway up his legs. And then the second step, which brought the water up to his belly. After some more coaxing, he finally took the leap of faith, and started swimming after Duchess, who had taken the toy to the opposite end, where she climbed out on the other stairs. She gave a mighty body shake to fling the water out of her fur. Then she presented her toy to Gordon, who tossed it back in the water to Amex. Clearly, fun outweighed grownup concerns like clogged pumps.

Next, I tried to coax Tyrion and Oreo into the water. I even got out and physically picked up Tyrion, who tensed up and splayed his legs straight out. I stepped down onto the first step, and gently set him in the water, which came up to about mid chest on him. He stood stock still in complete freak out. I tried praising him, and encouraging him to go further, but he seemed locked in place. So I just gently washed his sticky feet, without dunking him. Then I did the same with Oreo, who was also completely dismayed at the concept of being immersed in water.

I was still trying to happy talk the little ones into accepting the water, when Gordon had circled around from the opposite side of the pool, and was now behind me, where I sat at the top of the steps with my feet in the water. He pointed out, "You have to get all the way in the water, and tell them to follow you." At the same time, I felt his arms circle my waist, lift me up, and then leap us both into the water. We crashed with a huge splash. I did a lot of yelping. Somewhere in all of that, Oreo figured out how to jump up off the step, back onto the pool decking, and scampered away. Tyrion had also retreated to a distant point on the patio, well away from the pool. Both the little dogs were yapping at us intermittently. Zilla was still happily swimming around, and Amex and Duchess were taking turns climbing in and out and running around.

Sharon was laughing at us, from the opposite end of the pool. She sat on the edge, with her feet in the water, and likewise, tried to encourage Buster to go for a swim. The most he was interested in, was sitting down on the first step, which was enough to at least wet him down and get the watermelon juice off of him.

At first splash, the water seemed pretty cold. I was fully dressed for our earlier walk, but now that everything was wet, there didn't seem to be much hurry to get out. Within a few moments of splashing about, the water started to feel pretty nice.

Dillon and Micah finally appeared, still dressed in PJs. Our noise had finally woken them.

Gordon greeted them. "Oh, good, now that you're finally up, you can get started on your chores... Dillon, the water pump is going to need to be cleaned out regularly. And Micah, you get to mow the grass today."

Sunday mornings were our semi-regular chore time. If the guys weren't out doing line work, they tried to reserve the time to handle general household maintenance.

Dillon asked him, "And what exactly are you going to be doing?"

"I'm going to make sure the pool toys still float, and the mai tai's are strong" he said. Dillon tossed a pool noodle at him.

After playing with dogs for a little while more, and getting them completely tired out, Gordon told me what he really wanted to do today.

"I want to head up to the university, try the library over there. My contacts at the utility said there's a group of people on the main campus, that are pulling things together. I want to check out the engineering section of the library, see if they'll long term loan us some stuff."

Seemed like a reasonable request to me. "Okay, sounds like a plan."

We changed out of our wet clothes, finished our morning chores and then headed to school.

Chapter 15

I pondered the idea of a major state university as a survivor's enclave. Obviously, there was plenty of housing, if you liked small cramped dorm rooms. The other buildings might not be all that useful in an apocalypse: class rooms, labs, large scale cafeterias, offices. But there were also plenty of open lawns that could be replanted with food crops. It was situated in the middle of a suburban town, so packaged food and supplies could probably be collected relatively easily. Most of the students on campus had probably gone home when the Superflu started to peak, so there probably weren't that many bodies to clear. And of course, it had lots of libraries with a wealth of knowledge.

This particular university had made significant strides towards becoming a sustainable, zero carbon footprint institution. I'd read about some of its initiatives, like an extensive recycling collection program, and incentives to conserve paper usage and use public transportation, too. However, the most significant component of their plan, that made it a good target for our post-Superflu world, was the extensive array of solar panels on dozens of buildings, car park shelters, and other structures. I didn't know if the university was able to supply all of it's power needs from solar alone. But I figured anyone we encountered there would be able to answer that question.

Gordon had packed up his truck with several crates of fresh fruits and vegetables (which Carlos had already prepared for him when we stopped by his garden HQ). Some were intended for his contacts at the utility and the rest for whatever survivor group we found on campus. He was coming prepared to trade for what he wanted.

We approached the university via the main avenue that led onto campus from the east side. At the cross street that marked the start of campus proper, we discovered a road blockade, made from dinged up cars and trucks. A movable gate had been installed across the front, and was guarded by a team of people, who were well armed.

Gordon rolled down his window (and so did I), and approached slowly, waving calmly. When we were in shouting distance, he yelled;

"Hello! We've come to trade, and we have food to offer."

The guards yelled back at us to step out of the vehicle, for inspection. We both stepped out slowly. We were wearing our pistols in our open carry holsters (me on my shoulder, Gordon at his waist). We kept our hands well away from our guns, and did not act like criminals. Not that I knew anything about how criminals behaved.

The guards looked over the truck, noting the crates of fresh food in the back, and asked Gordon for more details. He explained about being interested in visiting the library, and that he wanted some engineering books.

The guards radioed our request to someone and after a few moments, we were permitted to pass. They directed us to the main concourse on campus, where others would meet us.

At the appointed location, we were met by a small delegation. They appeared mostly young, college aged, naturally, except for a couple of middle aged people. Maybe professors or administrators, I figured. We introduced ourselves, and where we were from. Their leader stepped forward and identified himself as the head librarian.

Again, Gordon explained his desire for access to the library, in more detail this time.

"I was hoping to trade the food for some books. Our city library is a nice one, but it's mostly focused on fiction and recreational stuff. It doesn't have a very good collection of engineering resources. We've got several projects going on, where we could really use some educational materials. I'm looking for stuff on solar power, water and fluid dynamics, and general construction."

The librarian nodded in understanding, and asked, "Are you looking to borrow or keep the books?"

"Well, I was thinking of it as a long term borrowing, if you're willing. We have several work crews that will need access to stuff. And we've got a lot of teenagers who are apprenticing in the trades, who need to learn stuff, too."

The guy nodded. He and Gordon dickered over terms. He explained that the university bookstore was still well stocked with course books, and we could take multiples of those. The library also sometimes had multiple copies of some books, and we could take one from a set, if we wished. However, if the library had only one copy of a title, it would have to stay on site. We were welcome to review the books, now or in the future, as needed, but they didn't want it leaving campus if it was a solo copy.

While they chatted, I looked about at the others of the team. "Are you also working in the library?" They nodded.

"Were you students, before?" A couple of them nodded, a couple shook their heads. "So, you're making this campus your survival place? Trading knowledge for supplies?"

"Sort of. Most of us just don't have anywhere else to go," one young woman responded. "We've collected a lot of supplies. And actually, we're working on planting gardens, too. But we kinda got a late start on it. So we're grateful for the food you've brought. We don't have a lot of our own fresh food, yet."

I nodded and smiled back. "So, is everyone living in the dorms, then?"

"Some of us are. There's some nice condos just on the south side of campus that we're using, too. They're much nicer than the dorm rooms."

"And, you're getting power from all the solar panels?" Kind of an obvious question, but I still had to check.

The young woman nodded again. "Yeah, mostly. We shut down some buildings, so that the rest of the campus could be powered by the panels in place."

"You know, the utility is still generating hydro-electric power at the dams. I'd think the university would be able to draw on some of that power, too."

"Uh, maybe. I dunno," responded the girl. Actually Gordon was asking more or less the same things. The lead librarian confirmed that yes, they were in contact with the small team at the utility company's headquarters (which was just a couple of miles up the road from the main campus). And, yes, the campus was still actively connected to the grid power system along with their solar generation. In fact, since they had shut down unused buildings, they were actually feeding some excess solar power back into the grid.

I wondered how they were fixed for water, but didn't have time to ask, as they led us to the university bookstore, to select course books. Gordon selected multiple copies of some of the most popular and basic titles on engineering topics, including civil, electrical, construction and other more obscure topics.

Next, we were led to the main library on campus. While there were several smaller, specialized libraries scattered about the campus, the main one, of course, had the largest collection. And, since their power was still running, we were not forced to use the prehistoric form of Google: the card catalog. With the assistants' help in checking the online library database, Gordon was directed to the engineering section to pick out some more esoteric titles. I asked for the section on gardening, and Native American cultures who had lived in the local area. I wanted to find books on growing, harvesting and preparing local native food plants that I could pass along to Carlos, or at least stash in our Chandler library, for anyone else to learn from, too.

Gordon and I each spent more than an hour in our respective title searches, and came away with boxes of extra copies that the library team was pleased to send away with us. We had, of course, explained the size of our own community, and what operations we had going. We also let them know that our hospital had recovered, and was staffed, and medical services were available if anyone needed anything. They were very intrigued by that idea. One girl pulled me aside, and asked if the hospital could help with birth control, and maybe check people for STDs? I assured her that, yes, that could be handled easily and discretely. She looked grateful.

***

After our university visit, we headed to the utility company's main office, which was not far from the campus. It was situated on a slight hill, just above the river, with wide views of the Valley all around.

We unloaded the remaining boxes of produce from the car, so that they wouldn't wilt in the car heat. Gordon led me in through the main entrance, and found a shady spot inside, to set down the boxes. Then he led me up a flight of stairs, down a hallway, and through a door into a room unlike anything I'd ever seen before.

We were standing on a walkway that circled a fairly large room. Below us, on the next level down, were clusters of desks with huge computer monitors lit up. Most were displaying colorful maps of lines or graphs that meant nothing to me. Gordon introduced me to what I was looking at.

"This is the control center for all system operations this company is responsible for. Those guys there," he waved at a few people at some of the desks, and they waved back, "are watching the power grid network for problems, and then responding to those problems. They can shut down, or reroute power around a house, neighborhood, or entire city, with just a few commands on the keyboard."

Gordon led me down another set of stairs, and over to one of the men working the computers. He introduced me to the men, and then said, "This is Jerry Llewelling. He's the head honcho for this team. Jerry, this is Maggie Shearin."

Jerry held out his hand to shake and smiled. "Good to meet you. Gordon has told me about you."

His smiled indicated it was just the good things, and not the embarrassing stuff.

Gordon prompted him. "I brought Maggie for a tour. Can you explain to her what's happening here?" he gestured around the room, speaking like a TV reporter turning over the microphone to an expert.

Jerry was a large man, with a big beer belly bulging over his belt. He wore a simple button down shirt and khaki pants, the basic office worker uniform. But it also looked like he hadn't shaved in a few days, and there were bags under his eyes, which where red rimmed with exhaustion. But he greeted us cheerfully and said, "Well, I can explain it about as well as an Englishman can explain cricket to a Yank." We all grinned at his joke.

Gordon interceded. "Can you bring up Chandler and show her the current status?"

"That I can do," Jerry responded. He turned to his computer, and with some unseen clicks of mouse and a few taps on a keyboard, brought up a shape that I recognized as our city borders. Bright lines trailed down from the north end of the city and exploded into a maze of color in the middle. Towards the bottom of the map, the lines petered out and large chunks were completely dark. Pockets of other areas scattered about were also dark, interspersed with more colored lines. A few were blinking.

"This is your city and the areas that are still actively receiving power. The different colors represent the different distribution lines that run through the area." He pressed another button on the keyboard. A series of numbers and dots appeared scattered about the city. "Those are the substations that convert the power from one phase to another and otherwise help route it around."

Next, he pointed his finger at the darkened areas. "And those are the areas that have been shut off by Gordon's teams," he said. I nodded as sagely as I could manage.

Gordon asked, "And how about the rest of the Valley?"

Jerry zoomed out the map, and pointed out various areas. "This is central Phoenix. As you can see, it's mostly dark, due to the damage from the riots and fires and things. A lot of distribution lines have gone down, and we haven't been able to repair them yet. Some things have been rerouted, and are working okay." He then pointed to other areas. "But then you have these other areas, like parts of Glendale, that we're shutting off, just like in Chandler. Gordon put us in touch with that group out there and the people at Luke Air Force Base. They're letting us know when they've cleared a neighborhood, and can turn it off."

I nodded some more. "So, Gordon's strategy of deliberately shutting off some areas, so that we can keep other areas on, is working then?" Not that I had ever doubted him, or anything.

"Yes, absolutely. Its going to happen anyway, with or without our intervention. It's better to do it in a controlled manner to minimize impact."

"And how does it happen if it's not controlled?" I asked.

"Well, demand for energy is starting to pick up, because AC is getting turned on. But it's happening very erratically. Here, lemme show you." He pulled up another window on his screen and zoomed in on a residential neighborhood in north Phoenix. "This was a couple of days ago." He started a time lapse video. Several lines on the map were moderately bright. Then one of the dots on the end point branching off the lines suddenly lit up brightly. It burned like that for a few moments and then winked out. The first segment of the line it was connected to darkened after it, followed by several more segments of the line going off, one after another, until it reached back to the junction point where it met up with several other lines.

Jerry explained, "That was a house, where some survivor just turned on the AC. The transformer wasn't prepared to provide that much power to it so it burned out the line segments in between. Now no one can use any power along that entire line."

"So, just to ask the obvious, why wasn't that transformer prepared to handle the load? I mean, it's mid-May, it's getting hot, people naturally turn on the AC at this time of the year."

"Yes, of course, but the system has no way of knowing where those people are. The coal burning plants and natural gas generating stations have gone off line. So we have a reduced quantity of power generation going into the system. We have to direct that to the places we know for certain are using it. Our relays and controls can open and close circuits upon command. And we have a lot of complicated automated software that's monitoring usage, and trying to predict where power will be needed. It monitors power usage over the entire geographic area for the recent period of time, and averages the current usage, to predict near term additional usage. Then it suggests adjustments to be made to meet those needs. We can also plug in things like weather information and other data that will also help predict demand. The problem is that the system looks at the entire neighborhood. It thinks all 200 houses on that line are going to use that power relatively evenly. Most of them are empty, and nothing is changing their current usage. So when one house spikes unexpectedly, the system was not expecting it, and was not prepared to handle it. Thus, it burns out."

"Huh." I squinted thoughtfully at the map.

Jerry went on. "Of course, when we know that neighborhoods are being deliberately turned off and disconnected, we can program the information in, and tell it to ignore segments. That's why Gordon's project is working. We know which areas he plans to black out, and which will stay on. And, he's reinforcing the distribution network with additional switches and transformers to regulate the flow, which helps insulate it from the spikes happening elsewhere."

"So, you've got a pretty solid handle on where active groups of survivors are, then?"

Jerry answerekd, "Kind of. We can tell where pockets of above average amounts of power are being consumed. At least, above historical average, and above recent activity. We can tell that people are gathering together in small groups or clusters of homes. That doesn't tell us anything about their situation, though. Just that they've turned on some appliances and things." Jerry zoomed the metro map back out, and pointed out several clusters of bright points and lighted lines.

"These are some of the bigger clusters of activities. Notice how they're all in really nice areas? North Scottsdale, Paradise Valley, Fountain Hills. Places where they have gated communities, large houses, and lots of nearby shopping that were well stocked with supplies."

Yeah, that made a lot of sense. I nodded.

"What about the economic side of things? I mean, electricity wasn't free, before. We all had to pay the bill or our power got cut off. Is anyone even still doing that? I haven't checked my bank account in months, but I was on auto-pay. I assume the system just kept deducting the money from my checking account, until it ran out of money. Then what?"

Jerry groaned. "Yeah, that's another whole headache for us." He stood up from his seat, and gestured at me to follow him. "Come on, I'll introduce you to Juanita. She's our accounting person." He walked us through another doorway, and down a different hall. I had pretty much lost track of where we were, in relation to the outside world.

Jerry opened a door to another large room, this one more typically furnished like a large office suite, with cubicles and window offices partitioned off with glass walls. At the end of the row, he entered a large corner office, with a middle aged woman sitting a desk. Several large computer monitors and a couple of keyboards were arrayed around her. To one side, a large comfy sofa was piled with several blankets and pillows. A large dresser stood beside it, looking very out of place. "This is Juanita. Juanita, this is Maggie. And you already know Gordon." Gordon was trailing behind us and waved at the new person.

Jerry explained who I was and that we were visiting. Then he told Juanita, "Maggie wants to know how billing is affecting the grid."

Juanita grinned, and said, "Ah. Well, basically, I'm trying to keep it from having any effect at all."

Huh? The woman was a middle aged Hispanic woman, somewhat large sized. She was dressed in a simple top and capri pants. Not very corporate, but I didn't hold that against her.

"What do you mean?" I asked.

She gazed at me for a moment and said, "You were probably on auto pay, right?" I nodded.

She explained, "Yeah, about 40% of our customers were. The rest paid by mailing in a check every month, or went to their local office and paid in person." Only 40% on auto-pay? That seemed ridiculously low, for such a simple and effective way to handle things. Never being late, never forgetting to put a check into the mail… But Juanita wasn't waiting for me to process my personal side bar opinions.

"We had a protocol for late payments. 15 days late, and first warning went out. 30 days late, and second warning went out. 45 days, and we'd inform the customer that they were at risk of getting their power shut off. 60 days, and we'd start making phone calls. At 90 days, if there was no payment and no other holds or statuses, the power would go off. Exceptions could be made if special conditions were met, like partial payments, notice of change in address, pending property sales, stuff like that."

I nodded. She continued.

"The system is still trying to do all of that. We're not physically printing and mailing the bills, but the system is ticking over the deadlines on the late accounts. It's trying to automatically shut off anything that reaches the 90 day mark. Unless I can put a stop on it, and reset the clock. So, most of my job is putting in statuses, like "change in ownership", and "partial payment received" and so on. We're still getting some bank transfers for auto-pays for some accounts…"

"Really?" I spluttered.

"Yeah, I'm shocked, too. Wells Fargo, and Chase Bank are still letting electronic transfers go through. Must be automated at their end, too. We can't seem to connect to the Bank of America servers, though. Of course, its only working if the account still has any funds in them. Once they empty out, well, they go into the deadbeat cycle, just like all the rest."

"But the economy has collapsed, money is basically worthless at the moment. How do you know how much to charge customers?" I asked.

"Yeah, but the computers don't know that money is worthless. To the computers, it's just numbers. And as for pricing, well, we just stopped adjusting rates. Before, we made micro adjustments to the rates daily, or hourly, usually just a few cents per kilowatt hour. That was based on supply and demand, and distribution…" She gestured back at Jerry, to indicate his side of the operation.

"But when Congress froze prices, back in November, that applied to us as well. So we just stopped the adjustments, and kept prices right where they were at that moment. And a lot of people died with plenty of cash still in their accounts and no one to tell us to stop the transfers. Nobody told the computers that the economy collapsed and the people died. They're still ticking along. But that's really a pretty small percentage of all of our accounts. I still have a lot of manual updating to do, to keep the system from shutting off things automatically for non-payment."

"Wouldn't automatic shut off be a good thing? Easier than doing it manually?" I asked.

"You'd think so, wouldn't you?" Juanita answered.

Jerry interrupted, "Actually, that's just another tool in our box. When we know an area is unoccupied and ready to be taken down, Juanita flips them over from paid to unpaid, and then they get shut off. We're working in batches, street by street, neighborhood by neighborhood. Remember, we don't always know for certain which sites are still occupied or not. Unless someone like our employees or Gordon's teams, confirm it to us."

"And you're doing all that work on your own?" I looked back out at the empty cubicles.

Juanita answered, "Oh, I have a couple of helpers. But they're off today. They needed some rest."

I smiled at her and thanked her for the explanation. "Listen, we brought you folks some food. We left it out in your main lobby. Didn't know where to take it."

Juanita and Jerry brightened at this. We led them back to where we had left the boxes. They were very excited to see to see the fresh produce.

"So, the people that are working here, are you all living together in some neighborhood nearby, too?

Jerry responded first. "Us? Nah, we've barely even left the building. There's only about 20 or so of us in the building. And too much work to do to leave. We've got another 75 or maybe 80 employees out trying to fix lines and things. But we're running out of replacement equipment. Which is another reason why Gordon's project is so important. He's been bringing in extra equipment that's been removed so that we can move it elsewhere."

"So, are you all actually living here in this building?" I asked them.

Juanita fielded this one. "Most of us are. We've got couches and stuff to sleep on. The fitness center downstairs has decent bathrooms with showers, to get cleaned up in. And since this is a vital resource, FEMA parked a whole semi-trailer truck with water and food on our loading dock last fall. There's still tons of that stuff to keep us going. But fresh food is certainly welcome!"

Gordon grinned at me. Clearly, he knew about their living situation and had thoughtfully planned ahead.

Gordon spent some time bringing Jerry up to date on his own projects, while I filled Juanita in on what I knew about some of the more distant communities around the state. I also asked Juanita if she had seen any of the zoo animals. I explained what my apprentices had seen and how they had discovered the open cages at the zoo. Since the zoo was just a block away from this office building, it was possible that some animals might have wandered by. Juanita's office did have an excellent view.

Juanita had not noticed any, but she said she would definitely be on the lookout for them from now on. Jerry spoke up and said, "Actually, one of the line men swore to me he saw elephants wandering around, but I thought it was just the exhaustion talking. I made him go get some sleep. I'll have to apologize to him."

We wrapped up the visit by extending open invitations to come to Chandler any time they needed more fresh food, or just time away from the office.

Chapter 16

The weeks after the first mayoral debate continued the same as before. Problems cropped up and either got solved, or not, depending on their complexity. Food was harvested from the garden or collected from homes and stores. Bodies were cremated. And, people came to open studio nights, made tiles and shared their stories. Some I already knew, some I did not.

Loren, the nurse who had helped with the dysentery outbreak diagnosis, backfilled me with more details on how the hospital had recovered after the flu burned out.

From her point of view, the rioting at our local hospital had been more like a series of bar fights than a true riot. A bunch of people would be sitting around one of the emergency waiting rooms, and someone would get frustrated at the lack of help being provided. They'd see their loved one struggling to breathe and get up to demand immediate attention. Their rage and frustration would overwhelm them. They'd start yelling, throw a chair, or punch a wall, or even try to hit a doctor or nurse or orderly. Other people would yell back at them, telling them to quiet down. Then security would come and guide the person, or maybe several people, outside. Once there, they'd kick at the tents in the parking lot, or maybe get a baseball bat from their car and start hitting ambulances and police cars. But the thing was, there were never enough people all at once to storm back into the building. At most, maybe 5 or 10 people would get enraged and lose control. Everyone else, while equally angry, were too sick to actually get up and pick up a rock or throw a punch. So the instigators would finally get sent away, usually leaving their family member alone in the waiting room. The incoming patients would either get admitted or get sent home. Within a few hours, a whole new crop of people would be sitting around, stewing in their germs and rage, and the cycle would start all over again.

I asked Loren how the medical staff had handled it. I knew it must have been stressful, probably way beyond anything I'd ever experienced. She explained that it had been the most traumatic experience of her life. For weeks and weeks, she and her colleagues had taken patients in and administered fluids and medicine, while the supply lasted. Every single bed had been occupied, including a lot of temporary cots. Rooms that normally were only supposed to hold one person, would have two or three people in them. Sometimes more, if a whole family was sick enough to be admitted.

She said most of the staff who were directly caring for patients stayed at the hospital for days on end. She admitted that some people eventually abandoned their jobs when their worry over their own families overwhelmed them. But the majority stayed until they got sick too. And when that happened, they just laid down in an empty bed, if they could find one, or on the floor if they couldn't.

The morgue had quickly been overwhelmed and had struggled to process the bodies and turn them over to the funeral homes. Bodies ended up getting stacked in the hallways and loading dock, just waiting for transfer. At the peak of the crisis, they were using semi trailer trucks just move the bodies. By that point, the city had carved out the cremation pits at the land fill, which were still in use now.

Loren also told me some things about the leadership at the hospital, that I had not been previously aware of. I knew who Doctor Reddy was and that he was an orthopedic surgeon. But Lauren informed me that he had been on the hospital's board of directors for years, and was effectively the last man standing, in terms of the management chain. She acknowledged that his people skills were a little under-developed. He was usually pretty brusque with most people, getting straight to the point of what he wanted to say, without much lead up or small talk. However, in addition to being an excellent surgeon, he was also a very qualified administrator. After the virus burned out, he made sure that the remaining staff got the rest they needed to recover and then put them back to work, cleaning up the place and recovering supplies. He didn't believe in coddling his staff. He felt the best path to recovery was to face the trauma and work through it. Literally.

Due to the sheer volume of patients that had passed through the hospital, it had been a mess. Linen service, housekeeping and maintenance had been completely overwhelmed. The kitchen that handled both patient meals and general cafeteria service for visitors and employees, was completely out of food and workers. Everyone had given up on record keeping. Billing of insurance companies had been the first administrative task to be abandoned. Doctors and nurses from any specialized area of medicine were reassigned to general palliative care of flu patients. Naturally, the pharmacy ran out of pain relievers, anti-inflammatories, hydration fluids, blood and anything else that might remotely have an impact on the flu virus.

After the dust settled and the few remaining staff survivors were back on their feet, Dr. Reddy essentially ran his own medical consolidation program. He inspected the entire hospital carefully. He directed his people to remove anything of value from several wings, and then closed those areas off. The remaining open areas were cleaned up, and put back in order. Linens were washed, floors were mopped, cots were packed away. Damaged cars were removed from the parking lots. Eventually, all the remaining bodies had been removed from the morgue to the cremation pits. By that point, the funeral homes had lost most of their personnel too, and had ceased to operate.

Dr. Reddy sent teams out to scavenge for drugs and supplies at local medical distribution warehouses, nursing homes and veterinary clinics. They tried the retail pharmacies, but those were mostly picked clean of useful stuff. They were able to recover abundant supplies of things like birth control, psychiatric drugs, cancer treatment drugs, bandages, and other esoteric health care supplies. By that point, he was in regular contact with the remaining city management team (meaning, Robert Ruckles and Ariana) and was working with them to actively get a functioning medical service up and running again. When the housing consolidation got underway, he insisted that his staff be assigned housing closest to the hospital, as well.

Loren told her story in a neutral tone. She had been right in the middle of the entire scene, throughout the cycle of the Superflu. It was clear that the hospital staff had been terrified, stressed, exhausted. And when the metaphorical storm cleared, the ones who were left picked themselves up, dusted themselves off and got back to work.

I asked Loren if she agreed that "Superflu Trauma" was a thing now, and if we could call it "ST" for short. She chided me for making up syndromes without any qualifications to do so, but she also acknowledge that as a term, it worked as well as any other, to describe the shell shock most people experienced in the aftermath. She also told me that they were still getting a steady stream of people having emotional freakouts over their grief and loss. People who had been functioning pretty well, just suddenly snapped and collapsed. Or people who were drinking themselves sick, or doing other illicit drugs that were still being found in personal stashes. The trauma was real, she agreed, and it wasn't over. They were doing the best that they could, one day at a time, one patient at a time.

I showed Loren the apothecary jars I was making at Dr. Reddy's request. She confirmed that they had taken in a pharmacist who'd been working retail before, who could compound and manufacture some drugs on a small scale, such as simple antibiotics, tetanus vaccines, and a few other things. But mostly, the medical team was focused on care of physical injuries and well-patient services.

Loren brightened when she pointed out that they had several dental hygienists and a dentist who had joined the team after the Superflu had flared out. She encouraged me to remind everyone to get back on a six month cycle of checkups and cleanings. I made a mental note to do so.

She was also excited at the prospect of the coming baby boom. Apparently several women around town were entering their second trimester of pregnancy. I'd heard of a few of them, but she wisely kept patient confidentiality, and did not name any names. Loren also let me know that it was good I was sending other women to them for birth control, as they had plenty of that, in many different forms, as well.

***

Loren was just one example of the many types of personal stories and experiences that people shared with me. Now that it was common knowledge that I was running for mayor, it seemed everyone wanted to share their personal experiences with the Superflu.

Some people told me they had come to Chandler during the winter, to find relatives, or to bug out from colder climates, and had gotten swooped up into the work crews, and were happy to be part of something positive. They liked having meaningful work to do, which kept their minds off of their grief trauma.

Some people told me they were planning on leaving Chandler soon, to get out of the heat, but would be back in the fall. They proclaimed themselves the new modern snow-birds, following a migratory path, wandering and working where ever they found opportunity.

Other people rather resented the hard work and wanted to make sure they would eventually be duly compensated for their labor. With those people, I turned it back around on them, and asked what form of compensation they wanted, given that cash was now worthless. Mostly they just hemmed and hawed, or talked about making sure they got to stay in a nice house with power, and food and water. Which they already had.

Other people told me stories about the people they had lost: charming grandparents, funny siblings, heroic parents. They wanted to share the details that a simple ceramic tile couldn't contain. With those people, I just listened.

Not everyone's stories were sad. People were starting to put together clubs, and movie nights and gaming sessions. One man was trying to start up a small intramural baseball league. Couples were pairing off, and there was much speculation about potential weddings in the future. Jenna even told me that Kyrene had been in touch with an old friend from college, who was staying in Phoenix, and was having a big party that coming weekend, and that she had invited Kaycee and Jenna to go with her. I smiled at her, and was happy to bask in normality of simple gossip.

***

Of course, not everything was sunshine and roses. Life was still life, and next it was Gordon's turn to suffer one of Murphy's pranks.

I had walked the dogs very early on Saturday morning. It was already getting very hot, so I had paused to lay down on the bed for just a moment, really, before taking my shower. The next thing I knew, a roaring yowl woke me from a sound sleep. I leapt up, and dashed outside, following the noise. It was coming from the side yard between the casita and the main house, just outside our bedroom. When I stepped outside, I found Gordon was hopping about on one foot, screaming "FUUUUCCCCKKKK!!!" at the top of his lungs.

"What on earth are you doing?" I tried to yell over him, not very successfully. Most of the dog pack had followed me out, and were quickly infected with Gordon's distress. They started barking and running around, looking for a threat to face down.

Gordon grabbed a nearby rake, and leaned on it, one foot still held up in the air. He was puffing and groaning. I looked around. Piles of leaves had been raked up along the walkway, and there was a pair of heavy duty clippers on the ground, along with an assortment of branches from the trees and bushes that shaded the pathway between the buildings.

Gordon finally managed to speak coherently. "Something bit me. I think it was a scorpion." He was hopping on one foot back towards the door into the main house. I could see that he was only wearing flip-flops. I tsked, but he didn't hear me. He should have known better than to go nearly barefoot while doing yard work.

"Okay, yeah, that's gonna hurt. Let's get you inside and take a look." While I was referring to checking for a bite mark on his foot, I also carefully looked at the ground around me but couldn't see anything. I was completely barefoot, so I quickly followed him inside and slammed the door behind us. Then I had to open it again to let the dogs back in. They were still agitated and ran off to check on everyone else in the house.

Gordon hobbled into our bedroom, and flopped down on the bed. I turned on the lights and inspected his foot. A large round red welt was rising up, just above the arch, on the side of his foot. It wasn't bleeding, though. Yeah, that could be a scorpion sting. Or maybe a spider. There were several vicious varieties about, including brown recluse spiders. But scorpion seemed as good a guess as any to me.

Gordon was still swearing, although somewhat more softly, and huffing and puffing. And he'd woken up Micah, who wandered in to see what the fuss was about.

I asked him, "Gord, do you want to go over to the hospital, to get this looked at?"

"Nah. It hurts like a son-of-a-bitch, but there's nothing they can do. Ice, and ibuprofen."

He was right. In a healthy adult, there wasn't much to be done about scorpion bites, except suffer through it.

"Okay. Micah, can you please calm the dogs down? Take them all outside and let them have a good sniff around the back yard. Keep them away from the side yard. I don't want them getting bitten, either. And take that rake back outside, it's getting leaves and junk all over the place. Then could you please go put on some real shoes and finish raking up the leaves he was working on?"

Micah got the confirmation nod from Gordon, to do as I asked, and headed off, rake in tow. I went to the kitchen, and wrapped some ice in a towel. I gave that to Gordon, which he applied. While he waited for his foot to go numb from the ice, I got the ibuprofen from the bathroom and a glass of water. I sat beside him. His face was still pretty red from the frustration and pain.

"Well, this sucks," he said. I tried to console him. He nodded, swallowed two pills with water, and scooched back on the bed to lay flat, with the ice pack on his foot.

He swore again, and said, "I'm not going to be able to do squat today. I was supposed to take a load of equipment back to Tempe. But I can't drive like this." The bite was on his right foot, his accelerator pedal foot. "I'm gonna need a cane, just to walk around for a day or two."

I thought about that for a moment. I hadn't seen a true cane anywhere in the house, but I figured we could improvise something. Maybe a broom or some other kind of stick? Of course, I could go out and get a cane, I supposed. I was sure the hospital would have one in their stash of medical supplies.

"All right. Let me see what I can come up with."

Dillon was next to check on us, just as groggy as Micah had been. "Dude, what was all the hollering for?" he asked.

We explained and Gordon gave him the marching orders for delivering the equipment in his place. I left Gordon to rest and let the ice and pain relievers do their job. I took my shower and mentally planned my errands for the day. In addition to finding a cane for Gordon, I was getting actually getting low on a few basic supplies, like shampoo, soap, laundry detergent and dog food. So it was time to go shopping.

I already knew that a lot of the town's retail stores had been consolidated into the nearby Costco warehouse. This was mostly for convenient ease of access. However, few people knew extra inventory was also stashed in a few other warehouses around town, which had been carefully treated to look abandoned and already looted. This program, to safeguard our resources by caching it in a few different locations, had been enacted after the raid on the Warner Road compound, at several people's recommendations. We didn't think looters would be foolish enough to go after a well protected supply location. But then… it was the apocalypse, after all.

I met Sharon in the kitchen, eating her breakfast, and explained about the scorpion bite. She winced in sympathy. "Yep, I've been stung before, too. It sucks."

I invited her to go shopping with me. She had not been to the supply warehouse since the consolidation started, so it was another opportunity to show her some of the changes that had happened since the Superflu. I checked with the rest of the guys to see if they needed anything and made up a formal list. And then Sharon and I headed out.

***

The Costco still looked remarkably like a Costco. The signs were still up and huge shopping carts were racked up outside the main entrance. The entry corridor was lined with big screen TVs packed in their boxes and strapped with that odd little security sensor device. The isles and huge industrial shelving units were filled with goods. But instead of cases and cases of just a few items in any one category, smaller shelving units had been setup inside the big racks, holding small quantities of many different things, stacked or stashed in tubs and baskets. Products were still clustered according to type, of course. So once you found the beauty supplies, it was pretty easy to locate the hair coloring and lipstick. Packaged food was still available, too, but quantities seemed to be dwindling. The produce and meat departments had chillers and freezers, and a decent supply of frozen meat was still available. A sign above a deep ice chest advertised fresh elk meat, brought back from Flagstaff area, by "Tom the Hunter." The dairy department had some blocks of a mild orange cheese packed in heavy duty vacuum seal thick plastic. A sign above the pile said, "One per customer, please." There was also some fresh goat cheese, small lumps wrapped in light saran wrap, with no sign that restricted quantities.

We wandered the aisles, inspecting the goods. In the bakery section, a woman was stacking forty pound bags of flour onto flat bed cart. She nodded at us in greeting. I think she must have recognized me, because she stood up straight, and smiled at us.

"Good morning," she greeted us. "I hope you weren't planning on getting any flour. We just found out this batch has got bugs in it."

Sharon's eyes widened, and she took a step or two back. I looked around in confusion for a moment, then asked, "You mean those little tiny ones?" I asked the woman. I examined the bags more closely, and could see some worn corners and creases, where tiny critters may have gotten in. Or out.

"Yeah, I don't know what they are. The tiny kind that get into flour if it sits around too long. Really gross. We're gonna have to trash these." She waved at the bags on the cart.

Flour, and by extension, any kind of baked good, had become a precious commodity. Wheat didn't grow here in the Valley, so the supply was limited. Until we could find a way to trade with a group that could grow it, who would be several states away from us, we'd been involuntarily weaning ourselves off of wheat. But it seemed like a criminal act to just toss this huge pallet's worth. There had to be a way to make use of it. I sure didn't want to eat buggy bread and no one I knew would do it, either. Well, almost no one. Then I could almost feel the warmth from the metaphorical light bulb over my head.

"Why don't you bake it into dog biscuits? Bugs are protein. And dogs won't care if they eat bugs. You could probably even bake it into cat kibble, too."

The woman gaped at me. I asked her, "You're doing a lot of baking right here on site, aren't you?" I already knew the store had a decent baking kitchen, as well as a butcher room.

I expanded on my idea. "Well, *some* baking, at least. You could get a few recipes for dog biscuits from a book or maybe online." I looked at Sharon, who shrugged her shoulders at me. "That flour can be mixed with oats, peanut butter, maybe a little ground meat of some kind. Roll it out, and cut into pieces and bake it until it's dry and crunchy. Or you could run it through a sausage machine, and cut it up into kibble. There's all kinds of recipes for dog biscuits and treats out there. And that flour is too precious to just throw it away. People don't want to eat bugs in their food, but dogs won't care."

The woman looked astonished. She called out to someone a few aisles away, a manager, apparently. She repeated my idea to the newcomer, who got a delighted look on her face. "That's brilliant!" She gushed. "There's a lot of pets around, and yeah, we are running low on pet food. We definitely need to supplement that."

The idea bulb over in my head was still glowing. "You'll want to keep the buggy flour separate from your other supplies, back in the kitchen. And the finished product too, naturally. Probably work in small test batches, until you come up with a good mix. You could mix in vegetable scraps, too – maybe Mercados can provide some, or the gardens might have excess veggies. And you'll need something to package the biscuits in, too – baggies or tubs or something. Make sure they're cooked really really well, too, to kill those bugs. Don't want to give anyone any intestinal parasites. Not sure if that kind of bug can even be a parasite, but still, just to be safe…" They nodded excitedly. I could practically see the implementation wheels spinning in their heads. The two women dashed off to the tables that stocked the bestsellers, to see if there were any dog recipe books. I wasn't sure that Costco had ever stocked that kind of book from before. But the women could easily make a run out to a bookstore or the library, too, if needed.

Sharon was staring at me. She said, "Okay, *now* I see why Ariana wants you to be Mayor. You *do* come up with all kinds of creative ideas."

I frowned at her. "You know, I really didn't want the Mayor job. I didn't go gunning for that. I only agreed to do it because they asked me to and I couldn't figure out how to turn it down without disappointing everyone. It's gonna be a pain in the arse kind of job if I get it."

"You'll get through it. And it's not an 'if,' it's a 'when.' You're leading the polls." She turned to head down another aisle.

"Polls? What polls? Since when we do have polls? There's no polls during the apocalypse!" I called after her, but Sharon just kept on shopping and smiling.

Chapter 17

After we returned home, Sharon worked on setting up a phone system for the house. From Costco's dwindling supply, she had grabbed a package system that included a console and six cordless remote phones. Even knowing about planned obsolescence and that this system might only work for a few years, she figured it was better for us to use it while it could be used, rather than be unreachable. She connected it to a small phone router she had scrounged, which was in turn, connected to the cable co-axial line, which the city VoIP communications network was also connected to. Then she waved her magic communications wand to give us an extension number on the city's phone network, and 'Ta Da!' we had a working phone system.

Well, not quite. I didn't fully understand everything that she did. I was just happy to have a phone system, so that people could call us, instead of actually having to come ring our door bell, in order to share important news, or drag one or another of us off to some meeting. If I was going to end up as mayor (shudder), I needed to be reachable, relatively speaking.

We had a fun time explaining the etiquette of a single-phone number household system to Micah. As a 12 year old, he had never lived in a world without cell phones, where everyone had their own number.

I started. "Okay, so rule number one: keep pen and paper handy near each phone, so that you can take a message for someone."

Micah asked, "Why don't we just text the message?"

"These phones don't do text. It's one line for the entire household."

Micah tried, "Well, can't they just leave a voice message?"

"If you answer the call, it might not be for you. If no one answers, then the answering machine picks up. If you listen to the messages, write it down and let whoever know about it, promptly."

Micah: "Why would I pick up the phone, if the call is not for me?"

"Incoming calls will ring on every extension. You won't know who it's for, unless you answer it. We don't have caller ID, for the moment."

Micah: "Can't I just transfer them to the answering machine?"

Sharon interrupted. "Uh, how do you know about transferring calls? That's not a regular cell phone feature. That's a network phone thing."

Micah looked at Sharon. "Something I heard my dad do all the time, before. He had a work phone in his home office."

We eyed him carefully. I wondered if he was playing us. He seemed to be picking up on Gordon's wicked smart sense of humor.

I redirected. "So, if you pick up a phone, and someone else is already using it, you should hang up immediately. That's a privacy thing. It's rude to listen in on other people's calls."

Micah made the innocent eyes at me. "Does that work both ways?" he asked.

Sharon responded. "Of course. No one will listen to your calls, either."

"Wait, what calls are you making? Who will you be calling?" I asked. I raised my eyebrows at him. "You wouldn't be planning on calling any *girls*, now, would you?"

Micah blushed. "Gross! Of course not!"

"Because, you know, if you can't handle the responsibility of a cordless phone, we could always get a corded one. You know, in my day, we had *one* phone in the house, and we all had to share it, and you could only go as far as the cord allowed, so everyone could hear you."

I gave him the hairy eyeball, to make it clear I was serious. Sharon busted out laughing, and Micah grinned when he saw through the teasing.

Gordon came hobbling into the room, leaning on his new cane. He'd finally managed to get a shower and was cleaned up. He wanted to know what we were giggling over, so Sharon showed him the new phones. The main console was in the kitchen, and a remote charging station, with phone, was positioned in each of the occupied bedrooms.

After that, Gordon settled himself on the couch in the living room. I needed to head out to the weekly Town Hall meeting, but I had a little time to kill before that. Gordon had already decided he wasn't going, as his foot hurt too much. I inspected the bite mark, and was relieved it had not swelled or spread too much. I was pretty sure that confirmed it was not a brown recluse spider bite, which was a huge relief. I brought him a fresh ice pack and got most of the dog pack settled around him. Tyrion and Zilla insisted on climbing on top of him, and snuggled in. Oreo hopped up on the couch, and settled near his feet, which he wasn't really prone to doing. Amex took the nearby chair, and Duchess stretched out on the floor.

I asked Gordon if he wanted anything else. I offered to setup the DVD player with some movies for him. He said he'd rather just have some music, instead. He'd been spiking a bit of fever and thought it might come back. He didn't think he'd be able to focus on a movie. And another nap was sounding like a good idea. So I got his tablet, which was stocked with his music collection. I nudged Oreo off the couch, so I could sit with Gordon's injured foot propped in my lap. I flicked through his music collection on his device.

"What do you want to hear?" I asked him.

Gordon said, "I dunno. Maybe just pick one of the playlists."

His music collection was pretty haphazardly organized. "Come on, this is mess, you can do better. You gotta classify, organize, thematicize them."

Gordon raised an eyebrow at me. "Is that a word? Thematicize?"

I shrugged. "Okay, I'm seeing lots of 70's and 80's rock here. Tell me what your favorites are."

Gordon said, "They all are. They wouldn't be there if I didn't like them."

"Really? You're telling me that 'N Synch and early Britney Spears are your favorites?"

"That was Jenny's music. She had to use my computer. So I could supervise, make sure she didn't overspend on iTunes. I copied the entire music library to that when I got it." He nodded at the tablet in my lap.

"Uh huh. Sure ya did." I smirked at him. "So, let's look at what else we have here… Billy Joel or Elton John?" I asked him.

Gordon: "Billy Joel."

"Metallica or Guns'n'Roses?"

Gordon: "Oh, that's a tough one… it's a tossup. Wait, do I even have Metallica in there?" He leaned up to try to take the tablet from me, but I pulled it out of his reach.

"Nirvana or Pearl Jam?" I asked.

Gordon: "Nirvana." He slumped back down on the couch.

"Michael Jackson or the Artist formerly known as Prince?"

Gordon: "Eh, neither. Couldn't stand either one of them. And neither of those are in there." He gestured at the tablet.

"Yes they are. Must be from Jenny's list. And it's still my turn. Neil Diamond or Frank Sinatra?"

Gordon: "Another toughie. I'll take both."

"Meatloaf or Queen?"

Gordon: "Also both."

"Bon Jovi or Aerosmith?"

Gordon: "Definitely Aerosmith."

"R.E.O. Speedwagon or R.E.M.?"

Gordon eyed me. "R.E.M. And you're mixing genres, now."

"I know. Peter Gabriel or Gabriel Byrne?"

Gordon raised an eyebrow at me. "Do you mean David Byrne?"

"Yes. Talking Heads. Burning down the house. I always get them mixed up."

Gordon let his head flop back on the cushion. "Yeah, both of them."

"Grateful Dead or Jimmy Buffet?"

Gordon said, "Grateful Dead was auditory genius. Did I ever tell you about the summer I went on the road with the Dead Heads?"

"No, you didn't. You're bullshitting me. The Who or The Stones?"

Gordon: "Also both."

"Okay, hang on, thinking…. Peter Gabriel or Phil Collins?"

"Now you're repeating yourself. Peter Gabriel, hands down.'"

"John, Paul, Ringo, or George?"

Gordon: "Paul. Next?"

"Free Bird or Stairway to Heaven?"

Gordon. "Ya know what, that's another 'both'. You're gonna have to come up with some real crap, to get me to pick out the good stuff. And I didn't buy crap." Then he smirked. "But I may have downloaded some of it from Napster, back in the day…"

I smacked him lightly on the leg, his good one, not the one with the injured foot. "Okay, I've built you a new custom play list of just your personal favorites. How's this." I started the first song, a Celine Dion ballad.

He grimaced, and cocked an eyebrow at me again. "That's not exactly a personal favorite, you know."

"Yeah, but it's good napping music." We sat for a bit. I scratched whichever dog happened to be sitting with me at the moment. I wondered if I had time for a nap, too, before going downtown to the meeting. Probably not.

Gordon nudged me with his good foot. "So, you've never told me what music you like."

"Well, I like all the stuff you've got here."

Gordon said, "Well, yeah, who doesn't. But what else? What's your secret musical indulgence, when no one is around to hear?"

"Uh…" Oh geez, did I really need to tell him this?

Gordon prodded me again. "Come on. You're gonna say you like Country, right?" I shook my head. Ugh, no.

Gordon went on: "Worse? Oh no, you like Rap, don't you? I knew it. I knew it deep down inside… This, this is the seed of destruction between us." He theatrically threw up his arms and flopped them back down on the couch. Tyrion grumbled at him reproachfully, as he was getting jiggled around.

I was still shaking my head, and struggling between giggling at his antics, and my true secret musical love.

"Come on, out with it. Tell me now."

I grimaced, and wrapped my arms around my stomach. In a tiny little voice, I finally said: "Bagpipes. I like bagpipes and drum corps stuff."

Gordon popped his eyes at me in surprise. "Seriously?" I nodded. He stared at me for a moment, and then said, "It's the kilts, isn't it?"

I struggled to keep the smirk off my face.

Gordon added, "Well, that actually kinda makes sense. You gotta thing for me, and I gotta thing for the drums, so, ergo, you like drummers. I can see that."

I grinned at him. "Actually, it's kinda like chocolate; you only need a little bit of it, to be happy. Too much of it, and you'll make yourself sick on it," I pointed out. He grinned back at me.

"I'll keep that in mind." He winked at me. Oh geez. He was planning something already. I could see the gears spinning inside his head. And I was going to get a sugar rush sick when it eventually happened, I was sure.

Sharon and I headed downtown to the weekly Town Hall meeting. They'd been moved to the school auditorium, which was air conditioned. 4pm on a Saturday afternoon in late May was much too hot for outdoor meetings.

Robert Ruckels was still nominally in charge of running these meetings. Ariana had single page agendas to hand out, covering the main talking points, which a lot of people folded up into fans and waved at themselves. The auditorium may have been air conditioned, but there were still a lot of bodies warming the place up. I made a wild guesstimate that there were about 200 people in attendance. That was actually down from some other meetings. These were getting routine enough that people didn't feel as much urgent need to show up for every one of them. I wondered if they could be scaled back to every other week, or maybe even monthly?

Robert called the meeting to order, and started out with an update on current progress of the work crews.

"I'm happy to report that we are about 95% finished with clearing the bodies out of homes inside the city limits. Crews are still checking on businesses, abandoned cars, and other structures, to make sure that all remains have been identified, and transferred for memorial cremation. I'd like to extend my heartfelt appreciation to all of the people who have worked on this project. I know it was an extraordinarily difficult job, and we are forever grateful for the tact and kindness these teams have demonstrated."

Robert started clapping his hands, nodding around to those he knew had been on body detail teams, and the audience promptly joined in.

When the round of appreciation applause started to die down, Ruckels resumed. "Pastor Daniel has requested a few moments to update us on the status of the cremations. Pastor?"

Pastor Daniel had been sitting in the first row. He stood up and quickly climbed up the few steps to the side of the stage, to join Ruckels. He spoke in a loud commanding voice.

"Folks, before I get to business, I'd like to have a moment of silence to commemorate those who have departed. Their physical bodies remain, and are being reduced to holy ash as we speak. Let us send their souls to their afterlife with the power of prayer."

Pastor Daniel bowed his head. Ruckels said, "Very well," and also bowed his head. Most of the crowd also did as prompted, turning their faces downward. I counted off about 30 seconds before I saw Daniel nodded back at Ruckels.

Pastor Daniel went on. "Thank you, everyone, for that. As you know, we have had to cremate the physical bodies of most of the victims of the Superflu. I know that this has distressed many of you, as you would have preferred burial in consecrated ground for your loved ones. As Mr. Ruckels has explained many times, it was an urgent public health matter to dispose of the bodies as quickly as possible. The nature of the emergency did not leave us much leeway for the niceties of formal burial, or even traditional cremation ovens. My people and I have kept extensive records of the people we have cremated, and also, where possible, we have kept ashes segregated, packaged and labeled. If groups of family members were brought to us, we cremated them together, again, for expediency. If anyone is still interested in reclaiming the ashes of your own loved ones, please come see me after wards." There was some murmuring in the crowd.

Daniel went on. "An idea was suggested to me a little while ago which I want to share with everyone. We still have many thousands of unclaimed cremains. I've been told that it's possible to mix ash into cement, for permanent disposal. In the correct proportions, it should not have any effect on the structural integrity of the cement. I propose that the unclaimed ashes of our departed citizens be used in the concrete that will form the memorial that is already starting to take shape in the park next door."

Excited murmuring fluttered around me. That actually was a pretty interesting idea. I looked around for the construction guys who were handling the job. I saw Ali a few rows behind me. I raised my eyebrows at him questioningly and he shrugged at me. He didn't know if it would work.

While I was looking at Ali, a man on the other side of the audience stood up and joined Daniel on stage. I recognized him as one of the construction guys on the project.

"Hey, I'm Max, and I'm helping with building the memorial." He nodded at Pastor Daniel and responded to the query in more detail.

"Yeah, we could do that. We're planning on pouring the foundation next week. Did you want ash mixed into that, too? I need to do some research on just how much foreign material we can mix into the concrete, and how it will affect it. My concern is that adding ash into it, might make it porous, which will weaken the structural matrix. But I can definitely see it working for the walls and body part."

The overall tone in the auditorium seemed mixed. I suspected some people were objecting. To me, it seemed like a good way to dispose of the ashes in a dignified way. The memorial would be a site of reverence and remembrance for generations to come. Encasing the cremains in a dedicated monument it seemed like a more dignified option than just leaving them in a pile at the landfill or abandoned in a warehouse.

After more audience chatter, Robert took control of the podium again.

"Okay, that takes care of the body disposal portion of our agenda. Next up: housing. Likewise, I'm happy to report that we are mostly caught up on making homes livable within the Power On zone. I believe that almost everyone who wants to move into the Zone, has done so, or is doing so now." He glanced back at Ariana, who was co-managing the meeting with him. She nodded, and stepped up next to him.

"Yes. If anyone is still living in a house outside the consolidation zone, and has lost power, or water pressure, please come see us afterwards. We can still place you. The crews are even preparing extra houses for future occupancy, or overflow. Or people who are just sick of their roommates." A few cheers went up from the audience. She grinned at them, waved and sat back down.

Robert resumed. "Okay, next: Water. You gotta keep boiling it. I know this is frustrating. Believe me, I'm probably the most frustrated person in the city, that the water, *my* water, isn't clean enough to drink straight from the tap. Here's what's happening: Our water comes from underground aquifers and from the Salt River, diverted through canals. It has to be treated at the processing plant to be clean enough to drink. We do that through a combination of processes, including filtration, sedimentation and chemical treatment. The problem is that my supply of chemicals is limited. Even with the scavenging and resource collection, I have to very carefully manage the treatment chemicals supply until we can find a source that can continue to provide them, reliably. That means that someone, somewhere, has to restart the manufacturing of those chemicals. And right now, I don't think that's happening. So, I've had to cut back on the quantities of chemicals used in the treatment process. We're putting in enough to be safe for bathing, but not enough for drinking it. Boiling it is the option of last resort, to make sure that any pathogens are killed and don't infect you. So please, keep on doing it and make sure your friends and neighbors know to do it, too."

The audience grumbled. That chore was kind of a pain in the rear.

Robert's next agenda topic was actually to introduce Sharon.

"Okay, everyone, I'd like to you to meet a new member of the management team. This is Sharon Walker." He gestured to her, and she stood up and joined him.

"Sharon is our telecommunications and networking leader. Our CIO, effectively. Sharon, explain the plan for restoring communications, if you would, please."

Sharon took over, and told the audience the same things she'd been telling me for several weeks. That cell phone networks were pretty much toast, that land line and cable line communications would have to be consolidated into a converged network. She said she'd be providing instructions and suggestions via the city website soon, and handouts would be available as well. She also had lists of recommended websites that still functioned and contained a wealth of survival information and news from other parts of the country. Most of those sites were blogs and wikis, produced and maintained by average citizens, and not experts, news reporters or government officials. The information available was very hodge-podge, and still coalescing, so she warned people to treat everything with a healthy dose of skepticism.

Sharon finished her announcements and turned the meeting back over to Robert. The meeting wrapped up on time, without too much audience chatter, and questioning. For once. I think the heat outside was having a soporific effect on people. Ali and the construction crew cornered me on the way out, to ask my opinion about the idea of mixing ash into the concrete. I explained to them that structurally, I knew nothing about how it would affect the monument's stability. Spiritually, I thought it was an excellent idea. Overall, I didn't think it would have any effect on the visual design, so I didn't have any additional input on the matter.

Afterwards, as usual, most people congregated on the patio outside Mercados and at the pub next door. They had the misters running full blast, and when beer was present, people seemed much more willing to tolerate the heat. Sharon got into a discussion with some people who apparently had some IT backgrounds in their former lives and were interested in helping her. She seemed to be conducting a group interview of them so I left her to it.

I found Ariana at a table with Cassandra. She was wheeling around on one of those little carts that goes under the knee, and lifts the foot and lower leg up behind her, to keep the weight off the healing bone. Ariana introduced me, as we had not officially met before, even though I knew who she was.

After the introductions, I asked her, "So, your dad made it back to Oak Creek okay?"

She nodded. "Yeah, he had to get back to taking care of our own people up there. We've got a garden too, but it's a lot smaller, and we're a few weeks behind. The Canyon doesn't get as much light as you do down here, so the growing season is a little behind. He wanted to supervise that."

I nodded. "And what's your role with the group? Do you have a specific job or anything?"

"Well, I studied accounting in school, but there doesn't seem to be much need for that now." She frowned. "Mostly, I just did whatever needed to be done. Helped out where it was needed. Did a lot of patrolling. Dad taught me all about guns and military procedure, so there's that." She trailed off.

"Did you help with the training exercise our newbies went to a few weeks ago?" I asked her.

"Yeah, I got partnered up in one of the teams, helped them work out the mechanics of going house to house in hostile conditions. It didn't seem to me they needed all that much training - they were pretty good, already knew a lot of stuff. Your Officer Adams, he's done a good job with them."

I smiled at that. "Yeah, he does know what he doing. But Jake also told me about how a housing compound was keeping a bunch of people as slaves? Is that accurate?" I had never doubted Jake's story, but I wanted her point of view on it.

"Yeah, a bunch of squatters were kidnapping others, making them work for them. They really need to be kicked out. I'm so grateful your people were able to help with that. It was a numbers game; between the Chandler people, and the Luke people, and ours, we way outnumbered them. And we saved a lot of innocent people, too." She was nodding earnestly.

I didn't press her much on the details of the raid. Then somehow the conversation wandered to other topics. Cassandra shared an interesting tidbit of information about harvesting acorns. She explained that Oak Creek Canyon was named that for a good reason, and where there were oak trees, there were acorns. Her people spent a lot of time gathering them where they had fallen. Spring was not the right season for acorn harvesting and so a lot of last fall's acorns had gone moldy sitting on the ground. But some had dried nicely, and were usable. They could be shelled, with the application of a little elbow grease. And then the nut meats could be leached of their bitter tannins, by soaking in water. Finally, they could be ground into a course meal or flour, and used in baked goods, either alone, or mixed with regular wheat flour.

I asked her what it tasted like, and she said it was kind of an acquired taste. She offered to bring some samples, when she had a chance. I also wondered aloud if it was going to be a future trade good for her people. She wasn't certain. It was an enormous amount of hand labor, for not a lot of finished product in the end. They would need to find ways to scale up production efficiently, and that would be a challenge, if they chose to pursue that.

We continued chatting for awhile. I noticed that our housing expert, Caleb, was sitting a few tables away, withMallorie, the young Mormon woman I'd met last fall. I nudged Ariana and nodded at the pair. "What's up with that? Did you know they knew each other?" The two were talking with several other people, but they were sitting side-by-side, very close together. Too close, for this heat.

Ariana grinned at me. "You didn't hear? They're engaged!"

"Engaged? I didn't even know they were acquainted! Huh! That seems awfully fast…"

Ariana said, "Not for Mormons, it's not. I've heard lots of meeting-to-marriage stories that happen within just a few months. When they know, they know."

Cassandra nodded in agreement. "I grew up in Mesa. Knew lots of Mormons in school. That's just how they roll."

I shrugged. "Huh. Well, that's fantastic news. I'm glad they found each other." Mallorie noticed me staring at them, and gave me a little wave. I smiled at her. Then I pointed at my ring finger, then her, smiled even more broadly, and gave her a thumbs up. She giggled, and told Caleb what I had communicated. He grinned at us and waved too, and then went back to the conversation going on at his table.

Another thought occurred me. "Ariana, does the city issue marriage licenses?"

"No, that was a county function before. And there's still no one over there, at the county administration building. At least, still no phone calls going through."

"Well, I guess that's another thing we're gonna have to start doing ourselves." I smiled at her.

"Yep. That's what we call 'a good problem to have'." She grinned back at me.

Chapter 18

On Monday morning I went to work in the studio as usual. I had been wondering how I was going to balance making pottery with being mayor. It was still unclear to me how much desk time the city work was going to require. But the studio had a very old air conditioner unit on the roof and it was not working well. I had a feeling the room would become very uncomfortable very soon. Which made the idea of going to an air conditioned office instead much more attractive.

My apprentices were not quite the early birds that I was. Which was fine. They had proven to me that they were capable of working unsupervised. So I came early and left early. Or I left at mid day for a siesta, and came back in the evenings. The apprentices were allowed to set their own routine as needed.

So I had already been at the wheel for a couple of hours when Jenna came in, alone. She came straight to me.

"Maggie, I'm really freaked out. I don't know where Kaycee and Kyrene are. They went out on Saturday and haven't come back."

She was visibly worried, distraught.

"What? I don't get it. Start at the beginning, please." I told her.

"Kyrene got a call, from a friend she knew at college. He's living in Phoenix, on Camelback Mountain, and they were throwing a huge party, and he wanted her to come, and bring all her friends. Ky invited me to go, but I didn't want to. But Kaycee went with her, and they haven't come back, and I'm really freakin' out. They're not answering their phones, and I can barely get any signal most of the time, and I don't know what to do…"

Jenna was practically crying now. I scratched my head, as I tried to parse the information. And then realized I'd just rubbed wet clay onto my forehead. Lovely.

"Okay, let's figure this out. It's going to be alright. We'll figure out what to do." I wiped my hands on my towel and stood up to give her a hug.

"Okay, do you know exactly where this party was?" I asked her.

Jenna answered, "I'm not sure. She kept saying it was at the castle on the mountain. I don't know what that means. There's no castles around here."

"What did she tell you about this friend who invited her?"

Jenna said, "Not much. Just some guy she knew from college."

"Was he a classmate, professor, something else?"

Jenna shook her head. She didn't know. I wondered what other information I could draw out.

"Did she say what kind of party it was? Movies and games? Pool party? Barbecue? Beer bash?"

"She just said it was some big wild party, a rager. She said the house was huge, so it would be like going to one of those really big clubs. Maggie, what if something happened to them?" Her voice was high pitched, and her eyes were getting red around the rims. I noticed slight bags under her eyes, too, as if she hadn't slept well.

"Okay, just breathe for a minute. Deep breath in… and out through the nose. Again."

Once she calmed down a little, I said, "Okay, let's think about this calmly. What else do you know about this party?"

Jenna paused, and then her eyes got big. She pulled her cell phone out of her pocket. "Wait, there was a Google+ post about it."

Jenna tapped at her phone for a few moments, and pulled up the post. The calendar item listed a title: "Memorial Day Weekend Blowout Party." It had Saturday's date, and start time of "12 noon." There was no end time listed. There was a photo of a medieval looking castle on the side of a mountain, and an address. There was a link to a Google Map of the location, but when I tapped it, nothing loaded. There was no wi-fi in the studio. She must have had the calendar post cached in her phone's local memory.

I studied the phone for a few moments, thinking. I had completely forgotten that it was Memorial Day today.

"Okay, we're going to need some help with this one. Come on, let's go across the street." City Hall was actually down a block and on the other side, but Jenna knew what I was referring to.

I had the little dogs with me today, so I leashed them up to come with us. I told Aaron where we were going and not to wait for us. He nodded and waved at us as we quickly walked out.

City Hall's main entrance lead to a large foyer with a security guard desk, which was unoccupied. I went straight up the stairs to the second floor to Ariana's suite of offices. She had several assistants to help with data processing and communications and such, and had them stashed in cubicles near her private office. Ariana was right where I expected to find her. We explained the situation to her, and Jenna showed her the phone, as well. Ariana was baffled, too.

"I think this is a police matter," she said. I agreed with her, so we all trooped back out of the office down the stairs again, and down the first floor hallway, where Zach had a suite of similar offices, cubicles and conference rooms. His conference room was equipped with computers, large monitors, and overhead projectors pointed at wall mounted screens. It was clearly a police operations command center. Luckily, Zach was actually in his office, instead of out on patrol.

One more time, we ran through the situation. He asked most of the same questions I had: where did the girls go, who was throwing this party, where was it, etc. He studied Jenna' phone, the picture and posted information. He tapped on his on computer keyboard. I was surprised to see a Google Maps image appear on screen.

"I thought Google was down?" I asked him.

He replied. "The main search site was down for a while, but just came back up a couple of weeks ago. Sharon's not sure what happened to bring it back. But actually, the Maps area has been working all along. So is the Google+ system. You just had to know the deep URL to get to it."

"Oh." I couldn't think of anything to add to that.

Zach zoomed in on the address of the house. It was, in fact, on Camelback Mountain in Phoenix. The area immediately surrounding the mountain had large, expensive houses built on large lots. They crept up the side of the mountain to about a third of the way up. Any higher, and the ground was too steep to build on. Or it was protected municipal property. I wasn't sure which. But I was sure it was the "high rent district" for the wealthy and famous.

Zach switched from map view, to street view. A distorted, slightly abstracted image of the front of the house appeared. It appeared to be constructed of stone, with towers at the corners, crenelations along the roof line, and an iron gate at the entrance. Yep, that was a castle all right.

We all stared at the image for a few moments. I looked at Zach. I could practically see the "Officer Adams" persona taking over his whole demeanor.

He turned to Jenna, "Tell me again what Kyrene said about the party at this house?"

"Just that it was going to be big. She said it would be a rager. Like at a club."

Zach thought for a few moments. He tapped the radio mic clipped to his collar. "HQ to Jake, Randy, come in."

I heard a click and then, "Randy to HQ. What's up, boss?"

Zach clicked his radio again. "I need you two to come in to the station ASAP. Got a project for you."

Randy clicked back. "On our way."

***

Zach moved us to the conference room, and had us sit down at the table. He woke up one of the computers, and connected it to the projector. He put the map of the castle's address onto the wall screen. Then he called Sharon on the inter-office phone line, and asked her to join us.

Sharon entered a few moments later. Zach said, "Can you help me dig up some information on this?" he pointed at the image of the castle, displayed next to the map. "I know Google is up, but it's not returning any search results."

"Yeah, I know. The home page is up, but the databases that power the searches are not back online yet." Sharon answered him. She studied the projection. "What is that?"

I blurted out first. "It's a castle on Camelback Mountain. You know Kaycee, right?" She nodded. As a graphic designer and communications specialist, Kaycee actually worked here at City Hall, so they were acquainted now.

"Well, she went with my apprentice, Kyrene, to a big party at that castle. On Saturday. They're not back yet."

Sharon's eyes bugged out. "Wow. Three days? That's some serious partying…" she trailed off. She read the stricken expression on Jenna's face.

"They weren't supposed to be gone that long, were they?"

We shook our heads.

"And you don't know why they haven't come back yet."

Jenna shook her head some more. "And I can't get them on their cell phones." She was struggling to hold back the crying.

Sharon turned back to the images. "Okay, let's try some other search tools, maybe a historical register." Sharon turned to another computer and began pushing keys, too. She sent URLs to Zach to try searches on, most of which didn't work. And the few that did, didn't produce very much information. After awhile, she finally tried an encyclopedia website, which had a listing of genuine castles built in the U.S. There weren't a lot of them. Mostly, they had been built as architectural eccentricities by wealthy people with more money than common sense.

From that information, she was able to click into an archive of old TV shows, and found an episode that toured the castle, and explained it's history. While we watched, Randy and Jake appeared. We backfilled them on what was going on, and then watched the recorded show again. That helped everyone understand the layout of building.

The castle had been the boondoggle project of a local wealthy philanthropist. It had been built mostly from the very same stone that was excavated out of the mountain side. Much of the interior furnishings were authentic period pieces, including a lot of iron gates, tapestries and heavy wooden furniture. It actually looked like a cool place to visit, but I certainly wouldn't want to live there. But I could also see how it would be attractive to any survivor, looking to live the lifestyle of the rich and famous, in the biggest house on the hill. And I could see how it would be a great place to throw a raging party, too.

The guys looked at each other.

Zach started first. "Okay, brainstorming time. How do we locate the girls, and get them out?"

Randy asked, "Are we sure they're still in the castle? Could they have left and gotten into an accident on the way home?"

Jake asked, "Are we sure they even made it to the castle in the first place? Do we know what route they took to get there?" Jenna shook her head at that.

Zach asked, "Is it possible they might have stopped off somewhere else, on their way home? Another friend to visit, maybe a boyfriend?"

Jenna shook her head again. "I don't know who they would have known that's not here in the zone," she said. Kyrene was around 20, I thought, and Kaycee was a few years older than that. The three girls were sharing a small house, so they had gotten very well acquainted. But Jenna was much younger than the other two, and didn't have quite as much life experience with things like partying and boys and living on their own. She looked up to the two girls like big sisters.

Randy asked another brainstorming question. "Is there any possibility that that they've been drugged, or got too drunk to keep control?"

We all looked around at each other. I finally admitted what everyone else was thinking. "Yeah, I think that's a real possibility."

Zach asked Jenna again to repeat what little she knew about the guy who issued the invitation. She didn't even have a name for him. Just that he was someone Kyrene had known from college.

"Are we sure this is the guy running the party, or is he just one of the people going to it?" Jenna shook her head some more. No, she was not sure that was the case.

Zach said, "I think we're going to have to go do some on site investigating, find out what's going on."

Jake said, "We're going to need more people." He unclipped his own radio mic from his collar, and stepped out of the room to summon some colleagues.

Randy suggested, "Maybe we should get the drones out, and do a fly over."

Zach nodded, "Good idea. And take a regular car, not the patrol cars. And change into street clothes. You might just have to walk up the front door and ask to join the party. In fact, take one of the big trucks, and bring some medical supplies. And food and water. I got a feeling there's something preventing those girls from leaving..."

Zach continued his own brainstorming, and giving orders for Jake and Randy. He was putting together a rescue mission by the seat of his pants. The plan was to try to get close to the mansion, observe for activity, and then evaluate. But if they had to pull one or more people out, or otherwise breakup the party, they were taking supplies and equipment with them. In the end, they took a large box truck, which would be parked a few streets away, out of sight of the house. They were preparing for all possible situations, from a bunch of passed out people with hangovers from hell, to an open portal to the underworld, and everything in between.

Other cops joined us in the control center room. They were briefed and given instructions. Everyone was going in street clothes, not cop uniform. They would carry concealed weapons, though. The castle location was out of our city jurisdiction, and our small police force didn't really have enough manpower to bust up a big house party, let alone the means to make any arrests. Ariana's face darkened at that realization. It was a continuous pain point for her. I wondered if we should call Luke AFB and ask for manpower assistance.

The control center buzzed with activity for awhile, as the cops went in and out gathering equipment, studying the map, images and video. They called over to the hospital, to get a medic to go with them, in case any emergency first aid would be required. They tested the drone's camera and made sure it was sending data to the controlling computer. They tested that computer to make sure it was sending data back to us. It was working, here in the local office, but everyone doubted it would do so once it got out in the field. It relied on wi-fi and satellite signals to communicate with the larger world.

Kyle had arrived at HQ as his training officer was one of the cops going on the mission. Keyl clearly expected to be included in the mission as well. However, Zach declined his request to go. He was too young, and not fully trained in under cover operations. It was unclear to me how much undercover work any of the other cops had done. Besides, how hard was it to walk into a party and ask for a beer?

Kyle seemed frustrated by the denial. I was studying him, and his reaction to disappointing news. He was very carefully not looking at Jenna on the opposite side of the room.

I was studying both of them, so I wasn't paying attention when the crowd of men at the other end of the room started laughing. One of them held up a bag and announced they had the perfect house warming present to get them in the front door. I looked at Zach He explained it was some of the meth they had seized from Petra's house after they had destroyed her lab.

Ariana, Jenna and I were sitting against the side wall in the conference room, watching the action around us. Ariana was tense, but quiet. I could tell she didn't like what was happening, but she was wearing her big girl pants. It wasn't like anyone had come up with a better way of getting into the house to see what was going on, and where our people had gone.

I shoulder bumped her. "It's gonna be okay. They're pro's. They know what they're doing." She nodded at me, but the frown lines remained. I scooped up Zilla from the floor and deposited her in Ariana's lap. Ariana settled the dog, and petted her. I did the same with Tyrion. They may not be trained therapy dogs but they were a comfort.

Finally, the cops had all their gear loaded and were ready to head out. Zach huddled them for final instructions.

"Okay, we really don't know what you're going to find when you get there. Watch the streets carefully on the approach. Look for recent car accidents. It could be something simple like that." Jenna shuddered and almost whimpered out loud.

Zach continued. "Send the drone over the house first, maximum distance. Don't approach too close, too quickly. I don't want the occupants to know they're being watched. Try coming at them from the north, down the side of the mountain. Try to find out how many people are about: count the cars on the drive, and the street below. Listen for music, or other noise, too. Once we can figure out how active the party is, we can evaluate and decide how many people to send in. If the party is still going on and is really crowded, you can probably slip in one or two at a time. Don't let on that you came together, or know each other. Find out where the girls are, and what their condition is, and then report back to me. We'll decide then what to do next. Any questions?"

He looked around at his men. They were solemn, and quiet for a moment.

Zach sent them off. "Okay, move out!"

As the guys were filing out of the room, one by one, I waved my hand, and said, in my best old-man Billy Crystal voice, "Have fun storming the castle!"

Beside me, Ariana groaned. "I can't believe you just said that! Out loud!"

Sharon snorted loudly, from across the room. Jenna looked confused. Zach smirked, and asked, "How long you been waiting to use that one?"

I glanced at my imaginary wrist watch, and said, "'Bout thirty minutes."

***

It would take the guys more than forty five minutes to even to get to the area around the mountain. That left the rest of us with time on our hands and little to do except worry.

I saw Zach pull Kyle aside, and give him some alternate instructions. I was still hanging out in the conference room, reviewing some of the data they had found online. So I heard Zach's instructions to Kyle. "I need you to go back out on patrol here in town. Drive the zone and ask anyone if they've seen or heard from the girls, or if they know anything about this party."

Kyle nodded. Zach continued his lecture. "I know you wanted to go on the mission but your training hasn't covered this kind of scenario. Frankly, no one's has. And I think we're outnumbered. In Sedona, we outnumbered that gang at least two to one. I suspect it's going to be the opposite here. And that means we're not looking to shut them down or kick them out. Since we're not looking to make any arrests, the end game is just to observe, locate and extract the girls."

Kyle nodded again. Zach said, "Okay, head out. If you get any solid information, radio it back in ASAP."

Kyle left. I turned to Jenna, who had just gotten back from a bathroom break. Ariana asked her to bring back a lunch order from Mercados, which she would call in, in just a moment. I glanced at the clock on the wall. I was surprised to see it was getting close to mid-day. It seemed like this whole thing had only started minutes ago.

I turned back to the computer, and tried to dig into some details about the guy who had posted the Google+ calendar event about the party. All I could find was a name (Lance), and a brief bio (grad student at the university) with a face shot of an ordinary looking guy. The links on his profile to other social media sites returned error messages. Those sites were still down.

Zach sat at the head of the conference table. "Ariana is not going to be happy with how this operation goes down, you know," he said.

I looked up. "Yeah, I know."

Sharon asked, "Why?"

I responded. "Ari likes law and order, due process. If there's a problem, if a law is being broken, she wants people to be arrested, tried, and imprisoned. But we don't have the means to do that."

Zach added, "It's more than that. One, we don't know that any laws have actually been broken. It's not illegal for girls to go to a party. They're over the age of consent, so they're allowed to drink, if they want to. Two, we don't know if the people holding the party are doing anything illegal, either. Three, they're out of our jurisdiction. We're Chandler, that's Phoenix. We quite literally don't have the right to make any arrests there. And four, as you said, we don't have any way to prosecute anyone, even if any arrests could be made."

"Yeah, I know." I repeated. "I've made that same point to Ari several times in the last few months."

I looked up at Zach. "Any luck on finding any lawyers or judges so far?"

He answered, "I've run into a couple of lawyers; but they were practicing corporate law, or estate planning, financial stuff. Not criminal lawyers. There's one guy I saw who I know used to be a defense lawyer, before the flu. I'm certain I saw him a few times when I was testifying in court on arrest charges. But now the guy is telling everyone he was a salesman. I think he doesn't want to go back to lawyering, and won't admit to having any experience."

I frowned at that. A lawyer who was disgusted with his own profession? Huh, who would have guessed it?

I sighed. Getting a criminal justice system back up and running was going to be daunting task.

***

After some time, the conference room phone console rang. It was a speaker phone in the middle of the table and could join together several incoming calls. The teams of guys were radioing into the dispatch system down the hall, and the staff person there was transferring the signal to the the conference room phone. The call was laced with static, and sometimes it was hard to understand what was being said. Mostly, I had to guess at some things from context, and from how Zach responded. They reported in their positions and preparations in turn.

There were two drone teams of two guys each. One went to the north side of Camelback, and prepared to fly up and over the camel's head, the rugged rock formation on the west side of the mountain. The other drone team navigated through the neighborhood to the southwest of the castle, and found an abandoned mansion driveway to park in, where they could see the castle from below.

Other guys, working alone or in pairs, parked farther away, and walked up the streets, and found hiding places in houses to the south and east of the castle. They had binoculars, and were prepared to radio their information back to a command vehicle parked a half mile away. That vehicle in turn was able to broadcast a stronger radio signal back to us here in Chandler. Zach had selected a radio frequency that was not regularly monitored by police scanners, and all the guys were tuned into it.

Zach instructed the drone teams to take turns with their flyovers, only one vehicle in the air at a time. The north side team, called "Alpha Team" went first. I wished I could see what the drone's camera was seeing. While the camera was beaming back signal to its controlling computer over its local wi-fi hotspot, there was not a strong enough cellular network connection between the laptop, and our offices. We had to rely on the operator verbally describing what he saw as he piloted the vehicle.

"Okay, drone is up and away." Pause, static. "Okay, there's the praying monk…" Pause. "Okay, we're flying over the camel's head… I'm swiveling around to see… yep, that's it, that's the castle. We're about a thousand feet above it; can't really see much yet. Going down, slowly…" Pause. "Okay, I'm about 500 feet above, and just a little north. I can see a lot of cars and things lining the driveway, and the street up to the castle… what are those things?" Mumbles from his team mate. "Yeah, yeah, you're right - those are bikes. Uh, I mean, motorcycles. Lots of motorcycles are parked around the place."

Zach asked, "Can you get a count of the vehicles, roughly?"

More static. "Uh, yeah, lemme see…" Mumbling. "I count about forty bikes, and maybe a dozen cars. Most of them look like big SUVs, a few sports cars."

Zach said, "Okay, that's a start. Can you make out any people on the property?"

"I'll have to take this down to about 200 feet, to get that kind of detail." Pause. "There's a big open area to the east of the main castle, looks like a pool and a patio area. I see some movement around there. Uh, yeah, there's people hanging out around there."

Zach said, "Okay, don't get too close. I don't want them to hear the noise. Pull up."

"Roger that. Pulling up."

We waited a bit. Zach was doodling on some scratch paper. He looked up at us. "Okay, I think the cars and bikes means there's at least 60 or 70 people on site at the moment. Maybe more if anyone walked in from farther away, if they're living in any of those other houses on the mountain."

Zach turned back to the speaker phone. "Okay, Alpha Team, good work. Bring it in, and recharge it. I'm sending in Beta Team next." Zach nodded at Sharon, who pressed a few buttons on the phone to switch calls, and nodded back to Zach.

"Beta Team, you're good to launch. Alpha Team is out of the area. Approach low and slow. There's people about on the patio on the east side of the building, so don't get too close."

The staticky voice of the next guy came over the phone. "Beta Team, launching now. And we're up." Pause. "Approaching... We're about 500 feet south-southwest of the main face. Using the building just below as cover." Pause. "Hey, can I land on this house, to steady the camera? Might get better footage. We could just park it and watch."

Zach considered and studied the Google Maps image. Sharon had zoomed in to a closeup of the castle and surrounding houses and was projecting it onto the wall screen.

Zach answered, "Negative, don't do that yet. I don't want a black drone sitting on top of a white roof; too easy to see." He stopped, thinking. "Beta Team, pull back a bit, and hold position."

He turned to Sharon, "Can you get Alpha Team back on the line please?"

She nodded. "Might as well just conference them all in on one."

Zach nodded back. "Alpha Team, you there?" They responded to confirm.

"Alpha Team, what color is your drone?" Zach asked.

"Uh, white, sir? Why?"

Zach gave them instructions to drive around to the south side of the mountain, and find a house and driveway that would concealed them, but would still have line of sight to a drone flying in the vicinity of the castle. He wanted the white drone to fly to the house just the east of the castle and land on its roof. The camera could be kept active and sending video back to the controller in the car. A white drone on a white roof would be less noticeable to the partiers. And if it wasn't flying, its battery would last a lot longer.

We waited some more, for Alpha Team to move position. Sharon tapped me and asked, "What did they mean about the praying monk?"

I looked at her. "Oh, that's a rock formation on the north side of the camel's head. Looks like a praying monk, when you see it from just the right angle."

Sharon frowned at me. "You've never seen it?" I asked her. She shook her head.

Ariana and Jenna returned to the conference room, with a package of sandwiches and side salads from the restaurant. They setup our lunch on a side table, and motioned to us to help ourselves, which we did.

While we served ourselves, Zach directed Beta Team to try some approaches from various angles from the south. The problem was that the castle was built into a hill, and the drone mostly had to fly up the side. It could have risen higher into the air, and come down from above. But it would have been very visible in the bright daylight, to anyone on the castle's patio or roof, who happened to be watching. We had no idea how much noise or music was happening in the castle. If they were playing loud music, they probably wouldn't hear the drone, and thus, not notice it. But the drone's own noise kept its operators from hearing any noise coming from the castle.

The best that Beta Team was able to confirm was that yes, there were some people hanging out around the pool. They also observed a couple of people leave the castle on motorcycles. And a new SUV pulled up to it, and two people unloaded something bulky and awkward. We guessed it was probably a beer keg.

I could see the turquoise shape of the pool on the Google map. Compared to the other images we'd seen of the castle earlier, from the TV episode we'd watched, it seemed pretty incongruous with the castle's style. Medieval Spanish castles weren't suppose to have pristine aqua pools surrounded by patios. But then, Arizona wasn't supposed to have medieval castles, either. I guessed HOA rules didn't apply to billionaires.

Beta Team's drone was hovering in the air, about 300 feet away from the castle, due south, when a staticky voice came back on the line. "Oh crap, I think we've been spotted. I can see someone on the roof, and they're pointing at us. Pulling back now."

Zach said, "Easy. Don't act suspicious. You're a hobby copter, a toy. Act like you're just out cruising the neighborhood, looking for a good place to live."

"Right. Turning westward, just cruising around, oh, look at that nice house over there…" Beta Team's voice was fake casual. "Uh, two more motorcycles just went under us, down the road…" Pause. "They're stopping, they're looking at us. Pulling up…" Beta Team switched to his fake casual voice, pretend talking to the bikers. "…nothing to see here, just looking around…"

Zach said, "Okay, return the drone to base, and pack it up. If the bikes find you, you're just a couple of guys looking around, looking to party. Got it?"

"Roger that. Returning drone to base." The line cut off, and it was several minutes more before we heard back from them. In the meantime, Alpha Team had driven their car back around the mountain and had found a shady driveway to hang out in, just south of the castle. They carefully navigated the white drone on a roundabout path up the mountain to the house just to the east of the castle and parked on the corner of the roof. Alpha Team was reasonably confident the drone was small enough to not be noticed by anyone in the castle, more than 300 feet away. It didn't have a view of the patio, as it was looking upwards at the supporting walls. But it could see the driveway up to the castle pretty well, they told us.

Beta Team came back after a bit and reported that the bikers had definitely spotted them. "Yeah, they came right up to us, and asked us what we were doing. I said, 'hey, we're just looking around, playing

with our toy.' And they bought it! They asked us if we had any beer!
Can you believe that? We told them we could go get some and bring it
back. So they said 'sure, as long as we don't come empty handed, we're
welcome to come to the party.' We're in."

Zach actually smiled. "Okay, I guess you're moving onto phase two
of the project. Good work, Randy. Go get some booze, and then just
walk in the front door." I hadn't realize that Jake & Randy were Beta
Team. I hadn't recognized their voices, over the static filled radio signal
patched to our phone line.

Alpha Team with the white drone settled in for observation. Teams
Charlie, Delta and Gamma hiked up the hill from their cars parked in
the neighborhood at the foot of the mountain. They were pretending
to be just some random guys who had been invited by a friend of a
friend, and were just there to party. They didn't want to all arrive at
once, so it took a while for everyone to get in the door.

Meanwhile, Randy and Jake broke into an empty house about mile
away, and grabbed a bunch of bottles of high end liquor for their
entry ticket. They took the case of bottles, and big dopey grins on
their faces up to the front door (which was actually on the back side
of the castle). They turned on their hidden body cameras and radios.
We could hear the conversation, but much of it was distorted. I
guessed the radio was in a pocket.

The front door opened, when they banged on it. They were asked
who they were, and what they brought. Randy and Jake introduced
themselves by first names only, and said they were friends of "John."
When Randy showed them the bottles, they were immediately
welcomed in.

Jake must have turned off his radio, or couldn't get any signal,
because the phone went silent for awhile. I finished off my lunch and
tossed the sandwich wrapping. I used the bathroom. When I got back
to the conference room, I could hear Jake, slightly garbled, speaking.

"…Yeah, there's about 50 or 60 men here, and some women.
They're kinda all scattered around, some out by the pool, some
hanging out inside. I don't see our targets yet. They got a shload of
beer and booze, though. I think this party has been going on for
awhile. One toilet I saw is clogged and overflowing, and nobody is
doing anything about it. And the pool is a mess; there's crap floating in

it. I think a lot of drinks have been spilled in there, maybe some other shit…"

Zach asked, "Are all our teams inside now?"

Speaker phone: "Yeah, confirmed, we got eight people inside now."

"Okay, have you located the bedrooms? Anywhere that someone might have gone for some privacy?"

Speaker phone: "Uh, not sure where those are yet. The floor plan is really confusing. Nothing is straight or square."

"Okay, finding those rooms is your next priority. Tell Charlie team to work on finding out who's in charge."

Speaker phone: "Roger that."

The phone went silent. I looked at Zach. He filled in, "He stepped outside for a smoke, found a private corner, and turned on his radio. There's too much noise to leave them on, and those thick stone walls are blocking the signal, anyways. So they're just going to call in progress reports."

I nodded my understanding.

Ariana had left after getting her own lunch. I took another break to go find her, in her office.

"You okay?" I asked her.

She shrugged. "Yeah. The waiting is getting to me. And it's really hard to follow the voices on speaker phone. I can barely understand anything they say."

"Yeah. It just takes a lot of concentration."

Ariana wasn't interested in having a deep heart-to-heart over the situation. So I left her to her own work and headed back to the conference room.

When I got back, I learned that Alpha Team had reported that the drone's microphone was picking up music more clearly. It was getting louder. Through the arched openings in the castle facade, the drone camera could also see more people mingling about on the pool patio.

Zach turned his attention to the supply truck team, waiting patiently in the area. "You seeing much traffic moving about?" he asked them.

Their radio signal was much clearer. "A little. Some motorcycles, a few pickup trucks. Looks like people making beer runs, I think."

"Okay. Anyone notice you yet?"

Truck Team: "Nope. We're just hiding in plain sight. We're parked in a driveway under a huge palo verde tree. They can't really see us, unless they know to look for us."

"You keeping cool? Got plenty of water?"

Truck team: "Of course, boss. Nice breeze in the shade, too."

Zach finished, "Okay, over and out." He turned his attention back to the castle.

After another period of waiting, Jake took another smoke break, and reported in. He had managed to find his way to the castle's lower level "dungeon", which was being used as a big game room. Since it was built well into the side of the mountain, it was actually very cool in there, compared to the 105 degree temperatures outside. He discovered a number of rooms branching off from the game room, down short hallways. He observed some guys going in to them, drinks in hand, and others coming out, with goofy grins on their faces, and zipping up their flys. Eventually, he asked the guy he was playing pool with, what the deal was. His opponent explained that was where the special entertainment was found, and whoever won the pool game, could have a turn in the rooms. Jake was not a very good pool player, and was not able to immediately confirm his suspicions.

Zach radioed his instructions back.

"Okay, I want you to work on getting as many people as possible out of the game room. Get the Delta and Gamma team down there with you. Get into your own little pool tournament. Hog the tables, and tell everyone else the action is happening up on the patio. You gotta sell it, make them want to be outside, not in the game room. Then you can try getting into those rooms."

This strategy turned out to be more challenging than expected. Partiers were coming and going constantly. The game room had 3 different pool tables, and an assortment of other arcade games. Eventually, one of the other cops managed to win a pool game and was granted access to one of the rooms. He discovered a young woman he did not recognize, who was passed out on the bed, nearly naked. After a quick conversation with Jake, he locked himself in the room with her for a while. His goal was to just keep the other partiers out. He also worked on trying to get the girl to wake up and drink some water, to sober her up.

As the afternoon wore on, the cop teams grew frustrated. Jenna's original assessment had been valid: the party was truly "raging." More and more people were arriving. The mess that was accumulating from empty cups, empty bottles, discarded clothing, and worse, made it clear this had been going on all weekend.

Charlie Team did finally manage to identify the core occupants and party sponsors. They slipped out to the quiet corner for a smoke, and also reported in.

"...There's not a lot of organization going on here. The guy who's running it is just some dude. Doesn't seem to be running any kind of operation here. It's not like Petra's people, or anything else. Just a guy who wanted to live in a big house and have a wild party."

Zach asked, "Is it just one guy, or more?"

Charlie team: "I think it's one guy, and then he found a few friends, and they spread the word. Hey, the weird thing, the guy, he said he was living in Chandler before he came up here. Can you believe that?"

I had a sudden image in my head, of the jerk neighbor who I had spoken with briefly, months ago. He'd said he was going to take off on a motorcycle and go party. It couldn't be, could it? That would be too weird.

The speaker phone was still squawking. "Anyway, he says he found the place, and it was abandoned, so he just moved in. He's got some generators below, running the electricity. Not sure where he's getting the gas from."

Zach asked, "So, he doesn't have any private security working the party, then?"

Charlie team: "Nah. Looks like people can pretty much do whatever they want..." The phone crackled for a moment, and then the voice came back. "...whoa, shit. Some chick just jumped in the pool, buck naked."

"Was it one of our targets?"

Charlie team: "Nah, just some chick. I think she got here about an hour ago."

"Okay, good report. Stay on the patio, and keep an eye out for anyone else who looks like they might get in the way of our operation."

And we waited some more. The party had grown to about 150 people, and we had only 8 people inside, and another 4 waiting outside, in the nearby houses, to help move the girls out. We still didn't have positive confirmation that either Kyrene or Kaycee were in the locked rooms. It was getting harder for our own guys to stay sober enough to function as well. They avoided drinking as much as they could, but for the sake of keeping up appearances, they had to consume some, just to blend in.

We didn't have the resources for a full frontal assault to shut down the party, but it was clear that there were several women trapped in those dungeon rooms. Some women had emerged from the rooms, usually hand in hand with a guy, and had gone upstairs, to jump in the pool or get fresh drinks. They were replaced by other women, who were dragged in by boyfriends or random drunks. The girls were too drunk or high to put up much protest.

Then Jake came back on the radio.

"Boss, we just got a confirmed sighting. Kaycee just walked out of one of the rooms. She looks really stoned, and didn't recognize us. She walked right past Randy, didn't even see him. Some guy was holding hands with her. I saw him go in there a little while ago, and he just led her back out. So I followed them. They went up the patio, and both got in the pool. They're just hanging out there, drinking beer."

Zach answered, "Okay, so we have confirmation. That's progress." He paused, thinking.

Ariana had returned to the conference room, during this final exchange. She stared at Zach. "This is taking too long. You have to do something. Just get them out of there."

That tipped Zach over the edge. He stared at her for a moment. Then he leaned over the speaker phone.

"Okay, let's proceed with 'Plan Big Guns'."

Speaker phone: "Roger that, boss. Bringing in the big guns."

Ariana and I looked at each other. I remembered that the guys had packed a grocery bag of crystal meth in their supplies.

After that, things moved quickly. Jake summarized the rest of the events afterwards. Randy retrieved the stash from the truck team, still stationed down the hill, and started distributing it around the party. He even thoughtfully provided the pipes and lighters for everyone to share. All of the cops encouraged their new "friends" to try it, best high they'd ever know. It took about an hour to get everyone so high they couldn't tell up from down, or scream from music. But once that was accomplished, they were able to quickly kick in the locked doors, and remove the women one by one. If any men were still in the rooms, they were sent out to the patio, to try the really good stuff.

The girls were walked or carried down the hill to where the truck team was waiting for them. Once in the van, the medic started IV drips to get them re-hydrated. Kyrene was one of the first girls taken out of the castle. She was too stoned to walk for herself and had to be carried. Charlie team managed to maneuver Kaycee away from her companion in the pool. She was still very drunk, so it took her a while to recognize the cute nice guy who was guiding her out of the castle, as someone she knew from home. Initially, she protested some but it was pretty ineffective and didn't last.

In all, eight girls were deliberately removed from the party. Randy and Jake had a quick conference with several team mates on site, to see if they felt anyone else was being held there against their will. They pretty much agreed that everyone else was there because they wanted to be, and weren't being forced to do anything they didn't want to do. That included additional women, as well as all the men. Before the remaining cop teams permanently left the vicinity, they made a final radio report to Zach.

"We've got 8 women out of the basement. It looks like they've been here for days. Everyone else by the pool seems to be here because they want to be here. Do you want us to get anyone else?"

Zach glanced at Ariana. Ariana shook her head.

"Nope, mission is accomplished. Head on back. Take the women to the hospital to get checked out. Everyone else report back here for debrief." He signed off.

***

It was fully dark out, when we finally left City Hall. I told Jenna she should go home, but she insisted that she wanted to come to the hospital with us to meet her roommates. I wanted to stop by my house first and drop off the dogs, and let Gordon know what was going on. I told Ariana and Jenna that I would meet them at the hospital. Zach stayed in his command center to debrief his guys when they got back.

Gordon had been home for a couple of hours already when I arrived. He limped out from the back rooms, supported on his cane, when he heard the dogs barking. He'd been playing video games with Micah and Dillon.

"Hey, Maggie! You're finally back! I was about to send out the search party for you!"

He had not yet noticed the tension I was dragging around, because he plunged ahead with what was on his own mind.

"Listen, what do you think of taking a short trip out of town with me? I need to go to San Diego to consult on something and thought you might like a get away…" He slowed down, when he finally noticed my face.

"…uh, what's wrong? What'd I say?" he asked.

I unhooked the little dogs, and hung up the leashes. I turned to Gordon. "It's not you. Just been a crappy day, is all. And it's not over yet."

I filled him in on what had happened. While I talked, we went into the kitchen. He poured me a glass of water and handed it to me. He gestured to a plate of food he pulled out of the fridge but I waved that off. My stomach didn't like to eat when I was stressed.

When I finished the story, I explained that I was expected over at the hospital, to welcome everyone back.

"So, why do you look so annoyed?" Gordon asked.

"Because Ari is acting like we're welcoming the conquering heroes home. But they're not heroes. I'm not even entirely sure they wanted to be rescued." I answered him.

Gordon drove me over the hospital. I found Ariana and Jenna in the waiting room, which was not a surprise. They confirmed that the girls had already arrived and had been moved to intake rooms for exams and initial treatment. We waited for a bit. After a time, Loren came out to update us.

She explained that everyone was on IV fluids, to take care of severe dehydration. They had taken samples and were pretty sure most of the women had been roofied, but they were just waiting for the official lab reports to confirm it. Physical exams also confirmed that they had all had sexual intercourse very recently, and it was most likely forced. None of the girls seemed to have been in a position to give consent, so yes, they were going to call it rape. Then Loren told us the doctor would be out shortly, with more detailed information on each patient, in a little bit.

We waited some more. And as stated, a doctor did appear, confirmed the information, and provide more. He said that, yes, lab tests shows that the girls had been given rohypnol at some point in the last 48 hours. And that they had appeared to have been raped. He then explained that he wanted to administer Mifeprex, saying it would probably be in everyone's best interests.

"Stop." I said. "You need informed consent, from each patient, to do that. They're all of legal age, they can decide for themselves. You can wait until tomorrow, or whenever they're clear minded enough, to administer it, if they want it."

Ariana looked at me, confused. "It's the "day after" drug. To prevent pregnancy." Her eyes got big. She nodded in understanding.

The doctor accepted this decision without complaint. He told us a couple of the women were awake enough to talk to, if we wanted, but most, including Kyrene, were still unconscious.

I wasn't sure I wanted to talk to any of them yet. Frankly, I was pretty pissed at Kyrene, for going to the party in the first place. And with Kaycee, for going, and then not dragging both of them back after the first night. I was angry that they had made some pretty poor choices, and had gotten themselves into very bad trouble. And I knew that was "blaming the victim", and that my attitude was not politically correct. I also knew perfectly well they were in for a hell of time, emotionally, in the next few weeks, maybe months.

It would be nice to think that this little adventure of theirs could be kept quiet but I highly doubted that would happen. More than a dozen cops, almost our entire police force, had been involved in the operation. Plus most of the city administrators had been in and out of the conference room, running errands or bringing us things. Jenna had probably already told other people before she had come to me that morning. She'd been worrying about their absence all day Sunday, too. So, it was highly likely news would spread. Our little community was just as gossipy as any other group. Juicy news never sat still. People would know what had happened. They might not get all the details, but it wouldn't be hard to come to accurate conclusions. Then the stares would start. The girls would be embarrassed. Shamed. On top of having to cope with being raped. They would need counseling, therapy.

There was a little seed of sympathy in my heart for them, but it was overshadowed by the frustration and anger. They were adults. They should have known better. They should have made better choices. Why had they so badly wanted to go to a party in a mansion on a hill? What was wrong with the local bar, and small house parties right here in our own town? Was this place not exciting enough for them? Not fancy enough?

These thoughts kept going round and round in my head. Sympathy for their pain. Anger at their choices. Guilt at myself for being angry with them. And round again. Ariana had to nudge me to get my attention.

"You coming?" she asked me.

"What?" I responded. "Who are you seeing first?"

"Kaycee is awake. Let's go see her" Ariana said.

I reluctantly followed Ariana. The hospital was keeping everyone overnight, so they had all been moved from the ER triage area, into individual rooms. Kaycee was sitting up in bed, but she looked exhausted. Her hair was lank, and she had been dressed in a hospital gown. The IV bag hung on a stand next to the bed. Ariana half sat on the bed beside Kaycee's legs, and took her hand. They talked in platitudes for a bit. Ariana assured her they would get any counseling they wanted. Finally, I couldn't help myself.

"Why did you go to that party?" I asked. I tried to keep my tone as neutral as possible, but I think a little bit of harshness crept in anyways.

She looked at me, looked away, looked around the room. She blinked back tears. Finally, she mumbled, "I dunno. I just wanted to go out, and have a good time. Have some fun. The guys there were all really nice at first, and it was such a cool place… I dunno what happened…" She trailed off.

I realized that I wasn't ever going to get an answer that satisfied. Much like why the Superflu had happened; no answer was ever going to be good enough. And beating up Kaycee or Kyrene, or any of the others, wasn't going to help them. So I got up and just walked out. I didn't storm, I didn't slam doors. I just left. I found Gordon in the waiting room, and told him to take me home.

Chapter 19

I had a very restless night, after leaving the hospital. It was too hot in the bedroom, so I kicked the covers off. Then I was too cold, because the ceiling fan was blowing on me. So I dragged them back over me. I turned over to switch sides several times an hour. At one point, I even accidentally knocked Tyrion off the bed. Gordon finally rolled over to spoon me, and wrapped me a bear hug. That finally helped me fall asleep, in spite of the sweaty skin-to-skin contact.

I woke up at oh-gawd-thirty in the morning and walked the dogs. My frustrations were still clawing at me enough to motivate me to go extra far so all the dogs were nice and tired.

I showered, ate breakfast, and headed off to meet the day, without hardly talking to any of my roomies. I headed straight to City Hall, and Zach.

"Conclusions?" I asked him as soon as I found him sitting at his desk in his office. He was in uniform this morning, per usual.

He looked up from his coffee mug. It was the one I had given him last Christmas, one that I had made. An extra large one, too.

"Well, 'Good Morning' to you too, Maggie," he said.

I gave him my best morning news show host smile, and said, "Good morning, Zach!"

Then I let the smile fall and looked a little more closely. He had bags under his eyes. I don't think he had slept any more than I had. I said, "So, what else did you learn, that I need to know about? Do we need to worry about retribution or retaliation from the party hosts?"

"Uh, you're not mayor yet, you know. Technically, I don't have to share anything with you yet."

"Come on, if you didn't want me to know the details, you would have kicked me out of the conference room 10 minutes after it started yesterday."

Zach shrugged and sat back in his chair. "Point. So, here's an interesting thing. Remember how we put the white drone on that house? Turns out, that house was not empty. There's a guy living there. When I had the guys retrieve the drone, he followed it down, and found their van. He walked right up to them, and asked them what they were doing. After talking a bit, he tells my guys - it was Brian and Jeff on Alpha Team, by the way - he tells them that he's owned that house next to the castle for more than 10 years, and that the guys in the castle just it took over a couple of months ago. They've been partying almost non-stop, to one degree or another, ever since. Booze, music, shouting, screaming, Harleys coming and going all day and night. This guy, he wants Brian and Jeff to do something about it, arrest them for noise violations! Wants city codes to be enforced! Wants all of my cops to come back, in uniform and patrol cars, and kick the guys out."

Zach stopped, and raised his eyebrows at me. I stared back. I frowned.

"We don't have jurisdiction" I said.

"Right. That's what Brian and Jeff said. But he's not buying it. So, the guy, he's planning on driving out here today, to talk to us, to me, to see if he can get us to take care of it."

I stared at him some more. I frowned. Zach waited patiently while I processed the information. Finally, I said, "Yeah, good luck with that!"

Zach grimaced back at me.

"So, *can* we do anything about the guys in the castle?"

Zach turned back into Officer Adams. "Well, technically, holding the girls against their will is kidnapping. That, and raping them, are felonies. But those are state or federal crimes, and as we keeping saying, we don't have jurisdiction. We'd need an FBI investigation team, just to get started on collecting evidence. And then they'd need to get a state or federal district attorney, to file charges. And we're back to needing judges and lawyers and courtrooms, and prisons and guards." He threw up his arms in disgust. This was frustrating him, too.

I slumped back in the chair in front of Zach's desk.

"Zach, there have to be consequences for their actions. They hurt a lot of women. They can't be allowed to just keep doing what they're doing. Other women will get lured in, and get trapped, too. How do we punish them? How do we drive them away so they never want to do it again? And not just out of that house; I mean, out of the city. Heck, out of the state."

253

Zach pursed his lips at me. "RPGs are probably overkill."

I stared at him. "Are you serious? Do you think we should have brought Bartosik and his guys in on this, right from the start?"

Zach shrugged again. "I dunno. I'm just spitballing ideas. When we started the operation, we had no reason to think anything illegal was going on. We just wanted to find our girls. That's not enough of a reason to bring in the military."

The administrative assistant assigned to the police suite came to Zach's door. "Uh, Officer Adams, there's a Mr. Frank Heffler here to see you?" she asked tentatively. Zack and I frowned at each other. He told her to send the guy in.

"The guy from the house?" I asked him. "That was fast!" I stood up, and moved to stand at the window, playing the part of silent observer.

After a few moments, a middle aged man was ushered in. He was dressed in a clean pressed white button down shirt, and khaki pants. He filled his clothes well; he clearly had been, and still was, in extremely good physical condition. He introduced himself as Frank Hemler and, yes, he was the guy living next door to the castle. Zach asked the assistant to bring in coffee and invited the man to have a seat. He had not yet introduced me so I kept quiet.

"So, what can I do for you, sir?" Zach asked the man.

He didn't waste a lot of time on small talk, and got straight to business. "I appreciate what your men did yesterday. I saw them taking those girls out of the castle. I hope they got proper medical care?" Zach nodded.

"That's good to know. So, as you might imagine, those a-holes in the castle have been making life a living hell for everyone in the neighborhood. They party all day and all night, there's loud Harleys going in an out, they're throwing their shit over the walls, the place is a complete mess. They need to be evicted."

Hemler stopped, to see if Zach would say anything. Finally Zach said, "You understand that we are Chandler police, not Phoenix police? I don't have any authority to do code enforcement in your neighborhood. Have you tried contacting your local police?" He kept his tone neutral. We had not heard from or about any reconstituted official police force in Phoenix. But anything was possible.

"No one around to report it to. I need help. I'm not the only person living in that neighborhood. Actually, a lot of the houses on the mountain are occupied. Mostly by other other survivors; they moved in after the owners died. I'm the only one who actually owned my house from before. Mostly, everyone else there are decent folks. It's just these jerks in the castle we're having a problem with."

Zach stared at him. "So, why don't you and your neighbors do something about it? Have you taken any steps at all?"

Hemler answered, "A couple of people have tried talking to them, but that did absolutely squat. They don't care what anyone else thinks."

I finally spoke up. "Are you working as a group, or just individually? The guys in the castle aren't going to pay any attention to a citizens committee from the local HOA. You need to present yourselves with a little more authority."

Zach introduced me. "Frank, this is Maggie Shearin." He did not explain my role further.

I started throwing out ideas and suggestions.

"Perhaps you could 'motivate' them to leave, go somewhere else. Try playing some really loud obnoxious music. Polka music. Or Swedish death metal. Or the theme song from the Barney the Dinosaur show. Maybe you could make their physical environment really unpleasant. Can you setup fans to blow manure odor at them? Can you get a hold of itching power, and spread it all over the place?"

Frank just stared at me. My prankster suggestions were not going over well.

"Or, maybe you want to get a little more hard core. Maybe blockade them and put them under siege; it is a castle, after all. You could block that entrance with some disabled trucks, drop a few boulders in the path so the cars can't leave. Trap them. Their food and booze and generator fuel will run out eventually. Tell them you'll only let them out if they agree to leave the state.

Frank was still staring at me. He turned to Zach. "Uh, is that even legal?"

Zach just shrugged. "We've been struggling with the concept of what is "legal", and how to enforce it, for awhile now. Remember that old line that goes, "first, let's kill all the lawyers."? Seems the Superflu took that to heart. We can't find a single judge, lawyer, court clerk, bailiff or mediator who can charge, prosecute and imprison a felon. In fact, just before you came in, we were talking about crime, and how to punish it. We didn't come up with any good solutions. And Maggie here is full of great solutions. For everything. Except how to punish a crime." Zach paused and eyed Frank.

"Do you get what I'm saying? We don't have any way to punish a crime." He said that last part very slowly. He waited for the idea to sink in. Frank finally got it. He was being given tacit permission to do whatever he wanted to solve his own problem.

Frank started nodding slowly. He squinted at me. He looked at Zach. I could see the light bulb growing brighter over his head. Guys who can afford to buy multi-million dollar homes on desert mountains are not dumb. They got their money through smarts and cunning. Frank would find a way. He stood up, preparing to leave. "Okay, I think I see what you're saying. Code enforcement is a non-starter."

Zach nodded back. "Exactly."

And then I saw that little gleam in Zach's eye. He added, "And if all else fails, we know a guy who has an RPG launcher, and loves to blow stuff up."

Frank's eyes bulged. "You're kidding, right?"

Zach just looked at him levelly. Then he pulled a business card out of his desk, and handed it over. "Give us call, let us know how things turn out. Or if you need that referral."

Frank showed himself out. Zach and I looked at each other. I perked up, and in my cheeriest Madam Mayor spokesperson voice, I said, "Oh darn, I forgot to tell him about the peaches in Queen Creek!"

Zach snorted at me.

***

I left Zach's office and started heading back to the studio. I saw a number of people across the street, at the memorial site, so I shifted directions.

Max, the head of the construction team, was directing people. There were several back hoes and front loaders moving about. I steered well around them and joined Max. He had to shout over the engine noise to be heard.

"Morning, Maggie. We're breaking ground for real today. We're going to start laying the foundation." The back hoe was digging furrows in the ground. The front loader was scraping away the dirt and depositing it into a dump truck to be moved elsewhere.

Max explained, in more detail than I really needed to know, how they would lay down layers of sand, gravel, iron rebar, and then concrete to form a solid foundation that could handle the weight of the monument. He pointed out the supply trucks that were waiting to spread their material into the exposed shallow pit.

The project was officially underway. I took a moment to just absorb the sense of it, to remind myself that this community was pulling together to turn my idea into a real and meaningful thing. And just when I felt like I was getting some peaceful equilibrium back, I inhaled a lungful of dust kicked up by the noisy machines and coughed vigorously for a few minutes. I thanked Max for the update and continued onto the studio.

I consoled Jenna for awhile. She was still processing what had happened and needed to vent her own frustrations. In addition to being mad at Kyrene and Kaycee, she was also pissed at Kyle. She had told him on Sunday, about the girls not being back, but he had refused to do anything about it, insisting they were fine and were just partying. I listened, and refrained from expressing my own personal judgments. It wouldn't help her.

I got back to work. As always, making pots was one of the few things that truly brought me any peace. Or at least some distraction.

***

After a couple of days, Jenna and Ariana both insisted that I go back to the hospital to see the girls. I didn't want to but Ariana said it was important that I make it clear the new women were welcome to stay. I told her she could do that just as easily but she still insisted.

When we arrived, all eight women were actually sitting together in a small family waiting room at the end of the hallway. They were dressed in sweats and t-shirts. A couple of them were still hooked up to IV bags, hanging on rolling stands. Ariana had timed our visit to arrive just after their first group therapy session, I discovered. I wondered who had led the session.

The other girls were introduced to me, one by one. As they went around the circle, I stared at the fourth one. She looked incredibly familiar, but I was having a hard time recalling why. When she said her name, though, I knew. Sasha. The girl I had encountered months before, in a grocery store near my home. We had helped each other scavenge a full meat locker. She recognized me, too, but didn't explain the connection to the others; she just gave me a little wave and a private smile.

I repeated Ariana's general welcome to the city, and told them they were welcome to stay as long as they liked. Once they returned to full health, and if they wanted to participate and work with us, they would be provided food and housing. I also told them they were free to go whenever they wanted, too.

One by one they told me their backgrounds and how they had come to be here.

Most of them had been living here in the Phoenix metro area for several years, if not their entire lives. They had been in school, or had just started working, before the Superflu. They were all young, mid-twenties and attractive.

Like Kyrene, they had heard about the party from a friend, or a friend of a friend. Or the Google+ postings. It turned out there had been several of postings, not just the one Kyrene had received. I suspected that Google+ was starting to become the post-pandemic version of Craigslist.

The girls were quite dismayed at what had happened. Individually, their memories were fuzzy, due to the alcohol and rohypnol. Collectively, they began to understand the magnitude of what had happened. As they shared their stories with each other, they saw how they had been manipulated, trapped. During the experience, their sense of time had been distorted. Now that they understood how much time they had spent in the castle (and some had been there for a day or two before Kyrene and Kaycee arrived), they were appalled.

I could see pain, guilt and remorse on their faces.

They asked me what was going to be done to the guys who had organized the party.

"Well, directly, there's not much we can do. You are all over age 18, so you have the legal right to go where you like. And most of you are legally allowed to drink alcohol, as well. So, you're not in trouble."

I thought for a moment. "They did violate you, and rape is a crime. And they held you against your will. That's also a crime. However, they're the kind of crimes that are prosecuted at the state or federal level. As you know, no one has the ability to do that at the moment. Frankly, I'm not sure what will happen to those guys." I said this as flatly as I could. There was no way I was going to drop hints about Frank and his neighbors. If he managed to succeed, I could tell them afterwards.

They accepted the non-answer calmly. For the moment. But I had to wonder if the issue would come back up again.

I repeated the message, about them being welcome to stay in Chandler as long as they liked, and that we would find something for them to do, while they healed.

The meeting broke up after that. Sasha grabbed my wrist before I could exit the room. "I'm really glad to see you here," she said. "I've wondered what happened to you. I kept going back to that store, for awhile, getting supplies, but I didn't see you again."

No, I had not gone back to that particular grocery, for scavenging. Shortly after our brief encounter, I had met Zach, who recruited me to start working with the City, and, well, one thing led to another, and it didn't seem that I needed any more supplies, after that.

"It's good to see you, too, Sasha." I said. I wanted to ask about her dogs, but if they had been left alone all this time… I didn't have high hopes for their welfare. Nor did I want to burden her with that, on top of everything else, either. I patted her on the shoulder, exchanged a few more pleasantries, and turned to try to leave again. Kyrene caught me on my other side.

She spoke up immediately. "You're probably really pissed at me, for going to that party." Her face was tight, her lip curling.

"Of course not." I white lied. "You had no way of knowing what would happen. It's not your fault. And, I'm not your mom, you didn't need my permission."

Kyrene's arms were crossed over her chest, and she was wiggling a slippered foot in agitation.

"I shouldn't have gone. I shouldn't have taken Kaycee, either. But I'm glad Jenna didn't come. At least, there's that."

Yes, there was that to be thankful for.

She stared at the floor. "I just wanted to have some fun. I've never been in a mansion before. It sounded so cool…"

I didn't know what to say. Finally, I stumbled into "Well, it's over now. Just focus on taking care of you, for now."

I made my excuses and struggled not to run out the door. I was still angry. I waited by Ariana's car.

When she finally joined me, she asked, "What is your problem?" She could see my agitation.

"Nothing." I did not want to say all the politically incorrect things running through my head. But then I did, anyways.

"I'm just really pissed. I can't understand why they had to go there in the first place. How could they not realize it would end badly? And if they had to go, why did they drink so much? Why weren't they paying attention? They got themselves into trouble, and now they're suffering consequences. But you know what's even worse? I'm not supposed to blame them. They're the victims. And we're not allowed to blame the victim. The victim can do no wrong. And that's such bullshit, because let's face it, they made choices early on, choices that put them in a position to be taken advantage of." I stopped, took a deep breath.

"That's what's going round in my head, round and round, and I can't get it to stop."

Ariana just put her arms around me and hugged me. And in an instant, the anger stepped aside and a rush of grief poured in. I started bawling. It was new grief. It was old grief. It was another round of stupid Superflu Trauma grief. Wouldn't this thing ever go away?

Was this what the girls were trying to escape, when they chose to go to a party? A distraction, an event, something new to get them to stop thinking about the old? Is that why they went? Everyone dealt with their grief in their own way. I released Ariana, while I pondered this potential explanation. My theory would need confirmation, but if true, it gave me a way out of my anger spiral. I chose to set it aside for further examination later on.

***

Life kept on going on, as it always does. The next Mayoral debate was scheduled for Saturday.

The election commission had advised us of the format this debate would take. This one was less of a traditional debate and more of a question and answer session. Attendees of the session could write out questions on cards and drop them in a large bin as they entered the auditorium. The moderator would randomly draw cards, and read the question, one per candidate, each in turn. Each candidate would have one minute to respond. There would be no counter response from other candidates.

The format struck me as a little odd. The moderator reserved the right to set aside questions if they were illegible, or inappropriate. That would keep the joke questions out so we could focus on the issues. However, it did leave some opportunity for similar or identical questions to be asked.

To prepare, Sharon drilled me by trying to ask the kinds of questions we thought might be brought up. I practiced answering them, calmly, clearly and succinctly. We also spent a little time trying to role play what the other candidates might do. I didn't know them well, yet, but since all but one of them would ultimately end up on the city council, it seemed like a good time to pull together a basic profile for each.

Richard Forchik was the first one to stand out in my mind. In the last debate I'd realized that he placed a premium on security and distribution of resources. He had been a CFO of a large company, before. He was highlighting that business experience as his primary credentials for the job.

And of course, I was acquainted with Pastor Daniel Johannsen. He was deeply committed to his faith, and tended to assume that everyone else felt the same as he did. He seemed surprised and disappointed whenever he discovered that they did not.

The remaining candidates were a bit of a mystery to me. Brad Lofkin, Victoria Allamilla, Roman Vance and Miguel Cisneros. Collectively, they all seemed to have good intentions and a desire to serve the community. For most of them, security and protection of resources seemed to be their primary areas of concern.

On Saturday, Team Maggie escorted me to the auditorium and turned in their own carefully worded questions into the bin (limit three per attendee). Cards had been made available around town for several days so that people could take their time to write out a thoughtful question.

At 4pm, the leader of the independent commission called the meeting to order, introduced the other members of the commission, and then introduced us. We were seated at tables on the stage, in no particular order, with name cards, microphones, bottled water, and paper and pens in front of us. The moderator explained the rules to the audience. A question would be drawn and the designated candidate would respond. Moving from stage left to stage right, each candidate would have their turn at a newly drawn question. We had one minute to respond. There would be four rounds.

Then the questions began. They were all over the place. They covered just about any topic one could think to lay at a potential Mayor's feet.

People are keeping goats and chickens in their backyards. They make a lot of noise, and they smell. Do you plan on restoring enforcement of city codes, and having livestock moved to properly zoned areas?

Now that the bodies have been removed within our city borders, will you be expanding the clearing process to the towns around us?

Will we be able to expand the consolidation zone, to include more houses, so that we don't have to share living quarters with total strangers?

How do you plan to stop unwanted visitors from coming into town?

Every night, I smell a lot of marijuana smoke in my neighborhood. Can we have the police come and confiscate the pot?

What steps will you take to publicly recognize the hard work performed by the body detail work crews?

When do you plan to restart the schools?

A lot of people are leaving town, to get out of the heat. What are your plans to make sure they return?

Some people have started having some really loud parties that go on until pretty late. When will noise regulations be enforced?

When will 911 start working, in case we have an emergency?

How are you going to keep strangers out of our town? Shouldn't there be some kind of screening process for visitors?

The houses all around the golf course are in a gated community. Are you going to build fences and gates around the other houses for equal protection?

What are you going to do about all the abandoned cars? They're becoming an eye sore.

My neighbors aren't keeping up with the yard maintenance. How do we get a new head of household who will keep up with things?

When can we go back to regular weekly trash pickups?

Some of the pools in my neighborhood are turning green and are breeding mosquitoes. Part of the consolidation plan was that people in the zone have to maintain their home. What do you plan to do to get the residents to take care of their own yards?

What's your plan for establishing a new currency?

I don't think that the allocation of housing was very fair. If elected, would you consider a lottery system to redistribute housing more fairly?

Is there any plan to start collecting recyclables again? How about city collection of compostables?

There's a lot of feral cats around, fighting and making a mess. What plans do you have to remove them?

Who gets to cast a vote in the election? How will you tell legal residents apart from visitors?

Our town has been emptied out, and it needs to be refilled. How will you encourage families to grow and repopulate this town?

How often will guard patrols pass through a neighborhood?

Do you plan to start collecting sales or property taxes again?

If someone wanted to restart a dairy operation, would it be possible to get the grid power turned on for a mini-farm, which is currently outside the consolidation zone?

My neighbor says he's going to paint his house purple. Doesn't he need approval from an architectural committee for that?

I'm interested in opening a new restaurant in the downtown area. Will there be an established procedure for claiming the unused business spaces inside the consolidation zone?

How much longer will the work crews be working?

Are there any plans to open up a car repair service? Just taking some other car, when one breaks down, is not sustainable in the long run.

At first I found them interesting. A few were repetitive. After an hour and a half, I was getting bored, and struggled to keep it from showing on my face. My fellow candidates and I answered them as best we could, in keeping with our own personal agendas and goals for the city. Richard was especially adept at turning his answers around to show how qualified he was for the position. Victoria and Brad also seemed competent. Roman and Miguel's responses were a little vague. Daniel, of course, was a master at public speaking, and managed to make his answers seem like solutions to world problems, not just city ordinance issues. And my responses, well, I thought they were okay, but it was hard to judge what others thought. I couldn't see faces well, because of the lights shining in my eyes.

After the meeting, we went to Mercados as we usually did. I positioned myself at one of the outdoor picnic tables, even though it was 105 degrees outside. Once the sun started setting, the buildings shaded the promenade, and it started to cool off. Misters were running, and that helped as well.

I picked the outside table so people could easily approach me to ask the inevitable followup questions. And they did. I phrased my answers a little less formally, since these were small conversations.

Question: "Maggie, you didn't get the question about the feral cats, but I can assure you, they're really becoming a problem. Do you have any alternatives?"

Answer: "Actually, I think we have a vet and some veterinary technicians as part of the medical crew. Maybe we could start a spay, neuter and release program. The cats help keep the mice and rats under control, so I don't want to completely eliminate them. But we do need to have some control on the population."

Question: "Do you think some of the work crews could be tasked to start helping with those green pools, and weeds and home maintenance, now that most of the clearing out is done? That would help the people who can't or won't take care of it on their own."

Answer: "Actually, that's a good idea. I think people benefit, when they have meaningful work to do, and the work crews' original mission is winding down now. Helping take care of the consolidation zone is in everyone's best interest."

Question: "The people who live down the street from me have been having parties on the weekends; I'm worried about them getting out of control. You know, like that one those girls went to in Phoenix? Do you think we can have a rule about no visitors after 9pm or something?"

Answer: "Well, I don't really think we can abridge people's rights to enjoy their home as they wish, including entertaining guests during the evenings. However, if their enjoyment of their home is having a negative impact on your enjoyment of yours, we do have noise and disturbance ordinances to address those issues."

And on it went. Gordon stayed close to me and kept pouring me lemonade to drink. He wouldn't let me have any beer while I was talking to strangers and unofficially campaigning. Which was fine. My other friends wandered off to visit with other people. Finally, the evening wore down and Gordon and I were able to leave. We walked home as we usually did.

Gordo prompted me, "You know, all these questions tonight makes me realize you never managed to answer my question, a couple of days ago."

"Please, I'm kinda questioned out. It's been a crazy long week, with way too many questions."

Gordon said, "About going to San Diego."

"What? Explain it again. That all went right over my head, last time."

Gordon said, "I need to go to San Diego, sometime soon, to do some consulting. Bartosik put me in touch with the Navy commander on the base over there. They want me to come look at some of their power generating options, and suggest which ones to decommission and which to try to keep running. I'd probably be there for a few days. I thought maybe we could make a weekend getaway out of it. Take a little break before you start mayoring up the place here."

"I don't think 'mayoring' is a verb. And I'm still not convinced I'm going to be elected. Did you watch that guy, Richard? He's slick. He may have won over a bunch of voters..."

Gordon shook his head. "Actually, that's exactly why he won't win. He's *too* slick. Too desperate and a braggart. He sounds too much like a politician. Nobody wants that. You come off as real, sincere. You're not afraid to admit when you've made a mistake, or that sometimes problems are complicated and don't have easy solutions. That really resonates with people."

"Yeah, what about Daniel? His colors shine through loud and clear. Do you think his base is large enough to take control?"

Gordon said, "Now who's mixing their metaphors? But yeah, Daniel's base is pretty solid, but I don't think he appeals to very many people outside his own congregation. And that's not a majority."

We walked in silence for a bit, and then reached our house. The dogs greeted us noisily, as always. Gordon shooed them all outside for a competitive peeing challenge, while I wandered into the kitchen. I could hear the sounds of video games from the back bedrooms. That meant Micah and probably Dillon, had roosted for the evening.

I stared into the fridge. I'd eaten dinner, but not very much. I contemplated the idea of a snack and was wondering if there was any ice cream left. Gordon and the dogs came back in.

"You know, that's not exactly very wise energy management policy, there, holding the fridge open."

"Yeah, I know." I closed the door. "I was thinking about ice cream. But it looks like we're out." I was a little disappointed, but not terribly surprised. The real surprise was that Gordon's stash had lasted as long as it had.

Then I asked Gordon, "Hey, did you notice that question about someone wanting to get a dairy farm started again? Do you think you could get power routed to a farm? No one wants those located close to town - too smelly."

"Yes, I did hear that one, and yes. Actually, that's one of the reasons why we've been collecting solar panels. To use them for special projects like that. And if they promise to make ice cream, I'll install the panels myself." Gordon grinned at me.

After a moment, Gordon asked, "So, are we going to San Diego, or what?" Gordon steered me back to his primary objective.

"Well, I can't go until after the election, and once the inauguration is done, I think I'm going to be too busy. I think there's only one free weekend, between election and inauguration; that's probably the only time I could get away. Unless I lose. Then we could spend the rest of the summer out there. Mmm. Cool ocean breezes." I closed my eyes as I pictured the waves.

Gordon answered: "I can work with that. Weekend after the

election. I'll set it up. They said they've got the Coronado Hotel cleaned up and able to take guests." He waggled his eyebrows at me.

I grinned back. That would be a lovely place to stay. Very historic. "You know, traveling together is usually a big relationship test. Tells us if we're compatible or not."

Gordon grinned at me. "Compatible? You can't tell if we're compatible yet? Come on, I'll show you how compatible we are." Gordon put his arms around me, and steered me back to our bedroom, while I giggled.

Chapter 20

The week leading up to the election was crazy. I didn't spend much time in the studio. Everyone told me to go out campaigning. I thought that was a little silly. There weren't any places to go campaigning; everyone hung out in the same downtown area. So, I just made myself as available as possible to people who wanted to ask questions or share their concerns.

It seemed to me that the number of people around town was dwindling. Partly I chalked that up to the heat keeping people inside their air conditioned houses. And partly, some people were heading out of town for extended camping trips in the cool mountains to the north. Or farther. Some people decided to go confirm the status of extended family members who had been living in other states. Other people objected to these people leaving, with a tankful of consolidated gas, but it seemed to me that was a pretty small contribution, for the potential information they might bring back in the fall. If any of them stopped to tell me their plans or say goodbye, I asked them to be on the lookout for information about oil refining getting restarted or sources for wheat or flour or seafood, that we might find a way to buy or trade for.

An early balloting box was setup in the City Hall foyer for anyone who wanted to vote, but was also eager to get out town. The in-person balloting process scheduled for Saturday was a bit of a mashup of procedures. Since Ariana and her people didn't have access to county voter registration lists, voters were required to show identification that included their name and a Chandler address, as it was established before the Superflu. Meaning, a driver's license. Once this was shown, the ballot card would be issued, one per person.

Of course, we also had some people in our community who had not been Chandler residents before the Superflu. Like Caleb, who had lived in Gilbert, the next town over, before going on his mission. These residents were provided provisional ballots where their names and identities would be checked against assigned housing inside the consolidation zone. Once confirmed as legitimate participating members of our community, their vote would be counted.

The election commission planned to count the ballots in a public setting, on the stage of the school auditorium. If anyone was interested in watching, to make sure no hanky panky was going on, they were welcome to do so, from the theater seats. The counting process would also be video recorded, for posterity.

Ariana also summoned all of the candidates for a briefing, as well. She wanted to give everyone an overview of ongoing city operations, so that the newly elected officials could get off to a running start. She also had some very complex procedures for running the various types of meetings that we would be required to participate in.

During the briefing, we were brought up to date on a lot things going on that had been omitted or only vaguely referenced, during the recent Town Hall public meetings.

She explained that body removal from homes within city limits was effectively completed. There was the possibility of still finding bodies in unexpected places, such as businesses, office buildings, abandoned cars, and outbuildings like barns or sheds. But now that it was summer, the few remaining bodies were quickly drying out so they were not the serious health threat that the hundreds of thousands of them had been six months ago. Now it was time to consider expanding the removal and cremation process to neighboring cities, county islands, and perhaps the Indian reservation to the south of the city. Pests and contamination didn't pay much attention to city borders so we would have to look at the area around us and assess the potential threat.

The next topic in her briefing was that we could consider expanding the consolidation zone to annex some additional neighborhoods for housing. The electrical and water teams had not specifically disconnected them from the grid. But they hadn't taken any steps to reinforce them, either. Should the Mayor and Council choose to do so, additional housing could quickly be made available. This would relieve overcrowding pressure. Most people had been patient and gracious about sharing homes with strangers, but that was starting to wear thin. A lot of people wanted to have some private space or at least more choice in who they got for roommates. Ariana told us that there were several plans being discussed for how to assign the new housing, including a lottery or perhaps a bidding process, where occupants pledged a certain amount of upkeep or labor, in exchange for nicer properties.

Additional points in the briefing covered basic city services. Trash pickup was moving to a regularly scheduled weekly interval inside the zone. Police patrols were being increased, thanks to new recruits completing their first round of training. More training would be provided but the new guards were ready to handle unarmed patrols outside the consolidation zone.

Communications continued to be a challenge. Sharon had developed a template and set of instructions for home phone systems to be installed or connected to the city telecommunications network, similar to what she had done in our own house. Some cell phone service was still functioning, but it was erratic and highly dependent on service carrier, location of nearest transmission tower and even time of day. At best, if it worked, it worked only for person to person phone calls. Access to the Internet via cell phone wi-fi was essentially unavailable for now on hand held devices. Happily, if a computer inside the zone was physically wired to a cable modem, it could connect to the Internet. Sharon had managed to reroute the nearest cable junctions to bypass the regional service providers and connect via the city's large capacity routers. High speed access was now effectively free.

Ariana handed out several pages of known working websites, and what we could expect to find on them. The list included a lot of blogs and wikis, where communities like ours were posting status reports, and instructional information on how to work with existing infrastructure to restore it. I noticed that several of the websites had military domains. I made a mental note to check them out very soon.

Ariana concluded the meeting by handing out an abbreviated guide to Roberts Rules of Order. She explained that these procedures would be followed during all official City Council meetings.

After the meeting, Ari and I had lunch together. In the interest of expanding our working relationship with the other candidates, we invited anyone who was interested to join us. Only Brad and Victoria accepted the invite; everyone else begged off, claiming they had other business to attend to.

During this lunch, I learned that Ariana and Brad were already casually acquainted with each other. Before the Superflu, Brad had been, and still was, working for our city library. He had been in charge of special programming, like scheduling public readings, free computer training classes and other special events. However, he was also a fully qualified librarian. I asked him what he was doing in the library now.

He explained, "Well, I've been working on acquisitions. I want our library to be a repository of knowledge that future generations are going to need. We didn't have a lot of technical or educational titles, before. The collection was mostly focused on consumer oriented things; popular fiction and non-fiction. I want to build up the collection in topic areas like medicine, agriculture, engineering and manufacturing. I've been scavenging from doctors offices, businesses and some homes, to find things and add them in."

"Huh. Did a big guy bring you a bunch of engineering books from the university, a few weeks ago?"

"Yes, Gordon. We're acquainted."

I nodded, but didn't not elaborate on my own connection to Gordon. No need to flaunt that if he was not already aware. "Have you thought about getting some law books, too? We've been struggling with how to restart a court system. If anyone wants to learn that from scratch, they're going to need lots of books on case law. There's gotta be a law firm office around here somewhere, with books on the shelves…"

Brad nodded back at me. "Sure. I'll put it on the list."

I turned to Victoria. "So, what did you do, before?" We were eating salads at Mercados. Inside, in the air conditioning. I waited for her to finish chewing before she answered.

"I worked in retail management. I was a regional manager for a big department chain. Did all kinds of things, hiring, firing, making recommendations, training people, rolling out promotions, that kind of thing."

I nodded. It was not an area I knew much about. Ariana drew her out. "Victoria has been working with the warehouse, advising them how to organize things. Setting up multiple sites, so we don't have all our resources in one place."

Victoria nodded at that. "Right. I'm worried about those gangs that are going around looting. Makes more sense to warehouse things in multiple locations, just in case."

Of course, one could make the case that we were looters just as much as the unspecified gangs were. But Victoria seemed to have drawn a pretty firm line between 'us' and 'them.'

"So, is there any other management left at the department stores? Anyone there going to be upset if we just take a bunch of linen sets, and maybe a blender?" I asked her.

She smirked, and shook her head. "No. There's a couple of sales clerks from the local stores around here, but I've not heard from any one higher up the management chain, than myself. And I say, there's plenty to go around."

That reminded me of something. "Ari, did you ever tell her about that break in we saw last winter, when those guys smashed and grabbed all the jewelry?"

Ariana wiped her lips with her napkin and shook her head. "No, sorry. Kinda slipped my mind."

Victoria said, "Now, see, that's the kind of thing that makes everyone nervous, about those outside gangs and looters. That why some people want more security fencing, like you have in that gated community."

Hmm… That was a little pointed. I straightened my back just a bit. My little shoulder devil also perked up and started paying attention.

Brad asked, "Speaking about that gated community… Ariana, I never did hear how you went about assigning housing. All I know, is that guy Caleb said I could have an apartment in that condo project over there, or I could be head of household in different house on Milagro, but that I'd be getting three roommates if I did that."

Ari squirmed a bit. "Yes, I know, it was a bit rushed, and haphazard. Caleb has done the best that he can, and he's been pretty good at it, I think. But we both realize it probably could have been handled differently."

Brad didn't want to let it go, yet. "I'm just confused. A lot of people got to claim the house they wanted, early on. This assigned housing thing only started happening later on. It would have been nice if everyone could have picked what they wanted."

My shoulder devil was tapping his chin thoughtfully.

Ariana responded calmly. "Yes, it would have been nice, but we were in a rush, during the last couple of months, once it started getting hot, and people needed air conditioning. We can still make adjustments. If you're not happy where you are, talk to Caleb about it. I'm sure he has some alternatives. And, of course, if you're elected, you'll be able to direct us to increase the zone. So, this is something that can be resolved. It's just going to take a little time."

Brad nodded and let the matter drop. I suspected it was just a temporary reprieve, though.

We finished our lunch. Brad and Victoria said their goodbyes and left to do other things. Since I was still trying to be "available" to the public, I thought I should hang out for a bit. Cassandra wheeled into the restaurant, just as Brad and Victoria were walking out the door. She waved and joined us.

"Hey, there you are, Ari! Patti has been wondering where you've been." Patti was one of Ariana's administrative people.

"Why? Is there a problem?" Ari asked her back.

"No, she just had some questions." She looked at me. "Hi Maggie. Hey, I wanted to tell you that I thought you did a really good job in the debate last weekend."

I smiled. "Thanks. Here, you can have a seat and join us, if you want. I'm pretending this is a coffee shop and we have nothing better to do than sit around and act like we're in a sitcom." I pushed out a chair for her, which she took. She grinned back at my self-deprecation.

"So, does Ariana have you slaving way in the offices with the rest of her girls?" She was dressed in the office casual uniform of capris and simple top.

"Yeah. I'm helping out with the database stuff. Recording all the names of the dead, trying to link it all up with other databases so we can confirm who's really gone, which houses are really abandoned, and so on. And get you the rest of the names for the bricks and tiles."

"Cool. That would be very helpful."

My little shoulder devil still hadn't settled down yet; he was needling me about Ari's big pink elephant in the room. I angled another question at Cassandra.

"So, is your dad coming back to visit soon? How long has it been since he checked up on you?"

"Uh, I think so. We actually managed to connect over the phone a few days ago. He said he wanted to observe the election this weekend, so he's trying to get down here for that."

"Cool. So, how are things up in the Canyon? Still catching lots of fish?" I asked.

"Some. The water level in the creek is going down; it usually does this time of year. And they're worried about forest fires. The whole forest is really, really dry."

Oh geez, another thing I had not thought about. The whole state, the whole Southwest region, had been in drought conditions for more than a decade. All of the forests were at high risk of fires. I nodded sympathetically at her.

Ariana interrupted. "Hey, did you know that Cass can sew? She's been helping me make a new set of curtains for the living room."

"You can?" I responded. "That could be a really valuable skill in the future! Someday, we're going to wear out all our clothes and will need new stuff."

"Yeah, maybe. Actually, I was kinda thinking I might like to try for the police force here…" Her voice trailed off as she said this.

I frowned. "Well, okay. Sure, you could do that. I know we need more. There's an application process, and training. That's a valuable skill set, too."

She was staring down at the table. "Well, whatever I end up doing, I think I kinda need to stick close to my dad, for while. He didn't take it well, losing my mom and my brother."

Huh. I hadn't realized Patrick had had a son. He hadn't said anything that night in the studio. I nodded at Cassandra. "You know, he did come into the studio a few weeks ago, and made a tile for your mom. It just got fired last week. It turned out really nice. I put a green celadon glaze on it. Thats a kind of a medium tone color, very translucent. Shows off the texture and writing he put on the tile."

Cassandra smiled at the mental image. "Green was mom's favorite color. Ari said I could make one for my brother, too?"

I nodded back at her. "Of course. You're welcome anytime. How about tonight? 6pm? I'll be there and can help you myself."

"Okay, that would be great!" Cassandra smiled at me.

Ariana finally announced that she needed to get back to the office and Cassandra went with her.

***

Ariana joined Cassandra that evening for the tile making session. I'd not even realized before now that she had not participated in one of the open studio sessions.

I got them settled at a table with a set of common tools. I also showed Cass the tile for her mom, which she was very pleased with. Then a largish group of about ten other people arrived together, so Ali and I did a group presentation, showing everyone some basic ideas for shapes, textures, carving, stamping and drawing to customize their own tiles.

After that, I sat down with Ariana and Cassandra. Ari actually spoke up. "I figured I should finally make a tile for Vargo and Miguel." I nodded. She seemed pretty hesitant. Which was a pretty common reaction. In this place, in this purpose, most everyone was forced to confront their personal losses.

"Any ideas on what you'd like to make? Did he have any hobbies or interests? Something you could use as a symbol?"

Ariana said, "Vargo, he and my son, Miguel, they both loved sports. Baseball, especially. And soccer."

"Okay, maybe a baseball glove, ball and bat motif?" I picked out some sports themed cookie cutters for the basic shape. Ariana cut a few shapes, was dissatisfied, and scrapped them for recycling. She tried drawing out her shapes freehand, and was much happier with that result. She drew in a few sketch marks to illustrate the the details of the glove and baseballs. And she then rolled out a thin strip to lay over them, like a banner. She lettered her husband and son's names, and their birth and death dates on it, and sat back to consider her work.

"You don't talk about them much." I said quietly.

She nodded. "My son... I just can't, yet." She paused for a moment. "You know, Micah reminds me of him in a lot of ways. His quick mind, his easy going attitude."

I nodded but just waited for her to go on. Soon, she did.

"Vargo... Well, Vargo was a real piece of work. He really knew how to push my buttons. He could get me all spun up over the stupidest crap. We had a lot of crazy fights. Did Zach ever tell you that was how we first met? A neighbor called the cops because we were arguing in the front yard. Zach was one of the patrol cops to respond to the 'domestic disturbance' call. But that was years and years ago, though."

She paused to wipe a damp sponge around her tile to soften and smooth the edges.

She continued in the middle. "It's not like we didn't have some good times, though. When things were good, they were good. But if he had a bad day at work or things weren't going his way, he'd vent his frustrations on me. And of course, I usually didn't take that very well. You may have noticed that I can have a bit of temper." She said this last part dryly.

"Really? I hadn't noticed." I said back, just as dryly. Cassandra eyed us sideways, but did not say anything.

"So. There's that. I don't know what more to really say about him. I wasn't really sure if I would stay with him after Miguel was grown and out of the house. But it never came to that and now they're both gone and here we are."

She sat back. There didn't seem to be much more to add.

Meanwhile, Cassandra had crafted another musical treble clef symbol, similar the one her dad had done, and written her brother's name on it, Ryan. There was no cryptic tag line, though. I complimented the work, and confirmed she wanted the same glaze color on it. I asked her about her brother, and she told me that he had been 16, almost 17, when he passed. Like lots of guys, he too loved sports and video games and music. But, she explained, he had gotten to that age where he was rebelling against his dad about almost everything; curfews, who he hung out with, what classes he was taking in school, what he wanted to do after high school. In the months leading up to the Superflu they'd been butting heads a lot. She was pretty sure her brother had started smoking pot and that her dad had been riding him about it.

Cassandra said, "I think Dad feels guilty, now, about it. He barely even mentions Ryan. He'll talk about Mom now and then but it seems like he's pretending that Ryan didn't even exist."

I looked at her. "Are you mad at him about it? What happens when you mention Ryan?"

"Mostly, he just changes the subject."

"Well, you realize the whole point of this memorial project is so that we don't have to pretend they never existed. Just the opposite. It's about making sure no one is forgotten. The names that go up on it don't have to be perfect people. They don't have to be saints. People have flaws. Sometimes we don't like people very much. But they existed, they had an impact on our lives, for better or for worse. The memorial is in honor of that."

Cassandra gave me a wan smile and nodded. She had tears in her eyes. Also a common experience in the studio. It was not the first time I'd heard such stories and confessions about the dead. And it wouldn't be the last, either.

Chapter 21

Election day arrived. It was Saturday and I had left the day open to publicly cast my own vote, and then sit around waiting for election results to be announced that evening. Several days before, Gordon had discovered my lack of any formal plans for the day, so he declared that we had to have a little pool party and invited a few friends over. He invited Robert Ruckles and Zach, but Zach was supervising the security around the election. Ariana took the idea and ran with it as well. She called Rob and Maddy MacDonald, and Ned and Irene from Coolidge, and invited them to join us. They had been planning on coming to serve as impartial observers of the election, anyways, so coming a few hours earlier to hang out in the pool was not a problem for them.

At nine in the morning, Gordon and I walked down to the school auditorium where everyone could drop their ballots into the secured boxes waiting there. Cameras were recording the boxes and admins stationed at laptops were carefully entering names and addresses, both current and former, of voters, and checking to make sure that duplicate, extra ballots were not issued to anyone who had previously obtained one. Ariana wanted to make sure no one could stuff the boxes with extra votes. She was running a scrupulously clean operation, to make sure no one had reason to accuse her, or anyone in city management, of rigging the election.

I waved to the assortment of people who were filling out their ballot cards and with a little flourish, dropped mine into the box. The cards didn't take long to fill out; it was a very small election; just the mayor and council positions to vote on. So, it was just a few check boxes to mark. Thus, people were in and out of the auditorium quickly.

After we voted, Gordon and I went home and made the house party ready. This required some cleaning. I had not been doing very much of that before. We all tidied up the normal clutter that living generated but I was not a very good housekeeper when it came to things like scrubbing toilets, mopping floors and dusting. But having company over required a little more effort. Sharon pitched in with the interior work, while Carlos and Gordon took care of the yard. The huge house and property required near constant landscape maintenance. Dillon and Micah were out on one more electrical disconnection project.

Finally, at noon, our guests started arriving. Gordon grilled hamburgers and fresh sweet corn on the cob for everyone. As usual, there was plenty of salad to go with it. Carlos' garden was still growing lettuce and other veggies in the shaded areas, although the areas in direct sun were mostly done until a fall crop could be rotated in.

In addition to that, Carlos had a special item that he wanted everyone's opinion on. Working from information in the books I'd brought back from the university library, he had collected several buckets of mesquite pods from nearby trees. Mesquite was a native, brushy, medium sized tree that was well adapted to thrive on a minimal amount of water. It flowered in spring and quickly grew seed pods that looked a little like a long pea pod. The pods turned tan and dried out on the tree, and were ready for harvesting in late June. It was important to get them before they fell off the trees naturally. Left to sit on the ground, in the shade, they could get moldy quickly. But it was fairly easy to position a plastic tarp under a tree, give the branches a solid shake, and catch the clean pods. After sorting through, to remove any that had bugs or other blemishes, he whirled the pods in small batches through a food processor until they were reduced to a course meal, a little moister than wheat flour.

Carlos was experimenting with ways to use this mesquite meal as a flour substitute. Since it had no gluten in it, he didn't think it would rise well in traditional leavened breads, so today he was focused on making tortillas with it. It wasn't going very well, though. He had mixed the meal with some water, and a little salt, and rolled out round flats about six inches wide. Unfortunately, they were tearing and breaking up, when he tried to cook them in a dry skillet.

We still gamely sampled the resulting fragments. They had a slightly sweet flavor, but the mealy texture was off-putting. One did not usually think of tortillas as being crumbly, so it was hard to get around that. We all agreed that frying them in oil and using them as chips would be a good alternative, though. We also suggested perhaps mixing the meal with regular flour, or other starches, might help with consistency. And other components in the mix, like oil or maybe even egg, would keep them from breaking up so much during cooking. Worst case scenario, the mesquite flour could be used for dog food. Carlos was still pretty pleased with his first attempts, though, and made extensive notes for himself.

I spent some time chattering with Ned, from Coolidge. He was explaining to me that most of his people had already gone up to the White Mountains for the summer. The few remaining people, including his friend Irene, would do the same once this election was complete. They were transporting some sheep who could graze up there and would be ready to shear for wool at the end of the summer. They were also going to try their hand at harvesting pine nuts from the pinon trees in the area in late September, just before they came back.

I saw Ariana stroll in, followed by Cassandra and Patrick Stettner. I had not realized she would be bringing them along, so I was a little startled to see them file in together. But I shifted gears quickly and invited them to help themselves to some food.

I pulled Ariana aside. "I thought you were going to supervise the election?"

She answered, "No need. Jill has it under control. I estimate we have about 500 votes in the box already. The rest of the turn out should be pretty slow for the rest of the afternoon. I've got my radio. They'll buzz me if they need me back there." She patted her hip.

"Okay then." I nodded, and turned to answer a question about where the napkins were.

People mingled on the patio, and ate their food. We had misters and ceiling fans circulating, but hot air moving fast is still hot air. Once everyone had digested a little bit, and was good and sweaty, the pool was inviting enough to overcome anyone's shyness over appearing in a bathing suit. One by one, everyone changed clothes, and waded or jumped into the pool.

While people took turns changing in the house bathrooms, Cassandra pulled me aside. "Ariana said you had a whole bunch of little dogs, but I don't see them around?"

Correct. The only one who was well behaved enough to be allowed to circulate among the guests was Duchess. And Jack was by Carlos, as always.

I said, "Oh, yeah, they're all in the bedroom. Come on, I'll introduce you. You can change in our bathroom." I led her to the other side of the house, and Ari trailed after us, also waiting for her turn to change.

"Uh, actually, I can't swim." Cassandra pointed to the cast that was still on her leg. "Not allowed to get it wet." She looked disappointed.

"Oh, right. Well, you can still meet the puppies." I told her. Ari held up her hand to indicate she wanted a dip in the pool, though.

We had closed all the dogs, including Buster, in the master bedroom. Without managing to let any of them out (and Amex tried), we slipped in. Tyrion, Oreo and Zilla had been sleeping on the bed. Buster was curled up on Amex's big dog bed in the corner of the room. The little dogs looked up, stood up and stretched, and happily greeted Ariana. I introduced them one by one to Cassandra. Tyrion started yapping at her, when he realized she was an unfamiliar intruder. It took me a few tries to grab him, pick him up, and put him into Cass' arms, where he stopped barking.

Cass cuddled and cooed to him. "I take it you're a dog person then?" I asked her.

"Yeah, I've always loved dogs. We used to have labs. But they passed a couple of years ago."

Ariana called out from the bathroom, "Tell her!"

I looked from Ari, in the bathroom, to Cassandra. "Tell me what?" I asked.

Cassandra said, "Well, Dad found this thing this morning, when he was leaving to drive down here. Back in Sedona. It's the littlest tiniest Chihuahua you've ever seen. She's about three pounds, maybe."

Ariana called from the bathroom again. "It's not a dog, it's a rat. A half drowned rat."

Cassandra called back, "It's not a rat. It's a dog." In a lower voice she said to me, "It's just a really weird looking dog. She doesn't have hardly any fur on her; her skin is all spotted and mottled. She's got these huge tufts sticking out of her ears and on her tail, and between her toes."

I squinted at her. "Maybe it's a Chinese Crested?"

Cassandra asked, "What's that?"

"Fancy dog breed. Very expensive. Hairless. They don't trigger dog allergies. Very popular with the Snottsdale swanky set. And probably the Sedona swanky types, too." I explained.

Ariana stepped out of the bathroom, tying a strip of material around her waist, as a sarong style beach coverup. "It's an ugly thing; I'm not completely sure it doesn't have mange, either."

Cassandra pouted. "She is not! She's so ugly she's cute."

"Maybe you should call her 'Gremlin'" I suggested. Ariana rolled her eyes at me.

"What's that?" Cassandra asked.

"Creature from an 80's movie. Cute as the dickens. Unless you fed them after midnight, which made them turn into little monsters." Cassandra still looked confused. "We'll find a video for you. Come on, let's go swim."

We shuffled back out again. Oreo and Amex tried to make a break for the party but I managed to grab them and shoo them back inside and closed the door on them. Tyrion barked in disappointment some more.

Outside the bedroom, I discovered that Dillon and Micah had returned home. They were wolfing down burgers and roasted corn on the cob at the kitchen counter. They stared at us as we waved and trooped past them and out to the pool patio. What was their deal? I wondered. I told them they could come join us after they ate, and oh, could they put their dirty dishes in the dishwasher when they were finished, pretty please?

Outside, Gordon, Sharon, Rob and Robert, and Stettner were already in the pool. Maddy and Carlos were still sitting at the huge patio table, chatting about gardening and mesquite flour.

Ari and I joined everyone in the pool. The water was delightful. Nothing better for beating the heat than just floating about in a nice clean pool.

Cassandra went around to the far side of the pool, which was shaded by a huge eucalyptus tree and sat on the edge. She propped her casted leg to the side, and swung her healthy leg into the water, which came halfway up her calf. Some of the guys had beers, but I wasn't about do any day drinking, on Election Day. We still had a few hours to kill, before I had to appear in public again.

Gordon had set out a some pool toys, but mostly, we just floated around on pool noodles. Cassandra confirmed that, yes, she was totally keeping the ugly/cute little dog. Ariana said that it had to stay quarantined away from her other pets, mostly cats and one exotic bird until they they were sure that it did not have mange or any other communicable disease.

Gordon and Stettner were talking on the other side of the pool. I heard Gordon say, "Yeah, if you want try a song or two with us, we're going to be playing a short set tonight."

"You sure you want to do that? We haven't practiced together, might be a total disaster." Stettner said.

"Just pick something simple, that no one can mess up. If you've got something you already know, I can call John, and tell him to pull the sheet music. He's talented enough to sight read, and I just have to keep a beat. Not that hard."

Patrick thought for a moment, but I didn't hear what he replied, because Micah had stepped out, and Amex came barreling out the sliding glass door with him, and took a running cannon ball leap into the pool, heading straight for Gordon. Several of us shrieked at the unexpected splashing. I heard Micah calling; "Sorry! He was crying, and wanted to come out, so I figured he needed to take care of business! Amex! Here, boy!"

Micah tried to get Amex to come to him, but the big goof ball was having none of it. Gordon grabbed him and played with him for a bit. I told Micah it was okay. He and Dillon were standing on the patio, looking around at all the people. I realized that they might not know very many of our guests. They didn't usually hang out with my core group, when we were out and about town.

I called to them, "Hey, boys, come over here, you should meet everyone." One by one, I introduced everyone, and explained their backgrounds. Dillon shook hands with the men, who were clustered at the edge near him. Micah followed his example, and did the same. But Cassandra was on the opposite side, with Ariana, Sharon and me. Neither of the boys could reach her. She just waved and let it go at that. Dillon kept looking at her, though.

"Why don't you guys get changed, and come join us?" I told them. They accepted the suggestion and returned within moments. They both cannon balled into the pool, just like Amex. We screeched at the splashing a little more, but honestly, I really didn't mind. It was cool and wet and felt good.

After a while, Amex got worn out enough to be shooed out of the pool. He laid down on the patio, in the shade near Carlos, and panted calmly for a bit, carefully supervising the rest of us. Duchess had retreated to the air conditioned interior of the house.

After a time, the conversation turned to a discussion about how crazy it was to be living here in Chandler, given how hot the summers were. Stettner was making the case that this was a really stupid place to live. In spite of his daughter pointing out that they'd been living here for almost 30 years. He reminded us that it was a desert, with an average rainfall of 7 to 10 inches per year. The soil was gravely, alkaline and hard, barely suitable for growing the hardiest crops on a large scale.

Ariana threw out the obvious question: "So, where is the perfect place to live? My great grandparents emigrated from Mexico, and thought this place was pretty awesome. If not here, then where should we be living?"

Ruckles answered first. "Oregon. Portland area. Lots of farmland, plenty of rain, doesn't get too cold in the winter. I think there are some small scale groups getting organized, up there, too. They might welcome new people."

Gordon had to add the obvious, "Nah, the West Coast is due for a huge earthquake any time now. I wouldn't want to spend years rebuilding a city, and then have it shaken apart. I think the smarter place to do the subsistence farming thing is anywhere in the Midwest. It's already cleared for farming. The former population density means there's plenty of housing to reclaim, factories, warehouses, leftover equipment. There's a lot of small and medium rivers for water and power, too."

Robert countered that. "A lot of the dams on those rivers are functionally obsolete. They were way past their sell-by date, even before the Superflu. Without constant maintenance, they're probably going to fall apart within the next ten or twenty years."

Gordon grimaced at that. He also conceded that he didn't like the cold winters and snow in the Midwest.

While we were chatting, I noticed that Dillon had moved around the rough circle of people in the pool, and had positioned himself beside Cassandra, who was still sitting in the shade on the far side, one foot in the water. They seemed to be having a bit of a sidebar conversation of their own. At one point, I heard her explain to Dillon that they'd been living in Mesa, before.

Sharon wondered aloud. "What about Texas, or anywhere in the Southeast? Louisiana, Florida? Plenty of farmland, rain, left over housing and businesses, no earthquakes."

"Hurricanes!" I said succinctly.

Everyone nodded, but I went on. "The East coast has the same problems, too: too cold, too old, possibly still too many people who might not take kindly to our relocation. Pockets of it here and there might still be nice and livable. But you know where the best place to live would be?" Everyone looked at me expectantly.

"Hawaii!" I grinned and raised my eyebrows, expecting everyone to get it instantly. They just stared blankly.

"It's perfect! The Big Island, Oahu and Maui already have a lot of cleared land for farming. The soil is rich, there's plenty of rain. Produce grows with barely any effort at all. It gets very few hurricanes, in spite of being in the middle of the ocean. Earthquakes are tiny, and directly tied to volcanic activity, and it's easy to stay away from that stuff. The climate is nearly perfect."

The gang was looking back and forth at each other speculatively. I went on.

"Hawaii could have been the fruit basket of the nation, but for the size and distance. When this country was expanding and growing over the last couple of centuries, it didn't have the transportation tech to overcome the distance. Only the most profitable industries could afford to grow or process stuff there and ship it over to the mainland. That's how it came to be known for stuff like whaling and sugar cane and pineapple. By the time shipping technology grew enough to be able to handle the distance, the population here on the mainland had grown beyond what the arable land in Hawaii could sustain, space-wise. Really, it was just a matter of circumstances. Well, that, and the development of plenty of good growing land all over this continent. But if Hawaii had been closer, it could have been a much bigger contributor to the country's agricultural economy. But that didn't happen. It's isolated and beautiful, so tourism and specialty crops like tropical fruit, became the dominant factors in the state's economy.

That, and the military, of course."

My friends were looking back and forth at each other, still processing.

"There's still plenty of housing leftover. 97-3, remember? It's so easy to grow food in the right parts of the islands, you don't really need a lot of equipment or supplies. Power requirements are minimal. You don't need much air conditioning. Or heat. Clean water is relatively easy to produce; there's springs and small rivers all over the place – it doesn't take a lot of filtration. Plenty of room for livestock, too. It could be a very leisurely way of life. Which, of course, is why it was so popular as a tourist and retirement destination."

Gordon had to start poking holes in my theory.

"What about the Hawaiians? They might not take very kindly to another colonial invasion. What did they call us gringos; 'Howlies'?"

I rolled my eyes. "Gordo; 97-3! The demographics on the island was a mix of native Hawaiians, Caucasian, and Asian. Mostly Japanese, I think. Invasion objections could probably be overcome, if we brought the right kinds of gifts. Medicine, antibiotics, skills."

Gordon was still skeptical. "Uh huh. And just how would we get there?"

"Boat, of course! Long Beach or L.A. or something has got to have marinas full of boats or yachts or ships that could be reclaimed and refurbished."

Gordon said, "I don't think any of us knows much about long distance ocean cruising…" He looked around at the others, who shook their heads. "And boat fuel is probably not the same as car gas. I think some boats, maybe a lot, use diesel, or other grades of fuel. And fuel goes bad."

I wasn't about to let transportation details sidetrack my paradise fantasy. I wanted him on board with my long term fantasy. "Gordon, do you know what else they grow in Hawaii?" I asked him.

"Uh, Maui Wowie?" he grinned at me. I smirked back at him and shook my head. Yeah, that grew there too, but it was not the answer I was looking for. He gestured for me to elaborate.

"Coffee. Kona Coffee. On the Big Island."

Gordon popped his eyes wide at me. "Oh! Well! I'm in then! Let's go!" He pretended to head for the steps.

Everyone busted out laughing. Gordon's love of coffee was well known and the dwindling supplies were causing some rationing already. Gordon had secured a large private stash early on, but he was already fretting about it running out one day.

The conversation meandered onto other topics, and I sat back, relaxing. I glanced around. Micah was practicing pool jump shots into a small basketball hoop, off to the side. Stettner was staring in his daughter's direction. He was wearing large sunglasses, so it was hard to read his expression, but I thought he might be frowning a bit. I looked at Cassandra. Dillon was still in the water beside her, looking up, chatting and gesturing around. I had moved to a sunnier spot and couldn't hear them clearly, but it looked pretty innocent to me. I made a mental note to keep observing but let it go for now.

***

Around 3 pm, I begged off from the party, telling people I needed a short nap, if I was going to be bright eyed and bushy tailed for the results counting. That cued people that it was time to clear out and do whatever they needed to get ready for the evening. I slipped away, while Gordon saw everyone else out.

I did lay down for about 20 minutes, but I was too wired to actually cat nap. After a bit, Gordon came in and took his shower. Then I cleaned the pool chlorine off as well and got dressed in my usual capris and top. I picked slightly dressier versions than usual, since I would probably have to make a brief speech. I had a mental list of points I wanted to make but I hadn't written anything down.

Gordon gathered everyone together to head out. Normally, we let Micah stay home during Saturday Town Halls; he thought they were boring. Usually, he and Dillon played video games instead. But this time, Dillon elected to go with us. Micah was rather put out by that choice, but he had the maturity not to whine about it.

We took two cars down to the school. Even though it was easy walking distance, I didn't want to get all sweaty on the short walk there.

Inside the theater, small groups were gathering. A beverage service with water, lemonade and iced tea had been setup in the lobby, but no snacks. Ariana had arranged for Mercados to have food ready later on.

We were not holding the regular Town Hall meeting that day, in favor of completing the election. But otherwise, it was a lot like most other Saturday afternoons.

Most of my fellow candidates had already arrived, along with their own support groups. While we waited, the last of them wandered in, as well. At 5pm, the polls officially closed, and the final counting could begin. They had already counted a couple of the boxes from early balloting and the morning drop offs. They just needed to do a final run down and finish the remaining box. It was actually rather boring, watching people look at cards, tap keys on a computer and pass it along to the next person. They had several people counting to make sure no errors occurred.

People mingled and chatted. I greeted my opponents politely, asked them how they were doing, made the usual small talk. Our independent election monitors, Rob and Maddy, Ned and Irene, and Stettner, circulated, chatted, and observed the counting.

At 6:30pm, the election commission summoned everyone who was waiting, into the auditorium. They announced the quantities of votes that each person had received. The candidate with the highest count was elected Mayor, and the next five highest counts earned the Council seats.

As everyone had told me I would, I did earn the highest quantity of votes. I had only half believed them that it would happen. Once it was officially written out on the big screen at the back of the stage, it suddenly became much more real. A little knot of disappointment swam around in my stomach. A part of me had kind of hoped I would lose, and thus, be off the hook for all the hard work and headache that I knew would be coming. My shoulder angel poked that attitude into submission and reminded me that I had accepted the challenge because I did care, because these people needed me, and that I could do the job.

The next highest counts listed my new Council: Richard Forchik, Daniel Johannsen, Victoria Allamilla, Brad Lofkin and Roman Vance. The seventh candidate, Miguel Cisneros, had not won enough votes to be seated on the Council. Overall, a little over 780 votes had been collected. That seemed like a surprisingly good turnout to me, compared to our overall population.

The audience called out for a victory speech, so I got on stage. While I had the main points in my head, it was mostly impromptu.

"Wow, thank you so much! Thank you to everyone who made this possible. A lot of hard work went into putting this together. And we still have a lot of hard work ahead of us. I know a lot people think the hard part is over, now that we've cleaned the place up. But I have a feeling the hard part is just getting started. In the coming months we're going to have to figure out how to restart an economy. We need to reconnect with the rest of the world. We need to keep on growing food. We need to balance our use of fuel, with our need to move about the area. We need to take precautions to keep our community safe, but still ensure we have the freedom to pursue our happiness. And, of course, we need to keep on healing from our grief."

I paused for a moment to collect my thoughts.

"I also want to congratulate my fellow candidates. I'm looking forward to working with the new Council. As mayor, I will have an 'open door' policy. Meaning, if you have concerns or ideas, you're always welcome to bring them to me." I had a feeling I was going to regret saying that. But it was the kind of thing that had to be said.

"And now, I believe the food is ready over at Mercados! Let's celebrate!" I grinned at everyone, who were also happy to move along to the fun part.

***

As usual, people mingled in the general party atmosphere of the restaurant, and adjacent pub space. People congratulated me on the victory. I shook hands and thanked supporters. When I had a moment, I drank down gulps of lemonade, and sat to catch my breath. I turned my head, to find Kaycee and Kyrene joining me at the table.

"Hey!" I greeted them. "You both look much better! How are you feeling?"

They nodded at me, and said they were doing much better. They told me that everyone had been released from the hospital. Three of the girls had taken off, going back to where ever they had been living before. But Sasha and two others had elected to take up residence in one of the apartments in the zone. They were starting work in the warehouse on Monday. Kaycee added, "I wanted to thank you for what you did. Jenna told us that you mobilized the police to come and get us."

"Well, I think they would have mobilized themselves, as soon as they knew they were needed. It probably wouldn't have mattered who brought the issue to them." My little shoulder devil wondered why Kyle had failed to take action when Jenna raised the issue within him on Sunday. His lack of action meant Jenna had waited to bring it to me on Monday. I kept that thought on the inside.

"So, are you back at work?" I asked Kaycee. She was a graphic designer and website designer for the city. She had assisted me with conceptual drawings of the memorial.

She nodded. "Yeah, Ariana said she had a whole bunch of stuff for me to do. I spent a few hours over there this morning, clearing some things off my to-do list."

I turned to Kyrene, with the same question on my face. "And will you be back in the studio soon?"

Kyrene looked a little sour. Uncomfortable. "Actually, that's what I wanted to talk to you about."

I waited patiently.

"I think I'm going to leave town for a while. I want to go back to California. I know my parents are gone but if they're still at the house, I want to bury them or burn them or something. I want to get some of my stuff, too."

I waited to see if she would add anything else. I thought maybe she was trying to run away from her problems. But then, going home to the desiccated corpses of her family was not exactly getting off the hook easily. Maybe she needed to confront her own past, her own losses, to get some perspective and insight into her own choices.

My silence made her uncomfortable. She added, "It's not like you really need me at the studio. You have everyone else, they can handle things there."

"You know you're always welcome to come back. You're an important part of our team. There's still more pots to be made." I said gently.

She nodded. She still had trouble meeting my eyes. I waited a bit, to see if she wanted to say anything else. It became clear that she did not.

Finally, I said, "Okay then. Listen, leave your contact info with us. And check in. Let us know that you're safe, okay?"

Kyrene nodded again.

"Okay. Good luck, then. Safe travels." I patted her on the arm, and they slipped away from the table. I hoped she would be safe. Kyrene was from the suburbs around Los Angles, and that area was a bit of a wasteland. We hadn't heard of any organized recovery on any significant scale in that area.

I turned to survey the party again. People were moving inside, and some people were dragging free chairs inside, as well. I followed them in. Gordon and his band were setting up on the stage in the corner. They had played one other gig a couple of weeks ago, but they still had a lot of practicing to do, to build up a collection of songs they could cover.

After a brief tune up, they launched into a rousing rendition of "Twist and Shout", followed by several other fun party tunes. Ariana dragged me out onto tiny dance floor, where we made silly fools of ourselves. Gawd, I could not keep a rhythm to save my life. But I made a game try of it. After a couple of songs, she let me go back to my seat.

Once everyone who was willing to publicly embarrass themselves was good and tired, the band paused. John, the lead guitarist addressed the crowd. "Folks, we're gonna slow things down here, give you all a chance to catch your breath. Please welcome a very special guest appearance by… uh… " He clearly didn't remember who he was supposed to introduce. From behind him, Gordon supplied the name.

"Right! Patrick Stettner is going to sing a song for us. We didn't have much time to practice this, so if we don't get it quite right, please have mercy!"

Patrick appeared from the back of the crowd, carrying a guitar. John unplugged his from the amplifiers, and Patrick plugged in the one he was carrying. John took over on the nearby electric keyboard. They tested their pitch, and nodded to Patrick to lead off when ready.

Patrick leaned into the microphone, and said, "This song is for everyone."

He launched into opening chords of a slow, simple ballad. It took me a few moments to recognize it. Finally, it came to me: "Dust in the

Wind" by Kansas. I immediately realized how well chosen the song was for our current circumstances.

Patrick sang the words in a beautiful tenor voice. I'd had no idea he could sing. Or play guitar. I think he may have missed a few notes of the melody, but he gracefully managed to carry on. As John had asked, everyone forgave them their minor mistakes.

When he concluded, everyone clapped enthusiastically. John took over lead position, and Patrick retreated to the back of the restaurant. I think he was putting the guitar away. John said they had a couple more songs in their repertoire. Next they played "Here Comes the Sun", a perfect choice to bring the mood of the room back up again. They finished off with "Old Time Rock'n'Roll", which Ariana made me get up and dance to again.

After the band wrapped up their live music set, they switched back over to some recorded music. Most people took this as a sign that it was okay to leave the party. They worked on finishing off their drinks and gathering their things. Gordon had rejoined me at our table and wanted one more beer before we headed home. Ariana located Cassandra who was at a nearby table with Dillon and several of his friends. She convinced Cass it was time go and Dillon stepped out with them, probably to walk them home. Meanwhile, Zach, who had been milling about the perimeter all evening in uniform, came over and sat down with us. He looked a little perturbed.

"Hey Zach. What's up? What's wrong?" I asked him.

He looked at me, and shook his head. "Nothing. I just don't understand that guy, Stettner."

"What do you mean?" Gordon asked.

"We had a little chat, earlier. Seems Ari and Cassandra told him some of the details of our castle rescue operation. He was giving me flak for not busting up that party sooner."

"How so?"

Zach answered, "He said we should never have let the girls go to the party in the first place."

"Like we could have stopped them! They didn't exactly ask permission!" I blurted out.

He kept going. "I know, I know, and I said that to him. Then he says we should have gone in riot gear, and busted it up, and kicked everyone out. Can you believe that? The guy has the nerve to tell me how to do my job!"

I frowned at him. I looked at Gordon. Gordon looked back at me. Neither of us were sure what to say.

Zach added, "And then he comes in here, and sings that song. That was beautiful! Did you guys practice that?" he asked Gordon.

"Yeah, just an hour ago. Went through it a couple of times. He's really rusty on the guitar, but he managed okay, I thought." Gordon answered.

Zach nodded that, yes, the song was well done. But he was still flummoxed over Stettner's attitudes.

"So, are you going to let it go?" I asked Zach.

"Yeah." He paused, looked at me, and then added, "Listen, I'm taking a day off tomorrow. I need a break."

"Of course. That's fine. Just be sure to get the PTO form onto my desk before you go." I winked at him.

He snorted back at me, and wandered off to make yet another check in with his guys.

Chapter 22

On Sunday morning after the election, I wanted to sleep in. At least, that's what I told my brain. However, I was still on the adrenaline rush from the night before. I was still having conversations inside my head, with all the people I'd already finished talking to.

As a result, I was up early and puttering about the house, when the doorbell rang. The fur alarm also rang, just to make sure I knew someone was at the door. I opened the front door to find Kevin. And he had a girl with him, who he introduced as Rochelle. They were holding hands. Well, alrighty then.

"You're back!" I exclaimed. I did a mental check, to recall when I'd last seen him. Geez, it had been a little over two months since he had left on his trip to go to the East coast.

Rochelle was a pretty girl, thin, short, with jet black hair and pale skin. Her hair cut had probably been a stylish bob, before, but it was growing out and looked a little uneven. She probably wasn't doing any better at finding a good stylist than I was.

The dogs, as always, greeted the new visitors enthusiastically. Rochelle didn't seem all that excited by their yapping leaping presence, so I shooed most of them into the bedroom and closed the door on them. They barked their protest at this, but I remained firm.

I invited Kevin and Rochelle into the kitchen, where I made them some breakfast. The rest of the house mates were off doing other things. I think Sharon was doing the weekly shopping for the house, picking up stuff from the gardens and the warehouse.

I fixed my guests omelets loaded with onions, peppers and tomato from the gardens and a little fresh goat cheese sprinkled on top. There was some fresh watermelon, too, so I sliced a bunch of that for them, as well. I also gave them some of Carlos' mesquite flour tortillas fragments to sample and made note of their opinions.

Then I sat down to listen to Kevin's update.

"Okay, so what do you want to tell me? What did you find?" I asked him.

He explained that he had gotten back yesterday just in time to vote, but was too tired to hang out at the restaurant, so he and Rochelle had just checked into the hotel and chilled for the evening. He had never officially moved out of his own house outside the zone, but it was too hot there right now, to stay. He was required to keep the hotel room clean as there there was no housekeeping service. But otherwise, it was a good option for his situation. Then he explained Rochelle's background. He said that she had been living in D.C., but was not interested in sticking around there any longer, so she had come along for the ride.

"Did you find any official federal government still operating?" I asked him.

"Yes. No. Sort of. There's FEMA camps around, but they're not what I expected. If FEMA is in charge of a spot, that just means a guy with a jacket with the letters on it is doing what you're doing here: mayoring, organizing people and collecting stuff. They're clearing out bodies and cleaning up towns. But it's weird. I'd drive through one town and it would be in pretty good condition. And then next one down the highway would be a complete wreck. Burned houses, boarded up windows, broken glass, cars left in the middle of street. Bullet holes in the walls."

"Did you run into any gangs, anyone try to take from you, or hurt you?"

"Nah, but only because I was paying attention. They're around, but I finally figured out how to avoid them. How to tell if a town was in good shape, and didn't have any gangs. See, it worked like this: If a town was a complete wreck, it was also probably empty. If a town was clean, no weeds, no trash, it was organized. But the ones in the middle, only partly cleaned up, those were the dangerous ones."

"How so?" I asked him.

"Say you drive into a little town. The cars are parked normally, there's only a few broken windows, but no glass on the ground. There's a few people walking around, but they're in small groups, and they're walking fast, hurrying. Then you see a bunch of guys clustered in a group in the middle of the town. They got AKs and sniper rifles, but they're not wearing any uniforms. You take a sniff of the air; see if you can still smell the dead bodies. Maybe it's there, but not real strong. Those are the towns you avoid. The gangs have done just enough to make it tolerable for themselves, but they're not exactly doing anything to help anyone else. Those are the towns you just drive on through, or around, if you can.

But a town that's pulling it together - they have cops in uniform, or maybe a homegrown militia, but they're at least in matching uniforms. They're patrolling in pairs, not just standing around. The people are walking easy, by themselves, not in groups. No one is in a hurry. They got gardens and little farms planted and growing food. They've patched up the broken glass, moved the abandoned cars. The trash is picked up. That's how you know the place is recovering."

I nodded thoughtfully. "Does that pattern apply to larger towns? Big cities? What route did you take?"

"Mostly I took I-40 eastward. But I'd get off and take the state routes sometimes, just so I could go through those little towns. The bigger cities are more of a mess, than the little ones. I went through Albuquerque, on the way out. That place is a wreck! But Amarillo wasn't too bad. They got people there, some real strong leadership. That was one of the bigger towns I saw that was pulling it together. Then a whole lot of little towns between Amarillo and Nashville. I went around Oklahoma City. I wanted to avoid Memphis, but I had to cross the Mississippi there, so I ended up going right through downtown. Also another wreck."

Kevin paused to drink some water.

"After that, things started to get more crowded. Lots of little farms, camps, settlements scattered all over the place, bigger towns abandoned, but the little towns were filled up. The people who bugged out from wherever, landing in those places. The, uh, - whats the word?" He looked to Rochelle.

"Housing density," she filled in.

"Right. The housing density got bigger the farther east I went. So, even though 97% died, people from elsewhere just moved in and filled up. I think a lot of people from here, or California, or West Texas ended up in that area."

Rochelle added in, "It's good farm land. People can grow enough food to feed themselves, and raise some animals, too, without exhausting themselves to do it."

I nodded. I looked back at Kevin.

He continued his narrative. "Oh, but the mountains!"

"Appalachians," Rochelle filled in again.

"Right! The Appalachians were filled with people hiding out in every cabin, and valley, and down every little pathway into some dark forest. And they weren't getting along. No one trusted anyone, and they're fighting over all the stuff that's left in the stores, and they're running out of gas already. I was really glad I had plenty of extra cans with me. One night, I camped near the Cherokee National Forest, three different groups came wandering through the campground, on foot, looking to get from one place to another, and looking at my Jeep, like they thought they needed it more than I did."

Kevin rolled his eyes, and snorted at his memories.

"After that, I just stuck to the main freeways, and high tailed it to D.C. Now, that is a town that has pulled it together! Can you believe it? The place is cleaned up, there's military patrolling the streets. A couple of the museums are even open! Coulda knocked me over with a feather!"

Well, I also found that news rather astonishing. At some cue that I did not see, Rochelle took over the narrative.

"I was in D.C. when the Superflu hit," she began.

"It was crazy there. Riots at the hospitals, protests outside the White House, and in front of Capitol Hill. People demanding a cure. But the government people - I was bar tending at this place in Georgetown, it gets a lot of government types, people who work for the Federal Reserve, or the letter agencies, like the EPA, HUD, or OSHA, or whatever. Mid level management bureaucrats. Anyway, the government people were just partying it up like it was the end of the world. Well, duh, it was the end of the world. A regular would come in the bar, get shit-faced, and then we'd never see him again. One by one, they just dropped off the face of the planet. But the weird thing is, I never got sick, even though I was around tons of people who were coughing and practically hacking out their lungs."

Rochelle kept going. I sat back to listen.

"My boss got sick. All the other waitresses got sick. Finally I was the last employee left. I just kept going in and serving drinks until the booze ran out. Some of the customers took pity on me and brought me food or more liquor to serve. Then a few weeks ago, Kevin walked into the bar." They grinned at each other.

So. They had each found their own true Mr./Ms. Right in a bar. Would miracles never cease? Well, whatever worked for them.

"How was food being distributed around the city? Was it all packaged food? Did they have much fresh food to go around?"

"Mostly packaged stuff, a lot of MREs. A couple of the larger federal departments had cafeterias serving hot cooked food. I could go in there, if I wanted. They were issuing ration cards, and people would give me some in exchange for keeping the bar open."

I thought. I had so many questions popping up in my head. "Cool. What about fuel? Transportation?"

"Uh huh." She shook her head. "They put the kibosh on that real quick, last winter. Most cars were seized, people were told to walk, or ride a bike. They said they needed to conserve all the gas. There were a few buses running people around, like from Capitol Hill to Georgetown and back. But not like it used to be. My apartment was a few blocks from the bar, so I walked most everywhere. I had a bike, too, if I wanted to go farther."

"What about bodies? Did they have to go house to house, clearing bodies?"

Rochelle got a very sad look on her face. "Some. But not like what it was here. Kev told me about the body clearing work you two did here. But D.C. is mostly a company town. It's all office buildings and government buildings. The proportion of residential housing to office space, is much lower than what you have here. My apartment was ridiculously expensive, before. I shared it with a couple of friends. But they died. In the hospital." The sad face settled on her for a moment.

"The hospitals there were bigger, too. And the CDC and WHO setup temporary facilities. I think a lot more people went to those, when they got sick, rather than staying home, like they did here. Of course, some people died at home, too. A lot, I guess. And eventually, someone went around cleaned it up. But I just kept serving drinks in the bar. It was like I was in a bubble, I couldn't feel or hear or see anything that was going on outside. Like the TV was on mute. People came in, drank, and left. They came back, or they didn't."

She stopped, but I could tell she had more to say. I waited. Kevin had his arm resting across the back of her chair. His thumb lightly brushed the back of her neck and shoulder, a tiny little massage. For comfort.

A new thought occurred to me. "Wait, you said they were confiscating vehicles, to conserve gas? Kevin, how did you keep yours? Do you still have the Jeep?"

He grinned at me. "Yeah, I heard about that before I even crossed the Beltway. I stashed it in a garage in an abandoned house. Rode a motorcycle that I, uh, 'found,' into town. They took that, too. We ended up riding bicycles back out to the house to get the Jeep."

I smiled back at his creativity and looked back to Rochelle.

Finally, she picked up the thread of her story. "One day, in February, the weather got nice, so I decided to go for a bike ride, before I opened up the bar. I was cruising around on the Island, the one in the middle of the Potomac. Good bike trails there. I saw this barge moving down the river. It was piled with stuff. Like logs wrapped in sheets and blankets and plastic bags. I'd heard about it before, but that was the only time I actually saw one. They were taking the bodies out to sea to dump them."

These last words came out slowly. Clearly, she was still horrified by what she had seen. I was horrified on her behalf. It seemed like a particularly heartless and crass way to dispose of bodies. But what better way to do it? Their crematoriums were probably overwhelmed, too, just like ours had been. And mass graves without embalming or coffins would contaminate their ground water. Outdoor cremation as we had done was probably not feasible, during a cold, wet East Coast winter. At least a burial at sea was clean and sanitary. It still seemed awfully cruel, though. But then, mixing cremains into concrete to make a memorial might seem equally cruel to Rochelle or anyone else for that matter. I kept my thoughts to myself.

"I'm sorry you had to see that." She nodded her thanks. I wanted to get more information, though. I waited a bit for her to recover her composure.

"Rochelle, what else can you tell me about the city? Was there any FBI presence, any activity from Homeland Security? Any kind of official law and order?"

"Well, the D.C. city police got conscripted by the military, to do patrols. They consolidated all the military branches into one, too. It's now just the 'U.S. Armed Military Forces.' U.S.A.M.F. It took them a while to get all their shit pulled together. Its been a real nightmare, transferring surviving personnel from around the country, heck, around the world, to the few remaining bases they were keeping open. I think they're still working on it. Norfolk is one of the main bases on the east coast. There's another one in Florida, I forget where. One in Texas. And San Diego, San Francisco, a few others. Mostly on the east and west coasts. The bases are responsible for general security, in their city or region. For them, that means mostly just breaking up fights, or scattering the gangs. Which hasn't been much of problem around D.C. The gangs are smart enough to not go anywhere near the Beltway. Anyway, U.S.A.M.F. is starting to send units out farther, to take care of those problems regionally. So, there's that."

"Okay, that's good to know. Gordon and I might be taking a quick trip to San Diego soon. Someone wants him for some consulting work. I'll probably get to meet with some muckity mucks there, so this is helpful to know, going in."

She smiled, pleased to have been able to provide some useful insight.

I looked back to Rochelle and asked, "Okay, so what about criminal prosecution? We had a situation; huge party in Phoenix went sideways. Some girls held against their will, assaulted, stuff like that. I'm hoping that someone somewhere, has a way to help arrest and punish the perps."

Rochelle's eyes widened. "Oh! Geez, how horrible! But no, there's no courts or anything, that I know of. All the police and military are doing is trying to restore order."

I nodded. "That reminds me, what about communications? Internet, telephones, cell phones? What do you know about federal plans for that? Anything?"

"Uh, nothing official. One guy at the bar did say that all the effort was going into cell phones. He thought regular phones were a lost cause."

Huh. That was contradictory to what I'd seen on some of the blogs Sharon had provided for me. And to what she had told me herself.

"Okay, next: any oil refining getting restarted? How desperate is the fuel crunch going to get?"

"Yes! That I do know! They are definitely getting an oil refinery restarted in Texas. But there's talk about a draft to get enough labor for it. They only need about a hundred men to drill for the oil on one of those off-shore platforms in the Gulf. But they need a few hundred more to run the refinery in Galveston. And they need *lots* more support people: maintenance, supply, trucking…" She glanced at Kevin. I had a feeling his OTR trucking days were not behind him, after all.

Kevin interrupted. "Some people I ran into in Texas had a real problem with being drafted for general labor. It was a real worry for them."

I nodded. Yeah, nobody likes being told what to do. Offer them a healthy incentive, and they might feel differently, though.

"What about the economy? Are they going to start a new currency system, or try to keep using dollars?" I asked both of them.

Rochelle answered, "Yeah, that's been a huge problem, too. Several different political factions and they all have different ideas about what to do. Some want a gold standard, some want to keep using regular dollars, some say let the market set its own price. And there's even a fringe group that says chuck it all and go with a crypto currency. At the bar, I was taking paper dollars or gold dollars, if people had them to offer. Food, bullets or booze, if they didn't."

"So, no one has come to any conclusions, so far?" I asked.

Rochelle shook her head. Great. I had really been counting on some help from above on that one.

Kevin spoke up. "We did hear there's going to be a presidential election this fall, though."

I nodded. "Yeah, I've heard that too. Pretty confusing. Only one guy running. Not sure how that's going to work."

Kevin nodded back at me. Rochelle looked down at her hands. I thought over everything they had told me so far.

"Kevin, anything else happen on the drive back?"

"Not really. We came back through central Ohio, Indiana, Illinois, all the way to the Rockies. Then back down to Albuquerque again, and back the way I left. More of the same. Little towns pulling together unless they got infected with a gang. Big towns emptied out and usually a complete mess. I cruised through some of the suburbs around the big cities too, looking for any that were like ours. Indianapolis had one on the north side, what was it called?" he looked to Rochelle.

"Carmel" she said.

"Right, that's it. Carmel. Cute little town. They seemed to be doing the same thing. Consolidating, moving people into a zone, turning off the power outside the zone."

"And how was the power situation, everywhere else?"

"Pretty bad. Mostly off." He said. "Generators, if they felt they could afford to use the fuel. Extreme rationing. Solar, if they get enough sun. Wind, too. Tennessee has a lot of dams on the rivers, and is getting electricity from those. But none of the big coal burning plants are running any more. No coal getting to them to be burned."

"Okay, I think that covers everything I need to know. Anything else?" I asked him. He shook his head. "You planning another trip yet?"

"Not sure" he responded. "Just need a couple of weeks to chill, figure out where to go next."

I thought about the conversation in the pool yesterday. "Kevin, how much do you know about piloting boats?" I asked him carefully.

He looked at me, very confused. "Boats? I don't know squat about boats," he said.

"Maybe you might want to think about them. Maybe go check out a marina, see if you can figure out how to figure them out. How to navigate, not just drive them."

He considered me. "Maggie, what do you have up your sleeve?" he asked.

"Just wondering about things elsewhere in the world. Just curious. It's not an emergency or anything. You don't have to. I'm just floating the idea out there. But for now, I have mayor work to do."

I gently shooed them out of the house and turned to my computer to study those websites and blogs some more.

Chapter 23

Dry summer in the Sonora desert can be brutal, but early July is when the real misery starts. That's the start of the summer monsoon season. The desert Native American tribes used to say there were two summers, the early dry summer, and the late wet summer. Monsoon is a bit of a misnomer, a cultural misappropriation of a word that originally described a much worse rainy cycle in India. Here in the desert, it means that the winds shift around to come from the southeast, and push moisture from the Gulf of Mexico into the region. The atmospheric heat, plus the additional heat that has baked into the ground, updrafts to cook up the huge cumulus clouds known as thunderheads. When enough energy collects, they roll over the desert, throwing back down wind, lightning, thunder and eventually, rain. It gets quite dramatic, and has been admired by many for generations. A collapsing thunderhead can push an enormous amount of air back down, which hits the ground, and pushes outward. If the ground is dry, it kicks up dust, which billows along in a wave known as a haboob (another word that was also appropriated from a different culture). Lots of dramatic videos of this phenomenon have been captured and were circulated on the Internet, before.

When the rain finally falls, it wets and compacts the dust, so that later in the season, the haboobs are not such an issue. But the wind still is. It can take down tree limbs, and sometimes whole trees. It blows trash around and generally makes a mess. Extremely intense rain, and sometimes hail, can fall in a relatively small area. Another favorite Valley joke revolves around getting rain in the front yard, but not the backyard, or variations on that concept. Intense rain can also cause localized flooding, as storm drains get quickly overwhelmed or clogged with debris. Water flows into arroyos and washes and minor river tributaries. Flash flooding can be sudden and dangerous. Quite a few years before the Superflu, Arizona enacted a "hillbilly in a wash" law, or more politely known as a "stupid motorist" law. Basically, if anyone was dumb enough to drive into a flooding wash, thinking it wasn't that deep, or that their vehicle could get through, but doesn't, they could be fined the cost of the rescue.

Those are just the overt dangers, though. The less obvious one, though, is just the sheer misery the heat and humidity cause. Heat stroke and heat exhaustion are real threats for anyone working outside. But just plain being sweaty and hot and uncomfortable all the time makes people cranky.

It's the kind of heat that makes it hard to sleep at night. The house only cools off enough to be comfortable in the early morning hours, which is its own dilemma. Early mornings, being the coolest time of the day, are the best time to get any vigorous outdoor work done, but they're also best time of the day for peaceful sleep. It's really hard to find the motivation to get up out of bed, to step outside in the swampy air, and walk the dogs or clean up the yard or pull weeds from the garden, during an Arizona monsoon season.

And this year, it was starting early.

The Mayoral Inauguration was set for July 4th, about 10 days after the election. Due to unexpected schedule conflicts of his own, Gordon decided to postpone the San Diego trip until after the inauguration. The actual swearing in would take place in the auditorium, which was blessedly air conditioned. Then the town was throwing a big Independence Day celebration, in the hotel ballroom.

Sharon and I went to the mall, to try to find appropriate lightweight party dresses for the occasion. The reduced quantity of carbs in our diet meant we were both still losing weight. All our older smaller clothes from the backs of our closets were years out of fashion. And were getting worn out or moth-eaten.

But the mall was still stocked with autumn colors and winter styles, which were very unappealing, in the heat.

So I reached out to Victoria Allamilla, who graciously gave me the address of a department store warehouse, and some information on how to navigate through it's stockpile of old overstock from prior seasons.

The warehouse was in South Chandler. I rarely left the downtown environment anymore, so to me it was like seeing a new place. As we drove, I observed the surroundings. The opens spaces to the sides of the streets were overgrown with weeds. Patches that used to be grass were yellow or brown. Occasionally bits of trash were tangled in trees and bushes that were in serious need of a trim. I wondered if I could redirect any work crews to city landscaping work.

We located the warehouse and broke in through a back door. We had to do some hunting and pecking to find the right boxes and racks for what we were looking for. And we were shopping in an dark, un-air conditioned building, with nothing more than a couple of camping lanterns for light. But eventually we found what we wanted. I, at least, was pretty pleased with our project. Nothing makes me feel more confident and assured, than wearing new clothes that are exactly perfect for the occasion.

When we left the warehouse, I asked Sharon to take a different route home so I could see more of the same overgrown weedy landscaping. It was kind of depressing. I turned my gaze to the skies surrounding the valley. Some thunderheads were already starting to build up to the south and east. To the north, a distant dark bank of clouds was also building up. That cloud bank appeared smudged from the distance. It was dark and ragged, compared to the bubbly white texture that thunderheads normally had when they formed. I assumed it meant that a storm cycle was winding down, and blowing away from us, rather than building up.

***

At the Mayoral swearing in, all of the new council members and I stood on stage and held up our right hands. There was a brief commotion when Pastor Daniel expected everyone to swear on a Bible. Of course, he had brought his own. He asked if there were any for the rest of us. The Election Commission politely informed him that swearing on a Bible was optional and as an alternative, the rest of us could hold our left hands over our chests to signify our solemnity. Daniel looked very sour at that.

The ceremony proceed and within moments, I was officially Mayor with a Council of five people to work with.

Of course, I was expected to make a speech. This one I had carefully written out ahead of time.

"Good evening, everyone. Thank you, for that." It took awhile for the applause to die down. I had to start over, once everyone had calmed down enough to listen to me.

"I'm very excited about this new phase in our recovery. It's been a long road. The calendar tells me it's been less than a year since the Superflu struck, but it certainly feels like much longer." Lots of head nodding in the audience.

"We still have a lot of work to do. In the next few weeks and months, I want to restart our economy. It's time to assign value to the work we've done, and the resources we have. If you work, you earn. If you earn, you can purchase. As a community, we can capitalize on the resources we do have, such as our hospital, and our abundant housing. Our winter climate is also an attraction. *(pause for applause)*. It won't be easy, but I firmly believe your patience will be rewarded in the end.

We've worked hard to cleanse our city of the deceased. I know it wasn't easy. But we need to expand our efforts to the surrounding communities. The bodies in the cities around us still pose a health threat to us.

Unclaimed fuel, food and water remain to be collected in the adjacent areas, as well. But we will not steal it from those who already possess it, who need it for their own survival. We are not alone. Isolated groups of survivors still need our assistance. We have the space, the capacity to extend a helping hand to others. And other communities have goods and services to trade with us. We need to establish good trading partnerships with them. Through trade, through generosity, by extending a helping hand, we can lift people up. And when we lift up others, we lift up ourselves, as well.

As residents of this community, you have the freedom to come and go as you please. Your safety is still a priority, though. Outside threats do exist. You have a responsibility to take care in your travels and interactions with other groups. And we, the city, have a responsibility to protect our residents from outside threats. We will meet those security challenges as they come.

While the outside threats are real, so are the opportunities. We need to reconnect with the rest of the country. Web sites are coming back on line. Networks are being rewired. A national election is scheduled for the fall. Fuel from the Gulf, wheat from the Midwest, seafood from the ocean. The riches of the nation can come to our door, if we welcome visitors to our community.

I hope everyone is prepared to roll up their sleeves, and get back to work. We still have a lot to do. I know it won't be easy. But the rewards are worth it. The Superflu took the future away from us. Now, we have to build a new future for ourselves and for our children.

Thank you, everyone."

I concluded my speech to a round of applause. The election commissioner added some closing remarks, reminding everyone that the celebration would continue in the nearby hotel ballroom, and everyone was welcome to join in.

***

Much like the New Year's Eve party six months ago, there was good food, music, bright lights, and dancing. Unlike the New Year's Eve party, the overall mood was much more sincerly cheerful, this time. I visited with friends, talked with strangers, answered questions as best I could. I made an effort to get better acquainted with my new Council members. Richard went on and on about resource allocation. Victoria complimented my outfit. Brad asked again about changing the way housing was assigned. Daniel asked if we were going to start a marriage license registry soon, as several couples had approached him about weddings. I assured him that would be one of the easier challenges to address.

Gordon's band had been invited to play a set, and they had prepared several new songs.

As they were taking the stage, someone in the crowd shouted out, "Hey, have you guys got a name yet?"

Gordon and John looked at each other. John shrugged, leaned into the microphone, and suggested, "How about: 'The Suburbanites'?"

Several boos hissed out from the crowd.

Gordon tried one. "Gordon and the Zappers?" he asked the crowd. That got a resounding "meh" from the audience.

"Okay, we'll work on it, and come up with something soon. So, let's play a song!" He took up his drumsticks and they launched into Bruce Springsteen's "Glory Days." The crowd clapped and sang along joyfully. They followed up with "Take it Easy" by the Eagles, and several other crowd pleasing standards.

I danced with friends for a few of songs, but then I slipped outside. A lot of bodies were packed into the room were giving off a lot of heat. Outside, some of the teenagers, including Micah, were setting off small scale fireworks in the parking lot, carefully supervised by our local police.

I was watching the sizzling spinners, when I noticed a small unfamiliar pickup truck careen into the parking lot, going way too fast. I frowned. Behind me, I heard a new voice. Ariana had come out the front doors, talking into her radio hand set. I stared at her, waiting for her to finish the radio call. I couldn't hear the voice on the other end. Ariana's face was stricken.

In the parking lot, a couple of guys had jumped out of the pickup, and were talking fast, gesturing their hands wildly, to the nearest police officer who had approached them. I looked to the guys. I looked back at Ariana. Zach stepped outside, behind her, also talking on his own radio. It appeared to be a different channel and conversation, as he was not in sync with Ari.

Ariana grabbed me by the arm, and said, "Come on, we have to get over to the hospital!"

"What's going on?" I asked her

"Oh, crap! I have to get Cass! Wait a sec!" She turned and ran back inside the hotel. I had last seen Cassandra dancing with Dillon (awkwardly, given her leg healing in it's plaster cast), and was pretty sure she was still there. I turned to Zach. "Can you tell me what's going on?" I asked him. He held up the "wait a sec" finger. After a moment, he moved his radio away from his ear.

"It's the Oak Creek Canyon people. There was a huge forest fire; it swept down off the cliffs into the canyon; they had to evacuate everyone out. They've got a lot of injuries, some burn victims. They brought them here."

While Zach relayed this to me, he snapped his fingers at his patrol cops in the parking lot and gestured for them to join him.

"Oh my gawd!" My exclamation was lost in the growing rush of activity around me. The kids with the fire works stopped what they were doing and looked around, trying to figure out what was going on. Zach started snapping out instructions to his cops.

"Okay, tell the kids the fireworks are done for the night; confiscate them if you have to. Darren, get over to the hospital and find out what they need. See if they left anyone on the road and if we need to go round them up. Brian, Jeff, go round up our extra first aid kits and meet people at the hospital parking lot. There might be minor injuries to be triaged."

Zach was still barking out orders to his men, when Ari came back out, with Cassandra wheeling along on her little cart as fast as she could manage.

"Come on, we have to get over to the hospital!" she repeated to me.

"Yeah, I know, I'm coming!" I helped Cassandra get herself into Ariana's car. I wondered if I should go back in and let Gordon know what was happening. But he was a big boy, he could figure out it and decide for himself if he needed to be there. I climbed into the car with Cass and Ari. Ari barely even waited for the door to close before she peeled out of the lot past the pickup truck.

The hospital was only a couple of miles from downtown. We were there within minutes. Cars, trucks and people were milling about the entry way. Medical techs in scrubs were kneeling over people laying on the ground. Gurneys were being wheeled outside. More cars followed us from the hotel. I saw Loren and some other medical staff climbing out, and rushing to join their colleagues in the triage session. They had been at the party with us. Dr. Reddy was shouting orders, prioritizing patients.

"Where's my Dad?" Cassandra wailed, only loud enough for us alone to hear. We had parked to the side, to stay clear of the vehicles still arriving. We were approaching the entrance on foot, but staying to the side, to keep out of people's way.

To my untrained eye, it appeared to be complete chaos, and it seemed to stay that way for a long time. After a while, though, I finally saw a pattern. The staff was categorizing the severity of injuries. The people who were most seriously injured were taken inside first, for emergency treatment. The rest were taken to the waiting room, where there was better lighting. There, the staff could apply bandages stop any minor bleeding, and hand out Ibruprofen.

Eventually, one of the hospital people directed us to the supply closet and told us to start handing out bottled water and clean towels to anyone who was in the waiting room. Lots of smoke smudged faces needed a wipe down. It was good to have something useful to do. I wondered if we needed to get blankets, too, but it was July 4th in the middle of the desert. No one was having a problem with hypothermia at the moment. Not even the ones in shock or coming down from their adrenaline rush.

"*Dad!*" I was talking to a woman with soot on her face, asking her what happened when I heard Cassandra shout from across the room.

I turned to see Stettner walking in, holding up another man, his shoulder under the man's arm. That man was also sooty and grimy. Cassandra abandoned her own rolling cart, hobbled over to the pair, and took the man's other side. Which was awkward for her, since she wasn't supposed to put any weight on her own broken leg. One of the nurses rushed to take her place, shooed her away and immediately took the two men into an emergency exam room.

I turned back to the woman I was helping. "You were saying?" I prompted her.

"It was a forest fire. It just came out of nowhere; it came over the lip and down the west side of the canyon, and cut us off. We couldn't go north. Someone said there was a rock slide blocking the road up the cliff. We had to drive right through the fire, to get out of the canyon! It was black as night, and embers were flying in the air everywhere." She was shuddering and practically wailing. I patted her shoulder, and tried to calm her. Another woman in the waiting room changed seats, and took the crying woman in her arms. Clearly, they were friends.

Stettner came back out of the emergency exam rooms area and spotted Cassandra. She had gone back to stand with Ariana. I joined them. I thrust a water bottle into Patrick's hand. He was wiping his forehead with the back of his hand, smearing ash around, and not really cleaning any of it off. He cracked open the water bottle and took a long gulp, draining about half of it. He looked around at us. He opened his mouth and closed it a few times. He couldn't figure out where to start.

Ariana spoke. "Come on, let's go sit down. Take a minute. Its going to be okay." Cassandra nodded and took her dad's arm for support. She hopped him over to a bench beside the door. Ariana sat down next to him. I sat next to Ari.

Patrick drank some more of the water, slowly this time. I handed him one of the clean towels I'd been carrying around, for people to wipe their faces with.

He started in the middle. "It just came down the sides so fast! We barely had time to sound the alarm, and get everyone to the cars. The last of the trucks pulling out were driving right through flaming embers landing on the road. We lost everything! No one had time to grab hardly anything - everyone just ran for their cars. I'm not even completely sure if everyone got out. We stopped in Sedona, to try and do a head count, and we're a few short. I think Timmy's group got stuck."

Patrick's face was stricken. I didn't know who Timmy was, but Cassandra also looked horrified. Maybe they were farther up in the canyon?

Patrick turned to Ariana and me. "I'm sorry, I didn't know where else to take everyone. A lot of this is minor burns, but some people were hurt pretty badly. Burning tree limbs were falling out of the sky, when people were trying to get into their vehicles. And the smoke - I hope they're treating for smoke inhalation…" He looked back at the exam room entrance door, and made to get up, but Ariana grabbed his arm and pulled him back down.

"They'll check for that, they're pros. They know what they're doing."

Stettner nodded. He finished the last of the water in his bottle.

"Dad, I don't see Javier's people here." She asked this quietly, like she didn't want to be overheard by others in the room.

"No, they decided to go around to I-17 and go up to Flag. They still don't think it's a good idea to come down to the desert."

Ariana and I looked at each other. We didn't know what that meant, but it wasn't any of our business at the moment.

Dr. Reddy appeared from the exam room. Several people around the waiting room recognized him and stood up, looking at him expectantly. Reddy looked around the room and didn't know who to address first.

"Who's in charge here?" he asked bluntly. Patrick stood up and raised his hand. Dr. Reddy addressed him, but spoke loudly enough for the entire room.

"Okay, we've completed the first phase of triage. The most serious cases are getting moved to patient rooms ASAP. Next we'll start bringing in the moderate injuries and treat those."

"Is everyone going to survive?" Stettner asked him.

Dr. Reddy looked a little surprised. "I believe so, yes. It's too early to tell for certain, though. The good news is that the burn injuries are on a relatively small proportion of the patients' bodies. That's a good indicator. I don't think anyone is over 25%. We've got them on oxygen, as well. We'll be starting antibiotics and pain meds immediately. We will get the burns bandaged as soon as we can clean them."

Other people from around the room started to speak up.

"When I can see Hank?"

"I think I need an X-ray, I think something might be broken."

"Is Susan in there? I didn't see her get taken in…"

Stettner stood to make the rounds of his people in the room, offering comfort, a touch on the shoulder, some soft words.

I went back to get more bottled water and clean towels. I wet the towels down in a sink I found in a prep room. I also noticed a rolling cart meant to hold soiled laundry. I dragged that with me back to the waiting room. I handed out clean towels for people to wipe down their faces and hands, and tossed the dirty ones into the laundry cart. Ariana was talking on her radio. At one point, I glanced up and saw Zach outside the waiting room entrance, talking to a couple of his patrol men and some of the newcomers.

Things were getting taken care of. People were being directed to where they were needed. It would be a long night, though. I noticed that several of the new City Council members had joined the waiting room. Daniel was in a corner, praying. Several people around him clasped their hands in their laps fervently. Victoria was also sitting with some people, listening to their stories and offering comfort.

In all, I figured about 125 people were processed through the hospital's service that night. Most only had minor singes, or cuts and scrapes. There were a couple of broken bones, too. A couple dozen patients had burns and injuries severe enough to get them admitted. In addition, more people from Oak Creek Canyon had evacuated, but did not require any medical treatment.

In small groups, we sent the uninjured and patients that had been treated and released, over to the hotel, to get checked into rooms for the night. Ariana had called back to the hotel to tell them to break up the party and start preparing rooms for guests. Zach and his cops drove people over there if they weren't up to driving their own vehicles.

Slowly, the waiting room emptied out. Stettner sat on the bench with his daughter, his arm over her shoulders, as she leaned on him.

Some time after midnight Gordon arrived and located me. The community grapevine had done it's job and he was mostly up to speed on what had happened. He just hugged me. He told me he had taken Dillon and Micah home. Then he sat down with Stettner, to wait for the final wrap up.

It was close to 3am when the last patient requiring a few stitches was released. Patrick stood up, and sent the young man to his truck, which was waiting outside. Dr. Reddy gave Patrick another private update on the patients that were staying. Stettner thanked the doctor, and then turned to us. His face was drawn. He was exhausted.

"I don't know how to thank you for this. I don't know what we would have done, if not for this." He waved his arm around, to indicate the entire hospital.

"It's okay. This is their mission. It's what they're here to do." I gestured back at the personnel, who I could see through the counter window to the admitting station. A couple of them, including Loren, looked up at me, and nodded.

Stettner went on. "I don't know what comes next. Our camp has been completely destroyed. I have no idea where to take any of them."

Ariana spoke up instantly. "You're staying here! You were always meant to be here, down here in the Valley. I've always known that. We've got houses cleared out and the power is on. I'm sure we can find plenty of work for your people. I know Zach would be happy to have more trained guards on patrol." Zach was standing in the entrance way leading to the parking lot. He was listening and did not object.

Stettner stared at Ariana.

Cassandra, standing next to her father, said, "She's right. We're supposed to be here. This is where we were meant to be all along. We're staying. We'll tell everyone else in the morning, get things settled then."

Ariana nodded in confirmation. She and Patrick were still staring each other in the eye.

Finally, Patrick nodded back at Ariana. "Okay. We'll stay. I'll make sure my people earn their keep. They're well trained and hard workers."

I nodded at both of them. I could see Ariana's ulterior motives, but it didn't seem like such a bad thing, now. Maybe the two of them really were meant to be together.

Gordon stepped forward from where he'd been standing behind me. "Glad to have you join the team!" He held out his hand to Patrick, who took it solemnly. Zach also came over, and shook hands in welcome.

Patrick looked to me. I told him, "I'm counting on you to help me. I can't mayor this place all by myself, you know." He nodded and held out his hand. I stepped past that, and wrapped my arms around his shoulders. I said, "You're one of ours now."

End of Book Two

About the Author

Lisa Harnish is a potter, writer and desk jockey. She has lived in Chandler, Arizona since 1995. When not pushing keys on a keyboard or playing in the mud, she can usually be found sprawled on the living room couch with her dogs, collectively known as the "The Jerky Boys." See her website at www.lisaharnish.com for more information.

CPSIA information can be obtained
at www.ICGtesting.com
Printed in the USA
BVHW031018280619
552219BV00001B/57/P

9 781733 141130